Beneath A Mountain Moon

"This is a delightful change from most fiction stories about the occult that focus on just the ritual and not the plot . . . I couldn't set the book down once I started reading it . . ."

—Accord, Council of the Magickal Arts

"This book is a 'good read' and we would highly recommend it to our friends . . . It grabs your attention and keeps you 'spellbound' until the very climax of the story."

—Phases

"Fast moving, superbly drawn characters. Magickal references and action are most enjoyable. You'll be swept away by the plot. The entire book moves like a cone of power. Recommendation? WOW . . . "

—The Hermit's Lantern

About the Author

Born in the heart of Pennsylvania, Silver has been interested in the magickal arts since childhood. "York, Cumberland, and Lancaster counties are alive with magick," she says.

"The best way for a magickal person to be accepted is to let people know you firsthand," explains Silver. "Once they get to know you and understand your personal values and principles, their attitudes on your alternative religious interests take a back seat. Let them know you—for you inside and the works that you do. It should be that way for everybody."

Born on September 11, 1956, Silver is a true Virgo: she adores making lists and arranging things. Definitely a lady of the 90s, she's hard to pin down. "I spend a great deal of my time with my four children," she says. "They come first in my life—everybody else, take a number!"

Silver teaches several magickal sciences as she tours the United States. She has attained Wiccan Priesthood, and is the Tradition Head of the Black Forest Clan, covering eight states, and an Elder of Family of Serphant Stone. She is the Director of the International Wiccan/Pagan Press Alliance. Be sure to visit her website at www.silverravenwolf.com.

To Write to the Author

If you wish to contact the author or would like more information about this book, please write to the author in care of Llewellyn Worldwide and we will forward your request. Both the author and publisher appreciate hearing from you and learning of your enjoyment of this book and how it has helped you. Llewellyn Worldwide cannot guarantee that every letter written to the author can be answered, but all will be forwarded. Please write to:

Silver RavenWolf
c/o Llewellyn Worldwide
P.O. Box 64383, Dept. 1–56718–722–6
St. Paul, MN 55164-0383, U.S.A.

Please enclose a self-addressed, stamped envelope for reply, or $1.00 to cover costs.
Silver cannot get back to you if you don't, so always include a SASE!

Beneath a Mountain Moon

Silver RavenWolf

2001
Llewellyn Publications
St. Paul, Minnesota 55164-0383 U.S.A.

FIRST EDITION
Second Printing, 2001

Cover design: Gavin Dayton Duffy
Cover photographs: © Digital Stock
Book design, layout, and editing: Jessica Thoreson

Library of Congress Cataloging-in-Publication Data
RavenWolf, Silver, 1956-
     Beneath a mountain moon / Silver RavenWolf. — 1st ed.
       p.   cm.
     ISBN 1-56718-722-6 (Trade pbk.)
     I. Title.
  PS3568.A833B46   1995
  831'.54—dc20   95-11763
                                               CIP

Llewellyn Publications
A Division of Llewellyn Worldwide, Ltd.
P.O. Box 64383, St. Paul, MN 55164-0383
www.llewellyn.com

Printed in the United States of America

Other Books by Silver RavenWolf

In the Silver's Spells Series

*This book is dedicated to
my mother,
Mozelle Strader Baker*

May she rest in peace ...

*Don't brag yet, Ma,
and keep an eye on those reviewers for me.*

chapter one

"DO YOU BELIEVE IN POSSESSION?" Elizabeyta Belladonna snapped her head around, her eyes raking across the woman standing in line behind her at Whiskey Springs' Market.

"I beg your pardon?" she asked, taking a deep breath and fighting off the urge to scream with frustration. Possession, indeed—if the woman only knew who she was talking to. After two long years, it seemed as if Elizabeyta may finally be bringing her agony home to rest. She did not need any complications; in her current state, even trivial conversation was too much to bear. Instead of screaming, or running, or strangling her—for a moment she thought she could do any of these things—she removed her credit card from its dirty plastic sleeve and flicked the edge of it with her fingernail, impatiently waiting to pay for her purchases and get out of there. Wherever she might choose to run, it would never be far enough.

The woman inched closer and smiled authoritatively. Her too-ruby lipstick clashed with her coifed mop of copper hair, giving her the appearance of a dime store mannequin. "Why, these tabloid newspapers here." She swept her gloved hand toward the newspaper display above the check-out counter. "This week's topic appears to be pos-*ses*-sion."

Elizabeyta tried to ignore her and edged closer to the counter. She was tired, hungry, and hanging on a ragged, emotional edge. She'd just driven almost non-stop from Oklahoma to this dead-end town in Pennsylvania, and even thinking was an effort. The tape in the cash register stuck and the clerk uttered a growl, thrusting open the machine and exposing its mechanized entrails. Oddly, the clerk's anger helped to assuage her own. She took a deep breath and centered herself. Better.

"Well, do you believe in possession?"

Elizabeyta straightened her shoulders and glanced at the woman as she spoke. "I think it could be true ... I guess. I mean I suppose it's all in what you believe, or don't." The clerk at the counter swore, ripped out the old tape, and scrabbled underneath the cash register for a new one. Elizabeyta suppressed a smile.

"My people have been in this town for over a hundred years," continued the woman beside her. "I've heard stories about all sorts of things like possession, ghosts, magick ... you name it. Let me tell you, there's no place in the world more magickal than Whiskey Springs. My grandma often talked about the Dark Men and the white witches they ran off back in her day." She nodded her head knowingly. The hair on the back of Elizabeyta's neck bristled.

"I hate the day after Christmas," grumbled the clerk. "Everything that can go wrong will go wrong."

"I know what you mean," answered Elizabeyta.

She glanced at the people standing behind the annoying woman. Most were looking straight at her, their curiosity overcoming the tedium of waiting. She grimaced. Terrific. On display at the grocery store. Exactly a predicament her family had warned her to avoid. A man in a long, black overcoat joined the end of the line. The woman, oblivious to Elizabeyta's discomfort, chattered on. "I bet I could write one heck of a novel just about the goings-on around here—past and present. I'd make a mint!" She shimmied her shoulders under her white fur coat. Heavy perfume hung in the air, tickling Elizabeyta's nose. She sneezed. Someone behind her said, "Bless you."

"Are you new around here?" asked the annoying woman.

Elizabeyta cleared her throat with effort. "Yes."

"Oh? You look so familiar. Visiting relatives?"

"You could say that."

The woman eyed her doubtfully. "But you look so familiar ..."

Elizabeyta looked past her. The line now numbered five deep and all of them seemed very interested in the conversation, especially the man in the black coat. He leaned forward as if hanging on every word. A Canon .35 millimeter camera hung on an embroidered black and red strap around his neck. When he caught Elizabeyta looking at him, he looked away, as if to survey the back of the store.

These were nameless faces Elizabeyta would probably never see again. Still, the last thing she wanted was an audience. She tried to turn away to discourage the woman, but that didn't do any good. The girl still had not fixed the cash register; instead, she reached over and flipped a switch. The lighted number "2" over the counter began to blink off and on, silently calling for managerial assistance. Unless she simply walked off without her purchases, Elizabeyta was stuck until help came. She ground her teeth in frustration.

"Coldest weather I can remember around here," the woman went on. "Oh, where was I? Yes, now I recall we were talking about magick in the area. Some people say that even our local law enforcement officers and town officials get caught up in some of that superstitious nonsense." A gasp escaped from someone in the growing customer line.

Why don't they open up another check-out? thought Elizabeyta with irritation.

The woman drew a deep breath and plunged on. "Why, there's a lady on South Mountain who's been doing faith healing for years. Her name's Emma something. And did you know that in York County, just past Route 15, the Pow-Wow doctors hung their shingles out for all to see only fifty years ago. 'Course, they don't do that now. It's against the law." Her badly-penciled eyebrows moved up and down emphatically.

A young fellow with more pimples than freckles materialized at the clerk's side, moving her out of the way. The plastic tag on his rumpled shirt read "Hi! I'm Bob. Happy to serve you." Bob didn't look overjoyed at the moment.

"Hardly anyone uses her anymore—the faith healing lady, I mean. Of course, my husband, Sam, says that faith healing and Dark Men and all are ridiculous. Even if they were around once, they're not here anymore. He says I should be spending my time worrying about things in the real world. We don't live in New York City anymore, so he says since there isn't any major crime here to keep my naturally quick mind busy, I'm apt to see things that aren't there at all. Still ..."

Elizabeyta nodded and closed her eyes for a moment. Weary from the long drive, she wanted to be home with her family in Oklahoma, not here in south-central Pennsylvania. And she wanted to be rid of the personal load of grief, to have some angel come and lift the heavy cloak of despair from her shoulders. A ridiculous wish, to be sure. She sighed. Actually, she just wanted to pick up a few supplies, get to the house, make a meal, and go to bed.

Bob slammed the lid on the repaired register and quickly strode away. The check-out girl resumed passing Elizabeyta's items over the OCR window. "That will be forty-eight dollars and sixty-two cents," she said. "Will that be a money access card or credit card?"

"Credit card, please," said Elizabeyta, handing over her credit card.

"I can't get over how familiar you look," pressed the woman beside her.

Elizabeyta ignored her and took the card back from the clerk, replaced it in its plastic sleeve, and dropped it into the yawning mouth of her black purse. She blinked, paused; her internal warning bells pealed impending danger. She looked at the faces behind the woman again. They floated, surreal in the harsh, neon light of the supermarket. Too many faces.

"Sign here, please," said the clerk loudly, holding the charge slip on the counter and producing a pen from a pocket in her blue smock. Had she asked before?

"How long will you be in town?" asked the woman beside her.

Elizabeyta shifted her booted feet and signed the slip, the pen working sloppily across the blue line. Elizabeyta could feel the woman peering over her shoulder, watching her sign her name. She didn't like the direction her chatter was taking. She handed the slip back to the clerk. The woman beside her may be a blabber mouth, but beneath all that green eye make-up lurked a pair of calculating brown eyes.

She said loudly, "Elizabeyta Belladonna! What a beautiful name!" Elizabeyta resisted the urge to slap her.

The clerk handed over Elizabeyta's copy of the slip. "Paper or plastic?"

"Paper," she mumbled.

"Well, my husband runs the local newspaper," said the woman sagely. Elizabeyta caught the hint of pride in the woman's voice as well as the warning. "I help him write up the society page. I know who you look like! You're a dead ringer for the Anderson girl. Do you know Terry Anderson?" persisted the woman beside her.

"No."

"Who did you say you were visiting? Are you sure you're not related to the Andersons? An older cousin, perhaps? I swear, you look just like little Terry Anderson. She must be twenty-five or six now." Elizabeyta moved to the other end of the counter. "Hold on, I'd love to chat with you a bit," said the woman, flapping her hand as if to bring Elizabeyta in for a landing. "My name's Mrs. Renard. Do give me a call. I'm in the book."

Elizabeyta tried to ignore her. The clerk began bagging the groceries. Elizabeyta offered to help but the girl shook her head. "I'm sorry you had to wait; this is the least I can do," she said, then pushed two full bags of groceries toward her. Quickly Elizabeyta picked them up, balancing them close to her face in an effort to shield herself from the onslaught of prying questions from the abominable woman.

Elizabeyta sidled out the door and into the bitter December cold, moving quickly to her rented Isuzu before Mrs. Renard could catch her. She rammed the bags into the passenger seat and scrambled into the driver's side. As she turned out of the parking lot she caught sight of Mrs. Renard's white fur coat emerging from the store. The face above the voluminous fur wore a puzzled expression. Immediately behind her stood the man in the long, black overcoat, its edges flapping slightly in the winter air.

chapter two

THIS IS A NIGHTMARE, THOUGHT ELIZABEYTA. *Things are going from bad to worse.* Don't make a spectacle of yourself, her family said! Don't draw any attention to what you are doing. Don't shop in town. Go to York or Harrisburg for any purchases. Just gather the research material and then we'll work together as a team. Don't think you are going to do this all by yourself. That's what family is for. We stick together.

So what had she done? Struck out on her own. She wasn't supposed to be here this time around. They were going to send someone else to tie up her research of the past two years because they said they couldn't afford to lose her. "It isn't wise to tempt fate," explained her brother. "You've taken this as far as you safely can. Let us finish it." The family had worked meticulously, planning how they would handle catching those who were systematically bringing despair to her family. She

5

was determined to find her grandmother's killer herself; somehow, she knew she had to be the one to do it. But now that she was here, shivering with cold in this little Pennsylvania town, she'd begun to think that maybe her family was right—it wasn't a good idea to do it on her own. Alone and unescorted. The mystery yet unsolved. Well, by now her family certainly knew she'd left, no mistake about that! She could feel their anger rolling in tempest blasts—an unfortunate circumstance when one belonged to a magickal family such as hers. She always felt their strong emotions no matter where she was.

Elizabeyta turned the Isuzu off Main Street and into the maple-lined driveway of the grey stone monstrosity. Her arms ached from so many hours of driving, her legs stiff and hard to control. She sat quietly for a moment in the gathering twilight, listening to the faint ticking of the engine as it cooled. The house loomed, dismal and deserted. The maple trees, so full of velvety greenery in the summer, now clawed at the winter-glass sky, defending the house of secrets, protecting the ghost within.

Her eyes strayed next door, where warm, lemon light spilled from the parsonage windows. She wondered vaguely if Pastor Lee Becker was home … and if he was watching her as he usually did. She'd lost count of how many times she'd almost told him her secret. The hours she'd laid in bed at night, thinking of him. Did she yearn for his friendship or more? She gave her head a little shake. If only someone could make the bad things in her life go away. So many silly thoughts in her head. It must be the endless strain.

She smiled to herself. Maybe she should send him a belated Christmas present. On the other hand, maybe she shouldn't be so friendly this time—cold-shoulder him for his own good. She wouldn't feel right if he got hurt. She liked him too much.

Chill tendrils of bitter air devoured the warmth inside the Isuzu, turning her mind to the task of unloading the vehicle and getting on with the business at hand. She headed for the side door that led in through the kitchen. It didn't take long to open the house and deposit her suitcases on the kitchen linoleum. Maybe she'd skip the meal and go straight to bed. The thought of resting her head on that pink, satin pillow gave added strength to finishing the job.

Her eyes roved slowly over both the neatly shoveled front and side walks. At least Lee had given her a good tip on a reliable teenager in September. The town council president's son, no less, but Mark seemed like a good kid and didn't ask her a lot of nosy questions. She'd paid him a lump sum to take care of the walks for the season; that way the place didn't look so empty and kept the town council from citing her for not clearing a path within twenty-four hours.

She trudged back to the Isuzu and grabbed the last grocery bag. The darkness crept around her while the sodium streetlights struggled vainly to illuminate the dreary atmosphere. She looked back at the greystone house. It stood at the top of the town, a sort of beacon at the crest of the hill that peered down over the various and sundry businesses of the three-block-long merchant district. Up the hill marched the rental properties, some sporting new siding from the autumn before, others dilapidated or downright gruesome. Her greystone, on a corner lot, marked the first of the privately-owned homes at the edge of the business district. Across the main street nestled the tiny town park, complete with gazebo, now entombed by vast drifts of snow and snarled icicles.

As she carried the groceries up to the house, she kept looking over her shoulder, straining her eyes in the winter gloom. Her skin crawled beneath her heavy, black wool coat. Was someone watching her? The man in black from the grocery store? She kicked off the notion. Probably bored neighbors who didn't have anything else to do the day after Christmas—Lee Becker in particular, she assured herself. She'd visited here a number of times over the past two years and no one had ever bothered her. Why should they start now? A quick look at the parsonage next door revealed thick panes full of bright light. No peeping pastor to be seen. She shivered and hurried up the walk. She opened the side door and flicked on the light when a floating male voice sent a jolt through her body.

"I thought at Thanksgiving you said you wouldn't be back until the weather let up?" A man stepped out from around a bush, laughing.

Elizabeyta's heart jumped, pounding in her chest, shooting adrenaline through her veins. "Lee! You nearly scared me witless."

He grinned, emerging from the gloom and into the pool of light cast by the open kitchen door. She noticed he wasn't wearing a coat and trying hard not to shiver.

"You big-time computer software ladies, hopping all over the country. I've been wondering how you were doing. I'm surprised to see you. Why aren't you at home with your family over the Christmas holiday?"

A brief smile touched her lips as her eyes swept his athletic figure. Tall, rugged, a body most women would swoon over, a voice one wanted to hear whispering endearments in her ear. Even if he was going a bit grey there on the sides and had put on a few pounds since she'd first met him two years ago, most women would consider him worth vying for. She'd thought about it herself plenty of times. "Business before pleasure," she said lightly, walking into the kitchen and setting down the groceries on the table. He trooped in behind her, shutting the door against the cold.

Over the past two years she and Lee had become more than acquaintances but less than friends—at least that's how she viewed their relationship. He thought she sold computer software for a living, was divorced, and primarily stayed with an old aunt in Nebraska. None of which held a fraction of the truth. Sometimes she regretted her lack of honesty, but circumstances dictated her actions—and her actions were to protect her family at all costs. No two worlds could be more different than those of a Witch and a Pastor.

Lee stood by the table, rocking on his heels. "Did you enjoy your holiday? Bet your aunt was upset that you had to leave the day after Christmas. Did you fly in?"

Elizabeyta held up her hands to feign off his questions. "I take it you are glad to see me. Parishioners getting to you over the holidays?"

"Yeah, all the old ladies are trying to marry me off to their spinster daughters," he said mischievously. "I've had enough cookies and egg nog to fill a barn." He patted his slightly protruding stomach as if to show her he'd gained at least an inch around the middle.

"A handsome thirty-seven-year-old unmarried minister is a little odd," she teased, avoiding his eyes, then turned away in embarrassment. She busied herself stowing away the last of the groceries, keeping her eyes away from his.

"Will you be in town long?"

"Oh, a week maybe," she said over her shoulder, hiding her face in the cupboard. "I have an important deal to close up. This, ah, may be my last time in the Eastern District. There's talk of my being transferred to the home office permanently."

A small sigh whooshed behind her. "Then someone else will be using this house?"

"Most likely. The company gives us the use of the houses so we don't have to stay in hotels. 'Course, I've told you all that before."

"Yeah. Right. So, you think maybe you won't be coming back?"

She closed the cupboard door and turned around, leaning against the counter. His grey eyes, soft as a humid summer afternoon, bored into hers. She looked away uncomfortably, mentally kicking herself for not telling him at Thanksgiving that she may not ever be back. It would have made things cleaner, easier to deal with. They could have said their good-byes then. The family would have sent in someone else and Lee Becker would have gone down in her memory as a nice man in the wrong place at the wrong time. Having him in the picture now was not a good idea. She was close to discovering who murdered her grandmother and why. Not that she had any concrete facts at this point, but she could feel that she was getting close. So close as to be dangerous. The memory of the man in black rose unbidden in her mind.

"I said, it's too bad you couldn't be with your aunt this Christmas," said Lee loudly.

"Huh? Oh. Yeah. Why aren't you with your family this Christmas?" she asked, trying to move the conversation away from the inevitable discussion of her leaving.

"My parents passed away two years ago. Remember, I told you?"

"I'm sorry," she said, feeling foolish. "I forgot. Listen, I'm really bushed from driving … I mean flying all that way. I'd like to make something to eat and then go to bed, or maybe just call it a night. Do you mind?" Irritation at his presence gnawed at her. She wanted him to go away before she let her defenses down and did, or said, something stupid.

His face collapsed a little. "Sure, no problem. Hey! Why don't I make a fire in the fireplace and cook you dinner? You sit down right here and relax, or even better, go take a shower and by the time you're done, dinner will be ready."

"I don't know …" He smiled so sweetly at her. She closed her eyes for a moment, then opened them. "I wouldn't be good company. Honestly, I'm in a very grumpy mood and this isn't the best time for you to be here."

"Oh come on," he said. His grey eyes were large and begging. "I'm a minister. You're safe with me."

chapter three

AFTER MORE PLEADING FROM LEE, SHE relented and took her bags to her room, showering as quickly as possible. A strange man in the house made her nervous. It wasn't that she feared him. She knew how to protect herself and had spent enough time with him to know his intentions were irritatingly honorable, but still, allowing him to stay was out of character for her. She blamed it on her fatigue and his cajoling. Dressing with speed, she'd pinned her heavy wet hair on top of her head and scurried down the stairs, hoping to get this dinner over quickly and find solace in her dreams as soon as possible. In her mind, there was much to be done in the days ahead and she wanted to get started.

It will be a shame to leave this place, thought Elizabeyta sadly. She liked the deep, wall-sized fireplace in the kitchen and the shiny linoleum floor with its pattern of tiny blue flowers on white that reflected the dancing flames on a cold night like this. She turned her attention to the table in the center of the kitchen. Made of blonde wood, it always looked so homey and inviting; its matching Windsor chairs curved comfortably to her back, the deep, plush blue cushions providing a delightfully easy seat. She wondered if she would have liked Great Aunt Beth Ann. She certainly loved her house.

She smiled at Lee approvingly. He'd set the table and even lit the glass oil lamp. Its graceful Tiffany panes cast soft, colored light over her aunt's best china. A tureen of steaming stew, French bread, a platter of assorted cold cuts, a large wooden bowl overflowing with salad, and a sugary shoe-fly pie graced the table. "You did all this while I took a shower?" she teased.

He held her chair out for her while she sat down, scooting it deftly underneath her as she edged closer to the table. "I cannot tell a lie," he said lightly. "The women of my parish have been cooking for me non-stop over the Christmas holiday. You are about to taste the best cuisine this side of South Mountain. Would you prefer tea or coffee? I brought a thermos of both."

She laughed. "Why, tea if you please. You mean you snuck out of the house and ran this stuff over?"

"Most certainly."

Elizabeyta and Lee dined on light conversation and heavy, rich stew. She asked him about his parish, who was ill, who had gotten married, and kept him busy answering questions about his life over the past month. The fatigue she'd felt earlier began to dissipate a bit. With the help of the food, she managed to catch a second wind.

During the conversation her psychic senses prodded Lee's mind, evaluating and determining what he felt and why. She methodically catalogued his attraction to her growing minute by minute, escalated, no doubt, by her earlier announcement that she would not be visiting this town again. No matter how she fielded questions or uttered witty remarks, the conversation kept twisting back to the subject she most definitely did not want to discuss—herself.

"I have a confession to make," said Lee, finishing his pie and pushing the plate to the side.

"Oh?" A mournful, whistling wind caressed the window panes, making them rattle and pop. The sound put her on edge.

"I've been watching you through my windows whenever you're around, and often when you're not, wishing you were here."

"Why Pastor Lee, I never dreamed!" she said, an impish smile falsely playing across her lips. Yes, her heart occasionally beat jungle drums when he looked at her, but she'd been around long enough to know lust when she felt it—something far different from the commitment of love. He sighed. "It's true; I don't want you to leave here. In fact, I wish you wouldn't take that promotion, but I know that's pure selfishness."

"So what do you see, when you look out your windows at my house?" she asked.

A shadow passed over his grey eyes.

"Oh come on. Tell me."

"I know you will think this is silly, but sometimes when you're not here, I think you are."

"Why is that?" Elizabeyta swallowed her last bit of pie, forcing it down her throat. Her uncle had been right to keep the family from attending Aunt Beth's funeral. Lee would have remembered her. As far as everyone in town knew, including Lee, a software corporation called MorningStar Inc. owned the property. No one knew that MorningStar Inc. was not a bunch of teckie geniuses, but an organization of Witches—namely Elizabeyta's family.

"Someone moves your curtains. Last week I thought I saw the lady who used to live here standing at your bedroom window. Her name was Beth Ann Baxter. Of course I know that's ridiculous because she's dead. I attended her funeral service over two years ago." He sat quietly for a moment, then said, "Does anyone else use this house when you're not here?"

"No. Do you believe in ghosts?" asked Elizabeyta, taking a long swallow from her tea cup.

"I'm not sure what I believe," remarked Lee. "At one time I thought ghosts were a figment of one's mind, either through wish fulfillment or fantasy. But honestly, now I'm not so sure. I can't deny what I saw. Have you ever—I mean, do you think there is a ghost in this house?"

Elizabeyta looked at him for a long time, weighing what she should and should not say. At home, she could speak her mind. The entire family immersed itself in the occult. Everyone, including herself, believed in and had talked to ghosts at one time or another, though she didn't consider herself a star pupil at it. But this was the other world—the world outside the covenstead—a place where not many people believed in such things as ghosts … or Witches.

"I believe there is a ghost here," she began carefully. "But I'm not afraid of her. I know it's a woman because I always smell lilacs when she's around. At least, I assume it's a woman. Could be the old lady who lived here before, as you say. I can honestly tell you she's never said anything to me and she's never manifested. I mean, I've never actually seen her."

"If you haven't seen her, how do you know she's here, other than the flower smell?"

Elizabeyta shrugged her shoulders. "Because she throws things around on occasion."

His eyes grew wide. "How long have you known about her?"

"Since the day I arrived. She wasn't pleased." Elizabeyta took the last sip of tea from her cup, setting it down daintily on its saucer.

"Really?"

"Really. She made my life miserable the first few visits to this house. She would hide my car keys and move my clothes. One time she dumped sugar on the floor. Even though I cleaned it up, I scrunched around in here for days." Smiling and shaking her head at the memory, Elizabeyta picked up some of the dirty dishes from the table and took them to the sink.

"And you're not frightened?"

"Would you be?" she asked, taking her seat again.

He thought about that for a moment. "I'll admit it makes me uneasy, but I can't say I'm scared of a ghost."

"In fact," said Elizabeyta, unable to resist testing his words, "she's probably listening to us right now. I bet she's hovering over there in the corner somewhere." She motioned languidly to the corner opposite her chair, sniffing the air mischievously. "Do you smell anything?"

Silence grew between the two of them as Lee sat back in his chair, his eyes casually shifting from left to right, his nostrils widening slightly. She sensed his nervousness growing, and felt sorry for him and the non-magickal people in the world like him. She knew she had to be careful, not too forward in her answers or he would misunderstand her. But she was so tired. So sick and tired of being on guard. When would it ever end? Psychically, though, she sensed his need for intimacy and that certainly needed squelching without hurting him.

She'd asked her grandmother once about the differences between her family and those she encountered outside of the covenstead. Her grandmother patted her on the knee. "Don't worry about it, little one; you'll get the hang of dealing with them. There will be some you will really like, and they will feel the same way about you. It will be like that with anyone you meet, magickal or not. You exist like the sacred circle—as above, so below … as within, so without … you know the Witch is the magick, and what you make of it, and yourself, is up to you, good or bad. May the Goddess be generous in her favors to you, Elizabeyta."

"Where do you really come from, Elizabeyta?"

She snapped back to the present, here with Lee, in her dead aunt's home, listening to the merry snap and pop of the logs in the fireplace, and the cruel winter wind snarling at the windows. Remembering her grandmother brought a deep sense of loss to her heart. No more tears. She could not shed another tear. "Whatever do you mean?" she asked quietly. A heavy tendril of hair loosened itself from the pile atop her head and slithered down around her cheek. She flicked it back over her shoulder, moving uncomfortably in her seat.

"Not many people would be so familiar with having a ghost in their home. Does everyone in Nebraska believe in ghosts, like they are an everyday occurrence?" He leaned one elbow on the table, cupping his chin in his hand. The soft light of the lamp pulled at the lines on his face, softening his features with a warm glow. "You are a very mysterious woman, Elizabeyta. Part of me wants to run and part of me wants to stay. Have you ever thought you've known someone all your life, but you really haven't? I realized when I saw you pull up in the driveway that I don't know you … I mean, really know you. Every time we are together I always talk about myself and you remain aloof, like a beautiful, unattainable object."

She raised her eyebrows. "That last part sounds like a quote from a book," she said uneasily.

"I don't mean it in a superior sense. It's more like, well, you're hiding something. Like you've built a wall around yourself and you don't want to let anyone in. Is it because of your divorce?"

She blinked. "Divorce? Divorce. Oh, no. That was a long time ago. I rarely think of it at all," she said, feeling a slight flush creep up her neck. She truly hated lying.

"Then what is it?" he pressed, his eyes catching and impaling her own.

Elizabeyta carefully considered how to proceed. She did a quick scan of Lee. His thoughts were cloudy and muddled—this could be good; then again, it could herald dangerous territory. One thing was certain, she couldn't carry this much further. Her own emotions threatened to get in the way. If she didn't think straight, she couldn't use her psychic gifts. Her power would get twisted and give her false information. That spelled disaster.

He reached over the table and captured her hand. She cleared her throat nervously. It was possible that even this visit of his could be putting his life in danger. She had to keep him at a distance—it would be safer for both of them, yet she wavered ever so slightly. What if she did tell him the truth? Maybe he would want to help her. Then she wouldn't be so alone. She ached to be forceful, unabashedly forward and lure him upstairs … Elizabeyta sighed internally, ventured a smile, and slowly withdrew her hand. What silliness was this? No, away he must go. This was not going to be easy.

"Have you been interested in religion all your life?" she asked. Once again she felt her irritation growing. If only he would go home now. Why did he make her so testy, so agitated? It was like waiting for a tornado you barely glimpse at the horizon, but you instinctively know is coming your way.

Obviously taken back by her remark about religion, he cleared his throat and moved to refill both their tea cups. "I find that most people are not as spiritual as they may like, simply because their busy schedules preclude it. I hope that I'm able to bring something to them, or at least open their minds a bit."

Elizabeyta could hardly sit still. What was wrong? She tapped her fingernails nervously on the side of her tea cup.

Lee kept talking, as if he didn't notice her fidgety behavior. "My mother was Catholic and my father a Methodist, but I had difficulty with needing a middle-man to God, which didn't make my mother too happy with me. Protestant studies have been more to my liking, which is why I'm pursuing a career there."

"A career?" Elizabeyta lifted the steaming cup toward her mouth. It jittered a bit before she caught it with her upper lip to steady the cup. What was her problem? Anger at herself and her lack of bodily control rose in her mind. He had to go home.

Lee hesitated. "Yes, it will be my life's work, so I've always seen it as a career, sort of." He grinned. "But see, you've turned the conversation again and I'm the topic. I want to know about you, because I want to marry you."

Time stopped dead for Elizabeyta. In a hiccup, she sputtered, spilling hot tea on herself and the table. "That's not possible!" she whispered. "Simply out of the question. You don't even know me!" She lowered the tea cup with a bang.

Lee smiled. "That's the point. I want to know everything about you!"

"Oh, no. You don't know what you're saying," she said, feeling her blood pressure rising. Not good. Not good. The fatigue she'd held off since she sat down to dinner crept insidiously over her. She rocked her head on her shoulders, fluttering her eyes. "I'm from a very religious family as well," she said, not meeting his gaze, trying to form logical words that stuck in her throat. "It's a rather unusual one, not so much in belief, rather in history. Unfortunately, people don't like us much, particularly over the last 2000 years …"

"Don't be ridiculous, Elizabeyta; there isn't a single reason, religious or otherwise, why I would change my mind about you."

She shook her head vehemently. More hair spilled over her ears. Cocking an eyebrow angrily, she said, "One of the things you didn't like about Terry Anderson, if I remember correctly, was her involvement in her New Age shop. You thought she was silly. Those were your exact words. 'Terry had some silly notions.'"

Lee looked at her, exasperated. "What does Terry have to do with this? That's old history. We stopped seeing each other over a year and a half ago."

"But you never got over her. Besides, you didn't appreciate her alternative beliefs," she snapped.

It was his turn to shake his head. "It wasn't like that at all. It's just, well, she would have been a minister's wife, my wife, My parish is … conservative. But I never said anything to her about it and religious choice was not the impetus for our breakup," he said firmly. "She was too young for me. Look, if you are worried I won't like you because of your religious preferences, you're wrong."

She saw the fear in his eyes. He really hadn't expected her to be anything but pleased at his proposal. She desperately tried to determine if this was a spur of the moment action on his part, or had he been considering it for awhile and simply not had the courage to tell her? For Goddess' sake, the man had never shared more than a meal with her! How could he ask her to marry him? She tried hard to scan him, but nothing came through. Her own emotions were increasingly hard to control. Maybe it was the long drive or the fact she was sure the end of her search for her grandmother's killer loomed ahead, or maybe, just maybe, she liked this man more than she wanted to admit.

"I don't care what you say, Elizabeyta, I'm going to marry you." His jaw set in a determined line. The desperation to make him stop rose in her throat like an upheaval of bile.

"You don't understand," she was nearly shouting now. "Everything I've told you about myself is a lie. You can't marry me! We're friends. Just friends. It can't go any further than that." Too late to stop. Too late. Too late. "I'm a Witch. W-I-T-C-H," she spelled with such force she nearly spit on the table. "Witch as in a person who casts spells. Witch as in someone who follows the Old Religion. I can't marry you, Lee. It simply isn't possible! I'm not here because I work for some stupid software company. I'm here to find my grandmother's killer." She half rose out of her chair and pointed her finger at his chest, poking him several times in the breastbone. "You, you, you are a problem right now. A pain. Leave me alone!" She flopped back down in her chair. A curling strand of hair fell across her face and she blew it away from her nose. Did she smell lilacs?

The words had flown from her mouth with such force she'd no idea what hit her. *Oh, good Goddess,* she thought. *Why in the world did I tell him? Could it be that I really do love him?* No, that was ridiculous. She was just plain tired and fed up.

Lee stared at her dumfounded. He rose slowly from the table, pacing the kitchen floor. "We are going to deal with this calmly and rationally. Let's leave the … ah … religious question alone for the moment and concentrate on the … so-called murder of your grandmother. I think you owe me an explanation." He leaned both arms stiffly on the table, palms outward, shoulders hunched toward her.

Elizabeyta rested both elbows on the table, massaging her eyes and forehead. She should never have come back. Why didn't she let the family deal with the problem? This would never have happened. Although the thought careened ridiculously around in her head, Lee could be a part of it. After all, he lived right next to Aunt Beth Ann. Didn't the newspaper man's wife, Mrs. Renard, say that county officials and even the police believed in the dark side of magick? What if Lee knew something, or was involved? Get real! She sniffed once. That damnable smell of lilacs again.

When she didn't answer him immediately, Lee stood and began pacing again. "I want to help you, Elizabeyta. Please, I'm in love with you!"

At that moment the half-filled tureen of stew levitated three inches off the table and dipped crazily forward and backward. Elizabeyta jumped out of her chair as the large bowl smashed back to the smooth surface, spewing broken china and bits of thick, brown gravy and vegetables everywhere. Lee, frozen in mid-pace, simply stared at the table.

They turned slowly to one another, eyes round.

"Looks like your ghost has been listening after all," remarked Lee.

"Indeed," whispered Elizabeyta. "Good evening, Aunt Beth Ann," she said between gritted teeth, "so nice of you to entertain us."

The scent of lilacs grew thick around them, then dissipated.

CHAPTER FOUR

HEY BOTH STOOD ABSOLUTELY STILL, WAIT-
ing for another outburst from the ghostly
Beth Ann. When nothing happened, Lee
took a deep breath and said, "Guess she didn't like
where the conversation was heading. I wonder if it
was my marriage proposal or your outburst?"

"I assume," said Elizabeyta, stooping to pick
up the shattered pieces of china, "that she didn't
care for either."

Lee looked cautiously around the room and
back to Elizabeyta. God, she was beautiful. High
cheekbones, large dark eyes that beckoned one to
drown in them given half the chance. Her long,
auburn hair, once swept high atop her head, gathered in an obvious hurry after her shower, now
tumbled delightfully across her shoulders. The
sultry highlights gleamed in the low light of the
kitchen. He resisted the urge to reach out and
touch her, controlling his actions as he'd done so

many times in the past when they were together. Instead, he said, "Do you think she'll do something else?"

Elizabeyta shook her head. "Moving things seems to tire her out. I doubt she'll do anything more. I've found her to be quiet for hours after a display like this."

"I've visited you many times," remarked Lee thoughtfully, "and she never took offense to anything we've said."

"Guess we got her riled up. Could be a lot of reasons," mumbled Elizabeyta, moving back and forth between the floor and the trash can. "Who knows with Beth Ann. I can't decide myself whether she is enemy or friend, though she's never done anything to outright hurt me. She's more of a pain than anything else."

"Where's your mop?" asked Lee, looking around the kitchen.

"In the pantry," said Elizabeyta, "the door's hanging open there." She pointed to one of the two doors behind him. "The bucket, I think, is beside it."

Lee fumbled around in the pantry gathering the mop and bucket, trying to make sense of the bizarre words she'd uttered. Normally, he didn't believe in the supernatural. Ghosts, murder, witches … but she'd always seemed so calm, secure in her life. Could he suspend his own beliefs to listen to her? He paused for a moment. He could hear her throwing more glass into the trash can. He stealthily peeked around the corner and thought of how he'd perceived her over the last two years, realizing now, more than ever, he knew nothing of this haughty creature mundanely picking up shards of glass on her hands and knees and tossing them with tiny clinks into the yellow rubber can. He'd perceived her as someone of great inner strength and delightfully pleasant—a fine woman of values and principles. She'd been so serious, so angry tonight. But she'd lied to him. What would keep her from lying to him again? As if she'd heard his thoughts, her head whirled in his direction. He hated it when she did that.

"You see how easy I am to domesticate?" said Lee, pasting a smile on his face as he emerged from the pantry.

Elizabeyta threw him an unreadable look, grabbed the bucket out of his hand and began filling it with hot water from the double, stainless steel sink.

He stood close to her shoulder, inhaling the exotic scent of her hair. "I want to know the truth, Elizabeyta. You can't leave me hanging after an outburst like that," said Lee firmly.

She stared at him. Finally she said, "I'll only explain if you give me your word, as a minister, that you won't repeat what I tell you. That means no cops, no newspaper people—absolutely no one."

"You've not been especially honest with me," he said.

"I must have your word or you can forget it and walk out that door for good." She turned off the tap and removed the bucket from the sink, staring at him with her lips pressed tightly together, holding the heavy plastic container with effort. Some of the water slopped on the floor and she ignored it.

He couldn't take his eyes off her. He had to know what mystery surrounded this woman. She entranced and enticed him, and he had to have more. "I promise I won't tell anyone," he said simply, never considering the impact her story may have on his life.

Her face softened a bit, the anxiety draining. He took the bucket from her and set it down on the floor. "I'll mop. You sit down and tell me," he said. She nodded, collapsing in a chair, propping her long legs on the one beside it.

"As far as anyone in this town knows, there never was a murder," she began. "A little over two years ago, my grandmother insisted she come here to see Aunt Beth Ann."

Lee dipped the mop in the bucket, squeezing out the excess water. He purposefully did not look at her, wanting her to tell the story in her own time.

"My grandmother and Beth Ann are—I mean were, sisters. They stopped talking to each other almost thirty years ago. Some big family fight that no one ever explained to the children." She took a deep breath and continued. "My grandmother did not entertain arguments over anything. You see, in our home, on the farm, she literally ran everything. It is the right of the chosen matriarch of the family to do as she pleases."

Lee stopped mopping, but didn't look up.

"I mean, Grandma wasn't cruel or anything. Everyone thought of her as a wise and kind person. The covenstead, where I live, is very big. We have several families with homes on the land. All of us are related. We depend on each other for religious as well as economic support. All of us are Witches."

Lee began mopping again, working hard to keep his face expressionless.

"So when Grandma up and told everyone she was coming back here to see Beth Ann, no one opposed her. What they thought privately, of course, is a different matter, but no one stopped her from coming. We thought it had to do with family business, and maybe it did; we aren't sure. It was only after she disappeared that we started putting the pieces together."

Lee leaned on the mop handle. "So Beth Ann Baxter, the woman who lived in this house, was your grandmother's sister?"

"Right. You see, before I was born all the family lived in this area. But there was so much trouble about their religion that they left and moved to another state."

"Nebraska?"

"No. None of us are allowed to reveal the location of the covenstead. I'm sorry." She looked legitimately dismayed at not being able to tell him, but it bothered him anyway. Another secret.

Lee resumed mopping the last bit of linoleum and squeezed the mop tightly. "Where do you want me to dump this water?" he asked.

"Oh, just leave it there. I'll get it later."

He pulled up a chair beside her and sat down. "And then what happened?" he prodded gently.

She sighed. "Well, Grandma flew in to the Harrisburg International Airport. She called to tell us that she was taking a cab to Aunt Beth's house and that she'd made it in okay. She was in a good mood and joked with the twins—that's my brother and sister back home. We thought everything was fine until my brother woke up in the middle of the night, screaming that Beth Ann and Grandma were dead."

Lee looked at her incredulously. Elizabeyta shook her head. "Oh, I know. Most people would have thought it was just a bad dream and sent him back to bed, but not in my house. My family believes in dreams and omens. We called here, to this very house … several times, and no one answered. Finally, we called my aunt's attorney and had him check on her. He's an old friend of the family. Or at least he was. He died about five months later of old age. Anyway, when he got here he found Beth Ann dead as a doornail. The local coroner ruled it natural causes—heart attack."

"And your grandmother?" asked Lee quietly.

"No sign of her. Nothing. The attorney asked all the neighbors and no one had seen her." She looked directly at Lee then, pinioning him with her dark, liquid eyes.

He could feel his eyebrows winging on his forehead. "I remember! Charles what's-his-name. He came over and asked me if I'd seen anyone around the house the day before!"

"And had you?"

Again she searched his eyes and he felt a little dizzy, not the first time this had happened with her. It was as if she could scoop those soft, pale fingers into his brain and pull out anything she pleased. It was unnerving, but it always left him intrigued. Sadly, he said, "No. I saw no one. I'm so sorry." He meant it.

She shrugged her shoulders and turned away to stare at the floor. "A large family debate ensued. Some of us wanted to call the local police immediately, but the elders held sway. They said they would handle it in their own way in their own time. To call the police was forbidden. None of us attended Beth Ann's funeral. She was, after all, an outcast of the family and since we didn't know the fate of Grandma for sure at the time, we didn't want to hurt her chances should she still be alive. We remained at the covenstead."

They sat in silence for a moment. A gust of wind rattled at the kitchen window. Neither of them looked up. Lee kept his mouth shut, not wanting to stop the momentum of the story. He watched as she twisted the bottom of her sweatshirt with the kneading motions of a lost child.

"Four days later," said Elizabeyta softly, "Grandma's suitcase showed up in an unused dumpster outside a train station in New York. It was a fluke anyone found it. No one knows what happened to Grandma, or how her suitcase got to New York. Her identification was in her suitcase along with her ritual bag. She never went anywhere without that ritual bag; that's why we assumed she was dead. After a horrid amount of red tape, the suitcase was returned to us." She looked at him with wide, moist eyes. He clenched his hands to keep from taking her in his arms, but unanswered questions loomed in his mind. He had to know the rest.

He waited until he felt sure she had finished. "I thought you said no one was supposed to know where the covenstead is? You said that her identification was in the suitcase. Surely the killer now knows where your family lives?"

She shook her head. "All of us carry the address of a safe house on our identification. Each safe house has an answering machine and is rented to non-magickal people through the corporation. Usually they are people we have helped somehow when the chips were really down. The line and machine are dedicated only to our use. When a call comes through the renters let us know immediately. If the cops should come knocking at the door for any reason looking for one of us, they are schooled on what to say. No one ever knows the difference. Their loyalty is unquestionable."

"Sounds like an extended amount of protection," said Lee. Did her people really live in fear like this? Surely this was another yarn, a tale too incredible to be believed. He pressed on. "Why didn't your family allow the police to have all the facts?"

Her shoulders slumped. "Because Grandma isn't the only member of our family to be murdered. Someone is picking us off, one by one, usually when we are alone or traveling. We think it started about five years ago. At least, that's when the first 'accidental' death occurred. We don't know who it is or why they are doing it, but my family feels that the police, at least the local ones here, may be involved somehow, or at least know about it and are keeping quiet. To date, all the deaths have been listed as accidental, except for Grandma's. Whoever killed her must have lost his or her head."

"There's got to be someone you could trust to handle this for you. A private investigator?"

She shook her head and her hair slid delicately around her pale face. "We tried that. He's conveniently missing. I think it got too hot for him and he just cut out." He noticed the trembling of her lower lip.

Lee leaned back in his chair. "Then for two years you've been out here, trying to find the killer or killers? How?"

Elizabeyta ran her hands over her face. "I've been going through the records in the attic. Beth Ann kept everything. She was the family archivist until she married her husband. She swore she'd burned everything that the family didn't take with them to the covenstead, but she lied. She never touched a thing. We thought by going through those records we could figure out who may be responsible for the murders."

"I don't understand. How could old records tell you who is responsible for the recent deaths in your family?"

Elizabeyta stared at the fire, and didn't answer.

"Elizabeyta?"

Without turning her head to look at him, she said, "Because we think whoever is responsible did it before."

"Before?"

He watched her closely, his breath catching in his chest. She appeared to be wrestling with something. She flung her head back, not looking at him, eyes slipping closed. Tears flowed beneath her long, black lashes onto her cheeks. "Yes, that's why the family left here in the first place. Someone started killing our children," she sobbed, then bit her trembling lower lip. She arched her neck, then slowly lowered her head, opening her eyes at the fire. "One at a time, through accidental deaths—just like now. We think that same someone is still living and for some reason has decided to continue the elimination." Her voice ended in a whisper.

"Who are the others who recently died?" He hoped in his heart they were not children.

"Adults. Those who were to take my grandmother's place." She swallowed hard. "My parents died in an auto accident a year ago, then my uncle last May in a freak hunting fiasco in Maine." She shook her head. "I don't want to talk about the others."

He touched her lightly on the cheek. "What about the others?"

"There were six all together, including Grandma, my parents and my uncle." She held up her fingers, counting off the macabre list. "A cousin in Texas and her husband, but I didn't count him because he wasn't officially a member of the covenstead. They died in a small plane crash. My cousin's husband was flying the plane. The last was my nephew. He'd just turned twenty-one. His tractor rolled on him."

"Surely the last was a legitimate accident."

"On a flat field?"

"Then why would they send you? Aren't you afraid?" He reached out and touched her slender shoulders, willing her to look at him. He believed her. Damn it, he truly believed her. She refused to meet his gaze. Her eyes were fixed on the fire. He could see the flames dancing on her pupils. Suddenly, he was afraid for her. "Why are you doing this?"

"Because I have been chosen to take my grandmother's place. The family is now my responsibility. In October a ceremony will be performed and I will officially lead the family tradition, for better or for worse. I've been groomed for it all my life, though they all thought I would be older when I assumed the position. You see, I can't marry you, or anyone outside of my religion. It's not like that for all of us. But it is like that for me. I couldn't stay here and be your wife; that opportunity is not now, and was never, open to me. My husband must be of my faith. It is the way. This has been my test, to see if I could survive and protect the family." She dipped her head like a queen, a small smile touching her full, lush lips. "A challenge, if you will," she said softly.

"That's ridiculous! Who would send a woman out to be slaughtered? What kind of people are they?"

Her head snapped up to face him. "Be careful what you say, preacher man. My family is loving and warm. I wasn't supposed to come this time. They were going to send others, but I know this is something I have to do. We take care of our own, don't make the mistake." Her perfectly formed teeth flashed against her sanguine lips. "The blood in our veins is thick and binding and we would die for one another. We are unified by ancestral lineage. We were warriors once, and if need be, we shall be warriors again!" She drew in close to him and looked him in the eye. "When the time is right, we will notify the proper authorities and let them render justice, if there is any left to be had. Make no mistake about it," she hissed.

Lee drew back from her deadly-glittering eyes. He could feel the power pulsating from her body and for the first time in his life, he feared another human being.

chapter five

"I'M A DEAD MAN," MUTTERED TIMOTHY REED to himself.

As the greater portion of the small town of Whiskey Springs slumbered, Timothy sat rigidly behind his desk, staring at nothing. Was he the only soul out of the 3,500 residents shaking in his slippers? Was he the only grown-up idiot in this town who sat shivering like a child, cowering in his leather desk chair as if some bogeyman lurked outside the door?

The only light in his study came from the lone lamp on the desk, a new-fangled thing that looked better than it worked. A little before midnight, his home squatted around him, as quiet as a condemned funeral parlor.

It was the day after Christmas. He'd always hated the day after Christmas. The world built excitement and energy for months, simply to expel

24

it on one single day. And for what? For bills and invoices that left monetary snail tracks in your life. For fatigue, nervous stomachs, and family squabbles over not being able to provide enough or giving too much. In fact, he despised the entire week after Christmas—a time when, statistically, suicides peaked and old people moved in spirit to wherever people go when the body's fed up with work, pain, and sickness. If there was such a place.

An involuntary shiver tickled his spine. There were all kinds of killers in life. Diseases killed you, accidents killed you, and people killed you, sometimes on purpose. He vaguely wondered if lack of sleep could kill you. If so, there was probably a death certificate waiting for him with his name on it. Every night for the last month, in an unwanted ritual, he always found himself here, facing the phone. He longed to take a walk, but of course it was dark outside. He didn't like the dark anymore.

He stared at the phone without really seeing it. His long, blunt fingers wound and unwound the coiling cord connecting the receiver to the base. It wasn't that he expected a call this very night, or even tomorrow. It would come. Sometime. Maybe soon. Maybe tonight.

A muffled tap on the door jolted him to his senses. The door swung quietly open and his wife, Marjorie, peered sleepily into the dim room. "Timothy?"

"Yeah?"

"Don't you think you should try to get some sleep, dear? You can't keep this up night after night. Why don't you come to bed?"

He smiled softly at his wife. She shook her dark, tousled head in dismay, sliding her hands into the pockets of her long, fuzzy blue robe. At forty she was still attractive—at least in his book. "I'm sorry, honey. I didn't want to keep you awake, so I thought I'd come down here and sit for awhile."

"Just sitting alone?"

"Seemed to be the thing to do."

The bitter December wind raked across the glass of the large picture window behind him. The pane billowed and rattled. He clenched his fists unconsciously. It was one thing to not be able to sleep, but quite another to be badgered in full wakefulness by the nasty weather.

He stood and stretched, pulling his heavy, black velour robe tightly around his body.

Marjorie padded softly across the carpet and sat on the edge of his desk, adjusting her robe. "Is it the upcoming campaign? Don't worry about it, Tim, we've been through this race before. You should feel relieved. You're the incumbent. You've done a good job and I'm sure you'll win."

Timothy turned his back to her and peered out the frost-etched window, beyond the daggers of glittering ice that hung from the eaves of the house. His fingers rolled lint balls at the bottom of his pockets. Insulated from the storm, he watched the willow trees in the backyard bend and sway.

Mark's old tire swing creaked under the heavy weight of snow and ice. "Maybe that, or maybe I'm going through male menopause or something." He tried to sound light, jovial, but his words fell flat against the glass.

"If not the campaign, then what?"

"Getting older. Thinking about life," *and death*, he thought. A gust of wind clawed against the window, and Timothy involuntarily stepped back, his own reflection now coming into focus. God, did he really look that bad? For an instant, he thought he saw them … their long black coats flapping among the trees.

His guts in a twist, he grabbed the drapery cord, and with a tight snap, obliterated the view. Maybe they would finally decide to do that to him, too. Obliterate the view.

In the beginning, he simply didn't believe. Not at all. Not one magickal bit of it. His brain wouldn't process it. He was used to dealing with facts and figures; statistics and numbers made his world a comfortable place to be. He had turned forty-two last May, a nice even number, without the fear or remorse most men felt.

The grandfather clock he had given Marjorie on their fifteenth anniversary began to chime, its sound reverberating from the darkened dining room at the front of the house as he turned to face her.

"The witching hour," she said quietly. "Want to come upstairs and tell me a ghost story?"

He smiled and shook his head. With his index finger he traced the meticulous printing on the manila folders stacked in perfect alignment in the OUT bin on his desk … each pencil, pen, pad, and paperclip precisely set in its appropriate place. The IN bin yawned empty and dustless. Just like his future, he mused … empty, void of hope. A lone tear escaped, slipping through the stubble of a day-old shadow.

"What's the matter, Timothy?"

"Marge, I think I've made a horrible mistake," he said, turning away from her.

"What kind of mistake? Is it us?" An almost hysterical timbre slipped into her voice. How many sleepless hours had she spent wondering what was going on with him?

He reached over and took her in his arms. "No, not us. God, never us." He kissed her and held her for a moment, then listlessly dropped his arms.

"Then is it money? You've made some bad investments, haven't you?" She looked him squarely in the eye. "Tell me the truth. I shouldn't have spent so much this Christmas. I'm sorry. With all that extra money we had this year I guess I went a little crazy. It was the first time in so long that I could just go anywhere I wanted and buy anything that struck my fancy. I'm so sorry, Timothy."

He looked at her in amazement. She thought it was her fault! "No, it's not the money you spent."

"I'll make it up, help you save," she rushed on. "We've been through tough times before, we can make it again. Do you remember those meatless spaghetti dinners we shared every night for a month when we were first married?" She chuckled. "To this day I can't eat spaghetti, but we'll get through it, you'll see."

Another gust of wind banged on the window, shaking the drapes.

"It's not the money, Marge." He tried to keep the irritation out of his voice. How could he expect her to understand or even relate to what he had done? It wasn't her fault. "Maybe you're right, maybe part of it is the elections. The mechanics are so tiresome. Dinners, speeches, advertising, and baby-kissing almost wore me to a frazzle the last time. The town is growing and I'm tired of the time-honored suck-up bit."

He looked over at Marjorie, who stared at him intently. Did she guess? She wasn't a stupid woman. Obviously she'd been wondering what was going on. Maybe he should let her think it was another woman after all? It wouldn't take her long to put the story together. Then what would she think? Would she simply separate and take their teenage son in an angry whoosh of skirts, or would she quietly file for divorce? If she did, what would they do to her?

Fear stung at him nastily. *Oh my God*, he thought. For the first time he realized what could happen to his wife and son if she found out. All this time he'd been worried about his own safety, selfishly wallowing in concern over his personal life expectancy, never thinking about Marjorie or Mark. Well, of course he thought of them. That was the reason for buying in, to give them a better life. But he thought of them as a living, loving family, not a pair of corpses. What to do? He must tell her nothing. It was the only way to ensure their safety.

Marjorie leaned into him. "Come to bed. I promise I'll make it worthwhile."

He rubbed her back affectionately as she slipped off the edge of the desk.

"Come to me," she said playfully, her extended hands running down his arm and capturing his fingertips with her own.

"No, not yet." He glanced at the phone.

"Are you sure there isn't something you have to tell me? You said you thought you'd made a mistake? Do you mean … is there—"

The phone purred. His thoughts tripped over each other, leaving his mind a momentary blank. Her fingers slipped from his and dropped to the sides of her bathrobe.

"Who would call after midnight?" she said, concern etching tiny lines around her eyes. "Were you expecting a call?" He thought he caught a guarded inflection in her voice. The phone continued to ring.

"Maybe somebody else can't sleep," he offered lamely.

She stared at him in disbelief. "What are you, a doctor for insomnia?"

He shrugged his shoulders. "Why don't you go on up to bed and I'll be there in a minute."

The phone continued to ring persistently. "Aren't you going to answer it?" she asked, not budging.

"Sure. In a second." He didn't move a muscle.

"Timothy?" Her eyes narrowed.

The ring of the phone haunted the space between them.

"I'll handle it. Don't worry."

"Why don't you want me to know who's calling?" She reached for the phone.

He snatched up the receiver, turning his back to her.

"Fine!" she growled, turned on her heel, and slammed the study door behind her.

chapter six

"REED HERE," HE MURMURED, CLASPING THE receiver with a moist palm.

"Good evening, Timothy."

His heart sank … he would know that voice anywhere. *Gotta be firm,* he thought. *Don't give him the upper hand any sooner than you have to.* He gathered his resolve to keep his voice calm and level. To give himself added assurance, he cradled the phone on his shoulder and cinched the belt of his bathrobe tighter around his middle. "Good evening, Jason," he said coolly.

"We have another small favor to ask of you."

Timothy jerked his head, the receiver slipping off his shoulder, clattering to the desktop. His face reddened. How utterly embarrassing. He swallowed hard and raised the receiver to his ear.

"Now, Tim my boy," he was saying, "all we're after is a little information. It will be totally painless on your part. And quite lucrative, as usual."

Timothy's heart pounded in his chest. So, it wasn't his time yet. Suddenly the thought that they may never be finished with him horrified him more than any nightmare he had ever thought possible. He gathered what shred of courage he had. "What is it this time?"

"Just some background on a possible new resident in our fair town," said Jason.

At that moment, Timothy was envisioning a large black creature slurping on a rotting carcass … his. He leaned heavily on the desk.

"How new?" Timothy was well aware that in this part of Pennsylvania, a "new resident" could have lived in the county for over twenty years and still be considered an outsider by some.

"We're not sure. But you'll be able to find out when you do the background check for us."

Timothy shifted his feet. Something very frightening indeed came to mind. "Jason, you're not going to … to dispose of this one are you? The last time I gave you 'just a little information,' the guy wound up dead at the bottom of Pinchot Lake." He could feel the hysteria rising, exploding toward the receiver that now shook in his bone-white hand. "That's not going to happen again, is it? I simply won't allow it! I will not be a party to such an event. Do you understand?" he shouted.

"For a man who can't even control the receiver he's holding," drawled Jason, "the concept of allowing or not allowing any event to take place is most likely beyond his control, wouldn't you think … Timothy?"

He fumbled for the desk chair and sat down hard. He was close to straight-jacket city. He knew the information he'd given had resulted in at least two murders. He didn't want to think about the other packets he'd handed over. How many were there? Six? Seven? They'd told him about the last two, just to keep him in line. It was working.

"Now, Timmy, you needn't be so flighty! A fuss you make. And for what? What we do is none of your concern. You have a nice, happy home, right?" Jason emphasized "happy," and Timothy didn't like the sound of that. Not one bit.

How he hated the Pennsylvania Dutch mannerisms and speech patterns! Flighty indeed—more like a one way ticket to hell. As his anger rose, his fear snapped back under control.

"And how is that fine son of yours doing?" continued Jason. "He must be almost seventeen now? And your wife, too; I'm sure she's proud of her home."

The hackles on the back of Timothy's neck rose. This was the ultimate threat, of course. Target the kid, then the wife. For release, his attention temporarily shifted to the sound of a high-pitched whine outside the window. The storm sounded like a pack of starving wolves out there. He shivered.

"Timothy?" drifted through the phone line.

Clearing his throat, Timothy answered a little louder than necessary.

"Ah, yes … Mark. Mark is doing fine. And Marge certainly does love the new additions. So good of you to inquire." He wanted to add "you bastard," but couldn't quite get it past his clenched teeth.

Jason continued smoothly, "I'll need this information as soon as possible. Will that be a problem?"

Tim didn't answer immediately.

"We'll give you three days. No more."

"You realize, Jason, that if the person hasn't bought any property, registered to vote, or filled out any official documents, he'll be difficult to find."

"Actually, I want you to call in some favors from the governor's office. I want an extensive search."

"That may take more than three days, Jason."

"If you care for your happy home, you will have the information to me in three days and no more."

Timothy's heart fluttered. He was also peeved at the leg work this request would entail. Especially during the week after Christmas, when most government employees were off and those who actually showed up at their jobs were performing the dance of the lame duck all over the country.

"Three days," mused Timothy. "Either you are running scared or this person has something you want very badly. I thought you people weren't afraid of anything? You've got the power, right? How come you can't simply do some hoodoo-voodoo and figure out where this person is and what he's into yourself?"

Dead silence greeted his outburst. Maybe he had pressed Jason too far. Better yet, maybe he had hit a nerve. He would have to think about this. Well, then, good! It was time he started to fight back, even if it was only a weak attempt at word play.

Jason broke into his thoughts. "Actually, I'll make it easier for you," said Jason. "Check out this address … 200 North Main Street, Whiskey Springs. I want everything. Deed information, liens, bank records, credit report on the current resident, social security number—the works."

Timothy quickly scratched the information down on top of one of the pristine manila folders on his desk. "The name?"

"Elizabeyta Belladonna," announced Jason.

Timothy sat up straight and sucked his breath between his teeth. "I thought you people didn't mess with women."

"A picture of the woman is already at your home, between the screen and the front door. I'm sure it will be most helpful to you."

The receiver went dead in Timothy's hands, leaving him to stare at it in dumbfounded silence. The hair on his arms waltzed to the serenade of the howling storm. He looked down at the name hastily jotted on the paper but couldn't bring himself to read it again. Perhaps she would get away if he didn't think about it right now. Avoiding the folder, he looked around the room to occupy his mind. Why on earth would Jason's people want to know about a woman? What could she have possibly done or have to merit their attention? He hoped to God that whatever she'd done had hurt Jason badly, and that she had sense enough to move on before she had nothing left to move with but her own coffin. Life was getting colder, definitely icy, and if he wasn't careful, well—how cold was insanity?

He'd better get that picture before Marge found it.

CHAPTER SEVEN

LIZABEYTA TOSSED AND TURNED BENEATH the voluminous quilt. Wide-eyed, furious at herself for not being able to calm her mind enough to slip into much-needed sleep, she kicked off the covers and sat on the windowseat in her bedroom, unblinking eyes entranced by the raging storm descending upon Whiskey Springs. It wasn't the wind tearing around the outside of the house, snuffling over the roof, creating whirlpools of new fallen snow in the depths of her yard that disturbed her. No—its power rode hot in her veins and she reveled in it. She closed her eyes and moved into its fury, indulging in the elemental intensity of the moment. What would it feel like to always be part of a storm of this magnitude? To have no cares for human frailties?

She sighed, shivering as the cold air around the window encircled her. What to do? Glancing at the clock on her night table, she realized that Lee had left over two hours ago, yet it seemed like he'd bent over and kissed her good-bye only moments before. Her fingers rose to her lips, delicately touching them, remembering his warm breath entangled with her own. Her fingers traced the frown that pulled at the corners of her mouth. Weren't you supposed to be happy when you were in love? Perhaps she was not in the throes of passion at all, but in the depths of loneliness, trying vainly to fill the hole with Lee's attentions. A somber thought indeed.

She gazed through the window. Much of Lee's house hid behind the violent curtain of wind and snow. One lone light shone from a second floor window, weakly piercing the veil of the storm. She wondered if he lay awake, thinking of her.

He'd said as he drew her into his arms that he didn't care about her religion at all, though when she scanned him, she felt an uncertainty. Of course, she dumped a lot on him tonight. It would take him some time to sort it all out. Guilt surfaced. How could she have allowed herself to pull an innocent person into this mess? Her karma was probably warped forever for that move. She wrapped her arms around herself and squeezed tightly. When she was a little girl, Grandma told her she would know when the right man came along. If Lee was the right man, why didn't she feel better?

The air filled with the scent of lilacs and she looked up expectantly. Any moment now Beth Ann might make her presence known. She waited hopefully. Perhaps this time Beth Ann would talk to her and unravel this damnable mystery once and for all. Then they could all get on with their lives, and if she was lucky, live happily ever after.

The room remained empty.

The wind screeched.

The cold limbs of the maple trees slapped at the sides of the house.

Inside, only her warm breath stirred the air.

The scent filtered slowly away.

She stretched her legs, pulling the grey flannel nightgown down around them. What would Grandma say if she were in a situation like this? What would Grandma do?

Grandma would tell her she'd lost her mind. A Protestant minister for a prospective husband—she'd certainly snort at that. Not that she didn't respect other religions, but other clergy usually didn't understand the mysteries, and even if they did, their parishioners wouldn't. A choice would eventually have to be made. As much as Lee made light of it, the import to Elizabeyta was obvious. One of them would have to choose.

Choose. That's what Beth Ann had done. Chosen not to stay with the family. Chosen to devote her life to the priest of another religion, to leave the magick and the mysteries behind her. Elizabeyta raised her head slowly. How stupid of her not to understand! That's what the argument must have been about all those years ago. Two sisters linked by lineage, blood, and magick. One choosing to stay, the other to leave. Why didn't she think of it before?

She slipped off the windowseat and circled the bed. Did the two sisters desire to see each other again because Beth Ann wanted to come back? There had been a few others in the family who left and returned once the passion for whatever they left for was over. Why not Beth Ann? But after thirty years? In frustration, she slapped her hands against her thighs. Who knew?

Beth Ann knew and she wasn't talking. Wasn't—or couldn't? All this time Elizabeyta had assumed Beth Ann was simply being stubborn. What if something stopped her from communicating as the mysteries had taught? Worse, what if she had forgotten? Thirty years out of practice and the complication of death would certainly have some sort of effect on the woman's abilities.

Elizabeyta flounced on the edge of the bed, reached over and turned on the light on the night table. The worn tarot cards she kept by the lamp were strewn in an uneven lump. Odd. She'd left them in their leather bag before she went to bed, meaning to throw a spread in the morning, when her mind could function without fatigue. She didn't remember taking them out and looking at them, and even if she did, she'd never leave them in a mess like that.

Her eyes flicked across the night table and down to the carpeted floor, looking for the leather bag that belonged to the cards. Not in sight, she got off the bed and crouched, running her hands under the dust ruffle of the bed. Her fingers bumped into the smooth leather and she stretched to retrieve the bag.

She straightened the cards on the table and moved to put them back in the bag when she realized a few cards nestled deep within the pouch. She drew them out slowly and set them on the quilt. She turned over the King of Wands first. Hmmm … fair-haired, communicative, likes working with people—that must be Lee. Swallowing nervously, she turned over the second card. The King of Swords. Who could that be? The third card revealed the embrace of the Lovers. This card meant a choice between two paths. She pondered this a moment along with the two kings. Perhaps a choice between two men … but she wasn't involved with two men right now. How strange. Confused, she flipped the next one up. The King of Cups reversed. Ugh. Usually a devious, shifty, dishonest man involved in illegal enterprises. If she was reading for someone else she'd tell her to stay away from this guy. Her hand reached over slowly and turned over another card. The Devil. Obviously the reversed King of Cups must be the man who threatened her family, mixed up in all sorts of nasty business. Maybe drugs, alcohol, or prostitution, or all three for all she knew. The last card sealed the image—the Tower with its crumbling foundation and lightning bolts of destruction. The King of Cups meant to do her in, no doubt about it.

Had Beth Ann left this message for her? On impulse she grabbed the remainder of the deck and extracted one card—the seven of Cups. "All that glitters is not gold," she mumbled to herself. "Choose wisely."

chapter eight

SARAH GOODLING SCRATCHED HER AMPLE HIP under her K-Mart brand nightie and heaved herself out of bed. Her stomach rumbled as she read the luminous dial of the clock on her nightstand: 1:15 AM. She searched the chilly floor for her furry pink slippers and finally found them, one at each corner of the room.

"Damn cat must've been playing with them again!" she muttered, and promptly tripped over a massive ball of spitting fur. "Zipper! You been playin' with my slippers?" She struggled to gently lift the feline monstrosity onto her bed, finally giving up by unceremoniously dumping him onto the floor at her feet.

Sarah lumbered through her tenement-style home, following the beam of light that filtered into the second floor hallway from a Mickey Mouse nightlight at the head of the stairs. She always kept the light on these days. She didn't like shadows.

The big yellow and white striped cat padded silently beside her.

Taking the stairs one at a time, she huffed and puffed at the exertion. He doctor said that she should take better care of herself—less cholesterol and more exercise. Did she want to live past age fifty-five? Her doctor, however, was not with her now.

She blinked at the strong overhead light as she entered the big, airy kitchen. Not yet ready to fix her gaze on the contents of the oversized brown enamel refrigerator, she wondered what the hell possessed her to rumble around at this ungodly hour.

Groggily she backtracked over the half hour she'd spent shivering under her bedding. It was one of those darn nightmares again. Another weird dream, just like the ones that had haunted her night after night, since Thanksgiving.

A creak at the bottom of the stairs made her whirl around and peer into the gloom beyond the kitchen doorway. "Morgan, that you?"

"Yeah. What are you doing up?"

"I had another nightmare," she announced to her husband.

Morgan swayed sleepily in the doorway, rubbing his tousled head. "Did you talk to the doctor about them last time you was there?"

"Nope. He'd think I'm crazy or something."

Morgan snorted. "That ain't nothin' new."

"Go back to bed, you old fool. I don't feel like arguing with you tonight."

Morgan moved stubbornly into the kitchen and leaned against the refrigerator. She knew he was blocking it on purpose, just to make her mad. She crossed her arms over her breasts, itching to shove him out of the way. Married twenty-five years, they hated each other. He'd turned out to be a lazy bum and she, well … she'd lost her self-respect and gained more pounds than she cared to count. In her mind, most men, except maybe a few of the cloth—and even then she wasn't so sure—were downright good for nothing.

"It's God condemning you for all the lives you've seen fit to ruin with that spiteful tongue of yours!" he said. "Time and time again I've told you to stay out of other people's business, but would you listen? Oh, no! Not Sarah Goodling! Not the gossip of the Universe. Not the woman who's mouth is as big as her—"

"That'll be enough, Morgan!"

"You can't keep your mouth shut about anything!"

She knew he was referring to her latest blunder. It was a perfectly honest mistake, understand. She thought she saw her daughter's husband with another woman down at the VFW on Country Music night, but it turned out the other woman was his cousin, a nun in from Texas for the holidays. She'd almost destroyed her daughter's marriage over that one. Not her fault nuns didn't always wear those habit things anymore.

"Even our own daughter won't talk to us!" Yep. There it was. She knew it. "You'd better get your act in gear, woman, before the hounds of hell themselves burst out of them damnable nightmares of yours and drag you down to Lucifer himself!"

"Go back to bed, Morgan," she snapped. "You're always grumpy if you don't get enough sleep."

He shook his head, an angry flush creeping up his neck. "I don't understand you Sarah. Just don't understand you." He opened the refrigerator door, reached in and pulled out a beer, popping the pull tab as he wandered out of the kitchen, leaving the fridge door hanging wide open. She could hear him muttering to himself as he climbed slowly up the stairs to his room on the second floor. They'd had separate bedrooms for the last ten years so at least she didn't have to hear his mouth once he shut his door.

She stared absently into the depths of the refrigerator. It was probably that Christian show on the television that had brought those nightmares to the surface tonight. Teenagers called in to the host to tell the listening audience how they had been involved in Satanism, drugs, and sex until the Lord Jesus had saved them. Well, praise God. Amen and hallelujah! She wished someone would come and save her from this miserable marriage.

She poured herself a glass of milk and sat down at the kitchen table, brushing off some turkey crumbs left over from dinner. The cat scurried between her feet to retrieve the prize. She reached down and patted Zipper on his large, square head. Loud, guttural purrs filled the kitchen.

In her latest dream she remembered a large, sparse room. It had snow-white walls with rough-hewn beams running the length of the ceiling. She didn't know where the room was, whether it was a church, a business, or even a residence, though she doubted the last. She did know that it was a place she did not recollect in her waking life.

There had been no pictures or paintings on the walls. A door at one end. Closed. There weren't any drapes on the windows. She remembered the night's darkness seeping through the panes of glass in sharp contrast to the bare walls. A low murmur of male voices surrounded her. They belonged to the men seated ramrod straight on wing-backed wooden chairs in a circle around the room. They were dressed in odd, dark clothing, cut plainly.

She couldn't be sure how many men were there. Dreams were woven of flimsy mental fabric and accuracy was never one of her strong points, even in her waking world.

The men ignored her, as if she couldn't be seen. They talked of hatred and power.

And death.

The wind screeched outside the window and Sarah sat bolt upright at the table, knocking over her glass of milk. Had she been dreaming again?

She looked around the room for Zipper, but didn't see him. Hadn't she been petting him only a second ago? The kitchen felt stark and cold.

Sarah rubbed her arms with ferocity. She had to clean up that milk. She half rose out of her chair, but the dream scene again flooded her memory.

Those men had cruel eyes. She definitely remembered that! They glittered like sharp bits of obsidian. Male voices rose in a chant, though she couldn't quite make it out. It sounded like a woman's name, maybe Ellen … no, that wasn't right. Lizzie! No, not it either. It eluded her, like that gingerbread man in the fairy tale. Catch me if you can!

Sarah shrugged and cleaned up the milk mess. Terry Anderson, that floozy she met down at the beauty parlor, told her she should write her nightmares down, then read them later. What a dizzy woman. She'd insisted the beautician play that water-plopping music while getting her hair done. Well, she didn't know diddly! Imagine, writin' down her nightmares! It would bring them to life, that's what it would do. It would make them real!

Oh, no.

Uh-uh.

No way.

Terry told her it would bring her en-lie-tin-ment. Poo on that. The only thing that kept gettin' lighter every week was Terry's hair, rat's nest that it was! 'Course, maybe it wouldn't hurt to have Terry do one of them rune readings for her. Naturally, she didn't put any stock in such nonsense. At this point, however, her only other avenue would be to visit Pastor Becker, and she didn't want to do that. He'd think she was downright crazy. He was one of those men of the cloth who weren't Satan in disguise. She'd been proud of him when she'd heard he dumped Terry. The girl never would have made an upstanding preacher's wife!

Zipper scooted into the kitchen from the darkened living room, running his back against Sarah's legs. Still, she had to do something to get rid of this scared shitless feeling that trailed after her like old Zipper. He lifted his head and sniffed her outstretched hand, purring loudly as she bent over to scratch under his chin.

She shivered as remnants of the dream tried to pry themselves into her conscious mind. Walking stiffly to the sink for the dish rag, she took a gander beyond the lemon yellow curtains that billowed slightly from the draft. "Land sakes, must be a heck of a storm out there!" she muttered. It was a good thing she'd stopped at the grocer's this morning in case those nasty winds brought more snow. As if they hadn't had enough of it already this winter. She shook her curlered head in distaste at the thought of a bad season, which is where this winter definitely headed. It made a body feel so lonely.

She decided to take a second glass of milk back to her room and almost stumbled over Zipper in the kitchen doorway. Ice-cold milk sloshed on her hand, but she held firm to the glass.

"Zipper! Well, don't just sit there. Are you coming or not?" The cat refused to follow her. Absently she turned off the kitchen light, forgetting her newfound fear of the dark.

Zipper's eyes flickered, luminous, like a neon bulb gone bad.

CHAPTER NINE

THE CAT GAVE SARAH THE CREEPS, IT DID, AND she refused to cajole it further to follow her. She shivered. "Should have put on a robe," she chided herself. A cold draft tickled the back of her neck as she reached the stairs. Although her nightlight fought the deep shadows bravely, she swallowed hard and mounted the stairs, a slight tremor running up the calves of her legs.

Zipper growled as she reached the halfway point on the stairs. "What's the matter with you?" she grumbled. The nightlight flickered once, then died. Her chest hitched as her eyes fought the syrupy blackness. "Just calm down," she said to herself. "After twenty-five years in this house you can find your way blindfolded to the bedroom if you have to." She'd just have to brave it and keep walking until she got to the top of the stairs where she could scrabble her fingers along the wall to find the light switch.

She clasped both hands tightly around the cold glass of sloshing milk and took a deep breath, placing one slippered foot slowly in front of the other. It was with the second scream of the cat that Sarah's world turned surreal.

The stairs spun; the steps swelled under her feet. If this was a new type of ride, Sarah definitely wanted to get off—now! Cold milk splattered across her chest. She grabbed at the front of her nightie and fell hard against the wall. The glass flew in slow motion from her hand, thumping on the carpeted stairs. She collapsed on one knee, then the other. Teetering on the stairs, reaching frantically for the railing she couldn't see, Sarah let out a low moan. Her eyes rolled back in her head. A dream. Another dream. Not possible. She fought it, but her will was too weak.

Now those men were talking to her. Those nasty fellows with the black, evil eyes. They demanded an answer, but she was too confused. She stood before them in the white room with the dark boring in from beyond. She felt both foolish and incensed. One of them commented to the others with wry distaste that commoners had no expertise in the astral. Another laughed at her old nightie.

She stood in the middle of the room with a burly guard on either side.

One man whispered loudly to the fellow beside him. "How many people came in answer to the ritual of calling tonight? I hope this is the last one."

"Dunno," answered the other, wiping his brow with a yellowed hand-kerchief. "I stopped counting over an hour ago."

"I say the entire evening has been a total waste of our time and energy," barked the first man, banging his cane on the wooden floor.

The man with the yellowed handkerchief folded it neatly and put it in his inside coat pocket. "There've been several who have touched by this Belladonna woman briefly, but none with definitive information. I say we call it an evening."

The other nodded. "Yes, but I'm not going to be the one to tell Jason; how about you?"

"Are you kidding? Not me. This is the last one anyway."

The first old fellow shook his cane. "Jason must have been desperate to call her in. She's shaking like a rabbit, fading in and out. She must deal with life only through her lower chakra centers. She doesn't know anything."

"Well, if you wouldn't have broken your concentration an hour ago, we wouldn't still be here."

"It's not my fault I've got asthma!"

"I want to go home!" wailed Sarah.

All eyes turned toward her. A tall, evil-looking man entered and whispered something to one of the guards. He seemed familiar to her, but she couldn't place his face. There was something odd about it—almost plastic. The questioning resumed. Did she know Elizabeyta Belladonna? That was the name she had tried to remember in the kitchen. Where was her kitchen? Where was she? She began to sweat. She felt herself wavering, as if she was about to dissolve. The smart-ass who had laughed at her nightie (she thought someone called him Luther) shouted, "Watchers, hold!" and she felt her body stabilize. "She's not leaving us until she gives us the information we need, even if it takes all night!" he sneered.

"Better be quick about it, Jason," muttered the old man with the cane. "Who knows how long we can fool her guardian."

"If she even has one," countered Jason. "The fact that we have gotten this far proves that it is either weak or incredibly new at its job!" His laughter filled the room, joined by numerous twitters of the others.

Again Jason asked her if she knew Elizabeyta Belladonna. Since Sarah had no desire to be wherever the hell she was all night, and hadn't the vaguest idea what a guardian was, she answered them.

"Well, I might know the girl."

"Have you ever held any long conversations with her?"

Sarah shifted uneasily. "No, keeps to herself, she does. Look, I'm not sure we're talking about the same girl."

Jason showed her a photograph. "This girl! This is the woman we are looking for. Does she look familiar to you?"

Sarah shrugged her shoulders. "I'm a Welcome Wagon lady. Everybody in town knows I'm their only representative in these parts," she said proudly. "I wouldn't remember her at all, 'cept she looks like another girl I know."

"We don't care about any other girls. We want to know about this girl!"

Sarah puffed out her chest. "I may have seen her, but that would be about two years ago. I want to go home now."

A hush fell over the room.

What was the matter with these fellas, anyway? thought Sarah.

"Two years?" said the man with the cane. "Two whole years?" He banged his cane on the floor so hard it split the handle. "This woman says the Belladonna girl has been around here for two years and we didn't know anything about it?" He threw a vicious glance at Jason. "What kind of leader are you that you could have missed this? Have the Gods deserted you? Perhaps we need a new leader!"

A shocked silence met his outburst. Sarah's guards stepped a little away from her. Now that they moved, she wished they would stay. Her eyes wide, she swallowed hard. All eyes in the room were now on that Jason man. At least that was a relief. Or was it?

Sarah felt increasingly uncomfortable, as if her body was being pulled in two opposite directions. It was giving her a headache, not to mention the heartburn that now set in. She didn't want to be here, but didn't know how to leave, either. Sweat trickled down the side of her face.

Jason turned to her with riveting dark eyes.

"The Elizabeyta woman is extraordinarily evil. Of course she could elude me. Her powers are great, but I shall overcome! We will have everything we've planned for. It is only a matter of time now."

In Sarah's mind, the odd circumstance she found herself in felt far more evil than the non-descript redhead who had shut the door in Sarah's face almost two years ago. Rude, maybe, but certainly not evil. At least the woman had used the mouth God gave her to say a none-too-polite "No thanks!" If it even was the same girl. The young woman at the door of the old Baxter house had never given her name, come to think of it.

"If you can remember the woman, you can tell us more. I command you to give me the information I need. You'd better answer for your own good!" spat the man with the broken cane.

Who did these old coots think they were, anyway? With her hands jabbed firmly onto her hips, she whirled to the one called Jason, and shouted, "Just who do you think you are, young man? Christ come down from the cross you're not, and I'll be darned if I answer any more of your stupid, idiotic questions! I don't know how I got here, but I'll be dipped if I'm stayin' any longer!"

With that, she moved toward her adversary to push him out of the way and promptly walked straight through him. It was then she realized there was no reality to her situation. Spiteful male laughter floated around her. Horrified, she stared at Jason, who looked vaguely familiar, but the memory didn't quite click. This didn't surprise her, considering the rate she was going on the issue of the young woman in the picture. Jason's visage wavered, melted, turned, snapped, and reformed into a mass of heaving fur and fangs. As quickly as it appeared, it changed, perceptively different from before—human again. Before her stood a six-foot-two, thirty-seven-year-old Jason Blackthorn, with black wavy hair and cold blue eyes.

Sarah gasped. She'd known this cruel man since he was a babe. Spawn of Satan himself, to be sure. How is it she didn't recognize him earlier? A wonder, it was. Why, he'd been the terror of the town in his teens, and even arrested for the murder of Chrissy Sheldon, a classmate the year he graduated. They let him go and he'd left town. Sarah never knew why they hadn't tried and convicted him. Everybody knew he'd done it. Now here he was, in this terrible nightmare of hers.

And then it hit her. Hadn't she read somewhere that one has complete control of their dreams? But she felt so weak.

"Speak, or you'll regret it," he whispered.

With fear or anger—Sarah didn't know—she theatrically clamped her lips shut and lifted her chin in defiance, even though she knew it was probably a big mistake.

An invisible fist jabbed her squarely in the belly. She doubled over, but not before an unseen punch smashed her nose. Sarah shrieked, her memory deserting her. She'd be damned if she'd talk now.

"Tell us more about her!" echoed in her brain. Her atrophied consciousness stirred briefly, but subsided stubbornly without answer. Again she was struck.

"Can't remember!" she burbled through the blood spurting from her twisted nose. "Just can't remember," she moaned. If she got into this dream, then she could get out of it. She closed her eyes and thought of her home, the carpeted stairs, her cat.

"Jason, you stupid fool," shouted the man with the broken cane, "now we're losing her!"

Jason whirled to pinpoint the idiot who dared to question him, breaking his focus on Sarah. It was enough time for her to shoot forward and grab him roughly from behind. She'd get this son-of-a-bitch if it was the last thing she did. Both tumbled in space as Jason punched his way free. She willed herself home, thinking of Zipper. Pitch black flooded before her eyes.

With labored breathing, Sarah forced her weary eyes open. Pain bolted through her head as she tried to move. Weak light filtered from Morgan's room at the top of the stairs. She was back in her home in a rumpled ball at the foot of the steps and Morgan was standing over her. She groaned.

"Sarah! What the hell were you doin' sneakin' up the stairs in the dark? I thought you was a burglar!"

"You blithering idiot," she hissed nasally as she cupped her nose. "I had a derrible pain in my head. I dink I blacked out, or somedin' …"

She struggled to rise, groping for a non-existent handhold on the wall. She slid back down, landing with a whump.

"Do you think anything is broken?" he asked.

"I don't dink so," she mumbled.

Morgan's eyes rounded as he helped her to her feet. She smoothed her bloody nightgown then wobbled off to the downstairs bathroom to assess the damage. Morgan's face loomed behind her in the medicine cabinet mirror.

"You don't look so good, Sarah." His gaze slid from her purpling face to study his bare toes. "Think maybe you ought to call the doc?"

"In case you haven't looked outside, there's a heck of a storm kicking up." She busied herself with a rag and cold water, dabbing the drying blood gently from around her nose. "What in tarnation woke you anyway? Usually you sleep like the dead!"

Morgan raised his head slowly. Their reflections stared at each other for a moment before his eyes again dropped to his bare feet. "A dream," he mumbled. "I had this dream … And then I heard this awful banging sound. I guess that was you taking a tumble down the stairs. Why didn't you put the light on before you came up?"

Sarah grasped the cold edge of the sink for support, ignoring his question. "Wha—what kind of dream?"

"There were these men. Bad men. I can't remember rightly! I mean, one minute I was dreamin' and the next you was lying at the bottom of the stairs!"

"What men?" snapped Sarah, whirling to face him.

"You know, men with funny eyes. Like in the movies!"

"How would I know such a thing?" She peered at him intently.

"Well I don't know, Sarah!" Morgan shrugged, hands raised protectively before him. "You said yourself you had nightmares lately. I just thought—"

Sarah turned back to the sink and doused the entire towel with cold water, checking Morgan's reflection to see if his expression showed even a hint of falsehood. Satisfied, she blocked out his mirrored image by covering her face with the cold towel. When she removed it he was gone. She stared in dismay at her reflected swollen nose. Black and blue coloring had begun to spread to her eye sockets. "Dear Gawd, Morgan, just look at my face! I'll have to use tons of make-up to hide this mess!" she shouted.

His head popped around the bathroom door. "Jesus, I'm sorry, Sarah!" he said.

"Don't just mill around there out in the hallway," barked Sarah. "Call Doc Baker and tell that answering service of his I fell down the stairs. Let 'em know I want the first available appointment after the snowplow goes through. And tell 'em I hurt my stomach, too. It aches terrible!"

Alone in the bathroom, Sarah examined the rest of herself. A nasty bruise stretched across her abdomen. Her nightie stuck to her ample chest. The dancing pink flowers on a once-blue background had been altered to a canvas of dried blood. Her favorite gown, too! *Don't that beat all*, she thought. She slipped the nightie over her head and groaned. With the shock wearing off, she wondered what on earth had happened to her. She had suffered the same injuries in her dream. Had real life and the dream coincided or had one happened before the other … and if so, which one? But the more she thought about the nightmare, the less she could remember. She tried to hold onto it, but bigger and bigger pieces slipped away.

"Oh for heaven's sake, Sarah, this isn't *Tales From the Crypt!*" she chided herself.

After she changed clothes, she met Morgan in the kitchen. Zipper was nowhere to be found and she assumed he'd high-tailed it under a piece of furniture somewhere. Morgan, seated at the kitchen table, had his broad back to her. His white tee-shirt was worn thin around the neck and there were small holes here and there across the back. She couldn't remember when she'd last shopped for him or took inventory of his clothes like she used to when they were first married. Sadness washed over her. All those years gone.

He had a mug of coffee waiting for her. He hadn't done that in years. Morgan was taking such great gulps from his own mug that Sarah suspected it held more than coffee. She bit her tongue on the issue and carefully settled herself across from him. Morgan didn't look up.

"Doc Baker says he'll see you two weeks from Monday. He's booked till then."

"What?" sputtered Sarah. "I could be dead by then!" The last snippets of the dream escaped with her anger.

Morgan scratched the stubble on his chin. "Doc says that if you think it's that bad, you're to go to the emergency room at St. Joseph's."

"Right, and spend a fortune if there's nothing wrong! Forget it, I'll wait," she said morosely.

Morgan drained his mug and left the kitchen. Never once did he look her straight in the eye. She should have thanked him for her coffee, but old habits were hard to break.

Sarah eased back in her chair, mug cupped between her pudgy hands. Her mind whirled. "Elizabeyta Belladonna and Jason Blackthorn." She rolled the names slowly on her tongue. Why should she be thinking of them? That woman, she wasn't sure if she even knew her. What did they have to do with Sarah's terrible nightmares? If things weren't so mixed up in her brain right now, she was sure she could figure this mess out once and for all!

Sarah tried to gather all the facts she had in her mental filing cabinet, which brimmed with hundreds of snippets of information on all sorts of people. The mental file on the Belladonna woman was totally blank. Wait, that was silly! She lived on … on … Sarah finished her coffee and rubbed her temples. This was ridiculous! The fall must have really rattled her brains. Maybe she was suffering from temporary amnesia or something. And why would she think of Jason Blackthorn after all these years? Someone said his parents had put him away in a loony place after that Chrissy Sheldon was found in little pieces on Ore Bank Road. What on earth would bring that crazy to mind? She shivered.

Evil was afoot. She was sure of it. Maybe those stories on the cable weren't all money-catchers after all. She toyed with the thought of calling her brother-in-law, Sam Renard. Although the *Whiskey Springs Gazette* was pretty respectable for a small newspaper, she knew there was a ton of gossip he was privy to that never got printed. She thought about asking her sister instead, but threw that idea out right away. If Sarah was bad at keeping things quiet, her sister was worse. If there was anything strange happening around town, Sam'd know about it and may not have told her sister. Maybe she could weasel it out of him. She'd give it a couple of days then ring him up, casually ask him if he knew Elizabeyta Belladonna … then again, maybe she wouldn't. She knew Sam despised her and only put up with her presence because of her sister.

Well, maybe she'd just ask him if he knew of any unusual things happening around town. Unfortunately, with the condition of her now purple and blue blooming face, all her snooping would have to be by phone. My, what will the neighbor's think? Shit, she didn't give a fig before, why should she now? There was a sense, though, that this had better be the quietest snooping she'd ever done. Maybe her life depended on it. Oh, that was just silly, but she intended to be careful, just the same.

chapter ten

L EE WENT THROUGH HIS SERVICE WITH practiced motions and no memory of what he was doing. The congregation never knew the difference and by 12:05 the few that had shown up were quickly shaking his hand at the back of the church and scurrying home out the large oak doors to heavy dinners and relaxing afternoons.

By half past noon, Lee sat in his parsonage office, tapping his fingers rhythmically on the desk. He believed Elizabeyta, but he didn't. No, that wasn't right. He believed her to a point, but felt she may be exaggerating her situation. No. No. He believed the part about … wait. Hell, he didn't know what to believe. He thought of her soft, supple body in his arms and his heart gave a lurch. To have her part of him like that for the rest of his life would certainly be heaven on earth.

He ruffled his hair furiously and arched his back. A knock at the outer parsonage door brought him to his feet, his hands flying to his head to smooth down his hair. "Mason, my man!" he said, throwing open the door. Mason owned the Whiskey Springs' Serenity Funeral Home and every now and then he stopped by on Sunday afternoons. He wasn't a church-going man. Lee's smile was genuine. He needed to talk to someone right now. "I hope business has been slow for you over the holiday season," said Lee with a light chuckle.

Mason grinned and shook his head. "'Tis the season; I always told you that after Christmas the oldsters drop dead like flies in a winter breeze." He winked and stepped through the door, stamping the snow off his boots. "Business booms over Yule and New Year's. In fact, we're so busy I had to schedule two for later this afternoon."

"How are the roads?" asked Lee. He took Mason's coat, brushed it off, and hung it in the closet. Mason switched his beige leather briefcase to his left hand and adjusted his suit coat with his right.

"Not too bad, actually. I made better time than I thought."

Lee ushered him into the office. "How's Louise?"

Mason pulled a wry face. "As godly as ever. I was in town on an errand and thought we'd get the arrangements for that Diamond funeral taken care of. I could have faxed them to you, but it's been a while since I've seen you. When Louise found out I'd be stopping here she insisted I ask you over for dinner next week." Mason took a comfortable leather chair opposite and set the briefcase on his lap.

Lee smiled. "Tell your wife my schedule is a little backed up right now but as soon as I get a free weekend, I'll give you a call."

Mason glanced at him oddly, nodded, and flicked the snaps on his briefcase open. "As I told you the other night when I called you, the Diamond woman didn't attend any particular church. Her family requested that I find a suitable pastor to conduct her funeral service tomorrow. I could have chosen good old Brother Hank, he'll do anything on the spur of the moment. But you know how I despise the bastard." He frowned and rummaged through the contents of his briefcase. "I'm so relieved you agreed to do it. Here is a little information on the woman, a list of passages the family would like read from the King James version of the Bible, some information about her service to the community, etc. You know the drill. Services are scheduled for 11:30 AM. Oh. She was also a member of the Order of the Eastern Star and those ladies have requested a separate ceremony that you don't need to attend."

Lee nodded and took the papers Mason handed him.

"I really appreciate you doing this," remarked Mason. "She had no immediate family left in the area and what relatives she did have are flying in from California as we speak. I checked with Harrisburg International and they'll be open as of twelve noon. When they get in and get settled in a hotel room they'll probably call you. I believe they'll be staying at that new hotel on Route 15, in case you want to see them before the service."

"No problem," said Lee, looking over the papers quickly, then dropping them on his desk. Lee studied the man across from him. Mason's black hair was cut in the latest flattering style, his suit immaculately chiseled to his body. Those roving sea-blue eyes flicked over the room as usual, taking in every minute detail, though his head never moved a millimeter. Terry once remarked that Mason was "lean and mean like a low-slung male machine." Lee had never understood this analogy. Mason always exhibited the most gentlemanly behavior, even on the racquetball court.

Mason shut the briefcase and set it on the floor beside his chair. "What's new with you? If you don't mind my saying so, you look like hell. The holiday season too much?" He grinned mischievously and relaxed back in the chair.

Lee looked at Mason through tired eyes. They'd been friends since Lee had taken on the parish four years ago. Around the same age, they held similar viewpoints on life, enjoyed various sports activities together when they could, and had both attended Penn State University—though not at the same time. Lee steepled his fingers and stared at Mason. "I asked Elizabeyta Belladonna to marry me last night."

Mason's jaw dropped.

"She said this was the last time her job would bring her here and … well … I think I lost my head."

"Does this mean I should be congratulating you or mourning your stupidity?"

Lee stared at Mason over his fingers. "I don't know."

"For a man who's finally decided to opt for marital bliss, you don't look too pleased."

"I know."

"What's the problem?"

Lee dropped his fingers and leaned on the desk top. "She has some … ah … difficulties."

Mason's eyebrows shot up. "As in … ?"

Lee hesitated. He'd given Elizabeyta his word he wouldn't tell anyone about her lifestyle or her search for the killer. He groaned internally. He really needed someone else's input. "Family problems … sort of," he said lamely.

Mason smoothed the front of his suit coat, studying the floor. Without looking up he said softly, "Is that all?"

Lee took a deep breath, trying to examine his feelings. "There is another minor problem, but I'm sure once she settles into life here, she'll forget about it and work with me."

"You mean she may not want to give up her job and move comfortably into the life of a pastor's wife?"

"Something like that. There are … religious differences."

Mason's eyes narrowed slightly. "Catholic, Jewish, something else?"

"Ah. Our views on religion aren't the same, but I'm confident we'll work that part out quickly."

"You don't sound so sure." Mason paused. "Do you love her?"

Lee squirmed uncomfortably in his chair. "I ... well ... I adore her."

"But do you love her?"

"You've never had a chance to meet her, have you?"

Mason shook his head. "You and I have talked about her on occasion and I knew of your interest in the woman—but marriage? That's a big commitment, Lee. You've almost been snagged before and that was a terrible fiasco. Terry Anderson literally stalked you for months after you broke your engagement to her."

Lee nodded his head. Terry, in the end, was too much for him. He'd cared for her deeply and they'd had a lot of good times together, but then she went on a diet, started that New Age store, and turned into a 90s hippie. She went from innocently beautiful to garishly provocative. His face reddened as he remembered how every Sunday the entire congregation would turn their heads to watch her waltz down the aisle to the first pew, her long peasant skirt swishing and the numerous bracelets on her arms jingling. He sighed. Mason hadn't fared much better with Louise, though she was the exact opposite of Terry—so prim and proper that she starched her white cotton blouses. He knew Mason's marriage was on the rocks but hadn't touched the subject. When Mason was ready to talk about it, he'd say something.

"You didn't mention whether she accepted or not," asked Mason, his eyes critiquing Lee.

"Actually, first she said no, then in the end, she said maybe."

"I see. And now that it is the cold light of day, which answer do you want to hear from her?"

"I don't know."

They sat in silence for a few moments.

"If I asked you a favor, Mason, would you do it?"

Mason grinned. "Ask away."

"Elizabeyta is working on sort of a family project that involves the history of this town. I know you're a buff on that sort of thing. Being the president of the historical society and all, you may be able to dig out some information that isn't ... well ... normally available."

"I thought you told me once that she isn't from around here. Arkansas or Nebraska or something?"

Lee chewed momentarily on his lips. "She found out she had extended family here at one time," he said evasively and knew he'd only piqued Mason's curiosity.

"From your tone of voice, I assume she's digging for skeletons in closets? An illegitimate birth or pregnancy before marriage in her family tree? Possible Indian heritage?"

"Not exactly. I don't know. I mean, I know, but she really should tell you about it. You'd have to talk to her. If I could convince her to meet you and let you help her piece a few things together, would you consider doing it?"

"Sure, be happy to. Just give me a call. I have several contacts through the historical society that have kept diaries, journals, and letters from relatives who helped to found this town. Another good source is Emma."

"You mean Emma Ward?"

Mason nodded. "She's a storehouse of information."

Lee thought that over for a moment. Emma, widowed at seventy and still spry at eighty, often took care of various members of the church when they were down and out. She'd carried quite a reputation in the old days of Whiskey Springs for her healing abilities and psychic gifts, but hadn't been out and about as much in the last few years. Lee never believed any of the rumors about her so-called supernatural gifts, but he liked her and found her to be a caring person. She might be the perfect person for Elizabeyta to meet, then again, maybe not. Emma was an upstanding church woman and Lee wasn't sure how she would handle Elizabeyta being a Witch. Of course, you never knew. He cleared his throat.

"I don't know," he said finally. "There may be some strings attached."

"Oh?"

"She may ask you for confidentiality in the matter."

"You know Emma keeps her mouth shut, I've never seen her gossip. She may be a little strange, but she has more town secrets locked away in that wizened grey head of hers than anybody at the downtown senior citizen center. She'd never utter a word if asked not to."

"You may be right," acknowledged Lee, "but I think we should take it one step at a time. You are the closest friend I have and I trust you."

Mason raised an eyebrow. "I see. I've worked with others before who have made a request for confidentiality."

"Really?" Lee said with surprise.

"Sure. Historical research can be lucrative if you get the right client. I do it for fun, but some fellows do it for their sole income. If I ever retire from Serenity, I may do it full time myself."

"If there is any charge, just give me the bill," said Lee. "I want to make sure you receive full compensation for your time."

"Don't worry about it. I owe you one for doing the Diamond funeral. When will Elizabeyta give you an answer—on the marriage proposal, I mean?" asked Mason, caution clearly edging his tone of voice.

Lee shrugged. "I think the outcome of that family problem I told you about has a lot to do with her decision."

"Oh. So if I help her, she might come up with an answer quicker?"

Lee hesitated. "Yeah."

"Isn't that good?"

Lee fingered the papers Mason had given him and pasted a weak smile on his face. "Yeah. Yeah, it's good. But I'm not sure if she'll go for you being involved."

Mason stood and stretched. Lee rounded the desk and they walked together to the door, stopping at the closet to pick up Mason's overcoat.

"Let me know if she's interested in my assistance," said Mason. "And keep it together, buddy. It'll work out."

Lee smiled, but he didn't mean it.

chapter eleven

A FEW MINUTES BEFORE THE MOST PSYCHIC experience of Terry's life happened, she was standing by her apartment window, looking out at the glistening blanket of new-fallen snow.

For the zillionth time in her life, she shut her eyes and whispered, "I want to be the best psychic in the universe. I want to see everything in the world of the living and the realm of the dead."

A smile played across her red-glossed lips as she slowly opened her eyes. She watched a snow plow rumble up the hill, past her window. Today was Sunday. Because of Pennsylvania's Blue Law she couldn't open her store, Rainbow's End, until noon. She hugged herself and twirled around. Perhaps today she would take a mental health day . . . maybe she wouldn't open the store at all. Maybe she would just kick back and be cozy. She bet not too many people would be out on the roads today, so she wouldn't be losing that much business . . .

Perhaps she could think up a real big storm. That way no one would want to go outside. Using the techniques she'd learned from self-hypnosis tapes, she'd already managed to make the repair shop next door to her store move out so she could expand her own enterprise. She grinned. Creative visualization at its best.

She rubbed her hands together and closed her eyes, willing more snow to appear so she wouldn't have to open the shop today.

Slowly, she opened her eyes. The clouds remained heavy and dark, yet no jettison of white tumbled from their slowly-moving depths.

She checked her watch. It was later than she thought—12:30. Lee would have finished with his Sunday service half an hour ago. She frowned, kicking the thought of him away. She'd taken control of her own life and he'd deserted her. Men! How she hated people who tried to control the actions of others for their own convenience. She tossed her heavy auburn hair with vehemence.

Maybe she should have followed up on her mother's suggestion and hired someone to help her at the store. Then she could stay in her warm apartment. However, she couldn't imagine that another person would be as dedicated as herself, nor did anyone else have the appropriate wisdom to do the rune readings. It was a special gift, you know. You can't up and call Kelly Girl and ask to employ a psychic for a day or two.

She continued to gaze out the window. A few large, lazy flakes brushed against the pane. Her eyes turned hopefully to the heavens, but as silently as the snow began, it stopped. Down below, across the street, she noticed a man in black leaning against the lamp post, a large yellow envelope in his outstretched hand. He looked from the envelope up to the windows of her building. She felt the urge to step back, but didn't. She had every right to live here and look out her own window. The hair bristled at the nape of her neck. A truck rumbled past and the lamp post stood alone, the yellow envelope crumpled in the mush of the gutter. She shrugged her shoulders and turned away.

Bracelets jingling, she lit the oil lamps on the tables sandwiching the bright floral patterned sofa, then flicked off the overhead light. The lamps cast warm pools of light that didn't quite reach her table on the other side of the room. She would never admit it, but she was intensely afraid of the dark. She had a lot to catch up on, and today presented the perfect opportunity to get a grip on things she'd let slide. The heck with the store. No one would be around today, anyway, with such threatening weather.

Her hands shook as she hastened to add more light to the room. She abhorred electric lamps. To cut down on the bills, she used candles and lamp oil from the store's merchandise. She recorded them as damaged goods. Who was to know? She shivered at the false darkness imposed by the leaden clouds of the winter day. Perhaps a reading to begin her projects would be pleasant.

"I want to be the best psychic in the universe," she said to herself. "In both the world of the living and the realm of the dead." Wrapping an electric-blue shawl close around her shoulders, she settled at her reading table. She was quite proud of it, and had one in the store just like it. She had spent many hours finding both round tables, sanding them, and painting them a soft pink enamel. Later she had stenciled zodiac figures, stars, and planets around the top. It was quite impressive, if she did say so herself.

She opened the single drawer of the table and scooped out her reading cloth and a green velvet drawstring bag. Carefully she spread the cloth on the table, smoothing out the folds. The personal ritual had begun. She seldom read for herself anymore. She was too busy, and besides, she now held the controlling strings of her fate in very secure hands. But this afternoon, she felt the urge to seek the wisdom of the runes.

The table drawer also held a collection of colored candles wrapped in tissue paper. She chose a silver one for psychism, and placed it in a candle-holder wrought in the shape of a large metal dragonfly, the totem symbol for vision quests and dreams.

Next she picked a rather large moonstone from among several gem stones that she kept in an old, flat jewelry case, rolling the smooth stone in her palm. Its milky shine was hypnotic. For a moment, she thought it tingled in her hand. Silly Terry! The books in her store told her that a moonstone should be placed with any divination tool for a truer reading. So be it.

She plopped it in the velvet drawstring bag, pulled the cord, and shook the contents. The tiny tiles clicked together with the moonstone. To give the power of the moonstone more time to work, she set the bag in the middle of the reading cloth, right on top of the six-pointed Star of David stitched in metallic gold embroidery floss.

Taking several deep breaths, she centered herself, then lit the silver candle with a lighter. (Matches were said to foul the air.) The single flame flickered, casting eerie grooves of light on the table.

Everything Terry used had a special meaning. The dragonfly was the bringer of messages, someone had told her, so she had searched over a dozen shops until she found such a design. Her circular reading cloth, about half the size of the table, was black satin—black chosen for its protective qualities. The silver and gold stitching represented the light from the heavens.

She slit her eyes, concentrating on the task at hand. She had begun to tell some of her prize customers (those with very open purses) that she was a Gypsy Witch, secretly adopted by her affluent parents when she was a small babe because her mother really couldn't have children. When the first one fell for it and gave her twenty extra bucks, the story became more elaborate, falling from her lips with ease.

Be careful what you wish for …

Terry knew she gave passable readings, learning the meanings of the tiles by rote. What she lacked was the mental thread that tied the runes together to bring into focus a logical line of divination, much like a short story. Her readings were about fifty percent accurate, enough to keep the blue-haired ladies and starstruck teens coming back for more. She had just the right amount of knowledge to make her dangerous. And she knew it.

The books and tapes said this special touch would come in time, like typing or something. One fine day she would wake up and channel with ease.

She was still waiting.

"I want to be the best psychic in the universe," she mumbled. "In the world of the living and in the realm of the dead. I want to see it all."

Terry picked up the velvet bag and relaxed in her chair. She shut her eyes, holding the bag tightly to her brow. Maybe this would be the day. Her heartbeat quickened. The gift could come through her "third eye," the energy center located on the forehead. There, it was foretold, a person could be struck dead from a malevolent force, or her consciousness could open to receive the psychic gift. She didn't believe one bit in the former, but hoped the latter was true. For a second, she thought she saw that man in black—or was it a man at all? Her mind wandered. She breathed evenly and slowly to focus herself, counting between breaths. The room was entirely forgotten. The winter day no longer touched her mind. Terry concentrated on the bag in her hands and the dark cloth before her.

She shook the bag once … twice … three times, and gently pulled the drawstring open. Her hand moved to scatter the tiles, her long, manicured fingernails flicked the drawstring back and forth in indecision. She thought better of it. They were too hard to read when dumped unceremoniously in a pile.

Carefully she dug into the bag, chose six tiles (without peeking), and set one face down at each of the various points of the embroidered star. She took another deep breath and turned the first rune over, the one at the top of the star. Terry's tongue pressed hard against her front teeth. This place stood for the past. This was not one of her favorite runes—Thurisz. It meant nasty stuff, like aggressive conflicts. She hadn't had any recently … she shivered. She hoped it wasn't something in the future … no … wait. Okay, that was right, considering all the horrible things she had gone through to get the store up and running smoothly. What bothered her most was that it may mean that old problems would again be resurfacing. Shit. She hesitated a few seconds, considering if she should continue. She didn't want to have a bad day because of a stupid reading. Maybe the next rune would be better.

She flipped over the second tile. This spot on the star was to tell her what bad things were happening that she wasn't aware of. Her heart sunk. Another yucky one—Hagalaz. A very disruptive force indeed. Not good. Not good. The "H" design with the crooked bar meant lightning would strike if she was not careful. It was known as the "Great Awakener." It could also have to do with the inclement weather. If that was the worst thing in her life right now, she could live with it.

The third tile now. This one for the good stuff around her that she didn't know about. She turned the rune. Her jaw dropped. A light shiver ran down her spine. No answer at this time. The tile was blank.

She turned over the next tile. A development in the recent past that should help her. This particular rune stood for a signal. What signal? She wasn't aware of any. Sometimes the signal was a physical object … nope, she couldn't think of a blessed thing. It never occurred to her that this reading could represent a warning, a flag of danger.

Another tile now. This one for any negative developments in her life. Perth. Initiation into something hidden. She usually told her customers it meant gossip. It sort of did, and the customers ate that up—hook, line, and open pocketbook.

Hmmmm. One more tile to go. So far, she didn't particularly care for this reading, and seriously thought of gathering everything up and sticking the runes back in the drawer. Curiosity got the better of her. The last rune represented the outcome of the situation at hand. Her fingers trembled as she turned over the tile. It popped over several times until she could see it properly in the flickering candlelight. Was there a draft in here?

She felt her stomach muscles constrict. The rune was Nauthiz. The necessity of pain.

Be careful what you wish for …

This was not a good reading. It was scary, and she hated to be afraid. A sense of black disquiet settled over her. Maybe it was the room. Too dark, that was all. Shadows. Abruptly she turned her attention back to the runes. Sometimes, when a customer was not satisfied with a reading, she would shake the bag and spill out a rune or two. She did so now. Both the moon-stone and Dagaz, the rune of transformation, fell onto the cloth. She stared first at the rune and then at the moonstone. Well! This rune was a little bet-ter. All she had to do was figure out what type of transformation was coming her way, or was here at the moment. She didn't think of the third interpreta-tion, that of death.

She drew her shawl tightly around her shoulders and knotted the ends at her chest. The candle before her guttered and spit, as if a door opened and closed somewhere within the apartment, though no sound had wavered in the air.

A headache niggled where that stupid third eye was supposed to be. Why couldn't she read these things any better? She absently picked up the moonstone and rolled it between her sweaty palms. It helped to dissipate her fear, but her head was really pounding now.

Terry placed the stone on her brow, hoping that it would ease the pain.

A flash of bright light cracked inside her head and Terry promptly tipped backward in the chair, her outstretched fingers clawing at the reading cloth, pulling it, the runes, and the bag down on top of her. Her head made a resounding smack as it struck the hardwood floor. The dragonfly candle-holder, left alone on the table, perched precariously on the edge. The candle burned on, without regard to its dangerous position in the world.

Terry's conscious mind vacillated between that of the earth plane and the mysteries of the astral—no mundane thoughts touched her.

Instead, she was watching Lee Becker as he struggled in the ice and snow. He stood over a casket . . . dropped a red rose in the yawning grave. It drifted down, down, down. In her astral state—and surely this was what all the books talked about—she observed him on his knees, falling to the ground—a man in black standing over him; a tire iron ready to deliver a crushing blow. But then the scene changed, and he was stumbling . . . the man in black gone … a mansion ahead. He was trying to run but the snow— so deep. An old woman was ahead of him, plowing through drifts, like a mini-tank. How odd, though, because this was Sunday afternoon, yet she watched them under a canopy of stars . . . and the snow and ice looked like bushels and bushels of glimmering diamonds . . .

chapter twelve

AT EIGHT O'CLOCK MONDAY MORNING, Marjorie looked out her kitchen window. An evening storm had dumped a few more inches of snow on the town of Whiskey Springs. Not enough to stop the world; just enough to make most adults miserable. The canopy of dirty clouds snuggled around South Mountain, hanging low over the valley nestled at its feet. If there was a sun up there, Marjorie wasn't aware of it.

The smell of steaming waffles and frying bacon wafted from the Reed kitchen. Marjorie bustled about with rosy cheeks, preparing breakfast for her only son, sixteen—and a half, mind you—year-old Mark. Timothy, poor man, was dead to the world, sleeping soundly for a change. Probably from utter exhaustion.

Mark sauntered in and flopped in the nearest chair.

"Good morning, my dear; did you sleep well?" she asked.

Mark, still rather bleary-eyed, nodded in assent.

She set a glass of orange juice in front of him and went back to the stove. "Why are you up so early today? I thought you'd sleep in during your school vacation," she asked above the sound of sizzling bacon.

"Figured I'd pick up a few bucks with Dad's snow blower. I've also got that place to do next to the parsonage. You know the one where the lady isn't around much? Do you think he'd mind? I'd ask him, but I know he's not been sleeping well, and I didn't want to disturb him."

Marjorie handed him a plate of waffles swimming in butter. "So you've noticed too, have you?" she asked as she plopped several strips of bacon onto his plate.

"Yeah. Has he told you what's bothering him?"

Marjorie's lips settled into a firm line. "No, not a word. How about you?"

"Nah. He still thinks I'm a kid. Whatever's keeping him awake is adult-type stuff." Mark dressed his waffles with syrup and concentrated on wolfing down his breakfast.

Marjorie shook her head. There was definitely something wrong—if only she could determine the nature of it. Timothy always consulted her when something was really bothering him, and they had been through some tough times. Their marriage lasted because they were truthful with each other in the things that really mattered. But this time, Timothy remained mute. Her stomping off to bed last night hadn't helped the situation.

Although he'd denied it, perhaps it was the amount of money they had both been spending lately. The new addition to the house including his study and the sun porch was finished in late fall. They had completely furnished both rooms, plus replaced the living room and dining room furniture. Then the holidays came and they'd spent a great deal on two parties—one for the family and one for political hob-nobbing. The holiday shopping consisted of a blur of malls and department stores. She had never seen the floor under the Christmas tree so tightly packed with gifts.

A mound of trash, a testament to the holiday buying spree, leaned neatly by the back kitchen door. She sidestepped a piece of stray ribbon that had somehow slithered out of one of the bags. "Mark, before you leave, would you mind taking the trash out? I meant to do it yesterday, but got so busy cleaning up, I left it."

Mouth jammed with waffles, Mark nodded. "No problem," he mumbled. "We missed the last pick-up. There's a lot of stuff out there already."

Marjorie sighed. "True, but I can't have it decorating my kitchen floor for the next week, either."

Mark grinned and waved a syrupy fork at her.

Marjorie succumbed once again to her brooding thoughts. Every time she asked Timothy if they had enough money, he told her not to worry about it. Supposedly, the stock market had been good to him this year.

She wasn't so sure. There were other ways to get that much money.

Marjorie felt both disappointed and hurt that he would not take her into his confidence, yet she allowed him to play his game by accepting the excuses he offered her. It was so good not to have to worry about money and to finally have some of the things that she had always wanted. Every appliance in the kitchen had been replaced, right down to the electric hand mixer. Sheets and towels worn thin from years of weekly washings were moved out of the linen cabinet to their new rank as rags in the basement, while twice as many new sets moved in.

Maybe there was another woman …

She was afraid to know the truth. It was safer to nestle in a cocoon of ignorance. She wanted to wear the blinders as long as possible, because in her heart, she knew that nothing lasts forever—everything eventually changes. As she removed the last of the sizzling bacon from the pan, she acknowledged that her wheel of fortune had finally gone up, and she didn't want to fall off—not just yet. But, gathering things around her could not take the place of their trust in each other. Soon she would have to make a choice. Timothy was slipping away while they stockpiled material items. There was a hole somewhere in the fabric of their marriage, and it was growing larger every day. Who had called him last night so late? Another woman? Oh dear God, don't let it be that.

Mark pushed away his empty plate. "So is it okay if I take the blower out? I promise I'll be careful, and I'll replace the gas I use from the money I earn."

Marjorie smiled. She was proud of her only son. He was certainly industrious, though his hair was rather too long and she didn't approve of some of his choices in clothing or friends lately. A sigh escaped from deep within her. All mothers probably thought the same things, why should she be any different? "Yes, go ahead, but dress warmly and do be careful!"

Mark grinned and raced upstairs, remembering to shout "Thanks!" somewhere between step five and step seven.

Marjorie winced. She hoped the noise didn't awaken Timothy. It wasn't until after he had barreled out the door that Marjorie feared she may have made a mistake by letting him go off on his own. The town always looked so bleak and deserted on days like this. She absently stretched a graying curl at her temple. *Another classic mother-worry*, she thought. He was young and strong. Bad things only happened to other people.

By 10:00 AM, Mark finished his fourth job, not counting his parents' place. His hands and feet were stiff from the biting cold. It was time for a break. He was close to Jeff Conner's house. Perfect. He had to see him anyway. Jeff was a late sleeper, but wouldn't care if Mark caught him while ladling some extra z's into his body.

Mrs. Conner let Mark in and pointed upstairs. A shy smile played across her lips. She was a small woman with habitual downcast eyes. Although Jeff and Mark had been inseparable since kindergarten, Mark always felt uneasy around her. It crossed his mind that he didn't know much about Jeff's mother at all. Maybe it was the vacant look in her eyes when she did look at you, or the fact that she rarely spoke. Maybe thinking strange shit like this was a part of growing up or something.

This morning, as usual, she was neatly attired in a country print dress with a white oversmock. Mark thought she looked like she had just stepped out of a time warp.

He shrugged and scooted up the stairs.

Jeff sat up in bed, his blond hair sticking out in various perpendicular directions. He looked at Mark with sallow eyes. "Yo," he mumbled.

"Man, you look like shit!"

"Too much partying, ya know," said Jeff as he pulled his crumpled black jeans off the nightstand, dragging the lamp dangerously close to the edge.

"Where's your dad?" asked Mark.

"Off in Chicago, I think. Some big city with some big deal. Like always." Jeff yawned and crawled stiffly out of his bed. "If you ask me, he's probably banging some slut. I hear through the grapevine he has one in every town." He padded off to his bathroom wearing a sheet for a robe.

Mark sprawled on the twin bed opposite Jeff's and stared at the ceiling. He hated to admit it, but his friend was getting a little weird. All the sports and sweet-girlie posters had been removed from the walls and replaced with themes from horror movies. The light blue curtains had disappeared. In their place hung black ones. Both quilts on the beds were solid black. Now that he thought about it, Jeff usually wore black jeans and shirts or sweaters these days along with some pretty crazy jewelry—like the death's head ring on his left hand and the heavy silver cross that swung like a pendulum around his neck when he worked on his car.

Jeff's newest hobby lay scattered across the bureau. Mark didn't think it was such a good idea to leave that stuff lying around, but there were no little kids in the house, so he guessed it was okay. Still, all those fancy daggers and knives out in the open like that gave him the creeps. There must be at least ten of them.

Nothing remains the same.

Jeff hopped out of the bathroom, wriggling into his jeans.

"Jesus, Jeff! When'd you get that gash on your arm?" exclaimed Mark, eyeing the ugly slice that wound across Jeff's right bicep. "And what's that above it, a tattoo?"

His friend examined the arm with indifference. "Guess the Circuit was a little hot last night. No big deal." He struggled into a clean black turtleneck. The chain of the cross got tangled in his hair.

"Let me see the tattoo," said Mark eagerly.

"Fuck off."

Both boys knew the dangers of the Circuit well. The recent economic recession had affected many York County families. Jobs were scarce and every week more businesses were either laying off or simply closing their doors for good. Only the bars and the pushers were doing a booming business. There were more people on the Circuit now than ever.

"Did you score?" Mark asked doubtfully. His opinion of the Circuit was divided. He was still young enough to worry about his parents' rules, and one of them strictly forbade him to go anywhere near the two one-way, inner-city streets that comprised the thirty-six-block stretch known as the Circuit. It was circled by fast cars, fast merchandise, and even faster girls. But he had to admit there was nothing like the thrill of cruising down Main Street, looking for action at any one of the twenty-five street lights, or dragging up Philadelphia Avenue to see who could make the fastest time to the next light. It was the only place that Mark knew where everyone wanted to stop at an intersection.

Jeff shut and locked his bedroom door. From his closet he withdrew a faded canvas bag and threw it at Mark. "Open it!" he commanded.

Mark pawed at the drawstrings and peered inside. He let out a long whistle. "Man, what a load of weed!"

"Some scum bucket tried to take it away from me after the buy. I left him hurting," sneered Jeff.

"Did the cops see you?" worried Mark.

"Nah! I got the power, man. I told you! Nobody fucks with me anymore." Jeff picked up one of the daggers and made slashing motions in front of the bureau mirror.

Mark stole another glance in the bag. He couldn't let his friend see how uneasy he felt. "How much profit do you think you'll make?" asked Mark. He made his eyes round with anticipation. His instincts told him it would be dangerous to let Jeff think he was scared. There had been a time when they shared practically everything from baseball cards to their fears of the dark—but not anymore.

Things change. Nothing remains the same.

"Plenty! I've got some shit to do this afternoon, but come over after supper and we'll take a drive. I'll have some excellent cash by then," said Jeff. "I hear there's a great party on Fifth Street. Plenty of booze and babes."

Mark hesitated. There was a new glitter in Jeff's eyes that didn't settle well. They used to be equal friends, one neither bullying nor overwhelming the other. It didn't seem that way anymore. Mark was beginning to feel like the underdog, as if there was a constant mental battle between them. If this was a war, he didn't particularly want to lose. The feeling that the stakes were higher than he wanted to pay was ever-present when he traveled in Jeff's sphere of influence.

All things revolve … even the planet.

Mark considered making a lame excuse about his parents not letting him go out, but he knew that Jeff would see right through it. Mark, like his father, was a terrible liar, especially with someone he'd known for so long. He had a tight knot in his stomach, like when he was a little kid and he had done something wrong and was sure to be caught. The anticipation of discovery was an excruciating experience of self-imposed guilt. "Sure! Why not?" he conceded. "I'll walk over around seven."

Jeff threw him a sly smile and tossed the dagger in the air, catching the handle neatly on the way down. "That's cool," he murmured. "Catch you later, bro."

The phone call came about an hour after Mark left. Jeff had been waiting for it in his father's den and snatched the receiver before his mother could get it, although he was pretty sure she was in the basement doing laundry.

"How did it go?" asked Jason.

"No problem. He believed everything, just like you said he would," said Jeff.

"Is everything ready for this evening? Will he go with you?"

"Yes on both counts. I told you, man, no problem. I got the power now, right? Just like you."

Jason laughed softly. "Sometimes your assumptions border on the childish, boy."

Jeff coughed nervously. "There's one hitch, though. He saw the initiation mark on my arm. And he got a glimpse of the tattoo."

There was a slight pause. "Continue," said Jason tightly.

"I—I told him I got it in a knife fight on the Circuit. He believed me. No problem, really. Actually, it made the story seem more real. He had to believe me. Let's face it, there's no way for him to check it out, even if he wanted to. Besides, once he took a look in the bag he forgot all about it." Jeff sat down in his father's chair behind the desk and swiveled it around to prop his feet on the bookcase. The back of the chair struck the desk, making a white gash on the wood.

"I think you are underestimating your friend," remarked Jason. "He is far more intelligent than you realize and his sense of morality is higher than your own."

"Bullshit. I've known Mark for years. I've got him where we want him! He'll do anything I tell him. I've been playing him for months. The kid's a dweeb, Jason. What do you want him for, anyway? He's not smart enough to be one of us. Besides, you said you'd help me settle my score with him."

"Don't worry, Jeff, it's not Mark we really want. It's his father we need. Your place with us will not be usurped by Mark, I assure you. He, unlike yourself, has a conscience. Whatever your reasons for disliking Mark, you can be assured that all will be settled. I have given you my word."

Jeff's eyes narrowed. "What do you want me to do tonight?"

"Do what we discussed earlier, then meet us at the old Mayville School House on Oxen Road. Do you know where that is?"

"Yeah, no problem. What do I need to see you guys for?" asked Jeff suspiciously.

"You'll be needing an alibi and a story. We will provide you with a flawless one," explained Jason patiently. "We will also extend payment to you at that time. The agreed upon price was $1,000, is that correct?"

"Yeah, and make it small bills, will ya? People around here will get suspicious if I wave around a couple of hundreds. Everybody knows I don't have a job. I thought you had the cops in your pocket."

"Not every man thinks as we do, Jeff. We have our connections, but one must always allow room for error. Therefore we plan carefully in case we must handle such an error. It is not your place to worry. We will handle any situation that may pop up unexpectedly."

"That's cool," said Jeff. "I'm not into taking any heat over this."

"I can assure you that, after tonight, you will no longer need to deal with Mark Reed," said Jason, and disconnected the call.

Jeff hung up the receiver. He hated being anyone's underling. He felt like a servant. It would be worth it, though. After tonight there would be heavy money in his pocket. There was plenty of time to climb through the ranks. After all, he was only sixteen. He dragged his feet off the bookcase and swerved the chair around to face the desk. He thought he saw his mother's smock flash quickly past the door but decided his eyes were only playing tricks on him.

Mark studied the driveway. It was long and winding, slithering around the back of the house, but the owner had paid him well in September to keep the sidewalks and drive clear of snow for the winter. He couldn't get Jeff off his mind. As he worked on the drive, he tried to determine exactly when Jeff started to change. Things hadn't really been right since the saga of Belinda last summer, and even after Belinda was out of the picture, his friendship with Jeff seemed continuously strained.

Timothy assured Mark that there would be many more girls in his life, but Mark had been devastated. It was a matter of pride that his father didn't seem to grasp. It still rankled him to see Belinda being slobbered on by that jerk, Bruce.

The image of Jeff floated in his mind. Mark knew that Mr. Conner wasn't around much, and when he was, his time was spent at an office in Harrisburg or at a bar in Coldwater Township. More than once Mark had seen ugly black bruises on Mrs. Conner when Jeff's dad had been in town for a few weeks. It was odd. They never appeared when he first returned from a trip, but she always had them when he left. While he was gone, sometimes months at a time, they would fade and none would reappear. Although Jeff had never come right out and said anything, Mark was sure that Mr. Conner beat his wife.

Mark had no first-hand experience with a dysfunctional family. Some of his school friends had trouble with alcoholic parents, drugs, and even abuse, but it was difficult to understand when your own family was pretty much the American Pie-type.

He missed Belinda.

He wished Jeff was himself, instead of a fledgling criminal.

He wondered why his dad had been so uncommunicative lately.

Things change.

Sometimes not for the better.

Mark finished the last swipe of the drive and stood up straight, surveying his handiwork. That should please the lady of the house. He'd been careful clearing the snow away from the brand new Isuzu in the drive. Time to head for home.

Elizabeyta let the front window curtain fall gently back a few inches to ensure the boy could not see her. Something told her that Mark was a very important key to the mystery that haunted her, but when she searched the threads of his possible futures, there was one that refused to reveal itself. It was the future made by fate—a path determined before he was born, and therefore could not be revealed. She watched him closely, drinking in his worry and his pain, but for now, he was not aware of the larger tapestry of events around him. She stayed at the window, watching as he pushed the snow blower up over the hill and out of sight.

Neither she nor Mark realized that by sunrise on the morrow, death would take on a new meaning to both of them.

chapter thirteen

ELIZABEYTA CLOSED THE HEAVY CURTAIN AND went back to the library. After two years of visiting this house, she felt so close to the answer. Half the attic was now clear and all the records in both the basement and the shed had been removed, sorted, and filed, but she still lacked the key to the knowledge that she sought. Somehow she knew the Reed kid was involved— no, that wasn't right. Someone near him was involved. She tried to scan the boy again, hoping for clues in his conscious mind, but either he hadn't put the pieces together yet himself, or she was definitely losing her touch.

What she did pick up was disconcerting. The more she focused on his life energy, the greater she felt he was in danger. Maybe she was just getting paranoid. Everybody she looked at these days had a flared aura of sorts. That usually meant the higher spirit of the person was working in overdrive to protect the stupid consciousness that blundered about the world in total ignorance. If ordinary humans knew how much danger they were in every breathing moment of their lives, they'd probably roll over and give up. That, of course, was why the conscious protected itself with petty thoughts and needless worries. Unfortunately, it usually did this too well, forcing the higher self to work into exhaustion. Then, bingo! Illness or accident hit. Sometimes it even resulted in death.

She wondered if this was happening to her. Would she be ready to face the killer or would he take her by surprise? Elizabeyta walked along the floor-to-ceiling bookcases that lined the right side of the room, dragging her fingertips lightly across the old bindings. The kid bothered her, but she had more distressing thoughts to consider.

The scent of lilacs wafted through the room. "I know you're here, Beth Ann!" she cried, whirling to face the empty room. "Why don't you just get it over with and show yourself?" Elizabeyta moved to the center of the library and spread her arms wide. "I command you to appear!"

Nothing happened.

"Damn you, Beth Ann! For two years you have played your pranks and pestered me. You've blocked every avenue to what I want. It just isn't fair. What the hell do you care, anyway? You're dead, dammit!"

She stomped her foot on the hardwood floor. Only the echo greeted her tirade.

"I'm not afraid of you, Beth Ann. You ought to have figured that out by now. That trick with the stew the other night was really cute."

Elizabeyta sashayed about the room, her hands on her hips. "You've behaved all this time with Lee until Saturday night. Afraid of being exorcised? You should be. He used to be a Catholic, you know. That's what normal people do with naughty ghosts—they try to get rid of them. It's known as celestial pest control!"

Cold air blew past Elizabeyta's long dark skirt, making it flap around her bare legs. An antique china plate flew off the mantle and crashed on the floor. Small bits of glass skidded on the smooth wooden surface. Elizabeyta cocked her eyebrow but didn't move.

"You can throw as many tantrums as you like, Beth Ann, but it won't matter. I came here to find the truth and I swear by the Goddess that I'll succeed, with or without your help!"

A second plate danced slowly down the mantle, wavered in the air a foot above the floor, then forcefully smashed like the first. Elizabeyta eyed the mess with disgust. "There are four more left, Beth Ann," she drawled. "Aren't you going to break them, too?" All four plates left on the mantle rattled. "And when you're done, clean up the mess, will you? You're such a sloppy housekeeper, Beth Ann. It's a wonder you lived to be eighty-nine. I'm surprised you didn't die in your own filth! My grandmother would be horrified if she had any idea what you've been doing. With your attitude, it's no wonder you two didn't talk to each other for over thirty years. At least she had the presence of mind to leave the earth plane and not get stuck here like some folks we know!"

Elizabeyta tossed her head and strode from the room, slamming the library door behind her. She rolled her eyes as each successive plate hit the floor. "One … two … three … four!" counted Elizabeyta to herself as she stood patiently outside the library door. One thing was certain, Beth Ann had a terrible temper.

She giggled.

Elizabeyta skipped up the stairs, two by two, to the attic. Temper tantrums left Beth Ann tired and quiet, so Elizabeyta knew she would be able to go through the records in peace, at least for a few hours. She must be getting close to the truth. Why else would Beth Ann have stepped up her disturbances? As her foot set down on the last stair, the phone rang. "Drat," she mumbled, walking into her bedroom and picking up the extension.

"Hey, hi …"

Her stomach did a quick flip-flop. Lee. She hadn't seen him since Saturday night, which was good. It gave her enough time to think about their relationship and firm her resolve to tell him they'd both made a mistake. "Oh, Lee. I'm glad you called. Are you coming over?"

"Wish I could, but I have a funeral this afternoon and counseling tonight."

"Tomorrow then?"

"I'll be on the train first thing Tuesday morning. I have some business to take care of in Larksburg. I could drive. It's only an hour away but I don't feel like maneuvering through all this slop."

"Oh. Um. I need to talk to you."

"Hey, don't sound so down. I'll be back by eight or nine tomorrow night. Then we can relax together and you can do all the talking you want."

She closed her eyes, resolve wavering.

"Listen—I called you because I think I found someone who can help you with all that research you told me about."

Immediately on guard, she said, "What do you mean?"

"You said you were looking into the history of the town. I've got a good friend who's an ace at that sort of stuff and I'm sure he'll help you."

"You told someone? How could you! You gave me your word."

"Hold on. I didn't give him any details, just said you were researching your family tree. He doesn't know anything else."

"So what am I supposed to tell him? Lie?"

"You managed to pull it off with me for two whole years; I can't see how that would make a difference to you now." Elizabeyta could clearly hear the hurt in his voice. Nope, they weren't going to be able to get past her deceit. *Wake up and smell the roses, kid,* she thought. *It ain't gonna happen.*

"I don't think it's such a good idea, Lee," she said, sitting down on the edge of her bed. "It might put him in danger."

"Oh come on, Elizabeyta. Mason Trout is an upstanding man in the community. No one is going to bother him. He's the funeral director at Serenity. No one will see him as a threat. Besides, who's going to know that he's helping you unless you tell?"

Elizabeyta twirled the phone cord. Don't speak to any outsiders more than you have to, said the family. She'd already broken the rule once and now look at the mess she'd gotten herself into.

"You told!"

"I did not! He doesn't know a thing! Look, the sooner you figure out this whole mess the better it will be for all of us. Please. I love you, Elizabeyta, more than anything in the world." Her heart did a nosedive. "Please let Mason help you. You don't have to give him any details. Just talk history. Please, do this for me. I promise we'll work this out together. You're not alone. Let him help you."

Mason Trout waited patiently outside of Elizabeyta Belladonna's residence. He rang the bell again. Lee warned him she was—how did he put it?—oh yes, emotionally distraught over the matter. Why would anyone be upset over their family history, unless of course, an ancestor had been involved in some sort of criminal activity, or perhaps an adoption had occurred and the woman's parentage was in question?

He adjusted his overcoat and straightened his shoulders. When she opened the door he found his tongue stuck uncomfortably to the roof of his mouth. The woman looked so much like Terry Anderson he'd lost the greeting he'd planned to say. A first for him. Funeral directors always knew what to say, and when.

His eyes swept her figure. Perhaps not quite as voluptuous as Terry, but the facial structure and the hair … tumbling auburn … delicate eyebrows—the two women could be twins, though this woman carried the knowing glint of maturity in her dark eyes, where Terry did not.

"Mason Trout?" she asked coolly.

Her dark eyes dug into his brain. He blinked for a moment, trying to understand why he suddenly felt—well, strange. Nodding his head, he followed her into the foyer. "Lee called me around eleven this morning and said you'd be expecting me this afternoon."

She smiled politely and offered to take his coat. He watched her put it meticulously onto a padded hanger and place it in the hall closet. Save for one other black coat, the closet was completely empty. Odd. Most people had all sorts of clutter in their closets. Then he remembered she didn't own the house and only stayed here on occasion. Stupid. Of course there wouldn't be many personal effects in the house. What was he thinking?

"I've been working in the attic lately," she was saying as she moved toward the staircase. It curved gently to the right, the heavy banister gleaming in the soft light of the house. "I'm not exactly sure what Lee told you." She hesitated, a tremble in her voice. "I've been going through a lot of old records, trying to piece together a sort of mystery. The attic is this way."

He followed her as she mounted the stairs. He noticed she was taller than Terry and far more slender at the waist. Those legs … longer and well shaped. She carried herself with a determined purpose, speaking in a well-modulated voice—the words soft-spoken, almost lilting. She and Terry may have similar faces and hair color, but that was about where the resemblance stopped. At times, Terry walked like a man. This woman almost waltzed with each step. Mason shook his head quickly. No, the women weren't the same.

Elizabeyta led Mason deep into the musty attic. "It looks like someone used this area for a bedroom at one time," she said.

Mason surveyed the area. Insulation and electrical outlets had been added, as well as a built-in bed under the eaves. Two glass shaded lights hugged the ceiling, one at each end of the attic. The area still held a decidedly male undercurrent. Dusty baseball trophies, a deflated football, and old track shoes were dumped unceremoniously in one corner. Probably a hideaway bedroom for a teenage boy in a large family.

Elizabeyta turned on the desk light and picked up a pile of old papers. "I got these from one of the trunks stacked against the inside wall." Several green ledgers embossed with the word "CASH" in brown sat on one side of the desk. She saw him eyeing them and said, "Although it is interesting to see the flow of cash in the family businesses and households through the years, they didn't help me."

"How do you think I can help?"

She shrugged. "Lee says you are an expert in the history of the area. You may see something that I've missed."

He teetered awkwardly behind her, as he leaned forward to look at the ledgers. The scent of musk perfume mixed with her sweat tickled his nose. Shutting his eyes tightly for a second, he brought the sudden urge to touch her under control. Eyes now open wide, he was shocked at his thoughts. He hadn't felt this way since high school, for heaven's sake. Taking a deep breath, he steadied himself, and caught her looking at him out of the corner of her eye.

"Last April," she said, politely ignoring the flush on his face, "I found over fifteen of these ledgers in the basement. Some were specifically financial records, like this one. Others were in journal format, but not specific. After I catalogued them, I sent them to the family to decide what to do with them. The postal service must love me. The amount of money I've spent shipping the paper contents of the shed out back, and the boxes and books in the basement was astronomical."

"I'm a little confused," admitted Mason. "I thought you worked for a software company. What do these family records have to do with you?"

She made a little "O" with her lips and raised her eyebrows. "The family who sold the house to the company is overseas. The company offers homes like these to their traveling employees as a perk. The family who originally owned the house are friends of the president of my company. I found these items when I first came here. The president is sort of a history buff and the family is trying to chart the history of the house. I believe they want to write a book to give to family and friends at their next family reunion. I've got a little extra time before I'm promoted and offered to do it for them."

"But you said you sent things out last April; did you know about your promotion then?" What was he saying? He was practically calling the woman a liar and he'd promised Lee he wouldn't ask too many questions. He wanted to melt right into the attic floor.

She gazed at him for a moment. Opening her mouth, she hesitated, then said, "It's sort of a hobby. I've been doing it a little each time I came to visit, around business, of course." She laughed. "Let's face it, there's not much to do in this town."

He grinned sheepishly. "Lee said you were working on some sort of mystery. I'm sorry, I thought it was going to be cloak and dagger stuff, at least that's what he led me to believe."

Another polite smile that didn't look quite true to him. "It's just that the family has a great deal of money and doesn't want, shall we say, some of the more tarnished histories to find their way out into the open."

He nodded. "So what have you got so far?"

She took a look at his expensive suit, then looked around the attic. "I'm afraid if you sit down, you're going to ruin your clothing."

"Don't worry about it. I've got plenty of suits. Part of the business."

She shrugged and pulled out a chair for him, dusted it off, then sat down in her chair at the desk. "It appears that two Scotch-Irish families arrived in America in 1720. They traveled with a primarily German group of immigrants and finally settled in this area, purchasing farm land from the native Indians and their German acquaintances in 1736. To date," she said, tapping the ledger, "I've determined that this house stayed in the Frampton family, one of the Scotch-Irish families, since it was built in the early 1800s, up until Beth Ann Frampton, the previous owner of this house, married Albert Baxter. It appears that the original dwelling was where the shed stands now."

"From the description in some of the old ledgers," she said, "the building was demolished when they built the new house, and a shed to hold a wagon, a carriage, and a few horses was constructed in its place."

"On trips to the local library and the York Historical Society, and while sorting out the contents of the house, I discovered that no other Scotch-Irish families settled here. All those who arrived after the original migration were of German descent. As I said before, the Framptons were one of the Scotch-Irish families."

"And the other?"

She looked at him uneasily. "I haven't been able to figure out why two Scotch-speaking families wanted to be surrounded with foreigners, or why the German families tolerated them. Even more of a mystery is that both Scotch-Irish family properties were located outside the stockade walls of the settlement. All the German families were located inside the settlement walls. Not one German family had property outside those walls. Discrimination, even then, or was it something else?"

Mason quietly crossed his arms and leaned back in the chair. He knew who that other family was, and so did this woman, yet she avoided telling him the truth. Should he play along with her game for Lee's sake, or should he call her on it? He debated for a moment, then decided to let it ride ... at least for the time being. "What does your research tell you?"

Her eyes flicked over to the papers on the desk than back to him. She clamped her lips together for a moment, then leaned forward in her chair. "At the York County Historical Society, I read that many of the settlers were driven off their land during the French and Indian War between 1755 and 1758, therefore they were not required to pay taxes on the acreage held by the enemy during that time. Neither of the two Scotch Irish families were listed among those families who had been forced to flee from South Mountain, this area, down into the stockade, yet the two farms lay directly between the mountain and the safety of the nucleus of the settlement. All their land was outside the stockade walls and within danger of attack, but neither family lost one life to either attack or sickness during that war."

"I'm familiar with that story," he said. "It appears you are saying that the Scotch-Irish were ostracized to the point that their lives were in jeopardy, but they survived just the same. I'd not heard that angle before. According to what I've been told, however, all the Scotch-Irish immigrants moved on, down into Virginia, around 1762." He steepled his fingers thoughtfully and waited for her to respond.

She took a deep breath, eyeing him closely. "They didn't go anywhere. Family records show that in 1762, to support a settlement population of seventy-five, Alexander Frampton built the first meeting house out of logs at the corner of his property closest to the stockade. The Indian trails beside the meeting house turned into well-worn roads for horseback riders and carriages traveling between York and Harrisburg. In 1773, he built a tavern beside the meeting house to accommodate such travelers. None of the official records, however, support this information I garnered from the family ledgers. It appears that the entire history of the settlement was rewritten at some time to exclude the two Scotch-Irish families. Why? It is as if they never existed."

"But they did exist, because Beth Ann Frampton owned this house previously."

"That's true, but unless she checked, how would she know what the records in the Historical Society held?"

Mason nodded, but threw her a critical glance. *How much further is she going to take this?* thought Mason.

She looked at him as though he'd just slapped her. Elizabeyta picked up a packet of yellowed papers tied with a faded blue ribbon and held them tightly. "You know it's all a lie, don't you?" she asked softly.

He surveyed her frankly for a moment. She reminded him of someone … not Terry, that was another matter. Someone else … Emma Ward! A much younger version of Emma Ward, of course. Emma had the gift. Mason knew it; sometimes they talked about it. She told him stories of fact and fiction on summer nights on her front porch on South Mountain. He never tired of listening to the old woman, and he cherished the time they spent together.

Slowly, he pointed his index finger at her. "You've been reading my mind the entire time. Are you satisfied?"

Her eyes fluttered; a frightened light flashed across her eyes. "How do you know?"

"I don't have the gift, but I have an old friend who does. You remind me a lot of her. It's okay, I won't tell anyone."

She fidgeted with the packet of letters. "What did Lee tell you … about me?"

"Basically he said you were emotionally distraught and that I should watch what I say. He's infatuated with you."

"I know."

"He'll never understand your gifts."

She sighed. "I'm aware of that."

"So, you love him?" Mason felt like an old marriage broker, playing middle man between two mismatched clients. It made him uncomfortable.

"I'm attracted to him."

"Not the same as love."

Snorting, she said, "How well I know."

"What's really going on here?"

Elizabeyta stood, stretched, and walked over to the large, free-standing bulletin board in the middle of the attic. "I think this entire mystery boils down to a three-way family feud. That's not quite right—a feud between the Scotch-Irish families and one German family. This family feud may still be on-going. As we've already discussed, there are some missing pieces, but I found more."

She opened the packet of letters and unfolded the first sheet, searched his face, and handed it slowly over to him. "The other family's name is Belladonna—my name. In 1788 a diploma from the University of Pennsylvania was awarded to a Martin Belladonna, proclaiming him a medical doctor. Here it is."

"And?"

She removed the canvas drop cloth covering the bulletin board. He looked in astonishment at the family trees she had drawn from copious notes over the last two years.

He looked at the top of two trees, one representing the Framptons and one headed by Alexander Belladonna. They covered the entire board. Martin was Alexander Belladonna's eldest son. He let out a soft whistle. "Excellent research," he muttered.

"Thanks. It's odd—the written history of the town I photocopied from the local library doesn't mention Martin Belladonna as the doctor of the settlement. If I remember correctly, it was a different name, but it doesn't seem to bear any relevance. Doesn't it strike you as strange that there were two doctors practicing in the settlement at the same time? A population of seventy-five did not require two physicians, unless …"

Elizabeyta rolled the bulletin board closer to the desk.

"That German family wouldn't be the Blackthorns, would it?" asked Mason.

"Why, yes, the very same."

"They have an incredibly long … ah … unscrupulous record. Quite a bunch of rednecks as I recall. In the 1920s they ran the only speakeasy and whorehouse in town. During World War II, it was the black market. A bad bunch all the way around. They've always been in trouble both with the law and their neighbors."

He took a deep breath. "Does any of your information tell you if the Belladonnas and the Framptons were Protestants or Catholics?" asked Mason.

"Oh, I can answer that one without looking at this stuff. They were both Catholic."

"Religion never made much difference to me, guess that's why I didn't think about it, but I believe the Blackthorns were the fire and brimstone kind of faith. They still are, what's left of them … mostly old folks, I think."

Elizabeyta looked up at him quickly. "I thought you ran a funeral home—I mean, aren't you religious?"

"Not me. That's my wife's department. She's really into it."

"Oh."

"After seeing so many people with so many faiths, I feel that sure, there's something out there making the universe work, but I can't see where one religion is any different than the other, so I practice none and talk to God in my own way."

Elizabeyta nodded. "Sounds like a logical approach to me."

"You still haven't told me why you're digging into all this stuff. If you did, I could probably help you better."

Elizabeyta leafed through the sheaf of photocopied papers, ignoring the question.

"The other doctor …"

"What was his name?"

"Jason Blackthorn. He graduated one year after Martin from the same university and set up his practice inside the stockade. I double-checked at the historical society—there was no mention of Martin Belladonna being a doctor, yet there was an item on the first pharmacy 'built outside the stockade, directly next to the meeting house.' The original ownership wasn't recorded, but I bet it belonged to Martin Belladonna."

"Okay. So, Jason was a part of the German family that didn't get along with your ancestors, right? But I'm curious, what was the relationship between the Framptons and Belladonnas other than their country of origin?"

"They were—I mean are—two clans, two extended families that have been pledged to each other for centuries. My father was a Belladonna and my mother, a Frampton."

"So when you are talking about families you weren't speaking of small families, but a large group of people—cousins, aunts, uncles, nieces, nephews, assorted grandparents ..."

"Yes."

Mason shook his head. "None of the historical records support that information."

Elizabeyta sighed. "How well I know."

"What are you looking for, Elizabeyta?"

Elizabeyta looked at the family tree again and back to Mason. "I can't tell you," she said quietly, "but sometimes I just wish this was all over with. Sometimes I wish I were dead."

Mason swallowed tightly. A connection was building between them. Slow. Deliciously insidious. Did she feel it too? He'd once heard the word "split-apart" from Emma. What she'd really meant was soul-mate. He'd always thought that was foolish talk, a woman's dream of a knight in shining armor that never appeared. A fantasy. Now, he wasn't so sure. He wanted to rescue this woman from her obvious torment.

Her large dark eyes looked at him painfully. "I mean it. I wish he would just get it all over with. I'm afraid he will kill us all."

"He who? Lee?"

She shook her head vehemently.

"Who?"

"It doesn't matter," she said, dropping the papers on the desk and walking away from him toward the attic stairs. "You won't be able to help. It's too dangerous."

Frustrated, Mason followed her. "If you don't tell me what you are looking for, of course I can't help you." He grabbed her by the arm; she whirled and fell against him. "You're shaking like a leaf." Instead of stepping back from him, she held on, as if he was the only life raft in a limitless ocean. They stood together for a timeless moment.

"I remember ..." he began dreamily, but she disentangled herself.

"I'm so sorry, Mason," she said. "I didn't do that on purpose. Perhaps you'd better go."

"Hey, it's okay. Everybody needs a little support now and then." His emotions were churning, Perhaps it was time for him to go. "Tell you what, when you feel more comfortable about sharing your research with me, just give me a call. If I can help you, I truly will. Why not give me something to go on and I can look in places you don't even know about. What do you say?"

She just looked at him.

"It's okay. If you want to read my thoughts, I don't mind. Emma does it all the time. In fact, sometimes we play this game where I try to read hers, too."

"Is Emma your wife?"

"No, she's the friend I told you about. The one that's a lot like you," he said, smiling.

"And in this game, how well do you do?"

He could see the interest in her eyes, which both pleased and amused him. "She says I do a little better than average. Come on, what do you say? Give me a little to go on and I promise you I'll do the best I can. If you're going to be my best friend's wife, it's the least I can do." He brushed off the front of his suit.

Her expression sobered, her brow wrinkling. "Find out about feuds, especially related to the Belladonnas, Framptons, or Blackthorns. Get a record of any unsolved murders that were recorded."

"Deep stuff."

"You don't know how deep."

Elizabeyta tapped her pencil on the desk. Evening shadows deepened into dusk, then turned to the blackness of a cold winter sky. The lamps surrounded her with pleasant, warm light.

She missed the twins, Amanda and Ben, and she missed the life of the covenstead. But they had pooled their money to buy this house, including its contents, and even borrowed from the covenstead accounts. She couldn't let them down. She'd have to stick it out.

She sighed and packed away the papers in a cardboard carton, addressing it in flowing handwriting to the post office box of the covenstead. Indeed, she thought as she wrote, she had taken an oath to find the truth—had sworn in her own running blood on the night of the Wolf Moon, when she had been told of her grandmother's death, that she would not give up until the mystery was solved. It was time to stop playing games with Beth Ann and get down to business. There were too many ugly things to confront.

She thought of the twins again, her brother and sister, now in their twenties—bright, inseparable, at times intolerable. She smiled sadly. Sworn to silence, they had begged her to not to take the trip this time. They had pleaded, cajoled, and threw tantrums to convince her to stay home. But they never told the rest of the family. She had almost given in, but a Witch was as good as her word, and she would simply have to fulfill it. She knew their lives depended upon it.

Maybe Mason would come up with something. He was a nice man. A handsome man. She selfishly wished it was he who lived next to her, who was single and unattached. They seemed to be able to communicate so well. By the time he'd left this afternoon they were exchanging jokes and mutual giggles. But he was a married man. Probably with children. Absolutely not available. She dropped the pencil and let it roll lazily across the desk. It was as if her long-dead feelings, awakened by Lee, had gone out of control. The image of Mason, his caring manner, his soft eyes … Why did her heart move in Mason's direction?

Time to worry about business. What to do? She ran the slender fingers of her right hand over her parted lips. There was one option yet left open to her, but meeting death face to face would be risky indeed.

chapter fourteen

ERRY WOKE AT NINE MONDAY MORNING with a splitting headache. She rolled over on her side, shocked to find herself lying on the living room floor. Muted daylight streamed through the windows. God, this was worse than any hangover. She got to her knees and bumped her head on the table. The dragonfly candleholder toppled to the floor, the candle long since burned to nothing.

She rubbed her head and stood unsteadily. The last thing she fully remembered was doing the reading for herself. After that, things were blurred. She thought she may have had some sort of vision, but it wasn't very clear. Something about Lee and snow. Terry massaged the back of her neck and headed for the bathroom.

Some aspirin and a hot shower should do the trick. She flicked on the television to discover it was not the Sunday afternoon news that greeted her sensitive ears, but Monday morning! The blood rushed to her head and she thought she might faint, but she recovered enough to sit on the edge of the bed and breathe deeply for a few moments. The shop wasn't open on Mondays, so she needn't rush around so as not to lose a day's business.

Two hours later, her headache had gone and she was busy going over the store accounts, trying to forget about the full day she'd lost and why. She was shocked at the numerical mess. How could she have let it go so long? Where was her head? Her kitchen table was cluttered with inventory files, invoices, and order forms. It would take her all day and half the night to even make a dent in this snarl of numbers! She groaned inwardly. She should have bought a computer months ago.

Her mother called her as the forgotten dusk sky deepened to a dirty black. She stood in front of the living room window, holding the cordless phone, watching as tiny pinpricks of stars appeared on the horizon.

"Thought I'd check in before your father and I leave for Philadelphia," said her mother. Terry had forgotten about her parents' plans. In fact, she had forgotten the time. Where had her day gone? Sodium streetlights flicked on in ghostly spasms, reflecting off the glassy surface of the street below her.

"Are you sure you should travel in this weather, Mother?"

"Your dad is driving the Jeep in to the Whiskey Springs Station. We've decided to take the train. That's one of the reasons why I called you. Would you mind terribly walking down tomorrow morning to pick it up?"

"Not at all. I'll see you off."

"No, dear, our train leaves at 5:00 AM. Don't trouble yourself. Do you still have the spare set of keys Daddy gave you?" Terry turned from the window and rooted through her purse. Dirty tissues, loose change, extra bracelets, a tube of half-used lipstick, eyeliner—ah, there they were … keys!

"Yes, Mother, I still have them."

"Good! Do you want us to pick anything up for you? I plan to hit as many of the stores that we don't have around here as possible. I'm going to shop until your father drops!"

Terry laughed. "Yeah? Well you can buy me a computer; that ought to turn the last few hairs on his head grey."

"A *what?*"

"Just kidding, Mother. I've been working on the store's accounting all day and it looks like I'll be burning the midnight oil and still be only half finished. I think I'll use the Jeep tomorrow and do some shopping myself. It's high time I bust in on technology and buy a computer for my business. I don't know why I've put it off for so long."

"What a wonderful idea!" her mother prattled. "You really should get away from that store more often." Terry rolled her eyes, expecting to get another lecture about hiring someone to help her with the store, but her mother was too excited about her shopping trip to carry the subject further. "We'll be back Thursday afternoon or Friday, depending on the weather. It's supposed to get milder toward the end of the week, so we may stay an extra day," said her mother. "I'll call you in plenty of time so that you can meet us at the station."

She looked down into the street again. Someone moved by the light post as if to avoid the pool of light, as if it were acid or something. Whoever it was slipped around the corner.

"Terry?"

"Yeah, Mom. That sounds fine," Terry replied. "Maybe I can snare Dad into helping me with the computer. I'm sure I'll not be able to make heads nor tails of it until he helps me. You be sure and have a good time and I'll see you when you get back."

Terry was ready to hang up at her mother's usual clipped good-bye, except it didn't come. Only a pregnant silence greeted her ear.

"Ah, Terry," hesitated her mother, "you will be careful, won't you?"

"Of course! Whatever would make you say that?"

"Oh … nothing. I just had an odd dream the other night. A silly thing, really! Forget I even mentioned it."

"Mother?" But her mother had already hung up.

Elizabeyta stepped into her boots and pulled on her black wool coat, buttoning it to the top, flipping the collar up, wrapping her head and neck in a warm, black knitted scarf. She checked her watch. Fifteen minutes until the post office closed. If she hurried, she could just make it. Picking up the box, she gave the house a once over, satisfied that all was peaceful and calm.

It took her only a few minutes to walk the three blocks downtown. The package got off with five minutes to spare. Pleased, she took her time walking back. A group of teenagers rounded the corner, throwing snowballs at each other. Across the street, just out of sight of the lamp light, stood a man in dark clothing, smoking a cigarette. The red flare as he drew deeply on the filter bounced in the darkness.

The kids drew closer and Elizabeyta got caught in the crossfire of their ice battle. Laughing, she picked up some snow, formed a ball and threw it back. In a few moments, amongst joyous yelling and screaming, the battle erupted into a full-scale war. Elizabeyta's scarf worked loose, letting her long auburn hair fly freely.

"Hey, it's Terry," shouted one of the kids.

Elizabeyta reeled, and moved in quickly to face him, snowball ready in her hand.

"I'm not Terry!" she said, giggling softly, "I'm someone else. See?" Then she promptly threw the snowball at him.

"Sorry for the mistake," said the boy. "You look just like Terry Anderson. My girlfriend goes to her shop for readings sometimes." He ducked as a snowball whizzed over his head, gathered up a missile of his own and shot it at one of his friends.

The kids traveled on and Elizabeyta leaned against a building, laughing and catching her breath. She sat down on the stoop and adjusted her scarf. The man loitering earlier across the street had disappeared.

Unbeknownst to Elizabeyta, she sat on the front step of Terry Anderson's apartment. After she felt reasonably revitalized, she tightened her scarf and trudged up the hill.

ChAPTER FIFTEEN

ERRY IMMERSED HERSELF IN PAPERWORK until past midnight. She tried to focus her aching eyes on the wall clock. The need for food finally tore her gaze away, before she figured out what time it was. After fumbling around in the refrigerator, she settled on zapping some egg rolls in the microwave. She returned to the table, plate in hand, and realized there was no place to eat. Piles of paper littered both the floor and the table top. She took her elbow and scattered everything with one tired swipe. What a mess! Well, a computer would keep this from ever happening again. She ate mechanically while the radio droned softly.

Leaving half the food on her plate, she stumbled to the bedroom. She moved to the bed, pausing to look out the second-story bedroom at the street below, a black ribbon of sparkling stillness. Cold air wafted off the window and she stepped back, hugging herself. A light snow dusted the sidewalks. She noticed the trail of footprints beneath the streetlight, but thought nothing of them. Above, stars littered the black sky, challenging the beauty of the earth below. She wondered briefly why her mother had sounded concerned about her welfare. She'd try to catch her parents at the train station instead of waiting and picking the car up later in the day.

Her alarm set for 4:30 AM, she slipped mercifully between the sheets. She snuggled deeper under the comforter, lazily deciding where she was going to put her new computer. Maybe in the corner by the window ...

She missed the train by ten minutes. Obviously they were running on time. Terry shook her head as she slipped and slid in the icy mush of the busy train station parking lot, searching for the Jeep. She was sure this monumental excellence in train scheduling would go down in Whiskey Springs history. She glanced at the sky. Last night's twinkling stars had been replaced by solid cloud cover. Dawn was still a few hours away and it didn't look promising. So much for the mild weather her mother had been wanting.

The parking lot was well lit and she found the Jeep with little difficulty. As she slid around to the driver's side, she spotted the Lehman twins hurriedly piling out of their father's pick-up, shouting orders to each other as they unloaded several yapping bloodhounds from the caged tailgate. Terry was going to holler a greeting over the din, but snapped her mouth shut as the implications of what they were doing hit her.

Someone was lost on the Jack Frost Ski Slopes. Gina and Tammy Lehman, robust and healthy at eighteen, were known for their expertise in tracking with the dogs. Their fluorescent orange parkas with Rescue Ski Patrol blazing across the backs gave her an ominous feeling as they snapped orders at the dogs and herded them into the station. Terry had a sudden desire to go back to bed and disappear under the covers.

Be careful what you wish for ...

The Jeep's engine purred as she rounded the first aisle in the parking lot, dodging a few oncoming cards with unsteady traction and numerous pedestrians who weren't faring much better. Where the hell were they all going? Well, she was out. Why shouldn't other people have business of their own? She blinked and swore as one man stepped right in front of the Jeep.

Brakes. Horn blowing. The look of exasperation she knew she wore on her face. The black overcoated man did not react. He just stood and stared at her. At least she thought he was staring at her, because the brim of his black hat completely shadowed his face from the harsh lights of the parking lot. A shiver danced between her shoulders. She imagined his eyes boring into her for what seemed like an eternity. In her swerve to avoid him, she missed the exit.

She grumbled at his stupidity and her own dumb reaction as she rounded the lot again, her bracelets tinkling merrily with every turn of the steering wheel. The man was nowhere to be seen the second trip around, but she did catch a glimpse of Lee as he disappeared briskly into the station.

Her heart bumped a bit, but she gripped the wheel as if to force him from her thoughts. Terry wondered if he had been called to the mountain, too. A sense of foreboding clasped cold fingers around her heart.

It was too early to shop and now she wasn't sure if she even wanted to go. None of the stores would be open for a few hours, if they were open at all. Maybe she would just pick up a new romance book and some hot chocolate and go home. Terry turned out on Main Street and stopped halfway up the hill at a convenience store. The young red-headed clerk smiled warmly as Terry stamped out her boots inside the door.

"I saved some of the new titles from the Silhouette line for you," she said brightly, reaching under the counter. She withdrew four pocket romance books and set them by the register.

"Hi, Kimmy! How's the promising senior doing?" asked Terry as she scooped up a box of Hershey's instant cocoa and headed toward the counter. She slipped on a puddle of slush, giggled, and recovered.

"Great!" Kim replied. "My mom is already talking about going into York to get a prom dress! Parents make such a big deal over that sort of stuff."

Terry smiled her best "I understand teenagers because I'm psychic, you know" smile and paid for her purchases. By the time she walked out the door, she had promised a free reading for Kim on the outcome of her prom. She figured if she gave one freebie, it would travel through the high school like wildfire and she'd be able to pick up extra bucks with lucrative speed. Maybe she would go shopping for that computer later this morning after all.

Seven hours later, Kim, through a veil of tears and swollen eyes, would remark, "Yes, officer; I guess I was the last person to see Terry Anderson alive."

CHAPTER SIXTEEN

EE CHECKED HIS WATCH AS HE EXITED THE train station and climbed into a cab. "University, please," he said, slamming the door.

The train was running a little behind schedule after that last stop. Something about unloading a bunch of dogs to be transported to Jack Frost, but the traffic from the station had been worse. His taxi wove around numerous accidents and near-misses. He hoped that Pauline hadn't given up on him. He smiled. It would be a pleasure to see her.

After twenty minutes he finally entered the University campus and marched into Southwood Hall. Lee greeted Diane, Pauline's secretary, with a wide grin.

"Good morning, Pastor Becker! Miss Pauline is waiting for you. Go right in," she said brightly. Diane was a heartbreaker with two kids, an amiable husband, and insatiable dimples. "I suppose that I should clear her schedule for the afternoon," she called after him. "Every time you show up, she's gone for hours!"

Lee smiled ruefully and turned the knob to his sister's office. As usual, the place was in an awful clutter.

Pauline's green eyes peeked over a mountain of books and papers on her desk. "About time you slithered in here. It's past ten, you know!" She grinned and barreled from behind the desk to give him a hug.

"I need the assistance of your esteemed education. You know, the one I helped pay for?" Lee grinned and broke their embrace.

"You braggart! I paid you back every cent, and then some!" She playfully punched him in the arm. Lee feigned pain and collapsed in her chair, the only empty one in the office. "Whatever it is, it must be important," she said. "I've been totally mystified since you called yesterday. What on earth could a lowly professor of archeology offer to her know-it-all brother? Not suddenly taking a leap in faith and questing after the Holy Grail, are you?"

Pauline pushed some of the papers over on the desk and plopped on the edge. Unlike her brother, she had inherited the stocky build and stick-straight hair of the family genes, though her height helped even out her appearance.

Lee set his scarf and gloves on the desk and steepled his fingers thoughtfully, the glimmer gone from his eyes.

"I recently became involved with someone—"

"Oh goody!" interrupted Pauline. "When do I get to meet her?"

Lee leaned back in the chair and playfully kicked his black loafered foot at her. "You disgust me sometimes, Paulie. You'd think that spending years in such a respectable science would have given you at least a veneer of maturity. Instead, you're frothing at the mouth about my sex life! Is your own so boring you have to stick your freckled little nose in mine?"

Pauline stuck out her tongue at him. "Mine's just peachy, thank you very much, Mister Minister. Correct me if I'm wrong, but your denomination does not demand the nasty practice of celibacy. Besides, I'd like to be an auntie one of these days, you know, then I don't have to have kids of my own. I can keep yours for a while and then give them back." She smiled mischievously.

"You're a terror, Paulie. No wonder Mother stopped after she had you!"

"You'd better watch it, Lee, or I'll write your number on every girls' restroom wall on the campus!"

Lee threw his gloves at her.

"Okay, okay," relinquished Pauline. "You met a girl, and what's wrong?"

"What do you know about Witchcraft, Paulie?"

She smirked at him. "You're asking me? I thought you pastor persons were experts on that stuff."

"Paulie!"

"Owwwww. I believe I've hit some sort of sore spot. So you've met a Witch; so what, they're all over the place these days. How romantic, the

Witch and the Priest, except you're not a priest, are you? It's not my fault you converted from Catholicism and don't know all about neat stuff … like magick!" She hopped off the desk before he could take a decent swipe at her.

"What do you mean, 'they're all over the place'?" asked Lee curiously.

"Just what I said. There's a revolution, my friend, and it's called the Age of Information. Today's Witches are very big on ecology and human rights," she explained. "There's one hell of a big underground of them."

"You're kidding."

"Heck, no. In fact, according to the latest statistics, it is the fastest growing religion in the United States. We even have a group of Dianic Witches on campus—at least they are trying to be Witches. Sometimes I think they are more interested in grabbing the fellas here with mysterious mumbo-jumbo just so they can be the most desirable catch, if you know what I mean."

Lee chuckled. "Any really serious?"

"I think a handful may be serious about understanding the religion. There are other colleges in the state that are incorporating Goddess religions in their curriculum, which often acts as a springboard for more mature seekers."

"But are they real?"

"Real in what sense?"

"Well, can they cast spells and things? You know, mind control and blood of hamster?"

"The girls here have cast one hell of a spell on most of the males, but the science department hasn't reported a shortage of hamsters," she giggled.

Lee wasn't laughing.

Paulie studied her brother for a moment. "You're not kidding about wanting to know about this stuff, are you?"

"Serious as death."

"That's pretty solemn," she remarked. "How much time have you got?"

"My day's open. The latest train leaves at nine tonight. Why?"

"There's someone you should meet. Gather up your gloves and scarf, kiddo, we're going to take a drive."

"If it's the little ladies on campus, I'm not interested, Paulie. I don't want someone who's playing games to put notches on bedposts," he said irritably.

"And let you lose your virginity? Nah. I've got someone else in mind. First, though, let's get you over to the campus library and find some reading material I think you'll find interesting. There's a book called *When God Was a Woman*. It's so popular here that the librarian keeps an extra copy in her private stash for college employees. I'll check it out for you, along with a few others she has hidden away. The librarian claims she can't keep the books on the shelves for more than a few hours at a time."

Lee loaded two stacks of books in the trunk of Paulie's black Saturn, pushing aside assorted camping gear and a bag of stale potato chips. "Go camping often these days?" he asked her as he climbed into the passenger seat. She floored it out of the parking space, fishtailing with glee, then rounded out of the campus proper.

"Not since the weather has turned so sour," she replied, never taking her gaze from the road.

"So where are we going? I hope your mysterious friend is a waitress at a local restaurant. Will she read my tea leaves?" His stomach growled and he rubbed it playfully.

Paulie only smiled and kept driving, using her horn with great gusto at almost every intersection.

A half hour later, Hartford County Police Barracks was the last place Lee expected to find himself.

"I'd like you to say hello to Detective Sergeant Daniel Bellovich, Lee," said Pauline as she ushered him into the spartan office. Lee removed his gloves and shook the detective's large hand. Daniel Bellovich was fortyish, with wavy dark hair barely graying at the temples and wore a smile a Lincoln Continental could have parked in. They were briefly interrupted as Bellovich answered a phone call and gave instructions to a smart-looking lieutenant with shiny black shoes that squeaked as he quickly entered and exited the office to complete an assignment. Lee was impressed by Bellovich's gentle presence of authority, something he rarely found these days, and noted that both the detective and the lieutenant were fit and trim. He'd heard from someone in his congregation that Hartford's police force was a cut above the rest in dress, mannerisms, and physical training. The rumor proved true if these two were an example of their fellow officers—and from Paulie's puppyish expression, Lee immediately understood that the relationship between Bellovich and herself was not solely professional.

"Daniel, this is my brother Lee." Pauline's eyes carried a hopeful expression of approval from both sides.

There was a moment of silence as each man sized up the other.

"So, Paulie, where have you been keeping this fellow?" grinned Lee.

Pauline hugged Daniel's arm and smiled. "If you would make a habit of visiting more often, I might have told you."

Lee put on the appropriate sheepish expression. Pauline turned to Daniel. "I told you he'd guess as soon as he saw you. He knows I'm a sucker for a man with authority!"

"I noticed you've dropped in around lunch time. Does that mean you're treating?" asked Daniel with a wry smile.

"How could I refuse to feed two starving men?" asked Pauline, wide-eyed. "Come on both of you, let's eat! How does shrimp at Mack's sound?"

After they had settled themselves at a quiet table in the corner of the restaurant, Pauline explained to Daniel that Lee was interested in the occult underground and had some questions that he might be able to answer. Over sporadic discussion of the menu, Pauline told Lee of Daniel's background studies. "He is the department's expert on occult criminal activity and has done intensive studies on various metaphysical religions, and I'm sure he would be delighted to help you. Daniel and I met on campus while he was taking a course in religious philosophy," she finished and lightly caressed the detective's hand.

The waitress appeared, decked in a short pirate costume, complete with fishnet stockings. They gave their order, hunger urging a hasty choice.

"Well," Lee began after the waitress scurried off with their order, "I've recently met a person who claims she is a Witch. My knowledge of the subject is not jiving with what Pauline has been telling me."

"Lee wants to know if Witches are real," Pauline interrupted.

Daniel considered the question thoughtfully. "I can best answer that by saying that some definitely are living a fantasy life, dabbling in the unusual so they will be noticed by other people as being something 'different.' They do not practice the religion as a matter of supporting religious belief nor do they have real psychic skills, but the role they have chosen fulfills a psychological need for them. In most circles they are considered dabblers. All fluff and no zap. Most of these people are not criminals, they're just a little flaky," explained Daniel.

"These people are like lots of the girls on our campus right now," broke in Paulie. "They wear pounds of make-up, odd clothing and jewelry, and enjoy calling attention to themselves. There are a few young men as well, and I've found they are always talking about power and money. Not the sort of thing that is unusual to the human species, but is exceptionally strange with the form of religion they say they follow."

"What about the ones who aren't 'living a fantasy life'?" asked Lee. "Are these people involved in criminal activities? And Paulie, what do you mean by 'religion'?"

Daniel laughed. "So many questions! Well, no, most likely they are not criminals in the justice system definition, or morally, either. Many of today's real Witches call themselves Goddess worshippers. Although they follow what's known as the 'Old Religion,' they don't become involved in any of the bloody rituals and evil intent that historians have pushed off on their ancestors. Today's Witches—the real ones, that is—are more interested in saving the planet from ecological serial killers than boiling babies in hot oil."

"Witches," said Pauline, "come in a variety of denominations, just like the standard religions. There are those who grow up in the religion with family training. They are called family traditionals, or fam-trads. The bulk of today's Witches, however, are people who have left the structured religions taught in their youth and choose to practice the Craft instead. In the sixties and seventies they were mostly initiated into a coven, which is a group of about thirteen to sixteen people, sometimes less. These days, with individual thought being so popular, a great deal of people are calling themselves eclectic Witches, meaning they study many of the denominations or sects, but do not choose to be a member of any single church or coven. Often they are called solitaries. Then, there is something new, called the open circle, where many of the different denominations or sects work together with some of the more standard religions, mostly Catholics and Jews."

Lee was astounded. "They have churches?"

"Yes," laughed Daniel, "even Witches have churches, though there aren't very many of them."

"But I thought devil worship was against the law?" exclaimed Lee.

"Hold on there, you really don't know that much about the occult, do you?" asked Daniel.

"He's a product of a staunch Catholic upbringing," interjected Pauline.

The trio waited until the waitress had served them heaping plates of shrimp and king crab legs and refilled their coffee cups before resuming their conversation.

"Regardless of what you have been told," continued Daniel, "Witches do not worship the Christian devil. In fact, they don't even believe in him. You are thinking of Satanists, but Witches and Satanists are two entirely different groups. Most Witches despise dark or negative magick almost as much as Christians do."

Lee chewed on his shrimp thoughtfully. Finally, he said, "You realize that this is entirely different from everything I've been taught."

Daniel nodded. "It is for most people. I had trouble swallowing a lot of the information myself when I first started studying this stuff, but after a while it begins to make sense. Remember that history is usually written by the victors of any battle or political disagreement. The church was powerful in medieval times and their chief concern was getting everyone to believe only one set of principles—theirs. Unfortunately, they were not interested in the spiritual well-being of the people, but in control, money, and property."

"Yes," said Pauline. "During what the Witches called The Burning Times, they say that the church officials murdered over nine million people, mostly women and children. Many were accused of Witchcraft to show the power of the church or to gain their fortunes. If someone was accused of Witchcraft, that person's money and property went to the church. It was the law."

"Although they stopped burning Witches," explained Daniel, "the officials of the church made sure that laws continued to make the practice of the Craft illegal in Europe up until the 1950s. They also continued to denounce the practice of the Old Religion so that they could remain free from retribution for the evil they had spread across the continent."

Lee looked at his sister suspiciously. "You are telling me that the church didn't want to admit that they murdered millions of people for money, so they taught their congregations that the Old Religion was nothing but a bunch of devil-worshipping fanatics."

"Read the books I'm sending home with you. They are footnoted with plenty of historical references and written by authors respected in their fields. Many are archeologists and folklorists, a few are individuals of various religious denominations."

Daniel nodded. "After all, you can't brag about the travesty of your own people being put in the lion's den when you do the same thing to others. Instead of using lions, they used fire. They had to make the other religion look evil to support their actions, even though Witchcraft was far from it."

When they were finished eating, Daniel ordered another pot of coffee and a round of cheesecake.

"But I've seen pictures of Witches worshipping a man with horns," said Lee. "Isn't that the devil?"

"No," said Pauline, "that is the God of the Hunt. You see, Witches believe in both male and female deities—who together make one energy, sometimes called The All. The Goddess of their religion is called 'The Lady,' and her equal half and consort is called 'The God' or 'The Horned Lord.' He has horns to represent nature; usually they are depicted like antlers on a stag, but sometimes you will see ram's horns. Most Witches prefer those of the stag because Satanists use ram's horns."

"Interesting," said Lee, enjoying a mouthful of cheesecake. "You seem to know a lot about the religion, sister of mine. For a moment there I thought I was getting a lecture."

She grinned and tossed her head.

"But the main question I have is, do these real Witches have any special powers?" asked Lee.

Daniel cleared his throat and looked at Pauline. "Some say yes, and some say no. Witches certainly believe they have special powers. They also believe these powers can be learned, that it doesn't take a gifted birth to have them."

"You're dancing around my question," said Lee.

Daniel smiled cryptically. "In my experience as a criminal investigator, I've found that supposed cult crimes are usually perpetrated by people who are trying to mimic an area of the occult that they really know nothing about. I've never arrested a 'real Witch,' as you say, for any of the crimes. It has always been some joker who gets off on being unusual."

"You still haven't answered my question."

"Well, let's just say I've seen some pretty strange things. I have sorted out a few murders with help from people involved in the occult, and these folks have been extremely helpful and generous, as long as they are not embarrassed or treated like fools. In one case, a fellow from New York, who claimed he was a family traditional Witch, helped me catch a murderer by doing a reading with Tarot cards and a few other skills he failed to mention."

"You're kidding!"

"No, I'm serious. I may have found the killer with a normal investigation, but this fellow knocked months off our inquiries by showing me which avenues to explore first."

Lee was fairly quiet during the ride back from the police barracks. On approval of the public relations department at the barracks, Lee and Pauline spent most of the afternoon with Daniel, discussing other areas of the occult. Daniel let Lee borrow several books on the subject.

"Now, you'll have to come back in short order to return all the books you are going to cart home with you," Pauline said brightly.

Lee held on to the dashboard as she turned sharply into the train station. "Your friend Daniel says that Witchcraft is the fastest growing religion in the United States today. You said the same thing. If that is true, why haven't I heard about it?"

"From what we can gather, the more standard religions aren't happy that something else is on their turf, especially since the Witches aren't into money. That kind of talk is very frightening to organizations who depend on large sums of guilt money," she said thoughtfully.

She rammed the Saturn into a parking space with an audible scream from the car.

"I hope you are easier on Daniel than you are on this car," kidded Lee.

Paulie turned around and rummaged among the junk stored in her back seat, pulling out a large, battered, brown suitcase. "We can fit most of your books in here. If you walk onto that train with all those occult books, they'll try to dump you off at the next stop." She slid the case into the front seat with difficulty, banging Lee on the elbow in the process. "Sorry," she quipped. Lee hadn't seemed to notice. He was staring at the fog on the window that grew with each breath.

"So," Pauline broke the silence. "Now you're probably ashamed that the lady who brought you here in the first place isn't the monster or idiot you thought she was. Remember, they believe in a positive higher power, just like we do."

"Thanks for not telling Daniel," Lee responded. "I do feel rather stupid. I guess I should have asked her about her religion, but at the time, it would have added fuel to the proverbial fire. I'm still not comfortable about it, though."

"Don't be so hard on yourself, Lee. You and I were brought up to believe one way, and one way only. Then, when you entered the seminary, you were not taught to have an open mind on other religions. Let's face it, you were there to learn a specific doctrine and that's what you did," said Pauline. She patted his knee. "I felt the same way until I met Daniel and took that course. I found out that no one specific way is right for everybody, but that all religions do focus on the same result. What makes you happy and comfortable is the one you ought to choose."

Lee didn't answer. Was he truly happy with the religion he had chosen? He thought so. But could he deal with Elizabeyta's? He wasn't so sure. He needed to know more before he could make that decision.

"What's her name?" asked Pauline.

"Elizabeyta. Elizabeyta Belladonna."

"Is she pretty?"

"Yes … she's very attractive."

"How come you've never mentioned her before?"

"How come I didn't know about Daniel?"

"Touché!" exclaimed Paulie as she jumped out of the car.

While Paulie and Lee packed the books into the briefcase, Lee proceeded to tell Pauline about Elizabeyta Belladonna, including her warning that he might be in some danger. He failed, however, to tell Paulie he'd asked Elizabeyta to marry him. Something held him back.

"You know, Lee, she may be trying to push you away because she feels her choice of religion would harm your reputation with the church if anyone found out you were associating with her," offered Pauline as she leaned on the suitcase to get it shut. "There, that ought to do it, but I wouldn't bump it. It could snap open, and then what a mess!"

Lee grabbed the suitcase, and together they walked arm and arm into the station. "The concern over my reputation is possible. You may be right."

They walked over to the newsstand. Lee wanted something to read on the way back to Whiskey Springs that he wouldn't have to hide from the other passengers. He picked up the *York Evening Times* and tucked it under his arm. Together they maneuvered around other commuters, though the traffic for 6:00 PM was relatively light.

"Guess not too many people like braving winter weather," remarked Paulie. The station faintly rumbled, and Paulie gave her brother a peck on the cheek.

"Don't be a stranger," she warned him, "and keep me posted. Your life is finally getting interesting and I certainly wouldn't want to miss a single detail!" she said gaily. He returned her kiss and squeezed her nose.

"I'll call you—collect," he smirked.

Paulie laughed and shoved him toward the waiting train. "You'd better do better than that. You have books to return and I don't think holding out on a detective is such a hot idea!" she called as he hustled onto his train.

Grinning, Paulie stepped back, her mind already covering her dinner engagement with a few female professors from college. Now, they would need red candles, some lavender … she thought Maven was bringing the pot … and she hoped Ivy would remember to pick up the fresh bread from the bakery. This was perfect—when the time came, perhaps this Elizabeyta Belladonna creature would have paved the way for her. Well, the Goddess does move in mysterious ways … "Oh, excuse me! I am so sorry!" she said in surprise as she collided with a man dressed in a long black coat hurrying toward the closing doors of the train. His turned-up collar and hat squashed down as far as it would go on his head precluded her from seeing his features. He clasped his hat to his head, spit at her feet, then bounded onto the train.

"Of all the nerve!" she meant to yell after him, but caught it in her throat, snapping her lips firmly shut. Something about that guy was not right. She worried about Lee for an instant, then thought, "How absurd!"

and fumbled for her gloves, which were no longer in her hands. She found them scattered on the platform near her feet. Bending to pick them up, she saw a credit card receipt stuck to her glove. "What's this?" She pulled it from her glove, its wet, sticky end tearing. Much of it was smeared, including the owner's name and card number. The name of the establishment, however, was plainly visible: Mack's Seafood and Fish Harbor. She knew it didn't belong to Lee because she had paid for the lunch in cash. Could it have possibly belonged to the stranger? Odd—she didn't remember seeing him there, but then again, they were sitting out of the way of regular traffic and intent on their conversation.

"Oh, it's just a coincidence," she muttered, and let it slip from her hand to the floor.

Lee sat back and breathed deeply. He'd picked up a great deal of information today and he desperately needed to get his thoughts in order. It appeared that Paulie finally had a decent companion, and he was pleased. She'd been on the single scene for so long he was afraid she'd become tired and worn like so many others in her field—up to their necks in books and papers, holed away in some classroom with changing faces that kept getting younger. She needed a decent relationship. A cop with an avid interest in the occult was certainly a switch from what he'd expected of her. That was great, though. She was into athletics, hiking, camping, that sort of thing. Perhaps this detective fellow shared some of the same interests.

He closed his eyes and let the motion of the train lull him into a semiconscious doze.

Elizabeyta Belladonna kept parading through his mind. God, she was beautiful, wasn't she? Both fire and ice …

He opened his eyes, gazing out at the gathering darkness rushing past the window. Lee unbuttoned his coat and opened the paper.

The bold headline read:

WHISKEY SPRINGS RESIDENT MURDERED!
CULT INVOLVEMENT SUSPECTED

He didn't notice the man in black who surreptitiously slipped into the seat behind him.

chapter seventeen

ARK SPENT ALL OF TUESDAY IN HIS ROOM. Marjorie was concerned; her son rarely squirreled himself away in the house. This was flu season and it had hit the community hard. She hoped he wasn't coming down with something serious. As the day progressed, however, she decided that whatever was wrong with Mark, it wasn't physical. *Probably girl trouble,* she thought, and prayed it wasn't another episode like the one with Belinda.

Although Marjorie was active in town politics for her husband's sake, she was not a newsy person. She disliked the television, believing that it was bad for your brain. Equally disturbing was the music on the radio. It rattled her eardrums. Neither did she read the newspaper, unless it carried information on town functions, which she was already privy to anyway.

There was too much evil in the world. If she didn't know about it, then it didn't exist in her universe. She felt that most media presentations were bought and sold long before the average reader got even a glimmer of the truth. Being the wife of a minor politician had a tendency to sour one's opinion on reporters, local or otherwise. These days she preferred her books to people, because none of the stories in the books she read were real.

It was not until three in the afternoon, then, that she heard about Jeff Conner's murder via phone call from her next-door neighbor.

She tapped on Mark's bedroom door.

There was no answer, but being a mother has its moments of ultimate dominion and she opened the door without invitation. Mark was huddled under a comforter in the corner of his bed next to the wall. Both the shades and curtains were tightly drawn. The room was cast in heavy shadows and she had trouble seeing as she made her way to the bed, tripping on a jumble of clothes and shoes.

"Mark, I'm so sorry about Jeffrey. Why didn't you tell me?" She sat gently on the edge of his bed. "I know you two were close." She moved to put her arm around her son but he drew away as if she carried the plague, staring past her, saying nothing.

Marjorie continued her soft dialogue. "Listen. Death is hard to understand when you haven't been exposed to it. It's tough. Often we feel sorrier for ourselves because of the hole that is left in our lives. That's normal, honey." She patted his knee.

Mark did not respond. "When death comes to one so young, it seems so unfair, doesn't it?" she asked.

Mark shifted and stared at her with hollow eyes.

Marjorie was silent for a moment. Grief was as individual as a fingerprint. She understood Mark would need some time to learn to deal with this new emotion, but there was something she needed to know. Something that had been bothering her since she hung up the phone. She figured she might as well dive in and get it over with.

"Mark, weren't you supposed to go out with Jeffrey last night? You left here at seven and didn't get back until eleven. I know what time you came in because I heard you." She paused a moment, letting what she had said sink in and giving him time to understand where the conversation was heading.

"Mark … do you know something about what happened to Jeff?"

"No!" Mark drew the comforter tighter around his body and turned to face the wall. "Just leave me alone. Leave me alone!"

Marjorie eyed him steadily, noticing the dull gleam of something metal in one of his clenched hands. "If you feel you can't tell me, you know you can tell your father. We're your parents and we love you very much. If you know something that would be important to the police, you should tell them, even if you think that for some reason you may have been in the wrong. I know that you would never do anything to intentionally harm another person. Your father and I would stand behind you."

Mark hugged himself tightly. Marjorie decided not to push any more. Her instincts told her there was something hidden concerning her son and that somehow Mark knew far more than his angry denial. Now was not the time to carry it further. You simply couldn't press Mark to talk when he didn't want to. When he was good and ready to tell you something, he would. Until then, wild horses couldn't drag it out of his mouth. He'd been like this since she could remember, and nothing she said would ever change this personality trait. She'd discuss this with Timothy when he got home.

"I didn't go with Jeffrey last night," he said, the words leaving his cracked lips in a spooky whisper that made Marjorie shiver. "He wanted to go to a party," Mark continued slowly, "but I chickened out at the last minute. Jeffrey seemed—well, strange. He was flashing around one of his knives, charging the air, talking about blood and killing …" Mark sobbed. "His mother was watching him through the living room window and she came out of the house with this real weird expression on her face. She told me to go, to leave, to get out of there because I was a bad influence on her son. She was crying. He turned around and punched her. So—so I left, see. No, I ran like a coward! I left him standing over his mother in his driveway, dancing like a maniac. I—I think he was on something, some kind of drug …"

Marjorie held her face in a calm mask. "Is that how you got the scratch on your face, from Jeffrey?"

Mark's hand flew to his cheek. "Yeah, I guess so."

Marjorie took a deep breath. "Do you think Jeffrey's mother might have something to do with his death?"

"No," he said sullenly. "When he realized I'd slipped away, I heard him screaming at her. She yelled something back, then limped into the house and slammed the door. He got in his car and drove off."

"Well, how would you know this, Mark, if you had already left?" she asked smoothly.

"I hid in a neighbor's yard and watched. I was afraid he would hurt her more. But he didn't. He just left."

Marjorie reached to brush his tears away, but he jerked back from her touch. Mark should tell the police what he had seen, but she didn't really think it had much bearing on what had happened to Jeffrey, other than it was drug-related, which they probably knew anyway. She would talk to Timothy about it when he got home. In the meantime, she'd keep a close eye on Mark. "Dinner will be ready at six. I know you probably won't be hungry, but you should try to put something in your stomach." She shut the bedroom door quietly behind her.

Something else bothered her, too. How did Mark know that Jeffrey was dead? Supposedly, the last time he'd seen Jeffrey, the boy was alive. Mark hadn't left his room all day. She shook her head. How silly she was; he probably heard it on the radio, or perhaps his television, though he must have had it on low, she mused, because his room had been quiet as a tomb all day.

Mark listened as his mother's footsteps retreated down the hall, fading on the staircase. He released the heavy pewter cross, letting it fall with a soft plop on the comforter.

Jeffrey had made the mistake of telling Mark where the party was—at the old school. Fearing Jeffrey would really hurt someone, Mark had bummed a ride from a friend who was heading out toward Jack Frost anyway. Before the turn to the school was a convenience store where many of the local teens hung out during ski season. The friend had left him there, but instead of going into the store, Mark waited until the parking lot was relatively empty, then slipped into the darkness. He avoided the road, and traveled several hundred yards on foot beside the road under cover of low brush and volumes of snow.

From a small rise a few hundred yards away from the school, he could view most of what was going on in back, where a new gravel parking lot had been laid this past fall. Someone had plowed it out, but none of this could be seen from the main highway. Jeffrey's car was already parked there, along with a battered pick-up truck and a snazzy black Bronco. Another pick-up pulled in, followed by a late-model black Eagle.

Only men alighted from the vehicles to join the six or seven already present. There was no music, no revelry, no women. If this was a party, it was more suited for a wake. From his secret vantage point he had seen every man present wearing one of those crosses ...

His mind returned to his room, cloaked now in near darkness. Burrowing deeper in his bed, he rubbed his eyes furiously with the heels of his hands. He felt like he was six years old again. God, to be so small with only small wrongs on his conscience. The necklace slipped from the comforter and plunked softly onto the carpet.

So much blood! He had never really considered how much blood was actually in the human body. When he was a child, both his mother and father swore there were no real monsters. They were wrong. Humans were capable of fitting the role perfectly, and he'd seen some last night.

So did Jeffrey.

Except Jeffrey didn't go home.

Jeffrey would never go home.

Slinking over the side of the bed, he retrieved the necklace, then scrambled back under the comforter. He ran his fingernail over the dried blood on the necklace, absently scraping, scraping. Mark sobbed. How could this have happened? How could things be so normal one day, and hellish the next? He would never forget Jeffrey's face ... or the blood. There was so much blood ...

For the second time that night he had stood silently by while violence was enacted before his eyes. Although the men spoke mostly in hushed voices, the countryside acted as a natural amplifier, and there was little he hadn't heard. Jason, the man who appeared to be the leader, was very angry with Jeffrey. It had been Jeffrey's job to lure Mark to them, these men dressed in black. They all wore long, black woolen coats, black scarves, black gloves, and black hats with wide brims pulled down over their eyes. A cold wind whistled through the hollow, lifting the edges of their coats, making them look like a flock of ravens ready to take flight.

Slowly they circled Jeffrey. Some were burly; others thin and gaunt. The Jason man was angry that Jeffrey had taken some sort of drug that had been meant for Mark. Jeffrey wheedled and pleaded, claiming he needed to check the stuff first. He hadn't needed to explain why Mark wasn't with him. Jason had little difficulty tracing the events prior to Jeffrey's arrival. A large man to Jason's right whispered something in his ear. Hearing this, Jason whirled with fury and struck Jeffrey, who immediately crumpled to his knees, crying and pleading for grace. Jason shouted something about Jeffrey's mother, and how could he be so stupid. Now people would ask questions. Jeffrey mumbled that his father always did it, what was the difference?

Jason kicked him in disgust. Jeffrey, now completely sprawled on the ground, wept in disgrace. The other men (by this time Mark had counted seven or eight, maybe nine) drew the circle closer, obliterating Mark's view of Jeffrey, but he could still hear.

Mark's body shook, his fingers working the edge of the comforter, squeezing and releasing in mindless repetition. He had to talk to someone. If he didn't, he'd surely lose his mind. His mother and father were out of the question—they were now part of the problem, not the solution. His anger flared. It was his father's fault that this had happened. He was involved!

He'd heard them talking after they'd beaten Jeff. They said they would have to find some other way to take care of Timothy, to move now on Mark would look suspicious, although some of them still felt, including Jason, that Mark would be a good candidate for initiation. However, it would have to be dealt with differently. There had been a great deal of low arguing, until Jason held up his hand for silence. They decided to leave the body, perhaps thinking he was dead. This would serve as a fair warning to all disciples not to bring disfavor to themselves or to the order. Jeffrey was useful after all, if not in the way intended.

There was a single piece of salvation in this mess ... they didn't know he'd followed Jeffrey. If they had, he'd be dead, too.

And there would have been more blood.

His.

All that blood ...

Mark squinted his eyes shut, frantically reviewing who he could trust. It had to be someone he could depend on. Someone who wouldn't talk. He looked up and stared at the ceiling with cold realization. Who would believe such a story from a sixteen-year-old kid? He turned his face to the pillow and screamed. Both grief and fear tumbled into the soft down. Wracking sobs tore from his body. Over and over in his head he replayed the rest of it. He heard them dragging Jeffrey into the brush. Without a further word they loaded into the vehicles, easing onto the highway in intervals as to not raise suspicion. Mark thought he waited at least ten minutes longer to move, but he was so cold he couldn't be sure how long he was out there.

Easing himself up from a stiff crouch, he stumbled toward Jeffrey's inert body. Trying not to look at the gory corpse, his trembling hand reached to pull at the end of a chain caught under the body. As he pulled it free, the cross whipped out and caught his cheek. It was then he heard Jeffrey gasp, and his heart practically burst from his mouth. Mark first stepped back, but moved closer with terrified fascination. Jeffrey clutched at him with a hand minus a few fingers and his grasp fell away weakly, flopping back into the snow.

There was blood everywhere.

Mark's stomach heaved, but he held on and leaned closer to Jeff.

"Sorry … sorry … Marky. It was that Belinda bitch who started it all …" his voice faded, he coughed, and Mark tried not to look at Jeffrey's face. Instead, he stared at the snow. The blood-red mush.

"I don't understand, Jeffrey, why you were jealous of a girl. We would have always been friends …" whispered Mark.

Jeffrey choked and blood burbled from his torn lips. "No, you fool. It's the genes. I hated her and I did everything to get her away from you, and I hated you because you chose her, of all people."

Mark was stunned. What was Jeffrey talking about? Genes?

Jeffrey gasped, "My poor mommy—I should've stopped him. Instead, I became him. I'm glad to die, Marky … I'm glad to die … tell Belinda … Belinda …"

So much blood.

Mark rolled over, pulling the comforter closer to his chin. He wanted someone to hold him, to love him, to tell him everything would work out. He needed someone to explain why this horror had impeded his life. He was sixteen; things like this just didn't happen to sixteen-year-olds. It wasn't fair! He clutched the cross to his chest. At that moment, he had never known hatred so strong as that he now felt toward his father. He had brought this down on them. But why?

The cross dug into his palm, cutting, cutting. Tiny droplets of blood fell on the comforter, blending into the patchwork pattern, as if they had always belonged. God, how he hated his father!

He reached for the phone on his night table and shakily dialed Belinda's number. It was a gamble, but maybe she would talk to him. And then he was going to find this Jason, and choke the life out of him.

chapter eighteen

ELIZABEYTA SET THE EVENING EDITION OF the *Whiskey Springs Gazette* down slowly. The house was unbearably quiet. Perhaps Beth Ann had been reading over her shoulder, and been shocked into silence by the headlines. Elizabeyta put her head back to relieve a cramp in her neck. It said "cult," but she could find nothing definitive in the article. Gut instinct told her the boy's death was associated with her grandmother's murder, but the needed connection wasn't apparent.

The kitchen was cozy just after dusk, illuminated only by a large Tiffany oil lamp and the merry fire in the hearth. A pot of spring water, dried rose petals, and cinnamon simmered gently on the stove, its pleasant fragrance hugging the air.

So sweet.

Closing her eyes and breathing deeply, Elizabeyta relaxed tense muscles throughout her body. Her sixth sense, well-honed by years of practice, told her that her privacy was secure. Even Beth Ann had disappeared. Elizabeyta reveled in the silence and for this one precious moment, pushed all the unanswered questions and fears from her conscious mind.

She thought of the covenstead and her family. The outside world did not know the covenstead existed. In the 1940s, her great grandparents bought a large tract of land, built a road, and set up twelve families from one end of the property to the other. The deed was kept secret, and homes and farms passed from one family to the next. Anyone traveling along old Route 12 thought each farm was separate from the next, never dreaming the lives of the people along this stretch of highway were linked by both religion and blood.

Naturally, none of the farms had gone up for sale, but families handing down their property to sons and daughters was commonplace. By plan, various members of each family attended the local churches. It was as their ancestors had done before them in many parts of the world under the popular faiths of the district. The covenstead, then, was not really the land, but the psychic and religious connection of the people on it. They dressed like everyone else, spoke the same dialect, and appeared profoundly religious. Outskirt neighbors and church members loved them as they were always the first to help in a crisis, the most dedicated in morality, and the most caring for their fellow humans. No one knew they were Witches by blood, by heart, and by soul.

She remember the day of her initiation. She was thirteen. The summer air clung warm and fragrant around her.

So sweet.

Her grandmother sat in a rocking chair, plaiting her hair with flowers. "When that time comes," said Grandma suddenly, "never forget who and what you are and the unlimited power that you hold within yourself. You must join your power with the positive forces of the universe. Your grandfather said it would be a mighty battle of wits and grit."

"Will I win, Grandma?" asked Elizabeyta solemnly, sensing a war of some sort but not really understanding. Cold shivers tickled up and down her spine, but all this talk of fighting seemed so far away. After all, Grandma would probably live for a very long time. It was difficult to envision herself involved in anything dark and dangerous and she was sure that Grandma, a very wise and powerful Witch herself, would never allow harm to come to her. In any case, she certainly hoped the danger wouldn't be too ferocious!

Grandma patted her head. "It depends on the choices you make and the path you take, my dear. Always remember that the Goddess gives each human the gift of choice. Nothing is carved in stone. Nothing is fixed or fated. Your future is what you make it." She smiled and rose from the rocker. "Oh, Elizabeyta?" She turned back a moment, her expression once again serious. "Never forget that fear is the killer of mental faculties. Once the beast gets hold of your mind, you are doomed. Learn to go beyond the fear, to fight the beast. Learn that you have a right to win and that fear is merely an animal who cowers at the feet of the strong. Conquer fear and you will always be the mistress of the forest—whether that forest be of trees or people."

Her grandmother had come here, to this house, for a reason. She had never returned home.

For the last year, the entire covenstead had noticed an increase in the number of outsiders on their properties. They were always men and they were always lost. Six months ago, the farmstead at the East end of the covenstead had been robbed. Last month, the family at the West lost a barn and most of their livestock to a mysterious fire. The family whose farm was at the South end of the covenstead was experiencing unexplained crop failure, and found poison in the fertilizer. Elizabeyta's family held the property at the North, and they were waiting. She felt sure the answer to these mysterious happenings was linked to her grandmother's death. Maybe the location of the covenstead wasn't a secret after all.

Elizabeyta opened her eyes and stared at the dying fire. She glanced at the wood pile, noting that the supply was lower than she thought. Damn! She'd have to bring more logs in from the back porch. She wasn't sure how long she had been daydreaming. The initiation ceremony hadn't crossed her mind in years. And how long could she stay here this time? Not much longer, she was sure. There were many children in the covenstead and they had to be protected. It was a general consensus that they would be targeted eventually, just like before.

She bundled up and stepped out on the back porch. Nothing stirred— not a branch or dead leaf. Elizabeyta filled her arms with a stack of wood and surveyed the yard. Although cold, this snow was comforting, quiet. The serenity of the landscape filled her and she smiled, turning to go back inside.

The firm grip on her shoulder stopped her in her tracks. Fear ripped through her for a paralyzing moment. She turned slowly to face the owner of the hand that still held her.

"Lee! You scared me half to death!" Her voice was a mixture of both fear and annoyance. "Did anyone ever tell you that you look like a character out of a horror film with that long, black coat?"

Lee released her shoulder and smiled. "Sorry," he said sheepishly, "you have those big earmuffs on. I guess you didn't hear me call you."

"Huh?"

Lee lifted one of her earmuffs. "I said, I called you, but you didn't hear me. I wouldn't advise wearing these things while driving. You might get run off the road by a fire truck or something."

Elizabeyta hugged the wood close to her body. "It's almost ten, I thought you would be around sooner. Actually, I was just getting ready to go to bed."

"I thought you wanted to talk to me? I haven't been able to see you for almost three whole days. I've missed you terribly."

She sighed internally. He looked crestfallen. She noticed the tired shadows under his eyes. He gently let go of the earmuff, leaving it cocked uncomfortably on the side of her head. She fumbled at the door, her mittened hand slipping on the knob.

Lee reached over her shoulder and opened the door for her. Elizabeyta walked through and dumped the logs with a clatter into the wood box. She took off her coat and slung it on a peg beside the door.

"Have a seat," she said.

He hesitated, moving, she knew, to try to take her in his arms. She concentrated on the spot between his eyebrows and mentally told him to sit down.

Lee sighed, took off his coat, and slung it on the back of the chair. "I just got off the train and thought I'd stop here before I went home. I know it's later than I promised. Sure could use a cup of coffee," he hinted, looking at the full pot on the counter. He plopped into the chair. "Did you see the article in the paper?"

"The *Whiskey Springs Gazette?* Yeah. I read it."

"Do you think it has anything to do with your grandmother?"

She shrugged her shoulders. "There wasn't much there, really, just a bunch of scary headlines. They found a kid murdered on the mountain. I'm not sure how the cult angle fits in, or why they even alluded to it."

"I thought the same thing," he said. "I think they got the words 'cult' and 'gang' mixed up. Probably a drug thing. How did it go with Mason?"

"He's a nice man," she said carefully, relieved that she had it in her to command him when necessary. She didn't like influencing other people like that, but occasionally it came in handy. "He's going to do a little research on family feuds for me. I didn't tell him anything important. Just let me get this fire rared up, and I'll pour you a cup of coffee," she offered. Talking about Mason made her uncomfortable. She was glad Lee hadn't sensed anything. All evening when she thought of kissing Lee, it was Mason's face that appeared in her mind's eye. Preposterous, of course, but there just the same. She wanted Lee to go home. She had business to take care of.

Facing the fire, she looked deep within its depths, envisioning Lee's handsome face. She thought of the blazing rune of flow, putting it over the picture of his face, and stoking up the fire at the same time. As the flames gathered strength, she chanted to herself. She replaced the rune visualization with that of a blazing blue pentacle.

Banish, banish, I banish thee home. Sleep. Sleep. Bring sweet dreams to thee. Sleep. Sleep. Go home and let me be. Rocking back and forth on her haunches, she repeated the words in her mind. When she turned to face him, Lee's head nodded and he was struggling to keep his eyes open.

"I'm sorry, Elizabeyta, I don't know what hit me." He yawned and grinned. "If you don't mind, I'll skip the coffee. Maybe tomorrow?"

Relief flooded through her. "No problem. Go home and get some rest, you must have had a big day." Elizabeyta mentally picked up the name Pauline—no, Paulie—but kept her mouth shut.

No wonder he was so easy to influence, she thought wryly, *a good woman will tire any man out.* She felt a twinge of jealousy but pushed it away. It would be better if he had met someone else. Obviously, he hadn't been serious about the marriage proposal.

"You've let yourself become too complacent, Elizabeyta dear," she said out loud after she ushered him out and shut the door. "For two years you've been banging and snooping around here and you've given yourself a false sense of security." Deep down she'd always thought that Beth Ann would warn her if real danger came to the house. But now she wasn't so sure of her safety. Lee may not be as trustworthy as he thought he was. She sensed he'd talked about her today to someone and she didn't like that at all. He could have put her in peril out of ignorance.

Beth Ann did want her out of the way. It was obvious from the constant chaos, but they were little things like broken dishes or missing notes. Even the episode with the stew had been worse than it looked. Beth Ann was making a great effort to show that she meant business, nothing more. If she wanted Elizabeyta dead, she would have killed her by now. Goddess knew the opportunity was always open. It had never occurred to her that the ghost posed any real threat, but Beth Ann may have decided to let someone else do her dirty work.

She felt the tug of fear. Elizabeyta hugged herself and paced the kitchen. The question of just who Pauline might be kept intruding on her thoughts. Now was not the time to worry about who Lee Becker was sleeping with or if he was right for her. In fact, no time was good for that thought. After all, he was a minister of a faith that abhorred her own. A relationship with him would be unworkable.

Others her age in the covenstead had already married, with prosperous families. Several had taken over the family farms. Elizabeyta yearned for the day when she could again set upright the family coat of arms above the altar, and begin the task of finding a suitable mate who would fulfill his destiny as her High Priest and co-facilitator of the covenstead business. There were male Witches all over the country from whom she could choose. She was the intended matriarch of the covenstead. She couldn't imagine not living there, nor would she ever think of taking an outsider into their closed environment, although a few had managed to do it without difficulty. Getting attached to Lee Becker was simply out of the question.

She thought about the ceremony where the family coat-of-arms had been inverted as a sign of the danger to their faith. As long as the mystery remained, there was no way the symbol could be hung properly, as it protected the entire covenstead from danger. An altar was erected to Eriu, Protectress of Covensteads, and a lamp was kept burning at all times.

Loneliness paced by her side.

The beast was growing. "Fight the beast," she muttered, "fight the beast." She needed a tool to draw Beth Ann out, something that would force her to communicate other than in temper tantrums.

For the hundredth time she wished she had Amanda's talent for finding lost things. Of course, if she knew exactly what she was looking for it
wouldn't be quite so difficult. As children they would play "Button, button"
or other games to test Amanda. She always won. When Cousin Laura lost
the pentacle necklace given to her at her initiation, Amanda came to the rescue and found it in the cold cellar, among the potatoes and apples. But it had
been agreed by the elders before Elizabeyta began her investigations that
she was to receive no magickal help from any of those living at the covenstead. They were afraid of being traced through her, should she be caught.
All ties to the group mind had been ritually cut every time she left the
covenstead to come here. She knew that as soon as the Elders discovered
she'd struck out on her own, they had performed the ceremony. She had no
psychic connection with her own. She felt sorry for the regular people in the
world, who had never experienced what a real family was like. How lonely
they must always be. No wonder there were so many crimes and so much
unhappiness in the world. It was the curse of abandonment, she was sure.

She gazed at the fire and knew it was time to do the ritual of death. It was
risky, but she had nothing left. She'd been putting it off in hopes of communicating with Beth Ann. She had tried everything from Tarot cards to the pendulum to shouting out loud, for Goddess' sake. All to no avail. The danger was
moving toward her; she could feel it coming, stalking her stealthily, sniffing
around, trying to find her. She really should have a High Priest to do this, but
since no trained male was available, she'd have to wing it on her own.

If death was on her personal highway, she was better off meeting him
in her own rig.

chapter nineteen

ACCORDING TO THE REALTOR WHO SOLD THE property to MorningStar Inc., no other home on the block contained sub-level servants' quarters. Elizabeyta took a set of keys off the hook by the refrigerator and unlocked the door beside the pantry. It was thought that, during the Civil War, the rooms beyond this locked door were used to harbor runaway slaves through the underground network. A large cupboard could be pushed in front of the door from the kitchen side and no one would know the difference. After all, Gettysburg was only thirty miles away. In later years, when it was no longer fashionable or affordable to accommodate servants, the rooms had been changed into a small apartment consisting of a sitting room, a small bedroom, and a bath. Elizabeyta now considered this area sacred space—her temple.

During Elizabeyta's research in the family journals, she discovered that friends of the family, mostly visiting pastors and missionaries, used the apartment in the fifties, giving them privacy from the rest of the household. In the seventies, Beth Ann converted the area into a sewing room, but that didn't last long. Almost immediately they became a sick room for her invalid husband until he died in '75. After that, Beth Ann never stepped foot in them again. Since she had few visitors in the last twenty years and most of the guests who had used the rooms were dead, Elizabeyta felt safer there than anywhere else in the house. From the kitchen, it simply looked like an additional storage door.

She was delighted with the bathroom. Here, her great aunt had spared no expense. A sunken bathtub, complete with whirlpool, awaited her use. Tiny green, blue, and white tiles graced most of the walls with intricate Celtic knot patterns that wove peacefully about the room.

Over the last two years Elizabeyta did her own remodeling, changing this area into her private temple and work room. The East wall of the sitting room was now lined with locked cabinets where she kept all her tools, robes, and other magickal implements and supplies. It also held her stereo and video equipment. She purchased a ready-made counter with storage compartments beneath and placed it along the West wall. Her computer, copier, and fax machine snuggled against the North wall, beside the door to her temple. A phone hung on the wall next to the desk. Elizabeyta prided herself in being a modern Witch, and often melded technology and magick together.

Tonight she locked the door securely behind her and threw the deadbolt. No one else had been in these rooms since she converted, cleansed, and consecrated them. This was her sacred space, her personal haven, her temple.

Total peace.

Total privacy.

As the bathroom was once a servant's bedroom, it was large, as bathrooms go, though it would have been quite small for a bedroom. She ran the bath water in the sunken tub and sprinkled a mixture of flowers, highly scented herbs, and oils into the water. This was the cleansing bath required before any major ritual. The body and spirit were to be completely pure before casting the circle. With the stereo piping soft music, she relaxed in the warm, fragrant water, releasing the stress and fear that clung so tightly to her thoughts.

An hour later, dressed in a soft, black shift, she opened the wall safe hidden behind a modernist painting of Diana and the Hunt above her desk. She removed a box of disks and sat down in front of the computer, busying herself at the keyboard. They would laugh at her at the covenstead if they knew she had put her Book of Shadows on disk, but in this environment, it was safer. It had taken her three full months to convert all her notes and studies to computer files, but the rewards were far worth the work.

Ah, there it was—Death. Service for—no, that wasn't it. Of a habit or addiction—nope. Second degree inversion work—almost. Here it was: Death, Emissary of—Ankou, akin to the Angel of Death known as Azrael.

She hit the enter key.

"WARNING! PASSWORD NEEDED TO ACCESS FILE" blinked nastily at her.

She typed in her magickal name, accessed the file, and pressed the print command. The printer beside her hummed softly. She loaded the second disk and searched for DIARY. She made notes of the day and time and what she planned to do, saved the file, and locked all the disks back up in the wall safe. Before she turned off the computer, she sent a brief message to Ben via modem to let him know what she was attempting and when she would contact him to let him know she was okay. If anything happened to her and she didn't send the message, he would fly out and remove all her personal belongings. Her contact with Ben was in direct conflict of the orders she had received from the Elders, but it was the only way she could keep Ben from worrying. She logged off quickly before he could send her a message in reply.

It was highly unlikely he was at the computer anyway, but she didn't want any lectures. She smiled to herself. The argument she went through with the family to get them to set up the computer on their end two years ago had been a massive one. After it was all said and done she knew many of them had found it useful, although no one would admit it. Now she could send her notes via disk, which took all the drudgery out of compiling and copying them. There was a rumor at the convenstead that Aunt Martha was using the computer to file her recipes and Uncle Homer was hooked on computer solitaire.

Each quarter family, as well as several of the others, now had a computer modem. Although they had been forbidden to hook up to any national computer boards, they had installed a network system, using the West computer as the server so that the families could talk to each other during bad weather or in an emergency.

Elizabeyta set about gathering the materials she would need for her ritual and moving them into her temple area. This room was bare, save for a large stone dolmen at the North wall, floor sconces to mark each quarter, and a thick black rug. The dolmen had been the most difficult item to move into the room and caused quite a discussion back at the convenstead. Some of the Elders insisted she have her own dolmen (their name for an altar) directly from the convenstead fields. It had taken Ben three months to design it from interlocking pieces of stone so that she could transport it and carry it into the house by herself. Transporting it had not been an easy task, and she finally resorted to a U-Haul to get it all the way to Pennsylvania. Each piece was marked, and they all fit together like a giant puzzle. It had taken Elizabeyta a full night to lug the pieces in and assemble it.

A large mirror, clothed now in black silk, hung on the wall above the dolmen. Track lighting, appropriately dimmed, filtered through the room. Although the dolmen at the convenstead was in the middle of the temple, Elizabeyta preferred hers as close to the North as possible. Her tradition used all quarters for the placement of the altar, depending upon the season, but Elizabeyta stuck with the North. As Grandpa once told her, "Child, everything comes from the North." So much the better; she didn't feel like dismantling and lugging the thing to a new quarter at the turn of each season. She believed her grandfather, anyway.

Once all her materials were on the dolmen, she double-checked her printout to ensure she hadn't forgotten anything. Black and white candles, dirt from a grave, an old skeleton key that had belonged to Beth Ann, orris root, assorted herbs, incense, nine yards of black gauze, the four elements, a silver bell, and a large silver pentacle to be placed in the center of the altar. Yes, it was all here. Oh, no—she almost forgot the most important item, for Goddess' sake, the cauldron! She debated between the stoneware or the iron, and finally chose the former.

From the safe in the workroom she withdrew a silver headband shaped like a crescent moon, two silver bracelets set with large crystals, and a heavy necklace made of amber and jet, its stunning central feature—a large bronze shield showing the family coat of arms (a wolf perched atop a triskele)—surrounded in intricate knotwork. Although she often found these props unnecessary, tonight's ritual was different. Not only would she enact the descent, but she would make it for real, not a parody or play for the benefit of heightened ritual theatrics. With determination, she buckled sheath and dagger around her right thigh.

From the cupboard under the counter, she chose a wand from ten different types, each lying on a bed of black velvet. This one had been fashioned from a yew tree, the tree of death. Pressing a button under the altar, a hidden panel on the wall to the right slid open to reveal a built-in closet. She removed her raiment of office, a white doeskin shawl and a set of twisted silken cords that bore the colors of her family—gold, silver, and black. These she placed at the foot of the altar, while reaching to press the button to close the closet door. One by one she began putting on the ritual items required, murmuring the appropriate prayers with each to align herself with the energies of the universe. She took a deep breath and adjusted the headband squarely on her head, then snapped the bracelets around her wrists so that each crystal lay on the pressure point of her wrist. The cords were wound from right shoulder to left hip, then around the waist, the ends left to dangle a foot from the floor. She lovingly caressed the shawl, and placed it around her shoulders.

The last piece of ritual attire, her necklace of office and symbol as matriarch, was carefully kissed and placed about her neck. It was now or never.

The purpose of this ritual was to align her soul with the Death Energy. She would follow the path of the Descent of the Goddess, often enacted in play form during a second-degree initiation. Tonight, it would be for real. She would attempt to contact Ankou, the Angel of Death.

Usually one worked with a male partner in the more intense rituals to ensure protection in case anything went wrong, but she was solitary here, and solitary the ritual would be performed. Normally this was an exhilarating experience. Now, she was filled with fear. She had never attempted melding her consciousness with that of the Ankou in a group, let alone by herself. Her grandmother had told stories about other Witches and magicians who had attempted and failed this ritual. Some had gone insane, others had simply disappeared without a trace, and a few had bled to death.

This was not a ritual designed for worship. Ankou required the participant to fully understand his mission. When she was a child, she had seen an aunt and uncle attempt to perform this same ritual in circle. No one actually saw the angel, although her aunt and uncle swore they had full sight of the angelic energy. Her uncle had used drugs, which Elizabeyta thought ridiculous, to induce an altered state. The ritual broke up in a shambles when her uncle flipped out, knocking over several people and sconces, nearly setting the entire place on fire. To acquire knowledge in this ritual, one simply had to give love—simply? To offer this, was to offer her consciousness. In the past, a few had sacrificed their own blood; never, however, with any success. She hoped her consciousness was all she would be required to offer this night.

The original notes on the ritual were rather sketchy, acquired from a family member who resided in Europe in the eighteenth century. So much for good record-keeping. There were only two elders alive who knew the keys of the ritual, and were not permitted to pass them to anyone but an elder like themselves to prevent the same disaster from happening again. As acting matriarch she had been given all the rituals, but not all the keys.

The only postscript was a rather dire sentence. "Once the link has been forged, it can never be broken."

Elizabeyta mildly wondered what had happened to Beth Ann. It had been too quiet, although Beth Ann, to Elizabeyta's knowledge, had never entered either her work room or the temple. Elizabeyta didn't think too much of a switched Witch, anyway. To be given the knowledge of the Craft and then opt for a different religion was unthinkable. Throwing away the mysteries would be like cutting off her own arm. How could anyone give up so much for so little? She must have really loved that fellow to throw away the Goddess like that.

Her supplies in place, Elizabeyta locked the temple door and proceeded to the dolmen. Her hands shook as she lighted the three-foot tall illuminator candles. They cast enough light about the room for her to see what she was doing. Besides, she could do the procedures of any basic ritual in her sleep. Her steps to turn off the track lighting were slow, almost feeble. The fear made her perspire. *Breathe deeply and center yourself, Elizabeyta,* she thought. *You've got a long way to go.*

She placed the three-legged cauldron, the symbol of birth, death, and rebirth, at the West quarter. Carefully, she stirred in water and the herbs of death—hemlock and nightshade. Beside the cauldron, she placed Beth Ann's key and the bowl of grave dirt. She was lucky she didn't get caught sneaking around the local graveyard last summer when she collected it.

As her tradition dictated, she began the altar devotion with her ritual dagger, opening the four elements upon the altar, cleansing, then blessing them. She prepared the holy water next, then sealed the altar with oil. Next she cleansed the temple area itself with the four elements. In the West corner of the room, beyond the cauldron, she drew a large yellow triangle on the floor with chalk. Dagger in both hands, she began to cast the circle, walking thrice in a clockwise direction, speaking the words in Gaelic that had become so dear to her. Most family traditions had converted their circle conjurations to English, but not Elizabeyta's family. There was an easier way to cast the circle and Elders often followed the practice, but she felt everything must be done in perfect sequence and all precautions taken against making a mistake in this ritual. The quarters were then acknowledged; she moved clockwise around the circle to light each candle. When she was finished, she returned to the altar and faced the center of the circle.

"Ye Guardians of the Spirit," she cried. "I summon you now to light my way and guard this circle!" A gentle breezed wafted through her hair. All was ready to meet Ankou, the emissary of death.

Elizabeyta breathed deeply and spoke the words of power. She allowed the golden light of the presence of universal love to fill her being.

She turned back to the altar, set down the dagger, and picked up the wand of yew. For a brief moment, she hesitated. Perhaps she should have brought the ritual sword into the circle? Well, it was too late now; besides, she didn't think she would have to battle any unusual entities or command dragons tonight.

Taking a deep breath, she pointed the wand of yew toward the shroud of black gauze that covered the temple mirror and stated, "I am now between the worlds, at the threshold of the gates of Death. I stand here before you, asking entrance to the realm of Tir-na-nog. My mission is to encounter the Angel of Death, he who is called Ankou." With that she reached over and pulled the black cloth from the mirror above the altar. It gleamed darkly in the sconce light. It was not like a normal mirror at all. Though its face was made of glass, the back had been painted black. Its surface was cool.

She paused and rang a silver bell on the altar three times, then walked clockwise to the West—the ritual Gate of Death. She raised the wand of yew before her, pointing it toward the cauldron.

"Ye Guardians of the Gates of Death, hear me now! I bring with me the key to thy world." She held up the skeleton key she had found that belonged to Beth Ann's bedroom, hoping like hell it would do, then dropped it into the cauldron. It plopped and sunk to the murky depths.

"Mighty Calliech, Blue-faced Crone, eyes of stone and fangs of bone, hear thy servant call thy name," she commanded in a steady sing-song, then sprinkled some of the grave dirt into the cauldron as well. "I, Elizabeyta, do summon, stir, and call ye forth. Queen of Heaven, Queen of Hell, I call thee now from Clan of Kelle, my mother's heritage I now do tell." Wadding up the nine yards of black gauze, she threw it outside the circle, into a heap in the center of the yellow chalked triangle, scooped up another handful of graveyard dirt, and pitched it on top of the gauze. Stepping back, arms outstretched, palms toward the heavens, she took the Goddess position.

"Mighty Crone, hear my cry, open the portals of your realm to thy humble servant!"

She felt the energy raising within her and without her. A sudden rushing feeling, like one gets on a roller coaster, filled her with power and strength. The cauldron began to boil, spitting bits of sizzling water and chunks of herb and dirt as high as her face. A little hit her cheek. She didn't flinch. The pot emanated a soft, green glow that grew in intensity. The temperature in the room dropped several degrees. The illuminator candle flames on the dolmen jumped and sputtered, keeping time with the quarter sconces.

"The door is open," she stated without a quiver. "And only those called have my permission to come in."

Elizabeyta walked in a clockwise direction back to the dolmen and lit the seven previously blessed and consecrated black candles that lined the rim of her altar, representing the seven gates to eternity. She stepped back and once again turned gracefully on her heel to face the West. She called out to the darkness, leveling the wand of yew at the still churning cauldron.

"Ankou, emissary of Death, I call you now. Join with my consciousness so that I may gain the answers I so desperately need. The fate of my clan is at stake." She raised her arms above her head, both hands now clutching the wand, and brought her wrists together so that the crystals on her bracelets touched. There was a loud cracking sound as the wand of yew split asunder. A cold gust of bitter air doused the sconces. The seven candles on the altar as well as the illuminator candles continued to burn brightly. Dizziness swept over her and she stumbled, stubbing her toe on the dolmen. She hopped about, lost her balance, and crashed to the floor, flipping the bowl of graveyard dirt everywhere. "Shit," she spat, as on hands and knees, she hurried to clean up the mess. The poor lighting made it even more difficult. She prayed silently to the Goddess she hadn't blown the ritual completely.

Returning to the dolmen, she took a few minutes to center herself before continuing.

"I now invoke the energy of the Sacred Mother into my body, so that I may take the legendary journey of descent." Slowly she raised her arms and took the Goddess position once again, feeling the energy of the divine feminine settling slowly into her body, covering her with a gleaming mantle of perfect love.

In trance now, she stepped forward. "Guardians of the City, I, Elizabeyta, do leave my gifts of spirit at your portal, seeking entrance into Tir-na-nog." She removed one of the bracelets and let it drop noiselessly on the black carpet. She moved to the next two quarters, calling the name of the portal city, and dropping first the other bracelet, then the crown. Finally, at the West, she dropped the necklace with the shield of her clan.

The world about her began to spin and she feared she would black out, never to return to reality. Her senses seemed to be functioning in slow motion. Plunging her hand in the cauldron to retrieve the key, she felt no pain. *I am going through the gate*, she thought. *It is only the gate.* Her heart trembled just the same.

Her eyes flicked to the grave dirt inside the triangle. It was shimmering, moving, mixing with the black gauze, pulling together.

It grew.

It formed.

The area around her feet twisted in an array of colors. With horror she realized she hadn't cleaned up all the dirt. A thin trail led over the boundary of the cast circle and into what used to be a pile of dirt and gauze, but was now … Ankou. Oh, shit! Her eyes widened as the pile slithered along the trail of dirt and into the circle itself. *Double shit, I'm a goner*, she thought.

At first the immense figure seemed to tower over her, his face covered by a silken cowl. It wavered, as if to swallow her in yards of gauze, but he stepped back and spoke softly. "Are you afraid of the specter of Death?"

Elizabeyta regained her footing and backed slightly away. If her courage slipped now, all would be lost, including her life. His figure was entirely cloaked in diaphanous black silk, no longer the cheap five-and-ten gauze of the pile.

"No," she spoke slowly. "I do not fear death, but am awed by his presence." She swallowed with some difficulty.

"I have appeared in a form that will be of pleasure to you," he said as he pushed back the cowl to reveal his face. Her hand flew instinctively to her mouth. Elizabeyta blinked in surprise and looked into his black, bottomless eyes. Perhaps she was mistaken, but bits of colored light swirled about him. He stood a head taller than she, the diaphanous silk now molding to his figure. It was not displeasing. Not by a long shot. She thought she heard a cackle outside of the circle, but couldn't be sure. Instead, she said softly, "You are most beautiful." *What a stupid, childish thing to say*, she thought to herself.

He sighed. "I am most lonely. Rumor has it that you are, too." He looked at her piercingly.

Elizabeyta's eyes widened. *News travels on the astral fast*, she thought, and didn't know whether she liked that at all.

He ignored her hesitation and continued. "Why have you sought my companionship on this night? Is it that you have given up hope and have called me for deliverance? Many do, you know. Sometimes I can honor their request, other times I cannot. If this is what you seek, I must tell you that it is not your time. Normally I would give you a good scare, but I just don't have the energy."

Elizabeyta cleared her throat delicately. He did look rather drawn around the edges, but she had simply assumed it was part of his mystique. She certainly hadn't expected him to look like some sort of textbook god. His hair was shoulder-length and wild, and shone like strands of black silk, laced with bits of stars woven around his temples. His eyebrows were heavy, his eyes now a kaleidoscope of color. His cheeks were perhaps too drawn and he was as pale as moonlight.

"I am Elizabeyta. You have taken those I deeply love to your world and on to the Summerland. I seek answers to why they were taken." She squared her shoulders and added, "No offense, sir, but I do not desire to accompany you. I am not yet ready to die. I have a vow to keep."

"I take all, eventually." He waved her words away with a delicate hand. "Why should I answer you when so many mortals ask the same questions?" He frowned and her heart sank. Her mind rushed to find the words to make him understand.

"You are a higher plane being, called an angel by some, one of the minions of the God-force, therefore you are bound by the laws of the Universe. Is this not so?"

He caressed his chin with slender fingers, considering where the conversation was heading. Finally, he said, "Yes, this is so. I am bound by the rules of the God-force, which is, as you know, neither male nor female as a whole."

"Nor are you a fallen angel," said Elizabeyta.

"Certainly not!" His eyes were molten on that one, but Elizabeyta rushed on.

"Yet you are the summoner of Death and therefore know all, when and why each human is taken."

"Of course."

"Then you would know if an injustice was done and that others are planned, and as an intricate part of the God-force being one of the minions of the positive universe, you would want to see this corrected. Is that not so?"

He looked at her with amusement. "If you wanted to see an injustice corrected, you should have called on Michael or perhaps my sister, Kele-de. Michael's the one who wields the sword of justice, you know. He's a bit flamboyant on occasion for my taste, but that's his job. And of course, Kele-de, probably more familiar to you, is known by many names. I believe there is one ethnic group that calls her Kali. She's a dickens, that one," he grinned mischievously. "My task is to take the humans back home when their time on this plane is completed. I don't kill them, I arrange for their transport. Sometimes I take them myself." He reached out and caressed her arm. Cold shivers ran throughout her body. He shook his head with sadness. "Everybody always thinks I'm the bad guy. Actually, I'm more like a very sophisticated travel agent, complete with my own transport system. Sometimes this job really stinks, you know?"

Elizabeyta looked at him in complete surprise. "But I thought, the scythe ... that you—"

"That's what everybody assumes, but it's not so," he said grumpily. "But at least you haven't fainted. So many of them faint, you know." He picked irritably at a fingernail.

"Oh, I am sorry," slipped out before Elizabeyta could catch it.

He glanced to see if she was baiting him, decided that she was not, and continued. "If you spend some time with me tonight, I will answer your questions, providing you don't go overboard. Where are we, anyway?"

"You are in my home. Actually, you are in my sacred space."

He looked around the room, then walked over and examined the top of the dolmen. "No wonder there isn't any furniture to sit on. You're one of the magickal crowd, obviously. Druid? Magician? Usually magicians try to put me in that damnable yellow triangle. No, wait." He held out his hand to stay her reply. "Let's see, you're not haughty enough for a ceremonial, they are always trying to command things." He looked around the temple again, tapping a finger on his forehead. "This place isn't set up right for a druid ritual ... a fairy, perhaps? I haven't encountered one of those in a long time. They live practically forever, you know. But no, that's not quite right. They do things in bands—prefer an audience so they can pat themselves on the back later. If you are a fairy, you are an unusual one."

She shook her head. "No, Witch."

He sat down with his back leaning against the dolmen and motioned for her to sit beside him. The candles on the altar cast a timid pool of light around them, as if they too were feeling the cold weight that had settled in the room.

"One of those Witches!" he snorted. "You're usually a rather skittish bunch. I don't hear from your kind very often, until it's time for you to move on, of course, and on that holiday of yours. What do you call it?"

"Samhain," she said, trying to keep the irritation out of her voice.

"You've got an awful lot of white-light bubble babblers in your crew these days. I think they call themselves New Agers or something, right?"

"Um, yes, something like that. There are a lot who aren't quite sure what they are, but that doesn't mean they are not trying to be serious," she snapped.

He arched his eyebrows. "Have I hit an uncomfortable subject for you?"

"I'm from a fam trad."

"I see." He paused for a moment. "A fam trad means family traditionalist. Ah, one of those stick in the muds," he grinned.

"Excuse me?" she said.

He waved his hand. "Always so touchy, you Witches—new or old, you do hold on tightly, don't you?" He didn't wait for her reply, but rushed on.

"Ah, yes, you mentioned ones who you loved. If you are talking about your grandmother, she's doing fine, by the way. Teaching the art of divination to a bunch of students who are slated to return to the earth plane in about twenty years. She's not coming back, unless, of course, fate is woven differently than is now planned." He eyed her closely.

Elizabeyta contemplated his words. She knew he had been playing with her all along. Her tilted head caught the light of the single flame, sending rainbows of color bouncing off her auburn hair. He reached over and touched it. She shivered. He was so cold!

"I'm sorry," he said. "You are very beautiful as well. At least I am thankful we are not in a morgue or at a grave site. I get so sick of being called there by humans. They think I delight in nothing else. Who wants to chat in one's work environment?"

Elizabeyta laughed. "I never thought about it, actually. I suppose you do get tired of the same routine. Do you get any kind of vacation?"

"Oh yes, Michael, Kele-de, and I visit other worlds quite often. We are very close, Michael and I." He grinned mysteriously. "We are all one in the universe, you know."

"Are you really so lonely?" asked Elizabeyta.

"How would you like to deal with frightened or sick people all the time? It takes patience, you know. Usually they are not in the mood to chat by the time I get to them. I hear complaints from my messengers and transporters all the time. They bitch constantly that their jobs are stressful. Death is a bit of a shock and most are not very talkative, if you know what I mean. When I first started, I was all puffed up because humans feared and respected me. But that gets old. Michael teases me that I've become much more compassionate these days. However, I'm sure that comment was driven by jealousy. I am in the limelight a lot."

They sat in silence for a few moments.

"It was different in the old days. People respected Ankou. They were delighted to see me. The old ones, they knew what my job really was and were proud when I came. But these new generations, year after year, they just don't understand …" he said quietly, staring past her.

Elizabeyta was having difficulty believing she was talking to the real, honest-to-god Ankou, and not feeling the least bit insane. Maybe that came later. Time seemed to be moving in slow motion. She couldn't pinpoint what day it was, even if her life depended on it—scratch that. She surveyed him out of the corner of her eye. Geez, he was beautiful, and for one ghastly second she wondered what he was like under that black cloak. Probably skeleton bones or something equally frightening. Weren't there starving little children hidden in death's cloak in Dickens' *A Christmas Carol?*

Yuck.

Ankou smiled at her with mischief in his glinting eyes, as if he could read her thoughts. It never occurred to her that an angel could scan, but of course they probably could, they were superior intelligences. Her face reddened. Ankou laughed and patted her knee. Her skin tingled under his touch.

"What is it you wish to ask me?" he said smiling.

"There isn't much point in asking out loud, is there?"

"No, but human conversation is pleasant and I need to practice. Go ahead."

"Can I see my grandmother? I've tried to contact her myself, but I haven't been able to get through. Neither have the Elders."

He paused for a moment, eyes fluttering closed. Then he opened them brightly and said, "Nope. She has gone too far beyond the veil, but she wishes you luck. She says for me to tell you to fight the beast." He cocked his head a little, as if listening to a voice Elizabeyta could not hear. "She also says that it's just like you to wonder what an angel is built like and to stick to business. Her message to you is that you have the strength to fight the beast, and he will come for you at the next full moon."

"But why?" Elizabeyta snapped her head so close to his lips that she could feel his chill breath. Rather than fear, she experienced the heady sensation of a cool breeze on a hot summer's day.

He was silent for a moment. "Because you are the only one who can stop him. She says that your meeting has been fated before you both were born. You are cleaning up old business and you'd better get it right this time around or else you'll have to go all through it again, without the aid of Witchcraft. And no dipping into any Mason jars, either!"

"Great." What did Mason jars have to do with anything? Her face colored. She must mean Mason Trout and the fact that he was married. "Tell her I have no intention of doing any such thing!"

"Trick or treat. I'm known to practice both."

Elizabeyta scrunched her nose, sighed, and moved to a more important topic. "How did she die?"

"Why not ask Beth Ann? She was responsible," hinted Ankou.

"Beth Ann is dead! That's why I called you. She refuses to talk to me!"

"She can't. It is forbidden."

"You're playing with me. You just told me to ask her, and now you say she can't talk to me. Why?"

"Because it was a condition at the time of her death. She had a choice. She could sleep for fifty years and return to the earth plane, or she could forgo the fifty years of rest and try to fix the damage she'd done. If she succeeds, she can go on to the Summerland. Your grandmother has already forgiven her, but the laws of the universe are not so forgiving."

Elizabeyta shifted position. The answers weren't making any sense.

"Why can't I talk to her? I certainly know she's around!"

Ankou, enjoying his human form, tried to touch his nose with his tongue. It was unnerving. "Beth Ann has been trying to protect you, Elizabeyta, in the only way she can. She was not given the ability to channel information to you herself, so she has been trying other ways to make you go home. She thinks that if you leave, you will no longer be in danger."

"Is that how she can fix what she messed up?"

"Actually, no. Beth Ann took a liking to you and decided that she would rather be forced to go through another life rather than see you die horribly in this one. If you go home, she goes to sleep for the remaining years, then will be born again. Beth Ann can only right her past wrongs if you stay here."

Does she know who is coming for me?"

"Yes, she knows quite well."

Elizabeyta swallowed hard. "Does that mean that if I stay here, I will die?"

Ankou gently took her hand. "Would you rather I take you now? Sometimes those who call me allow me to take them on ahead and they may serve with me for a time. You'd still have to come back. I can't erase your karma. However, I find your company delightful and wouldn't mind spending a few hundred years with you. Is that what you prefer? I promise it would be painless, like a deep and restful sleep. Of course, it will get us both into a lot of trouble, you know." He waved his hand in the air. "But they owe me one. However, if you do come with me now, then the order of things will be changed, and as I said before, it is not your time."

His eyes penetrated her mind. He was so soothing, loving. He leaned toward her, brushing the stray hair away from her cheek. Her eyelids fluttered and closed as he took her in his arms in a powerful embrace. His breath was so cold it felt warm on her face. He kissed her deeply as she melted into his strong physique. If this was death, she wondered what real life was like—as yet, she'd not experienced anything like it.

"I am not ready to die. I must stay here and take care of my clan," she whispered.

He gently caressed her cheek, his touch now poignantly hot. She felt his cool lips smile as he pressed them tightly to hers, his tongue gently forcing hers apart. For a hysterical moment, she plummeted into a polar wind.

Her consciousness melded with his. She felt his pain, his loneliness, and she struggled to fill that void with her own energy. She heard him whimper, not sure whether it was pleasure or agony. Their minds burst in orgasm. After what seemed like an eternity he disengaged himself from her arms, though she still sat heavily against him. Now he felt warm and glowing to her touch.

"You have given me love and energy without fear," he said. "The link between us has been forged. I will leave you with two gifts. From this day forward I will know you as Shadow and you will rule the shadows of this world, but only when you speak the words of power. You shall blend the shadows when the need arises and they will come when you beckon, but only after you have spoken the appropriate words of power."

His eyes penetrated her deliciously. "Be warned: To speak those words brings you to me—perhaps only for a while, perhaps forever. Only the true love of a soul like yourself can take you from my arms."

He tilted his head again and rose to his feet, pulling her up along with him. He held both her hands tightly and kissed her on the mouth. "The other gift is a surprise. Someone has asked that a wish be granted and I've just now thought about how I can do that. Someone who bears, shall we say, an association with you—though inadvertently."

He tapped a slender finger on his cheek and smiled. "Perhaps I could return another day for more of your delightful … ah … conversation," he said, winking roguishly, "but I will not be permitted to do so."

"You mean that when I see you again, it will be my time to use your travel services," said Elizabeyta.

He smiled. "Until we meet again," he whispered, and disappeared.

Elizabeyta stood with her mouth hanging open, staring bug-eyed at the empty room. "I bet you do that to all the girls," she whispered to the vacant air. "Humph, love 'em and leave 'em, that's the story of my life! Except I'm usually the one who does the leaving. Guess you turned the tables on me."

She went through the motions of closing the magickal circle and grounding her energy, what little was left. While putting away her tools, she realized that she had not asked all the questions she should have. Although her visit with Ankou was enlightening in some ways, other issues remained cryptic. Neither the black gauze nor the graveyard dirt were anywhere to be found. Both the key and the pieces of the wand were also gone without a trace. It was then she realized she had not asked a very important question—what were the words of power to access the gift? Shit!

As she moved to carry the cauldron out of the circle, a green light exploded from the pot. She fell backward, the pot rolling crazily across the floor. Above her floated a tremendous vision of a blue-faced hag—the Calliech.

"My Crone!" she cried.

The Calliech smiled grotesquely, her fangs dripping with red saliva, black robes undulating above Elizabeyta's head, moving through the air like a giant spider web. "You dare call the angel of death alone! Silly child. He lusts after you now. He'll not be sated until you are by his side. The true love of a mortal … indeed! He may be powerful, but he always had a lust for beautiful women." She spat on the floor, the gooey mess congealing, then vaporizing into nothing. "An angel … well … now you've really done it. My minions are a mighty lot and not to be trifled with!"

Elizabeyta stumbled slowly to her feet. "I cannot save my people without help. He was the only one I could think of. I've called to you hundreds of times and you have never appeared. I thought by calling one of your mighty ones I could help my family! The lives of our children are at stake, don't you understand?"

"You called him and he gave you nothing but a promise of astral lust and a few magickal presents that probably won't do you any good. You even forgot to ask him for the words of power, and he knew it. You should be ashamed of yourself. He's a magnificent being, but he, like all the rest of the astrals, has weaknesses!"

Elizabeyta hung her head.

The vision softened. "Oh, he'll see you through. He never breaks his word, I'll give him that, but I have been with you all the time, Elizabeyta. Just because you can't see me doesn't mean I'm not here, listening to your prayers and requests, helping you with your magick. But a human's life is governed by their choices. Neither Ankou nor I can interfere with the choices you make."

"I need your help."

"I will do the best I can for you. You must be strong and keep your faith."

And in less than a heartbeat, the crone goddess had vanished.

Elizabeyta was so tired she could hardly stand. She picked up the cauldron, locked the door to the temple, put away her tools, and sent a curt message to Ben on the computer—"STAND DOWN."

With little thought to unraveling any mystery this night, she made her way to the stairs, prepared to mount them and fall into bed. The phone rang. She looked at the mantle clock. Who would be calling her at this hour? She retraced her steps and picked up the phone in the kitchen.

Muffled sobbing traveled into her ear.

"Hello? Who is this? What's wrong?"

"It's … Lee."

"Lee? Are you crying?" Her heart did a little jump. What on earth was going on?"

"Terry."

"Something's wrong with Terry? Terry Anderson?"

"She's dead, Elizabeyta. Dead!"

"Oh, no. How did it happen? Are you okay? Do you want me to come over?"

"No. I don't want you to come over. I–I just need to be alone. I wanted to hear your voice. She died in a car accident early this morning. The papers held her name until they could get hold of her parents. They were in Philadelphia. They just got in and called me. Oh, God … I can't believe it. Dead."

"Are you sure you don't want me to come over?"

"Yeah. I'm sure."

"I'll call you in the morning, okay, Lee?"

"Right. In the morning."

chapter twenty

"WELL, YOUNG LADY, YOU GOT YOUR WISH," announced the woman hovering over her. Terry rubbed her temples, her thoughts miserably tangled. The darkness, the blaring lights, the grille of a black pick-up truck—or was it a tractor trailer? She groaned and squinted her eyes shut. Maybe if she kept them closed long enough, the woman shaking her would go away.

"Open your eyes, girl. You got yourself into this mess and only you can get yourself out."

Terry peeped one eye open, then quickly shut it. Where the hell was she, anyway? The old woman continued to shake her relentlessly. She supposed the only way to make her stop was to open her eyes and deal with it. She couldn't lay here forever, wherever here was. There had been an accident. Yes, that was it. She had been …

Terry opened her eyes wide, expecting a hospital environment. This rough-handed woman must be the night nurse or something.

She was not in a hospital.

The old woman was not dressed in a nurse's uniform or orderly whites.

The temptation to shut her eyes again was enormous.

"Oh no you don't, sweetie." The old woman grabbed both of Terry's arms, pulled her up to a sitting position, and shook her vigorously. "Snap out of it, kid. We've got a lot of work to do, you and I. I've been stuck here waiting for someone like you and I'll be damned if you're going to slip away and get lost somewhere. I haven't got time to bail you out and bring you back."

Terry eyed the woman with prim distaste. "I want to go back to sleep. I don't like it here!"

"Too bad. You don't get your fifty years until after you help me out."

"What on earth are you talking about? And who the hell are you, anyway? Where is my mother?"

"Oh dear, this is a setback." The old woman clicked her tongue. "You're not supposed to be feeling any desire to see your family."

"That's absurd. Why shouldn't I be asking for my family? This is some sort of—I mean, I am waiting for my family to pick me up, aren't I? My father is going to be just livid about the Jeep!"

The old woman simply frowned and moved to plump the pillows so that Terry could sit up, then pushed her back against them with gusto. Confused, Terry grabbed the thick comforter and clutched it more for solace than anything else. She didn't feel sick or injured, simply frustrated and a little afraid.

She pulled up a chair beside the bed and patted Terry's hand. "Look, honey, I've an awful lot of explaining to do in short order. I'll try to make this as easy on you as I can but there are just some things you are going to have to take my word on until you can acclimate yourself. I'm not going to hurt you. You're beyond that now."

Terry stuck out her lower lip. The old woman's touch was somehow calming, reassuring; she wanted more than anything to feel warm and safe. Terry sighed. "Okay, start explaining. I'll listen … for now."

"That's a good girl," the old woman smiled and Terry noticed for the first time that she was actually very beautiful … well, in her own way. Her blue eyes sparkled and her color was good for an old person. She had the longest white hair Terry had ever seen. She imagined the woman usually wore it up in knots or braids, but right now it was free-flowing and a little disheveled, but not straw-textured as some elderly locks were wont to be. The hair appeared flaxen and soft. In fact, the woman's entire countenance seemed to radiate warmth and freshness. Not at all like the feeling she often had around old people. Terry wondered what her own appearance was like. *Bound to be horrid*, she thought ruefully.

"Your name is Terry Anderson," said the old woman, "and you are here because you made a wish."

Terry looked at her quizzically.

"Yes, you made a wish to be psychic; extremely gifted, if I've got the story right. Is that true?"

Terry nodded her head slowly. Yes, she had made such a wish, but that didn't explain her current situation, even though she wasn't exactly sure what that situation was. Terry was growing uncomfortable with the direction of the conversation. She was beginning to feel she knew the truth ... and it was an awful thought.

"Oh my, this is so difficult, I just don't know where to begin," muttered the old woman as she gazed off into space. "Actually, I didn't expect you at all. I thought it would be someone else. Someone more—no offense intended—capable." She drummed her fingers on the silk comforter. "They don't tell you everything here, you know. Just because you're dead people think it's from God's mouth to your ear ... Oh, I'm sorry, dear, you look like you've just seen a ghost!" She laughed heartily while Terry stared at her, stupefied.

"Dead? You're a ghost?" sputtered Terry, her hands involuntarily flying to her open mouth.

"Well, you don't have to get so rattled about it, dearie. You are, too, you know!" huffed the older woman.

Terry sunk into the pillows, her hand unconsciously drifting, curling to wipe eyes that were threatening to well over at any moment. How could she be dead? She hadn't even lived yet! It was so unfair! But wait ... who's to say it's true? Some nutty old woman. She could be trapped in someone's house, for Christ's sake! Fear flooded her mind as she cowered against the headboard of the bed.

The old woman's laughter had long since died and she was eyeing Terry with a worried expression. It was obvious that Terry's reaction was far more than she had anticipated. She leaned forward, her face mere inches from Terry's. The younger woman felt a strong sense of peace. The smell of lilacs wafted about her.

"Listen, my little miss," she whispered. "I can hear your thoughts just like they were on an intercom system. That's one of the perks around here. You'll get used to it. You must understand that I'm not going to hurt you. You are not in a farmhouse somewhere being held for slaughter. I'm just as confused as you are right now, but on a different level, so to speak," she sighed and sat back. "You are dead," she said matter-of-factly. "There is no doubt about that, and you are welcome to check out your surroundings for yourself. It was my understanding that all this would be explained to you before they sent you here. Evidently something drastic has happened on the earth plane and, in the meantime, someone made the decision to drop you here without ceremony. And dimes to dollars somebody in the system is going to get their butt kicked." She rolled her eyes heavenward.

"However, they never leave you in the dark for long, and I'm sure we will be contacted soon. What disturbs me is your obvious connection to the earth plane and those still on it. Normally we don't feel such attachments. All that is removed so that we can continue our work, whatever it may be. Perhaps if we put our heads together we can figure out why this attachment persists. Obviously, your silly wish has something to do with all this."

Terry slowly digested the information. Supposedly she was dead, and had been offered the chance to investigate her new world without limitations, most likely at a later date. The knowledge of freedom was rather comforting, but loneliness enveloped her. The tears flowed.

The old woman rose and brought her a tissue. "Perhaps a hot cup of tea?" she asked.

Terry sniffled, nodding. "If I'm dead, how come I can eat and drink?"

The old woman paused at the doorway of the bedroom. "Right now, you and I are between the worlds, as they say. You are living in my reality. This is my house. Well, it was my house. The intake of food and drink is not necessary, but an act of habit. I learned early on to set up some type of routine for myself. It gets boring floating around with nothing to do. To be blunt with you, we don't even have bodies, really. Actually we are pure consciousness. However, it's far more comforting to keep some of our earthly thought-forms, like the body. Our reality, for the time being, is superimposed over that of the earth plane. Since we are stuck here, we might as well make the two planes work as closely together as we can. You'll understand more after you are here for awhile, but it won't last forever." She smiled wryly. "When you have completed the task that brought you here, they will come for you."

"What about you?" asked Terry. "Won't they come for you, too?"

The old woman shook her head sadly. "I really don't know. I made a very bad choice before I died and some people were killed because of my folly. I've got to try to fix it. If I don't, I'll have to do it all over again in the next life. Instead of sleeping for fifty years, I chose to be here."

"I don't understand," said Terry, "why would you choose to be stuck … ah … between the worlds?"

"It's a long story and I'll explain it later. First, let's get you used to your new environment."

"Wait, don't go yet!" She didn't want the woman to leave. Perhaps she would disappear and never come back! "What's your name?"

The old woman chuckled. "All my friends in the last incarnation called me Beth Ann."

"What do you mean … in the last incarnation?"

"You know. Reincarnation. Where you live one life, die, then come back for another, and another, until you work out all the things you need to. It's the human's way of evolving toward the divine. I usually come back and take up the same religion. I'm a Witch. In fact, I've been Craft for nine consecutive lifetimes," she said proudly.

Terry's eyes rounded. "You mean there really is reincarnation? I'm not going to be dead forever?" Terry wasn't sure which was more astounding, the choice of this woman's religion or the promise that she would live again.

"My, my, for one who was supposed to be so engulfed in that New Age stuff, you mean to tell me you really didn't believe in reincarnation?"

Terry felt sheepish but the urge to defend herself won out. "You said yourself that the dead don't know everything, how do you expect the living to be any more sure of things than you are?"

"Point well taken. While I'm in the kitchen, why don't you open that closet over there and choose something to wear? Unless you are used to being a naturist, I think you'll want to dress before you begin your ghostly wanderings. Everything is already in your size, and I believe to your taste as well. This will be your room for the duration of your stay here. Mine is across the hall."

After she was alone, Terry stole a glance under the covers to make sure all the right equipment was where she remembered it. Yup. "Great," she thought, "stark naked and dead, too." At least she didn't feel the least bit cold. Evidently physical discomforts didn't exist in this world.

She scrambled out of bed and promptly floated toward the ceiling. Frantically she kicked her arms and legs trying to perfect some sort of landing. Instead, she bobbed around the room like a drunken fish. When she tried to dive downward, her behind kept smacking into the ceiling.

Peals of laughter echoed below her. Tears were streaming down Beth Ann's cheeks. She was laughing so hard she couldn't speak. The tea tray she held jiggled threateningly.

"Think—" Beth Ann's laughter erupted again and she couldn't finish her sentence. "Think yourself down!"

She set the tray on the nightstand and held her sides for dear life.

Terry did as she was told and landed with an ungraceful thump.

Beth Ann took a tissue out of her apron pocket and wiped her eyes. "I'm sorry, I should have told you about that. I forgot you didn't get any orientation period at all. Oh my ..." She sat down in the chair and fanned herself with her apron, then caught herself. "Force of habit," she said. "What you think is real, becomes real. It's like that on the earth plane, but at a much slower rate. Here, everything is instantaneous. You'll get used to it."

Terry started to float again and grabbed for the nearest piece of furniture—a big oak dresser with an oval mirror. "I can see myself!" she exclaimed.

"Heavens, child, you're not a vampire, you know. Of course you can see yourself."

Terry scrutinized her appearance and was pleased to see that she radiated with that same inner glow that Beth Ann appeared to have. A few things were different. That longer, thicker hair she'd always envied on other women now shined on her own head, the cut ending just below the shoulder blades. Her eyes appeared a little larger than normal and her waist a bit slimmer. If her legs were a little longer she'd have taken any beauty pageant by storm.

Beth Ann appeared behind her in the mirror, a hint of a smile playing at her lips. "Like I said, it's your own reality. Think it, and it becomes so." She put her hand on Terry's shoulder and spun her toward the closet. "You can prance around in front of the mirror later, kiddo. Right now take a hike to that closet. You can dress behind the screen over there while I drink my tea before it gets cold, providing I haven't spilled the bulk of it while you were doing your flying act."

Terry half-floated, half-walked to the closet.

"What about underwear?" she called from behind the screen.

"What ghost needs underwear? You're never going to sag and hygiene isn't a problem on this side."

"Oh. Yeah, guess you're right." Terry emerged from behind the screen wearing a light blue flowing dress.

"That color suits you. It also tells me a little about your personality. Had you chosen red, I would have worried," remarked Beth Ann.

"Red? Why?"

Beth Ann delicately sipped her tea. "Red is a very passionate, emotional color. Had you chosen it I would have worried about your self-control in the situations ahead we will be forced to deal with. You'll need a level head and the soft blue you have chosen indicates that you are capable of cool and logical thought. We are going to need it, believe me."

Terry settled herself on the edge of the bed and lifted her tea cup, only to drop it as a vivacious redhead dressed from head to toe in black burst into the room. "Who are you?" shouted the wide-eyed woman. "What in Goddess' name are you doing here? I command you to speak immediately!"

CHAPTER TWENTY-ONE

ETH ANN AND TERRY STARED AT Elizabeyta in disbelief, alternately swinging their heads from Elizabeyta back to each other.

"Is this one of the people you said would tell us what was next?" asked Terry.

Beth Ann didn't answer—she looked like she'd seen a ghost.

Elizabeyta leaned against the door frame and glared into the room. "Who are you?" she demanded again. She thought the girl in her guest room must be daft because she was muttering something to the air.

Terry was in the process of requesting an answer from Beth Ann when she turned to answer Elizabeyta. "I'm Terry Anderson, or at least I think I am. Beth here seems to have lost her brains for the moment. Are you here to tell me what I'm supposed to do next?"

Elizabeyta's expression was a mixture between shocked and quizzical. Who the hell was Beth?

Terry looked at Beth Ann again. She was working her mouth, but nothing was coming out.

"I don't understand why you both are acting so strange," snapped Terry. "I mean, this is a strange place, but you are here to see me, aren't you?" insisted Terry.

"Terry," Elizabeyta began slowly, "only you and I are in this room and you aren't supposed to be here. You're dead."

"I know I'm dead!" Terry retorted. "Who are you?"

Beth Ann vented a long whoosh of air. "Terry, can you see Elizabeyta clearly?"

"Of course!"

"And she can see you?"

"So it appears. Can't she see you?"

"No."

"What is going on here?" Terry was getting irritated. "First I'm dead, now I'm in a fucking fun house!"

Elizabeyta stomped into the guest room. "Fun house? This is my house, Terry. What are you doing here?" This was just too weird.

"Elizabeyta is living, Terry. She's not a ghost, she's flesh and bone. She's also my grandniece. She's never been able to see me or talk to me. In fact, I've been trying to scare her away," whispered Beth.

"Apparently I can talk to her," remarked Terry. "Do you want me to scare her? And why the hell are you whispering, Beth?"

"Talk to who? Scare me?" asked Elizabeyta.

"If I didn't know better, I'd think we were rehearsing for *Blithe Spirit*," muttered Beth Ann.

"Blithe … what?" asked Terry.

"Never mind; it was a play, you're too young to remember it." Beth Ann's mind was racing, trying to make sense of the situation.

"Did you say *Blithe Spirit?*" piped Elizabeyta.

"Yes; your great aunt says its a play or something."

"Beth—you mean Beth Ann is here, too?" asked Elizabeyta excitedly as she advanced into the room.

"Don't tell me you can't see her, either." Terry rolled her eyes.

"Either?"

"Beth Ann says you're blurry to her."

"I didn't say that," hissed Beth Ann.

"No, you thought it."

"Oh."

Elizabeyta started to sit in Beth Ann's chair. Beth Ann promptly shoved it back and Elizabeyta ended up on the floor.

"You were going to sit on her," said Terry.

It was Elizabeyta's turn for eye rolling. "I've just about had enough of you, Beth Ann," she growled. "Terry, what are you doing here? Why aren't you in the Summerland?"

"What's that?" snapped Terry with obvious irritation.

"It's a place you go after your physical body dies, like heaven," whispered Beth Ann.

Terry tilted her head back and glanced at Beth Ann, who wore a dour expression. "Beth Ann says it's because I wished for it."

"You wished to be dead and in my house?" Elizabeyta was incredulous. "Why would you do that?"

"No, silly! I wished to be psychic and this," she motioned to her ghostly form, "is what I got."

"Oh no!" breathed Elizabeyta, sitting slowly on the edge of the bed next to Terry. "Let me get this straight. You are dead because you wanted to be psychic. Beth Ann can see you and talk to you but she can't see me very well, but you can."

"She says that, for her, looking into the real world is like looking through a pane of frosted glass," explained Terry. "She doesn't even know what you really look like. You are just a blob of color to her."

"Can she hear me?" Elizabeyta asked, looking about the room.

Beth Ann sniffed. "Tell her that her language has been atrocious over the past few months and her grandmother would roll over in her grave!"

Terry complied and gave her the message.

Elizabeyta threw a haughty glance around the room. "If you wouldn't have been such a bitch I would have treated you better!" She smoothed out her black dress over her lap. Something wasn't quite right here; her dress shimmered under her touch. Oh, shit, maybe they were all a bunch of ghosts stuck in Beth Ann's house. My, wouldn't that be a world-class event.

Terry noticed it, too. "Elizabeyta, if you aren't a ghost, how come there are some moments when you seem transparent?"

"Uh-oh," said Beth Ann. "I bet she's sleeping, but don't tell her. The thought might wake her up. I'll go check. You keep her talking. We may not have much time with her." Beth Ann floated out of the room. Elizabeyta felt a chill pass by her.

"Did Beth Ann go somewhere?" asked Elizabeyta.

"She thinks you are sleeping. I'm supposed to make like a chatter box and so are you. Oops!"

"That would explain some of this," said Elizabeyta thoughtfully; her form shimmered again and Terry realized she'd done exactly what Beth Ann told her not to do—tell Elizabeyta she may be sleeping. But Elizabeyta's form grew firm again. "I did a ritual tonight and the last thing I remember was coming upstairs and going to my own room. I don't come in here too often, and I don't remember stopping here. I went to bed, too tired to change clothes, and the next thing I know I was coming through that door. We, or at least I, must be on the astral plane."

"I know what that is!" said Terry. "I always wanted to do that!"

"It's easy. All you do is—oh, I'm sorry, I forgot. You don't need to know anymore."

"Yeah. Right."

There was an uncomfortable pause. Beth Ann whisked back into the room. "Dead to the world, she is. Definitely in the astral, which means we are working on borrowed time. This may be the one and only opportunity we have to save her."

"Save her?"

"Save me?"

"Tell her she is in grave danger. The man after her is Jason Black-thorn—a real bad character. Tell her it's karmic, she'll get the picture."

"Why should I tell her that?"

"Tell me what?"

"Don't ask questions now!" snapped Beth Ann, who was floating behind Elizabeyta and above her head. "If I have the chance, I'll tell you later. If I don't, and spend all my time bellyaching to you, we're all going down the tubes!"

Terry sullenly gave Elizabeyta the message.

"What about my grandmother?" grilled Elizabeyta.

Beth Ann looked uncomfortable.

"What did she say?" pressed Elizabeyta. She was getting very tired; the room looked fuzzy.

"She hasn't said anything yet."

"She's going!" wailed Beth Ann, clawing at the air in an effort to hold Elizabeyta back. "Tell her he's coming for her on the full moon. He's not like anything she's ever encountered before. He's as evil as they come!"

Elizabeyta's head was nodding, but she made a concerted effort to keep focused while Terry spoke. "What kind of magick does he use?" she asked drowsily.

"Tell her I know he uses Pow-Wow magick, but he's not one of the heal-ers, he's the dark artist, the Dark Man!" Beth Ann frantically wrung the edges of her shawl. Elizabeyta was becoming more transparent by the second.

Her senses stabilized and she rubbed her eyes. "What is a Pow-Wow artist?" she mumbled.

"Pow-Wow is a magickal system that ordinarily uses the Christian reli-gion, but can encompass the dark side of ceremonial magick. Usually it deals with healing, helping neighbors, stopping gossip, that sort of thing—it's really a bastardized form of the Craft. Tell her this man is why her grand-mother and our people left the area in the thirties. They fled for their lives! And if she knew what was good for her she'd get her behind out of this town and back to where she belongs!"

Terry told Elizabeyta, but she was afraid the words were not getting through. Elizabeyta's head was lolling, but she valiantly struggled to hang on.

"I'm dealing with an old magickal coot?" she smiled dreamily.

"No, no!" shouted Beth Ann. "Tell her to think! Tell her Beth Ann says to think! He's not—oh, shit!"

Terry rushed to repeat what Beth Ann had said, but Elizabeyta had already faded away. "Now what? Can't we wake her up or something?"

Beth Ann floated down and sat beside Terry on the bed. "No, if we scare her she might lose everything we told her."

"I thought you said you wanted to scare her? I don't understand!" wailed Terry.

Beth Ann's shoulders slumped. "At first I wanted to scare her, to make her go home to safety. But now I understand it's gone too far. If she goes home, they'll eventually find them. No. We'll just have to wait and watch, protect her if we can, but even that is a long shot. Most likely he'll try to get her away from this house. Her power base is here right now, and mine was here before hers, and my mother's before me, and so on. This house has been in our family for generations and the power here is good and strong. Everything has been protected with centuries of warding. She is safe from outsiders as long as she is in the house, but she doesn't seem to know that. And, considering her station at the covenstead, she should be well aware of what she can and cannot do here. Evidently my sister never had the chance to tell her, or believed she didn't need to know."

Terry disregarded everything Beth had said. Instead, she spoke wistfully. "I wish I could have given her a message for my parents."

Beth Ann patted her knee. "I never thought. So selfish of me. I'm sorry, Terry. Maybe we'll get another chance."

They floated into Elizabeyta's room. The single candle by the bedside was guttering. Elizabeyta was sprawled out on the bed, her gentle breathing echoing softly. Beth Ann chuckled and picked up a blanket from the end of the bed and tucked her in.

"I thought you couldn't see her very well."

"I can't, but just like a blind person learns to live with disability and adjust accordingly, so have I. I rely a lot on sound and energy currents."

"Do you think she'll be able to see me when she wakes up?" asked Terry.

"I honestly don't know. If she doesn't, let's hope she remembers what we told her. Since you can see everything so well, check the windows for me. Then I'll give you a tour through the house, so you can get the lay of the land, so to speak."

Terry drifted about the room, inspecting the latches on the windows. "Beth Ann, if Jason Blackthorn is such an adept magickal person and is so hellbent on destroying your family, a few little latches aren't going to stop him."

"I know, but it makes me feel better."

"How come Jason didn't kill you?"

"He did, and Elizabeyta's grandmother, too. We died together. In the end, I tried to stop him … but my sister went on to the Summerland," Beth Ann's voice quavered and lapsed into silence.

Terry, sensing deep undercurrents of despair, grew quiet. She suddenly realized that her own short life was spent lolling in self-satisfaction and vapid pursuits. For one moment of clarity she rose above the little trials of normal thought and was gripped with a sense of disgust at herself. She had wasted the little time she'd had.

Without speaking, they moved into the hallway and glided side by side down the steps. Terry was having trouble navigating and kept zipping toward the ceiling. "You'll get used to it," assured Beth Ann. After a moment, she said, "Terry, what do you remember about dying?"

"I remember pulling out of the parking lot at the convenience store. The roads were really slippery but I wasn't afraid or anything because I was in my father's Jeep. It was early in the morning, I think, and there weren't many cars on the road …" She stopped at the landing and waited to see which direction Beth Ann would go, then followed her toward what she thought must be the kitchen.

"I was on Main Street," she said, her voice growing tremulous, "heading up the hill when this black—no, it was blue—pick-up truck tore out of the alley and blindsided me. It was a souped-up job and I remember the grille of the truck was so close to my head I could reach out and touch it. The next thing I knew, the truck was replaced by a telephone pole. I can remember the sound of the impact, like a loud whump and then a crack, and tinkling glass, like hundreds of wind chimes … I could smell smoke, but everything was so dim. I couldn't see or hear right …" she shuddered. "I—I knew I was dying." She hesitated. "I wasn't afraid of death, but I knew I didn't want to burn …"

"Did you?" whispered Beth.

"I'm not sure. I read once that the spirit actually separates itself from the body and that you don't feel any pain. I mean, the body does and reacts, like screaming, but the spirit is already gone so the pain doesn't affect it. Crazy, huh? I guess the answer is yes and no then. I just remember a feeling of peace, and then one of sadness. I really did love my parents, you know."

They had reached the kitchen and Beth Ann pulled out a chair for her. Embers in the fireplace glowed pumpkin orange. Terry felt the energy of the fire and watched passively as Beth Ann threw on a few small logs. The flames took hold, licking the air. Terry held out her hands. Although she couldn't feel heat, she could sense the energy the fire expelled and it made her feel good. She also knew Beth Ann was thinking the stoked fire would also keep the kitchen warm and toasty for Elizabeyta when she woke up.

"It thinks, you know," remarked Beth Ann.

Terry raised her bowed head. "What thinks?"

"Fire. It thinks, it breathes, it breeds. It is an entity all of its own."

"It kills," said Terry matter-of-factly. "It killed me." Her ghostly form started to shake, making her look more like a collection of luminous particles than a person.

"No, it was a tool, Terry. Everything in the universe can be controlled, even fire. But it has to be a part of you first. Fire cleanses, fire ignites passion, fire is a process of rebirth. It can create or destroy. It is a living element and demands respect, like any other living thing."

Terry looked at her doubtfully, but the shakes were receding. Beth Ann continued to stand in front of the fire. "What else do you remember?"

"That's about all."

"How about before. What were you doing before?"

"I was at the train station. I picked up the Jeep there. Why?"

Beth Ann drew up a chair beside Terry. They both gazed at the fire. "It is kinda pretty, isn't it?" asked Terry.

Beth Ann ignored her. "Did you talk to anyone? See anything strange?"

Terry thought a moment. "I saw the twins with their dogs, but they were so busy they didn't see me. I saw Lee, but he didn't see me, either. You know, I read somewhere that up to twenty-four hours before you die the spirit is in the process of leaving the body, and in the case of murder, the only person who really sees you is the killer. No one else can really see you once your fate has been set in motion. I'm glad I got to see Lee."

"It appears you've read a variety of unusual material," sniffed Beth Ann. "You mean Lee Baxter, the minister fellow?"

Terry smiled. "Yes. I was engaged to be married to him once. Now that I think about it, he was a nice man. Just a little too controlling."

Beth Ann cleared her throat politely. "He's Elizabeyta's neighbor."

"Really? Oh yes, this is the big stone house on the corner, isn't it?"

Beth Ann nodded. "Do you think you could handle seeing him?"

"It would make me sad, I guess. Why?"

"Because he comes over here to visit."

Terry surveyed the other woman. "Visit ... how?"

"Oh dear," mumbled Beth Ann.

Terry rolled her eyes. "You mean he's interested in Elizabeyta?" She thought about that for a moment. "Guess it shouldn't matter to me one way or the other, huh? I mean, I'm dead. He's still puttering around on the other side. Sort of like two different species now, I suppose."

They both stared at the fire.

"That certainly does put an interesting twist on things, doesn't it?" Terry finally said.

Tell me, Beth Ann, is she a Witch like you?"

"Yes, but she's better at it."

"Does he know?"

"Yes, I heard them talking. He knows."

"How did he take it?"

Beth Ann cocked her head. "I'm not sure. He acted like it didn't phase him, but …" She sighed. "I turned away from the Craft in this incarnation. I gave it up because I thought I loved someone and felt my involvement with him could overcome everything, including my personal religious beliefs." Beth Ann gathered her shawl around her. "I was wrong. One should never give up their shields, it makes them powerless." Beth Ann picked at the fringes of her shawl. Terry eyed her curiously.

"Habit again." She shrugged and smiled. "You know, you look a lot like Elizabeyta. I mean, you're younger and all. But the hair color and facial bones are very similar. Keep thinking about the people you saw before you passed; anybody else?"

"Well, now that you mention it," her eyes grew round. "I saw the Dark Man! I mean, I saw a man all dressed in black. He walked right out in front of my Jeep!"

Beth Ann sat up straight. "Did he say anything?"

"I don't know, the heater was running and the windows were shut. I thought he was just muttering and making funny motions like he was drunk or crazy or something. In fact, he really gave me the creeps."

"Oh, hell! He got you, too!" exclaimed Beth Ann. "If you saw him again, would you recognize him?"

Terry mushed her mouth like an accordion and ignored her question. "That's ridiculous. Why would anyone want to kill me? Besides, you told me I'm dead because I wished for it."

"That's just it!" Beth Ann exclaimed. "You had to wish for it first. He must have somehow picked up on your desire to be psychic."

Terry leaned forward, putting her elbows on her knees, chin cupped in her hands. "It still doesn't make sense. Why would he care if I were psychic or not?"

"You're right. That is a little far-fetched." Beth Ann looked at Terry closely, then slapped her knee. "That's it. That's it!"

"What. What!"

"He must have thought you were Elizabeyta!"

"That's ridiculous. He couldn't think I was Elizabeyta because my parents have lived in this town all their lives. Are you saying that he doesn't know what Elizabeyta looks like?"

"I honestly don't know," sighed Beth Ann. "I do know, however, that he's spent the last several years trying to find our people. He's not found the covenstead yet, although some of his people did get through several years ago and nearly burned the place down. The elders caught them and dispensed with them before they could let him know anything. Luckily for us, the gentlemen in question were acting on their own and hadn't reported in for several days. The last time anyone had heard from them they were in another state."

"Then maybe it wasn't Jason but one of his people who caused my accident?"

"Possibly."

"But that's not fair! Elizabeyta is the one who is supposed to be dead, not me! It's all a mistake. Where are those people who run everything? We've got to find them. They can fix this mess and maybe send me back!"

Beth Ann shook her head sadly, allowing Terry to rant and rave while she floated about the room, sobbing.

"Come here, child."

Terry drifted down to her chair again, hiccuping occasionally.

"Listen, Terry. Certain things in our lives are fated. It was your time to go. How you got here is really unimportant right now. You are here. You can't go back to the life you had. Your body is gone. Now you have to look ahead."

"You said that word before," muttered Terry.

"What word?"

"Covenstead," intoned Terry carefully.

"Oh, just the place where Elizabeyta and her parents grew up. I know Jason has found some of those who left the group, who chose to separate from the main body. That's how he knew about the covenstead in the first place. They were told that it was dangerous, but they wouldn't listen. My sister told me. That's why she came here, to warn me. He'd been picking them off, one by one, and she found out about it while trying to trace them for Elizabeyta's eldering ceremony. The reigns and government of the fam trad are to be passed to her for guidance and safe-keeping, the only problem was that tradition demanded certain family members to appear. At first, no one could find them. Elizabeyta's grandmother got suspicious and started to track them down. She used everything she could think of from magick to private detectives. They either came up permanently missing or dead. Then he really came out of the closet, so to speak, and killed Elizabeyta's parents and her uncle. You see, Elizabeyta doesn't know that she was the one chosen from the beginning to take over the trad. She thinks it has happened because of the recent deaths."

"So why is the lineage so important?" asked Terry.

"Well," Beth Ann sat back in her chair. "The fam trad is our family tradition—our lineage which includes magickal expertise held by our family for over nine hundred years as well as four million dollars in property and stocks, both here and in Oklahoma."

Terry whistled between clenched teeth. "Wow! Does Elizabeyta know all this?"

"No."

"The woman is exorbitantly rich and she doesn't know it?" breathed Terry incredulously.

"You must understand that Elizabeyta will be the caretaker of the people at the covenstead. The money really belongs to all of them. If they want to leave, they are set up in businesses of their own, but ties are broken after that unless they are in real trouble. The covenstead will also college educate the children of those who leave, as well as provide homes for all of them when the time comes. It takes a level head to ensure the safety of all those people. Unfortunately, only a few stragglers outside the covenstead are left, and of course the sixty or so people who remain at the Oklahoma holdings."

The shawl slipped from Beth Ann's shoulders as she continued her story. "Jason has managed to set up several accidents much like yours when he could, or worse if he had to. The only ones left that we know of are those at the covenstead and three others we can't find. Either they sensed the danger and went deep underground, or they and their families are dead like the rest."

Terry looked confused. "If they are dead, wouldn't you know about it? I mean, you say you hear things from the great beyond or whatever it is, how come you haven't heard anything about these people?"

Beth Ann looked at her thoughtfully. "I don't know. I get messages from a light being now and then, but it isn't like talking to you. Sometimes it is just a feeling of what I should know. It's hard to explain. I know I'm here to help Elizabeyta because I chose to stay."

"Why are you trying to scare her away? If you are supposed to help her fight this Jason guy, why are you trying to get rid of her? If I remember correctly, she wasn't happy with you this evening. She thinks you are some astral monster trying to force her back home. What did you do to her, anyway?"

"Pranks, mostly. Unfortunately, I've taken a liking to the kid."

The fire crackled in the hearth and Beth Ann threw on another log. "Did Elizabeyta say anything interesting when I went to check on her body?"

"Just that she had been really tired and apologized because I was dead. She also said she did a ritual before she went to bed."

"Did she say which one?"

"No, not that I recall. Why, is it important?"

"Could be. I feel something different in the house. Not bad, but different. Like someone's been here and gone. Someone or something that left power in its wake."

"I thought since you were dead you would know automatically what's going on in the house and investigate anything unusual right away," said Terry dubiously. She was still having trouble getting the hang of this dead business.

Beth Ann chuckled. "First off, I can't get through Elizabeyta's wards— her protection magick. She's very good at it. Second, there are powers greater than a little old ghostie in this universe, young one, and if they or it don't want me to know what's going on, I don't."

Is there any way we can check it out?"

"I can't get into her ritual room. My sister taught her well. It's barred from both human and non-human entrance, save for her. I can't get over the threshold. All her notes are in there. She keeps them on that newfangled box; I believe it's called a PDC."

"PDC? Oh, a PC!" Terry laughed. "That's a computer, Beth Ann. But if you can't get into the room, how do you know that?"

"I stand at the door and listen. She talks to herself. She talked a lot when she first got the thing. Swore at it like a trooper until she figured it out." Beth Ann laughed at the memory.

"What do we do now?"

"We wait. We watch. We do what we can. We hope to hell you can communicate with her better than I can." Beth Ann slapped her knee firmly. "And we find out what the devil you are doing here!"

The two wraiths talked into the night, educating each other on times past and present. As the grandfather clock in the hall struck 7:00 AM, Beth lifted her head. "She's awake and coming down the stairs. Here we go."

Terry rose, but Beth Ann motioned for her to sit down. "You don't want to scare her half to death. We don't know what she remembers."

Terry twisted her hands in her lap. Soft footsteps grew closer. The anticipation was terrible. She felt like a little kid waiting for her mother to pick her up from a babysitter's.

Elizabeyta entered the kitchen, scratching her head. She looked at the roaring fire. She looked at the chairs facing the hearth, walked over to them, and turned them around to face the table, where they belonged.

Beth Ann and Terry floated up to the ceiling.

"So much for that!" sputtered Beth Ann.

"She didn't see me!" Terry cried. "She didn't see me ..."

Elizabeyta turned and headed toward the coffee maker, bleary eyes staring at nothing. She paused for a moment, confused. Where did the coffee come from? She didn't remember making any. The odd dream came snaking back to her. She rubbed her eyes.

"I think I now have two ghosts instead of one."

A coffee cup disengaged itself from the rack and floated to the counter. At the same time the refrigerator door opened, allowing the cream to come out and meander across the room, and hang in front of her. Elizabeyta grabbed it in case Beth Ann was up to her old tricks and decided to throw it at her.

"That was pretty good, Terry," said Beth Ann. "You catch on fast."

"I almost dropped it," replied Terry.

"Listen," said Beth Ann, "I want you to try to go out that door." She pointed to the back door.

"You mean you want me to open it and go out?"

"No, I want you to try to walk through it. I can't, but maybe you can."

Terry looked doubtful but floated over to the door, hovered in front of it for a few moments, then melted right through it. She popped back a couple of seconds later.

"How was it?" asked Beth Ann breathlessly.

"Well, it wasn't exactly like I expected. Things sort of glow and shimmer, and I don't see them the way I used to."

"But you got out?"

"Yes, no problem there."

Beth Ann clapped her hands. "Maybe there's hope for all of us, then. We need someone who can help us. You are going to have to find this person."

"How am I going to do that?"

"Look for someone who glows very brightly. There will be a strong white or blue light around them."

Terry raised her right eyebrow. "You mean to tell me you want me to go outside and wander around, looking for someone who glows? And, if I do find someone, what am I supposed to do with them?"

"Bring them here," said Beth Ann simply.

"Bring them here? How am I supposed to do that?"

Beth Ann stood up straighter. "You'll think of something. Now, shoo!"

"But—"

"I said shoo, get on with it! Time is short." Her hand made little circles toward the door. "Shoo, shoo, shoo!"

"Maybe I'll just float away and never come back!" taunted Terry.

"Then a curse on you!"

"Cute, Beth Ann. You couldn't curse anyone if you tried. You don't have it in you. But, I'll go and try to find someone. Maybe I'll even stop in and see my parents."

"I don't think that would be such a good idea," said Beth Ann, "but you do what you think you have to. Just don't let us down, hear?"

Terry looked at Beth Ann. Her cheeks were wet, her mouth quivering.

"I won't let you down, Beth Ann," said Terry quietly as she disappeared through the door once again.

"May the Great Goddess guide and care for you," murmured Beth Ann.

chapter twenty-two

SAM RENARD, OWNER, PUBLISHER, AND EDITOR of the *Whiskey Springs Gazette*, hunched at the computer, fingers dashing madly over the keypad. He could milk this murder bit for at least two weeks. If he was lucky, they wouldn't catch the killers right away, then he could get a good month's worth of press on it. He estimated his counter sales would double in the next two days. That meant advertisers would be screaming for space. *Yummy, yummy, money, money,* he thought.

His newspaper hadn't experienced such a boost in sales since that farmer's wife, Edna Patterson, stabbed a knife in her husband's throat over five years ago. Sam whizzed the computer mouse across the screen, setting the type for the next installment on the murder, entitled "BODY PARTS MISSING: CULT MURDERERS STILL AT LARGE," for the Wednesday evening edition. That ought to get 'em. Yessir!

"Grace!" he screamed.

Grace Richards, secretary, reporter, sometimes layout person, general gofer, one-time mistress, and daily verbal punching bag, appeared in the doorway of his office. She looked at him stoically over her horn-rimmed glasses. As usual, her silver hair was perfectly coiffed; her navy blue suit neat and clean.

"Yes, Mr. Renard?"

"Get that college kid who aspires to television journalism—you know, what's-his-name. If we're lucky, he didn't party too hard last night and he'll hear the phone. Tell him to get his butt out to the victim's neighborhood. Tell him to bang on every damned door. I want a human interest piece on the family and any information he can find on the victim. Tell him to dig. I want some kinky stuff, not that 'such a sweet person' shit. Nobody's a nice person all the time. Got that, Richards?"

Grace glared at him. "What's-his-name is Vincent."

"Yeah, yeah, Vincent. Just call him!"

Grace's lips settled into a permanent pucker as she disappeared from the doorway.

Sam rubbed his hands and picked up the photographs on his desk. What a lucky man he was. Two murders in one week! Here were the pictures on the Terry Anderson hit-and-run. God, what a mess that was. Good shots, though. Lou had done well. He was still waiting for the cult murder prints taken at Jack Frost Ski Slopes. They should be in early this afternoon. Plenty of carnage on that one, too. Lucky dog, lucky dog!

"Grace!" he hollered.

She scowled at him from around the doorframe, her lips still puckered.

"Did you get that copy ready on the Anderson death?"

"Almost done, Mr. Renard. We're waiting for the obit from the funeral home so we can add the service and surviving family info to the article. It should be faxed to us in about an hour." Although Grace was the only full-time employee in the office and alone most of the time, she always spoke of herself as if she were a group. She turned on her sensible flat heel and disappeared into the depths of the outer office.

The phone rang. Sam heard a bit of stiletto conversation, but he couldn't make out who was on the phone. After a moment, Grace buzzed him on the intercom.

"Your sister-in-law's on the phone," she said.

"What the hell does she want?"

"How the bloody hell should I know?" snapped Grace. "We're busy out here. I haven't got time for chatting with that jabberbox!"

"Tell her I'm busy and I'll call her back."

"Oh no, I won't. She'll be calling every fifteen minutes if you don't talk to her now. If you want me to drum up more advertising you'll get on that phone and find out what she wants so she doesn't tie up the line for the rest of the day!"

"Grace, I should have married you instead of Jackie. Then I wouldn't be cursed with Sarah."

"Your loss. That'll teach you to fall in love with your mistress when you haven't the slightest intention of leaving your wife. Besides, you had your chance twenty years ago," quipped Grace. "Now pick up the damn phone so we can get back to work out here!"

Sam punched the blinking button. "What is it, Sarah?"

"Oh, Sam, I'm so glad I caught you. Isn't this just awful? Poor Terry Anderson, and that boy, too. There's evil in this town, Sam."

"That's what the paper says," drawled Sam. "What is it you want, Sarah? I'm very busy here." He slowly extracted a large gob of wax from his free ear with a blunt pencil, then twirled it in the air for minor amusement.

"Well, I just wondered if the police have checked out that woman, Elizabeyta Belladonna, in connection with the murder on Jack Frost ..." baited Sarah.

Sam's irritation was going beyond his control. She was such a bag of wind, but something tugged at his instincts. He might as well pursue it. "Who is Elizabeyta—ah, whatever her name is."

"Belladonna, Elizabeyta Belladonna," said Sarah. "There's something real odd about her, and I think someone should check her out. She may be involved in that cult murder thing."

Sam sighed—just as he thought, this was going no place. If the police investigated every odd person in Whiskey Springs, they'd be investigating half the town. "Could you be more specific? What connection did she have to the victim?" he asked.

"Well, I don't know. But she's unusual," said Sarah lamely.

"Does she live near the victim?"

"I, ah, I don't know. I mean, I know, but I forgot ... somehow. But I'm tellin' ya, Sam, there's stink in this town, the stink of the devil. Why, I wouldn't be surprised if you found demon hoofprints all around that body up in the snow, melted clean through to the ground. Why, I bet if someone talked to Brother Hank, he'd do something about it ..."

"Right, Sarah," Sam interrupted. "Listen, if it will make you happy, I'll pass your tip on to the police." He could almost hear Sarah beaming. It made him uneasy that she mentioned talking to that fundamentalist nut, Hank Johnson. No good ever came out of that man's mouth. God's minion or not, he was sure to start up unnecessary trouble. There was something about the sleazy minister that stuck a thorn in Sam's usually thick hide. How people could listen to that man's drivel was beyond Sam.

Of course, those were exactly the people who were slavering over his own headlines. He had a touch of momentary guilt. It passed quickly; envisioning the boat he was going to buy was a much brighter thought.

"Oh, thank you, Sam! And you will let me know if something new develops, won't you?" she asked sweetly.

"Sure. Sure, Sarah. I'll call you right away." He hung up the phone with a quick snap. He had no intention of following Sarah's advice. Most likely that Belladonna woman had done something in the past to piss Sarah off. It would be just like her to bring pain and suffering to the unsuspecting doorstep of another woman in town (as she had done numerous times before) and make him the laughing stock of the police station.

They were already upset with the capitalization on the cult angle, but he could handle that. After all, it wasn't his fault that young rookie cop said it looked like a cult murder in front of a bunch of reporters, including himself. He was only quoting the official source at the crime scene. Let the police brass handle that one. Nobody could blame him for riding the media wave— it was his job.

Sam also knew how far he could push the PR people at the cop station, who usually provided him with good copy on most of the local police activities. Sending them off on a wild witch-hunt would be very bad for Sam's carefully constructed network. A newspaper without local, up-to-date crime news was no better than kitty litter. People thrived on the evil in the world. He had strong competition he definitely could not overlook. Because Whiskey Springs was a growing suburb to nothing, set smack dab between two fairly large cities but belonging to neither, it was imperative to keep on his toes. Some days it was all he could do to drum up enough good copy to keep from being overtaken by the big boys. And he wasn't going to allow Sarah—or anybody else, for that matter—to screw it up.

Sam looked up at the elongated shadow outside the frosted pane on his office door. He'd recognize that physique anywhere.

"Hey Lou!" he called.

Lou Strader tentatively opened the door. "Grace says for me to tell you she just landed the Moyer Bank ad, full page. She also says I should come in here with a cross in front of me. She seems to feel you're sucking the life blood right out of her. I take it you've been pretty busy."

Lou grinned and handed over a manila envelope. He settled his tall but pudgy form in the chair opposite Sam's desk, propping his feet on the edge.

"When are you going to get rid of that baggy tweed coat, Lou? Even your patches need patches," Sam snorted.

"My, my, aren't we malicious today." Lou checked both inside pockets of his coat. "Nope, must have left it at home."

"Left what?"

"My cross, man!"

Sam snorted. "What's in the envelope?"

Lou's eyes glinted. "You asked for high school photos, you got 'em. Both Terry Anderson's and … the kid's. They're good, too, nice and clear."

Sam scrabbled at the seal on the envelope. "I thought the Conner kid's parents and the school board refused to release the yearbook photo? How'd you get hold of it?" There was a real run-around when Sam first asked for the photo of the kid. The pictures were taken in the fall. When the kid's mother saw them, she'd refused to pay and demanded a retake, which never materialized. The photographer on the project had quit, gone off to shoot some war somewhere, and the school was still scrambling on the subject.

Sam withdrew the two pictures and laid them side by side on his desk. There was Terry Anderson, her chubby face smiling happily for the camera. And there was Jeff Conner, stringy hair hanging over slit eyes, a heavy metal cross prominent on his black tee-shirt. He was giving the camera lens the finger, which was more in focus than the boy's face.

Sam whistled. He had the perfect subtitle for the photo—LAST GREAT ACT OF DEFIANCE—So old and corny he knew it would be a smash! He could see his boat moored at the lake already. "You done good, Lou. Real good."

"Seriously," said Lou. "Got any clues on either murder?"

Sam leaned back in his chair, fingering the pictures. "Well," he tapped Terry Anderson's photo, "this one is probably a hit-and-run by a drunk. There are several bars along Route 1. Cops often call it death highway. In fact, right around where she bought it there are three white crosses set up by families of previous traffic accident victims. It's a real bad stretch of macadam. She was driving home before sunrise on a sheet of ice. It was dark and that road is known to be a killer. Some drunk coming off an all-night binge probably popped her off and doesn't even remember it. They are on the look out for a large dark blue vehicle, possibly a pick-up, that's banged up pretty bad."

He popped his knuckles and stretched. "The other one," he leaned forward and picked up the photograph, studying it for a few moments, "could be the end result of drug involvement or the beginning of a real fanatical mess."

Lou scratched his head thoughtfully. "You don't really believe that comment about cult involvement, do you?" asked Lou skeptically.

"On the surface? No, not really. There's been an influx of undesirables from Baltimore and Philly lately in the drug trade. They are even coming from New York and Washington, D.C.—mostly middlemen and runners. The general population hasn't really gotten on to the fact that we've got serious company, save for that self-defense shooting up in Paxtang and the car chase that killed an innocent bystander down in Spring City last summer.

"Both incidents involved non-locals and their drugs. It could be that this kid tapped into something like that and either snitched, or learned too much of the operation too fast and threatened someone he shouldn't have. Most likely, someone was trying to make an example of him."

"Looks like they did a very effective job," said Lou, eyeing the crime scene photos littering Sam's desk.

"Still," hesitated Sam, "there's something here that twists my nose and for the life of me, I haven't figured it out. There was a real bad deal several years ago when I was working in New York that's ringing a bell, but I can't put my finger on it. Something familiar … anyway, the cops are playing this one real close to the chest."

"What's Sargeant Jamieson had to say about it?"

"That's just it," mused Sam. "He's not been his usual talkative self. I've only managed to get the straight, standard line out of him on the Conner murder because he hopes the press can drum up somebody who either saw the accident or knew something about it. He's more than willing to talk about Anderson, and constantly switches the subject back to her. But," Sam stood up and walked over to the window, placing his hands behind his back, "he can't dodge the media's questions forever, or the town's, for that matter. They're going to have to say something definitive soon. Either it is or it isn't a cult murder. If it is, you can bet your bottom dollar newspeople from all over the country are going to gather here like flies on a workhorse."

" How is good old Sarah doing, anyway?"

"Grace told you that, too?" Sam rolled his eyes in disgust. "I was on the phone with her when you walked in. Grace gets a kick out of her."

"What's she up to this time?"

"Trying to dig me an early grave, the old battle axe. If it weren't for Jackie, I'd have told that woman off permanently years ago. But she's the only family Jackie has, so I put up with her. She tried to tell me that she thinks some woman who lives in town by the name of Elizabeyta … can't think of it … anyway, is involved with the murder of the Conner boy."

"Gee, what a solid tip. Did she tell you why?"

"Said the woman was odd. An excellent reason to finger somebody for a murder, isn't it?" sneered Sam.

chapter twenty-three

SARAH GOODLING MANEUVERED HER GIRTH through the double glass doors of the Heavenly Springs Fellowship Church. Her appointment with Brother Hank Johnson was at precisely 10:00 AM. She was five minutes early. The place appeared deserted, but the lights were on, and she followed the familiar crimson carpeted hallway to Brother Hank's office. She peeped in and found him on the phone, in the midst of a low-toned, yet heated discussion. His free arm flailed at the ceiling. He abruptly dropped it and smiled sheepishly when he saw Sarah. He held up his index finger, indicating he'd be just a moment, then turned his back to her. She slipped back into the hall. It was impolite to obviously listen to a minister's conversation, so she moved out of his field of vision but not out of earshot.

Sarah had heard rumors of financial difficulties at Heavenly Springs, but on the surface, Brother Hank had kept the gossip to a minimum. She was hoping to catch the drift of his conversation so she could take the news back to her cronies at Pastor Becker's flock. To her disappointment, he quickly ended the conversation and called her in.

"Sister Sarah, so good to see you!" he smiled warmly.

Sarah preened. Brother Hank was so-o-o-o handsome and a servant of the Almighty. If she were only twenty years younger! She was a bit embarrassed that she had left his flock in the first place, but when Tiffany Lou fell down at the altar two weeks before Christmas, supposedly stricken in the spirit, with her skirt hiked up practically over her head, Sarah had had enough. Church was a place to pray for forgiveness for your sins, not create them in front of the entire congregation.

"I'm glad you could take some time out of your schedule to see me." She eyed the couch to the right, decided that it would be too tough to get out of— let alone sit lady-like on—and settled herself in the nearest chair. She set her black plastic pocketbook on her lap, her hands primly folded over its clasp.

Brother Hank flashed her his perfect minister smile with his perfectly capped minister teeth. He pulled up a chair and relaxed his lanky, six-foot frame opposite her.

"What can I do for you, Sister?"

Sarah took in his expensive navy blue suit and cleared her throat nervously.

"It's all right, Sister; does it have something to do with your accident?" He leaned forward.

"Accident?" Sarah's hands flew to her face. She had tried to cover up the bruises from her fall with a heavy foundation. "Oh, that ..." she drifted. "No, not really, but thank you for inquiring."

"Then how may I assist you? Are you coming back to the fold?" He stole a glance at his goldplated watch.

Sarah missed nothing and she didn't like being pressured by anyone, not even Brother Hank. She started to rise awkwardly from her chair. "Perhaps I'm keeping you from more important matters."

Brother Hank's hand flashed out and touched her knee. "Please don't go, Sister Sarah; I don't have another appointment until eleven."

She eased herself back into the chair, but she was still rather miffed.

"I've come to you because I don't think Pastor Becker will want to hear what I have to say." Actually, she didn't have the guts to tell her own minister about her dreams. It was far easier to talk to someone she didn't have to stare at every Sunday. "There's been two terrible murders in this town," she said solemnly, "and I think there is going to be another one."

"Why do you think that, Sister?" His curiosity was immediately aroused.

"Well," she hesitated. "I've been having these dreams ... nightmares." She looked at him closely. She silently swore that if he made fun of her in any way she'd march right out the door.

He didn't. Instead, he took her hand in his. "Tell me about the dreams."

"There's these men, all dressed in black, sitting in a circle in a room."

"Satanists!" he said angrily. "Yes, Sister, there is darkness all around. Even as we speak there are thousands plotting against us."

"Yeah. Anyway, these men are trying to find a woman—"

"Their priestess of darkness! Yes, Sister, these wicked women will try to coerce us, but we will overcome!"

"I have all sorts of dreams like this and—"

"You must fight this evil, Sister. They are trying to take over your mind!"

Sarah's eyes grew round and large. "You mean I'm having these nightmares because they want me to be one of them?"

"Yes! Yes! They are trying to recruit you!"

"I know there will be another murder," she cried. "I can feel it!"

"Yes, we will stand against Satan, Sister. We will fight the evil that has come to our fair town. I will hold a prayer vigil and a march! We will call God's servants together! God has sent you here to give me a message. The Lord often relates knowledge to us in the dreams of his chosen. You are a chosen vessel of God, Sister Sarah!"

He stood up and marched around the room. "We will strike this evil. We will fight the demons of the underworld!" he exclaimed.

He turned and smiled his most ministerly smile. He placed his hand on her head. "Thou art a messenger of God, Sarah. Speak to me now. Tell me who you think is involved in this plan of Satan!"

Sarah, rather taken aback at this display of religious zealousness, licked her lips. Her eyes roved frantically around the room. She was supposed to say something important, but what? Maybe it wasn't such a good idea to come here after all.

"Speak! Speak!" cried Brother Hank. "The Lord will speak through you. Open your heart and he will use you!"

Sarah began to sweat. She didn't feel any different. She didn't feel God. Instead, she felt stupid and small.

"Oh Holy Father!" shouted Brother Hank. "Speak through this woman, I pray thee. Who is Satan's warrior?"

"Elizabeyta Belladonna," croaked Sarah. There—it was out and she had no idea why she said it. It was just the first name that popped into her head.

Brother Hank looked totally blank and a bit disappointed. "Who," he asked, "is Elizabeyta Belladonna?"

Sarah paled. She realized what she had done and now it was too late. What if this woman was innocent?

"Sister, it is the Lord speaking through you! I know it!" He grasped her by her shoulders and hauled her up from the chair, his pale blue eyes boring into hers. "Speak, Sister Sarah; it is the will of God!"

Sarah trembled and clutched her purse. For some strange reason the image of Zipper crossed her mind.

Curiosity killed the cat. A cat has nine lives; you don't.

"She lives in town. At the grey stone house across from the park. I checked this morning, just to be sure," mumbled Sarah.

Sarah felt tired. There was a growing fear in the pit of her stomach, the kind you get when you know you've done something wrong and boy, are you going to pay for it.

"Don't worry, Sister," Hank released his hold on her. "All will be well, but you must come to the prayer meeting on Friday night."

"Oh, I don't know," said Sarah fearfully. What would her friends think?

"Come to the meeting, Sarah," wheedled Brother Hank, "and we will pray for your dreams."

Sarah looked at him hopefully. Anything was better than the nightmares. If Brother Hank and his prayer meeting could get rid of those, she would be forever in his debt, theatrics and all.

Sarah left Brother Hank's office at exactly 10:25, in time to see Tiffany rushing through the parking lot in her Bronco, screeching around the corner so close to the gigantic Heavenly Springs Church sign that Sarah could have sworn she hit it. She zipped into a parking space and killed the motor, glancing up to see Sarah.

Sarah could tell Tiffany was not pleased at her presence. Nose in the air, Tiffany slid out of the Bronco, nodded a polite but reserved how-do, then turned on her heel and marched through the church doors. They slammed shut with a resounding bang. Sarah unconsciously drew her own coat closer.

Not slow on the uptake, Sarah clicked her tongue. Tiffany was now separated from her husband—still, a minister? Perhaps Brother Hank was not all he was cracked up to be. But those nightmares ... well, she'd overlook this piece of gossip until after Friday night, at least.

As she hefted herself into the old Volvo, the temptation to return to the church and ferret out the relationship between Tiffany and Brother Hank almost overcame her.

Curiosity killed the cat.

She looked in her rearview mirror and could have sworn she saw an old woman dressed all in black with a tattered, flowing cape and long white hair testing the door handle of the church. When she couldn't get it opened, her old head glanced to the street. Her face was blue!

Sarah rammed the key in the ignition and sped off, resisting the urge to follow the woman inside. She didn't even look in the rearview mirror.

Inside, Tiffany was stripping off her coat, as well as her slacks and blouse. Fearing Sarah would return, Brother Hank glanced out in the hall as he pulled the door shut, just in time to catch a glimpse of the old woman as she moved quickly to the right side of the hallway and into the sanctuary. Brother Hank blinked and opened his mouth to speak to her, but the woman was gone.

Tiffany mentioned that she'd seen Sarah, and more importantly, Sarah had seen her. If Sarah came back and caught them together like this, it would blow everything. Tiffany dragged him away from the door over to the leather couch. What a lusty woman she was! She was equally stupid and money hungry. As long as he permitted these dangerous rendezvous and gave her her weekly cut from the offering plate, she'd do anything.

She was also great during the summer when they went on the road to neighboring towns and cities. Not only did she keep him satisfied and his hands off the innocents of the world, she was also a marvelous little actress. She had been healed so many times of so many ailments that she could have had a career on stage if she had the brains to know it. She was unbelievably believable. Her wardrobe and costume make-up could turn her into anything from a blind old woman to a pubescent prostitute. Some people were just grand at sleaze—that was Tiffany.

Tiffany looked fantastic in white, and at the moment, she was peeling off a white lace push-up bra. Her dusky skin shone with the sweat of anticipation. You could believe that if the spirit didn't strike the male members of his congregation, raven-haired Tiffany would. He often sent her around to the back of the gathering with the offering plate where most of the single men hibernated. Dress her in a pure white peasant blouse with a diaphanous white skirt and she'd make a mint every time she bent over to gratefully thank the wallet holder, her large breasts threatening to pop right out of that elastic and into the plate, her white panties showing through to the fella behind her. An offering to the Gods indeed!

Brother Hank did not feel guilty about using her. His daddy had always taught him that the Lord helps those who help themselves, and he helped himself to a lot of things—like other people's money, their wives, daughters, girlfriends, and anything else he could get his hands on. Tiffany was the best thing that had ever happened to him. She basically kept him out of jail and away from some dumb farmer's shotgun.

Tiffany straddled him and he moaned. At this moment in his life, nothing could be better. Any sort of nightmare was far from his occupied mind.

Neither of them saw the old woman as she silently opened the office door and peeked in, taking in the entire scene. She made a few quick motions with the long, curved nail of her index finger, then melted into the hallway.

chapter twenty-four

INKY CARLISLE TOOLED DOWN THE ROAD IN his Ford pick-up, banging the dashboard in time to a Bob Seeger tune. He'd spent all morning hooking up his new stereo system and he was taking it, and his truck, out for a spin. He was supposed to tell Jason the job was done, but he wanted his new tunes in before he went up to the compound. The music was so loud it vibrated the pebbles on the road as he whizzed through town and up toward South Mountain.

A lady with a blue Dodge Aries slowed his progress. He eased the monster grille of the truck close to her bumper until he saw a kid in the car beside her. Shit. Jason had told him to stay away from the family types. He backed off, gave himself room to pass, and sped around her, his extended side mirror almost kissing the side of her car.

She completely ignored him.

Pennsylvania bitches, his friends from out of state said, always had their noses stuck up in the air. Although Binky wasn't the family type himself, he remembered how his parents had brought up his sisters, all blessed five of them. Girls in this state weren't really stuck up. They were just following what they had been taught—never talk to strange men, never hitchhike, and be wary of guys with out-of-state plates, even if you think you know 'em.

Everybody knew somebody around here. You could always canvass your friends and check a person out. Strangers were an oddity. If the grapevine didn't reveal anything, you shied away from that person until you could get a line on them. If you couldn't, you ignored them. Simple. Safe. All his sisters had done well, either marryin' half decent stock or movin' to better places. Only Binky, out on his own at sixteen by choice, had been the major fuck-up of the family. He liked it that way. He looked in his rearview mirror, thought he glimpsed something, but when he double-checked, there was nothing there.

Binky swung around Dead Man's Curve on two wheels, his rear end fishtailing a bit when he pulled onto the straight stretch of road. Most of the pavement was dry, but sooty banks of snow lined the highway. The sky overhead remained leaden. He looked in the rearview mirror again. This time he saw it a little better—an old lady with a blue face and fangs. He jerked his head around. The road and the truck bed were empty, save for a few rolling beer cans and a handful of snow. Nothing. Too much drinkin', he guessed, and smiled.

Despite the single-degree temperature, Binky wore only a black tee-shirt, black jeans, and of course, his famous shit-kicker boots. A heavy silver chain connected the wallet in his back pocket to a belt loop on his jeans, cutting into his skinny backside. He cracked the window and lit a Camel, blowing smoke at the yellowed windshield.

Binky liked to think of himself as the visage of Death. Everybody called him The Wraith, because there was not much to his build and his skin remained pale as ivory, even in the summer. He was proud of the long way he'd come since joining up with old Jason and his gang. At eighteen he was so down and out he had to use safety pins on the broken zipper of his only pair of jeans. Now he looked forward to his twenty-first birthday in two weeks, cruising in a hot set of wheels. He could buy what he needed—basically booze, drugs, and truck parts—whenever he needed it.

He didn't like pushin', so he did other tasks for Jason. Like getting rid of that bitch yesterday morning. A piece of cake. He'd get at least $5,000 for that job, knocking off that Elizabeyta broad.

He flexed his thin arm admiringly. The tattoo of the Star of David with a bat over it covered most of his bicep. If he flexed his arm just right, the wings would flap. The other guys did it all the time to get the chicks, but Binky's physique was not particularly tantalizing, tattoo or no. By the time he got to them, they were either so drunk they didn't care or they punched him out.

Pennsylvania bitches.

The smoke was making his eyes water. He rolled down the window. Cold air blasted him. Seeger over, he popped in a Springsteen CD. He couldn't wait for warmer weather and good roads. He was saving up for a Harley and as soon as he picked up that payment Jason owed him this morning, he'd just about have enough. The job had gone oh-so-smooth: no witnesses, no foul-ups, save for a scratch above the grille of his truck, but a little touch-up fixed the problem in no time. Yeah, man! Did that bitch scream or what!

He tromped on the gas pedal and passed another broad. This one was in one of those Saturn jobs. She had two little girls in the back. They shoved their dollies up to the window and waved. When he didn't respond, they stuck out their tongues at him.

Pennsylvania bitches.

He checked the rearview again. This time he could have sworn there was a bitch dressed in black and grey, hangin' on the tail of his truck. Her face was blue, mouth open to show hellish fangs, and she was screamin'—no, laughin'—he blinked his eyes and she was gone. He whirled his head back around and nearly missed another bend in the road, almost shooting out over a ditch. Damn! Must have been some shit in that booze!

Well, soon he'd have his legs wrapped around his mean dream machine. Clamping his cigarette between his teeth, he gunned the engine, took his half out of the middle of a side road and zoomed toward Route 15 until the Saturn was only a pinpoint in the rearview mirror. At least there was no old bitch back there this time.

The head of his cigarette dropped in his lap. He banged at it and it rolled to the floor among discarded McDonald's napkins, Wendy's burger papers, and crushed cigarette wrappers. A thin line of smoke reached up from somewhere underneath the paper. Bending his head to see, he took his foot off the gas pedal and tried to stomp at the smoldering mess. Just as he decided to straighten and pull off the road, a pick-up materialized in front him, the large grille of his own truck nearly kissing the bumper of the one ahead. In a half-crouch position he jerked the wheel to the left side, barely missing the truck as he veered into the oncoming lane, catching the pewter cross around his neck on the gear shift. He breathed a short sigh of relief until he realized the pewter cross was tangled on the gear shift. Frantically he pulled himself up, clutching the wheel and letting up on the gas, just in time to see a garbage truck heading dead-on toward him. The woman driving the truck turned white as a sheet, and on top of the truck—no, it couldn't be— was that old lady, black coat flapping in the wind, white hair streaming behind her, her mouth open in an evil scream … face bluer than a summer sky …

Pennsylvania bitches …

Get ya every time.

CHAPTER TWENTY-FIVE

AM RENARD CHEWED THE END OF HIS PENCIL, working on the copy to go with the high school photos of the two victims. Grace buzzed him from the outer office.

"It's Lou and he says he got something hot," she said evenly. Not much rattled good old Grace. "Oh, and the scanner went off. Major pile-up on Falcon Road. Somebody thinks it's Binky Carlisle, or what's left of him, under Bertha Jones' garbage truck. Bertha's okay, but she won't be picking up trash for two weeks."

Sam grimaced. "Binky Carlisle—isn't that Meridith and Tom Carlisle's only boy?"

"Yep," came the matter-of-fact reply.

"When the obit comes in, send flowers. You still got Lou on the phone?"

"Yep."

Sam snatched up the phone. "Yeah, Ace, what's up?"

"If you plan to hit the jackpot you'd better get your carcass down to my studio!"

Ordinarily Sam would have told Lou to lay off the dramatics and cut to the chase, but there was something in the photographer's voice that squelched his usual attitude. "Ten minutes," was all he said and slammed down the phone.

"Grace!"

He was already throwing on his overcoat when she rounded through the door. "Anything else on the monitor this morning I should know about?"

Grace thought for a moment. "There was a contained fire at the Hardee's restaurant off Route 64, and Molly, the school crossing guard, beat the shit out of a farmer in a red pick-up who tried to go through her stop sign. I hear the cop fined the driver eight hundred bucks. Other than that, nothing very interesting."

Sam tightened his scarf and plopped his hat over his ears and checked his watch. "It's after one now. Listen, I'm going over to Lou's studio but I don't want a soul to know where I'm at. Got it?"

Grace smiled. "Sure; you went out for lunch and you'll be back when the spirit moves you."

Sam pinched her cheek. "Atta girl!"

Grace rolled her eyes.

The snow started just as Sam pulled into the parking lot of the old school administration building now converted into a fancy set of offices; the lot was full. Irritated, he parked along the street, between the hardware store and the pharmacy.

Sam circled around the side of the building and carefully maneuvered the steep steps at the old janitor's entrance. His crepe-soled shoes left a lonely path in the fresh snow. Turning the knob on the steel door, he found it locked. Funny; Lou never locked the entrance when he was in. Sam pounded on the door.

Lou answered within seconds, opening the door a meager foot. "Keep the racket down, man. If the cops knew you were here my ass would be in a sling. Where'd you park?"

"Where'd you think, wise guy? Down the street, of course!"

Lou let out a sigh of relief and yanked Sam through the doorway, almost pulling the buttons off his coat.

"What the hell is your problem?" snapped Sam as he rearranged his coat. But Lou was already double-timing it down the cinder-blocked hallway toward his offices. Sam had no choice but to trail at a steady clip.

Lou grabbed a group of photos off his desk and shoved them at Sam. "This!" he exclaimed.

Sam whistled as he leafed through the photos. "Is this truck a fuckin' pancake or what? Whose is it?" He riffled through the photos until he saw the front of the garbage truck. "You took these pictures this morning?"

"Keep going. That close-up—there—the deceased's arm!"

"Ho-ly shit! It's the same tattoo the Conner kid had. And look at this!" he waved another photo in the air. It was a picture of what was left of the gear shift, covered in blood. A necklace with a mangled chain was caught around it. "Isn't that the same necklace the Conner kid had on in his school pics?"

"The very same. Looks like this guy and Jeffrey Conner were linked into the same thing—whatever it is!" Lou was grinning from ear to ear.

"How the hell did you get these?" he asked, waving the photos.

"Cops needed color photos. Their usual photographer is down with a bad case of the flu. Since I'm the only guy close, they asked me to take the pictures and process them. I'm to drop them off at the station in ten minutes. They just called to ask me what was taking so long."

"Have they seen the necklace and the tattoo?"

"Yes on the necklace, but as far as the tattoo, not at the scene. They were too busy taking care of Bertha. Man, does that woman have a set of lungs on her! Screaming like a banshee, she was. It took three of them just to keep her immobilized until the EMS team came." Lou pointed to one of the pictures showing what was left of Binky. "It was obvious this yo-yo was dead, all twisted up like a pretzel." He pointed to one of the photos Sam was holding.

"Any witnesses?"

"Just Bertha and the broad with two kids who pulled her out of the garbage truck." Lou pointed to a non-descript, thirtyish brunette bending over Bertha. In the background was a Saturn with two little girls peering fearfully over the back seat. Lou smiled. "Good for a sidebar—LOCAL RESIDENT RESCUES ACCIDENT VICTIM—that sort of thing. Her name is Vicky Peters. I already checked, she's in the book, so you'll have no trouble reaching her."

"So this is—I mean was—Binky Carlisle!" Lou asked.

Sam nodded.

"Always knew he was trouble. Didn't he have some strange nickname or something?"

"Yeah, fellas at Cold Springs Bar called him The Wraith," grinned Sam. His eyes gleamed. "Well, he's certainly one now. This'll make great copy, Lou my boy!" He slapped Lou on the shoulder.

"Ah, just a minute, boss. You can have the standard wreck pictures; I shot them in black and white." He walked into the darkroom and emerged with another slew of pictures. But you can't have those you're holding. If the cops even find out I showed them to you, I'll be in deep shit. Especially when they see the tattoo shot."

"Can't you hold that one out?" Sam pointed to the close-up of the tattoo. "Then they wouldn't know you have it," wheedled Sam.

"Wish I could, but they checked what I was using. I have to turn in everything, even the duds. Got two of them. Both aren't worth the paper they're printed on."

"Can't condemn a man for dreaming," smiled Sam as he walked back down the hall. "Call me later and we'll get the story together. Let me know if the cops let anything slip."

"They won't, pal. They are well aware I do freelance for you and you're on their shit list these days."

"Really," Sam exaggerated. "See if they'll clear the picture of the owner of the Saturn, that Peters woman, bending over bloody Bertha for the paper."

"Yeah? They told me that if their trained dogs smelled you anywhere near here in the next twelve hours I'd spend the next thirty days in jail."

Sam tipped the brim of his hat, held his index finger to his lips, and quietly left down the corridor and out the door.

No one saw him come or go, save for the man in black.

Lou shook his head and locked the door. He spent the next few minutes packing up the photos and documentation for the police. What he hadn't told Sam was that he had a spare set of the color pics. They'd be useful some time, but one didn't dangle a banana in front of an ape like Sam and expect to walk away with it intact. Lou learned long ago that you held some of your cards when you played with Sam.

He leafed through his set of pictures. Weird. Really weird. On that tattoo, wasn't that the Star of David? Binky wasn't Jewish; he wasn't even religious. Where the hell did that come from, and why?

Lou had some pretty good connections. Tomorrow he'd check out who was doing tattoos these days. Whoever the artist was, he'd done a damn good job. It was a work of art, if you were into that sort of thing. The tattoo consisted of a bat superimposed over the Star of David. The outer edges of the star were yellow flecked in orange and red. The bat itself was a two-toned affair, with purple melting into black. Tricky stuff, considering the tattoo itself was the size of a baseball. Must've taken a long time (and a lot of pain) to do. He really ought to let Sam do the rock-turning on this one; he had more experience and the paper protected him from getting bumped off too easily, but the smell of big money was like a woman with a nice ass—he couldn't resist tagging after either one.

Lou wasn't stupid. When the rookie had rushed in and snatched the jewelry from the kid's neck, even an idiot would have smelled something bad gone to worse. But jewelry is jewelry and he'd seen the same type of baroque crap at several stores up and down the mall. It wasn't anything special in itself and the puppy cop was probably thinking Lou would do something stupid, like touch it. The real key was the tattoo.

Now, what to do with these photos? Almost every police force in the universe has some hidden method of gathering information, whether it stems from pillow talk or downright crooked cops. As long as he kept a low profile and wasn't caught snooping around, he'd be safe. But, if this was what he thought it was, his career in amateur detecting would go down the tubes, possibly with the addition of cement overshoes or a lethal overdose of drugs, depending what the hell Binky was mixed up in.

At the moment, the police were most likely going to rule accidental death on this one. Newspaper readers would cluck their tongues and voraciously read the copy when it hit the stands in the morning. Further investigation into Binky's habits would be done very quietly.

Lou put the extra set of prints in his camera bag. Better to carry them with him for the moment. If someone did get suspicious, the first place they'd look would be here; the second place would be his apartment. He'd figure out where to stash them later, but right now he'd better get his butt to the station and turn in the originals.

Lou grabbed his coat, turned on the answering machine, and doused the lights. The strap of his camera bag was uncomfortable and he fought it until he was well out the door. He didn't notice there were two sets of footprints in the snow—one with crepe designs and one set that had melted the snow clean through to the cement.

chapter twenty-six

TIMOTHY REED DRUMMED HIS FINGERS ON THE desktop. It was late Wednesday afternoon and the snow fell in sporadic bits. *What a winter wonderland*, he thought to himself. All he did these days was wonder. He continued to stare out the window behind his desk, his mind idly flitting from thought to thought.

One of the first people called about Bertha's accident was Timothy. It took him most of the morning to line up a company that would be willing to pick up the town's trash for two weeks while Bertha and her truck were out of commission. He had to cash in some favors he'd been holding for emergency snow relief, but every resident in town would be screaming if he didn't see to the trash pickup. He'd also arranged for flowers to be sent to the home of Binky's parents. Binky's father had worked on the town maintenance crew for over twenty years. A likable enough fellow, but not very

160

bright. He jotted a few notes on his actions to be reviewed by the town council and slid them into a manila folder and placed it neatly at the edge of his desk. Too bad about Carlisle's son.

Too many things were happening too fast, and he didn't understand most of them. Timothy hated to be mentally hanging on a limb. He put his face in his hands, trying to rub away the agony his life had become.

The problem was he couldn't pin anything down. Mark had been distant, gliding through the house like a ghost. When Timothy did manage to catch his attention, the boy looked at him like he had done something terrible. Timothy wanted to disintegrate on the spot every time Mark's eyes connected with his own.

He did try to talk to him, especially since Marjorie was so distraught. She kept telling him something was very wrong. This morning she finally confided that she felt Mark was somehow involved with Jeff Conner's death, and this afternoon she swore someone in a black coat and hat was watching the house. Naturally he blew it off in front of her, but worried why Jason was applying the pressure. He'd done what he said he would and made the obligatory call this afternoon to tell Jason the envelope was ready.

Jason seemed preoccupied, but his tone emitted pleasure that the task was done. "Don't tell me over the phone," ordered Jason. "I'll send someone by as usual," he said, explained where he wanted the documents left for pickup, then slammed down the receiver.

Why was he after the Belladonna woman? More importantly, what would handing over the information to Jason cost both Elizabeyta Belladonna and himself? He already knew what the price would be if he didn't, and it wasn't one he wanted to pay. What disturbed him was that there was no guarantee. He knew the last package ended in the accidental death of the individual named. With growing sickness in the pit of his stomach, he wondered about the other information he had compiled. Over ten packets had been for people out of state. What had happened to them? He had never bothered to follow up on his initial investigations, just turned over the information and washed his hands of it, choosing to believe it was a matter of business deals, financial stability, etc. Now he wasn't so sure.

He fingered the report. The instructions were clear. He was to leave the information in the shed out back at precisely 3:00 PM.

If there was only some way he could warn this woman, tell her to get out of town. He shook his head—this wasn't the wild west. He was pretty sure his phone was tapped and with the disturbing news that someone was watching the house, it was clear every move he made was being monitored. A trip over to her house was too big of a risk. Besides, what would he say to her when she opened the door? "Excuse me, Miss Belladonna, but a group of mad men are asking questions about you"? Right.

Jason had contacts all over, so the post office was out. If there was only some way he could warn her ...

What would they do to her when they got her?

He felt like he was like playing a new video game without the instructions. There were too many moves that could be made, with no codes to decipher them. He jammed the report in a manila envelope, sealed it shut, and slammed it on his desk. Checking his watch, he determined he still had half an hour before he had to take the envelope to the shed. Sometimes it was picked up on the dot; other times it would sit there for days. Since there was someone watching the house, he assumed it would be retrieved on the dot. Well, fuck 'em all. He'd wait until one minute of to take the damn thing out there!

The aroma of baking meat filtered into his office. Absently he pushed the manila envelope to the edge of his desk, rose, and stretched. As he walked by the desk, his hip knocked the envelope in the trash can. *I'm so tired. So very tired*, he thought. Was one good night's sleep so much to ask for? All he really wanted was a clear head. Perhaps then he could somehow beat Jason at his own game. He wandered aimlessly through the house, eventually treading a heavy path to the kitchen.

Marjorie was half-heartedly stirring a large pot of bubbling stew. She looked pale, the worry lines around her eyes etched deeper than usual. Her usually crisp apron was rumpled and one of the buttons on the back of her dress was misbuttoned.

It was his intention to walk up behind her and put his arms around her, to lean into her while she was cooking. It was a game they played for years. She'd giggle and he would tell her the dinner wasn't the only thing cooking in the kitchen. Instead she jumped as if struck, the stirring spoon clattering hollowly to the floor.

"Oh, Tim, I'm sorry," she murmured, stooping to retrieve the spoon. Tim tore a paper towel off the rack above the stove and handed it to her.

"I didn't mean to scare you."

"S'okay." She wiped up the mess and returned to the stove, averting her eyes.

"Where's Mark?"

She stopped in mid-stir and stared at the pot. "He went out about five minutes ago. Didn't you hear the door slam?"

"No."

"Did you talk to him?"

Tim sat down at the breakfast bar and absently worked one of the quilting threads on an orange placemat. "Couldn't get a thing out of him. He looks at me like it's all my fault."

"Is it?" Her tone was cold but she didn't look at him. The wooden spoon slowly swished through the stew.

Tim jerked at the thread. It pulled right out of the material, leaving a big unquilted spot down the middle of the placemat. He didn't even notice. "What makes you think I had something to do with the boy's death?" he asked quietly.

The spoon picked up speed, circling the pot, faster and faster, then stopped. The only sound in the kitchen was the bubbling of the stew.

"What has happened to us, Timothy? When did it all go wrong?"

He shifted uncomfortably, avoiding her question. "Where did Mark go?"

The stirring resumed. Marjorie moved protectively closer to the pot, her back to him. "I have no idea," came the answer. "I was grateful he got out of the house."

Tim nodded and glanced out the kitchen window. He shivered. "Any coffee?"

Marjorie tapped the wooden spoon on the edge of the pot and took it over to the sink. "Just made a pot; help yourself." She rinsed the spoon and let it fall aimlessly in the sink. The entire time she kept her back to him, shoulders slumped. "I made up the guest room for you. It probably doesn't matter to you because you never sleep; however, I don't want you interrupting mine anymore."

Tim froze. He'd heard of husbands being relegated to the couch or guest room. It was a standard joke in a small town. He supposed it wasn't any different—in the big city, either—the woman's ultimate weapon, like chaining a dog outside when it's messed in the house or chewed your favorite pair of tennies. No muss, no fuss, no violence—just a clean sheet, your own pillow, and a mothball-scented blanket from the closet.

He could have told her he was sorry. He could have told her the truth. His mouth opened, but snapped shut. She was already wiping her hands on her apron and hustling out of the kitchen.

He bypassed the coffee pot and fished for the Jack Daniels in the corner cupboard where Marjorie kept all the booze. She called it the cocktail cabinet. The full bottle was behind an assortment of party favors, stirring sticks, and leftover New Year's napkins. He knocked over a box of straws trying to maneuver the bottle out. He didn't bother to pick them up.

Water glass in one hand and the bottle in the other, he slammed his office door with his foot and poured himself a double, throwing it down like it was soda pop. Why hadn't he told her? He tilted the bottle and filled the water glass to the top. His hands were shaking so badly he sloshed booze all over the carpet. Maybe if he drank himself into oblivion everything would just fade away. In the depths of the house he heard the vacuum cleaner rumbling. Why was she doing that? They had a cleaning woman, for Christ's sake! Maybe that's how Marjorie dealt with stress, cleaning everything in hopes that all the bad stuff would get mixed with the dust and dirt and find its way outside.

He polished off half the glass and rounded the corner of his desk. It was spotless, absolutely clean, as usual, but something was missing—the Belladonna woman's envelope, it was gone! The booze was kicking in and he reeled toward the door. Had Marjorie taken it? He turned around and rushed back to the desk, checking all the drawers and the floor, and then vaguely remembered brushing against the desk. Maybe he'd knocked the envelope in the trash can? He bent over and realized the unthinkable. The trash can was empty.

"Marjorie! Marjorie!"

The vacuum cleaner continued to drone somewhere upstairs. He took the steps in threes, which was difficult on a spiral staircase and a gut sloshing with whiskey. He tripped on the next to the last one from the top, grabbed for the banister and slipped, his knee popping painfully as he twisted. A growl passed from his lips as he struggled to regain his balance, his fingers only brushing against the railing as he tipped over. His heart banged against his chest, exploding in pain. Gasping for air, he croaked one word.

"Shit."

Marjorie switched off the vacuum cleaner in the guest room. Had she heard a banging sound? She was so rattled after her non-conversation with Timothy that she wasn't sure if she was hearing mythical beasts or what. She wound the cord around the metal tongues on the handle and rolled the vacuum out into the hall.

All the rooms on this floor were to her right. A white and gold banister ran the length of the hallway on her left, giving one a good view of the sunken living room if you were so inclined. The door to the master bedroom at the opposite end hung open, just as she had left it, giving her a full view of the empty room. The staircase, what she could see of it from here, was empty as well. Mark's door was open, too. Dirty socks, underwear, and a pair of muddy jeans spilled out into the hall, as if the room had quite enough and was voluntarily regurgitating the mess.

The house sat dead-quiet.

She scouted the bedrooms for additional laundry, found none, and picked up the hefty pile, peering over it as she carefully stepped toward the stairs. She was sorry she had begged Timothy for these stupid stairs. They may be enchanting to view but were a bitch to negotiate.

It was on the third step from the top that she saw him, sprawled on the parquet tile below, congealed blood forming a devilish ring around his head. Her mouth worked, but no sound came out. She dropped the laundry and nearly tripped down the stairs. A dirty sock clung to the toe of her sneaker and she flew off the bottom step. Her hands hit the floor and came back up filled with blood. The smell of whiskey wafted up to her flared nostrils.

A high whirring sound resounded in her head. Her heart pounded; her breath came in uneven gasps. Timothy was white, his lips blue. She didn't touch him but flew to the kitchen and dialed 911.

The grandfather clock ticked off the minutes. She knelt by his side, too stunned to do anything but stare at nothing and hold his lifeless hand.

CHAPTER TWENTY-SEVEN

ELINDA THOMPSON PEERED THROUGH THE oval window of her front door and felt her heart sink. It was too late to pretend she wasn't home; Mark had already seen her. Now what?

Her mother was in Ohio at a speaking engagement and wouldn't be home for a few days, leaving Belinda to fend for herself. The last person she wanted to talk to today was Mark. Jeffrey was dead, and today of all days, Bruce had dumped her, which was probably why Mark was here. Her mother often told her that teenagers, including Belinda, were far more dramatic than situations required. But honestly, today had to be the worst day of her life.

She opened the door about four inches. "What do you want?"

Mark simply stared at her.

"If it's about Bruce Goodling and how sorry you are, I don't want to hear it," she snapped.

Mark looked perplexed and it dawned on her the rumor she'd heard was possibly true. It was going around that Mark was so shocked by Jeff's death that he hadn't talked to any of his usual friends, which was the believable part of the rumor. The other part of the rumor, about Mark and Jeff's "special" relationship, wasn't worth considering since Belinda was well aware of Mark's sexual preferences.

She opened the door a few inches wider. Mark opened his mouth and shut it again.

God, he was pale!

Finally, his vocal chords connected with his mouth. "What's wrong with Bruce Goodling?"

Gee, she thought, *he sounds kinda of frantic.*

She said, "Nothing's wrong with him. We had a fight, is all," which wasn't entirely true. The truth was Bruce was probably banging the stuffing out of Jenny Griffin right now, the slut. In fact, both of them were sluts!

Most parents in this dead-end town thought teens only dreamed about sex and were too interested in sports. A lot they knew! Her lip quivered, but she caught herself and returned her senses to dealing with the immediate problem—Mark, who seemed to be having difficulty standing on his own two feet. Was he swaying or was it a trick of the snow? Big flakes stuck on his long, beautiful lashes … oh no, not this again, no way.

"Mark—" she stopped, noting the vacant look in his eyes and the black circles underneath. She changed her mind. "Won't you come in?" she offered, and swung the door open.

He nodded and brushed past her. He waited in the hallway, taking his cue from her on which way he was to go. That in itself was uncomfortable, as she remembered him slouching in, giving her a secretive kiss, and heading toward the rec room downstairs all in one swoop. Things are always tough when two people go from intimacy directly to enmity—even grown-ups can't seem to handle it satisfactorily.

"How about we go downstairs?" she asked.

"That will be fine."

Just polite. No questions. No nasty remarks. Nothing. He waited patiently for her to lead the way. You could have knocked Belinda over with a feather.

"Want a Coke?" she asked, heading for the fridge behind the bar.

"No, thanks."

Belinda got herself one and popped the tab. She hated soda without ice—it burned her throat—so she busied herself searching for ice. There wasn't any. "Just a sec," she said, and walked across the room to the mud-room that lead to the garage. "It'll only take me a minute. Mom bought a new freezer and stuck it out in the garage." She disappeared through the mudroom, resurfacing a few moments later with a large bag of ice. Mark remained standing in the middle of the room. He looked like a lost puppy.

No laughter. No crossing to the big screen T.V. No turning on the Sega Genesis. No rooting through her mom's collection of dirty movies. No sprawling on the sofa and patting his crotch, making big eyes at her. Belinda considered if she had an alien in the house.

"Want me to turn on the CD player?" she asked.

He shook his head.

"The radio?"

"Nope."

My, aren't we full of trivial conversation today!

"Ohhh-kay." She moved around the bar and sat on the sofa, more to see what he would do than anything else. He sat heavily on the chair opposite her. Belinda didn't know whether she should be insulted or relieved.

Dead silence hung between them. Mark and Belinda were both products of one-child families. In the past, it was not unusual for them to sit quietly in each other's company; the necessary chatter of being heard over the din of a big family was not part of their repertoire. Silence was enjoyable, if you understood it.

Belinda did not understand this, however. He had come to see her, and here he sat. They hadn't talked to each other in months, hadn't passed a note to a friend to deliver to the other—nothing. To be honest, both played the avoidance routine with great care. Even looking at each other was a painful reminder of lost love, if it was ever really there in the first place.

She jumped when he broke the silence. "I came here because there is no one else to talk to," he said quietly. "All I want is someone to listen. I know a lot of bad things have happened between us, and I don't understand that, either, but what I really need now is to find out if I'm crazy."

Belinda started to speak, but he held up his hand and plowed on. "Tell me right now before I get into this if you are going to hear me out. If not, I know my way home and I'll never bother you again. I promise."

Belinda sucked on her bottom lip. This was not a good day to ask her this. With reservation, she said, "Okay. I'll listen."

"You have to promise me you won't tell anybody."

Belinda shrugged, her blonde bangs tickling her eyebrows. "First you asked me to listen, now you ask me not to tell. You've taken all the fun out of it." She smiled. He didn't. So much for humor.

Dead silence hung between them. "All right, I swear. Now what's up, Sherlock?" That, at least, used to get a smile out of him. Today his face made a granite statue of a gargoyle look more appealing.

"I need to know what happened between you and Jeffrey."

Uh-oh. This was dangerous territory. "I thought you said I was going to do the listening and you were going to do the talking? If we are going to go over this, you can forget it."

For the first time in her experience of knowing Mark, he looked like he was going to cry. This was a switch. If the spoiled brat had shed at least one tear a few months back she might have reconsidered. The thought of the-atrics crossed her mind, but he recovered with effort, so she threw that out.

Mark rose and walked over to the bar. She thought he was going to leave and wasn't sure if she wanted that to happen or not. "Mark, wait."

He leaned against the bar and put his head down on the soft padding around the edge. "I ... really need to know." His voice was soft and muffled because of the padding. She could hardly hear him.

Her mother taught her one very important lesson in life so far: Do not ever, ever tell one man the details of a relationship you have had with some-one else. It leads to more divorces than the number of dead people in the universe, and it also leads to dead people. Domestic violence was a nasty reality. She figured her mother ought to know, she'd been married three times, working on number four, who happened—luckily—to be Belinda's natural father. How that came about was too confusing for Belinda to con-sider, so she just let it go and figured she'd take what she could get out of the whole situation. At least her mother hadn't allowed him to move in here—yet. She was sick and tired of all the freeloaders.

Which did not solve the dilemma before her now. "Why is it so impor-tant that you know all the sordid details?"

"Because Jeffrey called out your name when he died," Mark said flatly.

Belinda felt like she had been hit by a truck. No one knew how Jeffrey died. Wasn't that the idea of the police investigation, the interviews being con-ducted at the school, even though they were all on vacation? Belinda had been one of the first to be scheduled. Unfortunately, she was no help and the cops only spoke to her for a few moments. She wondered if Mark had been called in, or maybe his father had refused to let him go.

She shuddered. What if Mark were the killer? That was ridiculous. He couldn't kill anything, not even in his dreams.

She rose to the bait. "I'll tell you if you promise to be straight with me. I want to know everything that happened. No lies, not exaggerations, just cut to the chase."

He raised his head and stared at her. His cheeks were glistening and it wasn't from sweat. "If I tell you, you may be in danger. They might try to kill you, too."

"Who's 'they'?" asked Belinda.

Mark didn't answer her.

She shrugged. "Don't be ridiculous; how would anyone know you are here? Did you tell your parents you were coming to see me?"

"No. But Mom swears a guy in a black coat and hat has been watching the house. Dad told her she was imagining things. I overheard her last night and this morning she broke down and told me because Dad won't listen to her. I believe her. I saw him, too, but split through the wood lot behind the school and came around that way. I don't think he saw me leave the house."

"Someone is watching your house? Why didn't you call the police?"

"I can't!" he sobbed. "I just can't!"

"Why not? Have you lost your senses entirely? That is what police are for, to bust killers, for God's sake! Why can't you call the police, Mark?"

"Because my father is part of it."

Belinda flipped her bangs out of her eyes, tossing her head. "Oh, right. Mr. Clean is an axe murderer. Get real, Mark, you know that's impossible. Your father is so squeaky he is utterly boring. He doesn't even drink on New Year's, for Christ's sake!"

"I'm telling you it's true. I heard them talking about him." His fists were balled and tucked close to his heaving chest.

Belinda thought he was going to hyperventilate or something. She reached over and touched his balled fists. When he didn't pull away she put her hands over his and lead him to the sofa. "Here," she said, and proceeded to unzip his coat. With her fumbling, a manila envelope slipped out from underneath the jacket. "What's that?"

"Something I stole off my father's desk."

Belinda's blue eyes rounded. "You stole a file from your father?"

Mark ignored her and picked up the envelope. He sniffled and sat down on top of his coat. "You haven't answered my question yet," he said.

"Back to that again, are we? What exactly do you want to know?"

"How—no, why—what was Jeffrey's involvement in your dropping me?"

"Me drop *you?*" Belinda stared at him incredulously. "You were the one who told Jeff to tell me to bug off!"

"What?" Mark almost screeched.

Belinda, mouth slightly parted, eyes contracting to a slit, moved back ever so slightly and sat perfectly still. The color drained from her face as her eyes widened. So now she knew it was true, for sure. "He came over here one night last August with a six-pack of beer," she said with a dead voice. "My mom was down in Atlantic City speaking at that gay rights symposium, and you were at camp, counseling those church kids, remember?"

Mark nodded.

"He'd been visiting me almost every night since you were away. He was just as bored as I was and I didn't really feel we should go out to the movies or anything because I didn't want you to get the wrong idea, should you come back and someone tell you they saw us out."

Mark shook his head; he knew what was coming.

Belinda leaned back in the sofa, tucking one blue-jeaned leg underneath herself. "Anyway, you had been gone for two weeks and you still had a week to go. Jeffrey got to the house around eight. He said he'd gotten a letter from you that day and he was dropping by to give me the news. I thought he meant camp news, the same drivel you were writing to me," she glanced at his hurt expression. "Sorry, I didn't think it was drivel at the time, of course."

She took a piece of her white-blonde hair and curled it around her finger, lazily letting it slid through her fingertips. It was impossible to look at Mark for this next part of the saga, so she looked to his left and spoke to the air, concentrating on how to phrase her words. "Jeffrey told me you had found another girl at camp and went into all the sordid details, including the lovemaking process, which he swore you wrote, word for word, waving the envelope under my nose. I asked to see the letter, but he said he was so incensed at what you did to me that he burned it. I got roaring drunk and we hit my mom's stash in the bar here when the six-pack was gone."

"But why didn't you tell me any of this when I got home?" Mark wailed. "I would have told you it wasn't true!"

Belinda gave him a hard look. "Because number one, I wouldn't have believed you, at first anyway—and two, it gets worse."

"What do you mean, worse?"

Belinda resumed talking to the air. "Jeffrey didn't look weird then, you know? No black tees or jeans, no crosses—anyway, he told me he had loved me for a long time but was afraid to say anything because he didn't want to ruin his friendship with you. I was drunk off my ass, the first and the last time."

"Oh no." Mark groaned.

"Actually, if it makes you feel any better, I don't remember most of it."

"You didn't!"

"Well, I thought you did!" she shot nastily.

"Belinda, that's the oldest con in the book!"

"So said my mother."

"You told your mother?"

"Of course I told her. She had too many questions when she got back. I figured if I hit her with the truth she'd be so touched by the fact that I was honest with her, things would go better around here in the future. Besides, she's been through more shit than I want to know about and she's always given me a straight answer when I ask her for the truth. It wouldn't be fair to lie."

Mark shook his head and ran both his hands through his hair. "But why didn't you return my calls?"

"Because if Jeffrey was right, there wouldn't be any point in speaking to you. If he was wrong, I'd just laid the biggest creep in town. I'm sure you would have approved," she said snidely.

"Well."

"There's more."

"More?"

"Jeffrey came here a week after you got back. My mother convinced me that he played me for a fool. I confronted him with it out in the front yard. He laughed, told me he'd had better girls than me and threatened to tell the whole town if I ever said anything to you or anyone else. But he did stick by his story about your new girlfriend."

"What did you say?"

"We got into an argument. I didn't know my mom was around the side of the house watering the garden. It was dark and there was a water ration on and she didn't want anyone to know. Said she spent over two hundred bucks on the garden and the township could be damned. Anyway, she heard the commotion and snuck around the side of the house. Jeffrey threw a punch at me, I ducked and my mom hit him on the back of the head with a hoe. Knocked him out cold," Belinda giggled. When he came to, my mother picked him up by the seat of his pants and told him that if she ever caught him so much as breathing in my direction she'd make a woman out of him!"

"And he stood for that?"

"He didn't stand, he ran like the wicked witch of the west set him afire!" They both laughed. "And he never came back?"

"Never."

"But you never told me, either."

"I didn't want to press my luck."

"I would have protected you," he said thoughtfully.

"Not after you found out what I had done."

They sat in silence for several minutes.

"Looks like he conned both of us," Mark said. "Too late now," he whispered.

"Too late now," Belinda parroted. "Mom always says that if humans fail to rectify the problem, the universe eventually will." She was having difficulty making eye contact. "I'm sorry, Mark. I don't know what more I can say—you'll find another girl. One who hasn't been had by your best friend …" her voice trailed off as she mustered the courage to look at him. She felt him flinch.

He was really crying now, for whom she wasn't sure. Her fear that he would move away from her if she touched him kept her hands poised politely in her lap. It was a fact that she missed him terribly; she wanted to gather him up in her arms in the worst way and stroke his hair, kiss away his tears. She couldn't even produce the courage to shift her weight from the leg that was going to sleep. If he treated her like she had the plague now, it would kill her.

Mark dried his eyes on the sleeve of his sweater. "What about Bruce Goodling?"

"What?"

"Goodling. What happened between you two?"

"If I told you, you probably wouldn't believe me."

"Try me."

"In a nutshell? I wouldn't put out. He called me a tease and a bunch of other assorted, less appealing names, and walked off with his hand down Jennifer Griffen's shirt."

"Oh."

She arched her back and rubbed the kink out of it, then struggled to wake her leg up. "Hey, what can I say. If they don't hang on for the duration of the chase they were never worth it in the first place."

"You sound like your mother," Mark said tiredly.

Belinda's smile was a bit crooked. "So I do. Now," she said seriously, "it's your turn."

He studied her for a moment, obviously weighing something. Belinda could feel the internal conflict. The energy in the room was almost tangible. Was he going to tell her or not? She sat motionless, waiting for the verdict.

Finally, he took her hands in his. She felt the tremors in his grasp. "I missed you, Belinda. God, you don't know how many nights I cried myself to sleep. Yes, cried—over you. I want everything between us to be the same as before."

Belinda closed her eyes. "You know that's not possible, Mark."

Mark sighed and flopped back into the sofa. "You're right, I can't ask you to be with me now. I'd be putting you in a lot of danger."

Belinda's eyebrows flew up in surprise. That wasn't exactly why she thought they couldn't be together again. She had momentarily forgotten about why Mark had really come here. She extricated her heart from her mouth and turned on her common sense. "How about we talk about this later, and you tell me exactly why you came here tonight. Explain what is going on here. Your father, Jeffrey's murder, the guy watching your house—everything, including what's in that envelope. We'll try to make sense out of it, you and I."

Mark closed his eyes for a moment, trying to get his thoughts in order. Then slowly he opened his eyes, took a deep breath, and told her everything.

Forty-five minutes later, Belinda was no longer worrying about their relationship, rather she was wondering if they would both make it through this mess alive. Not only had Mark stolen the folder, he had also been systematically going through his father's files. He knew enough of the family finances to figure out that what was in the bank account did not match his father's earnings or stock holdings. The renovations to the house, the great Christmas, the furniture—none of these things had been purchased either by checking account or credit. All transactions had been done in cash. He was also able to figure out that his father had been snooping on people, because he found receipts for various private detectives in other states. Although Mark didn't exactly know who all this information was being funneled to, or why, he did know the people directly related to Jeffrey's death were the recipients. He just didn't know their names—yet. Mark concluded his father hadn't stolen any money from the town outright, rather he had been selling information and taking kick-backs, which was just as bad.

"So, what's in the envelope?" she asked matter-of-factly.

"It's a report on a woman by the name of Elizabeyta Belladonna. From what I can gather, she's connected with a lot of dough. They probably want to shake her down or something." He tossed the envelope in Belinda's lap. She fingered through the papers gingerly.

"How'd you get it? Don't you think your dad will know it's missing?" she asked solemnly.

Mark's eyes flashed. "At this point, I don't give a damn!" he spat. "I walked out the back door while Mom was cooking dinner, then went around to the front and into the den from the living room. Dad was in the kitchen with her and they were having one of their low-level arguments. Neither of them heard or saw me."

"But why did you take the envelope?" asked Belinda.

"I needed to prove to you I was telling the truth, and since it was sealed I figured he was ready to deliver it. Funny thing, though; I found it in the trash can."

"Well, maybe he was having second thoughts," murmured Belinda.

"I doubt it," sighed Mark, "or he would have burned it. That's what he does with stuff he doesn't want us to find—he burns it in the fireplace. I've seen the ashes and even watched him from the hallway once. No, if he wanted to destroy it, he'd have done it right away."

"What's he going to do when he finds it missing?" breathed Belinda.

"I don't know. Probably search the house, for starters. Ask my mom. Then start looking for me. I'm going to tell him I don't know anything about it. He can't prove I took it."

Belinda shook her head doubtfully. "Only kids don't have the pleasure of hiding behind brothers and sisters, Mark; he's going to know you took it."

Mark's lips tightened as he turned away from Belinda. "Well, he's not going to find it!" He gathered up the pages and stuffed them back in the envelope. "It's not on his computer, either," he said evilly.

"How could you know that?"

"Because I reformatted the hard drive so it can't be retrieved, then ran a magnet over the floppies he had in his desk drawer. Gone—everything is gone." When he turned to face her, his face was flushed and wet with tears.

Belinda rose from the couch and put her arms around Mark. He sobbed into her shoulder for several minutes while she murmured unintelligible words of comfort. A creaking board overhead made him pull quickly from her.

"When's your mother coming home?" he asked.

"My mother?" replied Belinda with hesitation. "She's not coming back tonight, Mark; she's in Ohio at a speaking engagement."

"Then who's in the house?"

"Why, nobody." Belinda's eyes grew round with fear.

"I think we'd better get out of here," whispered Mark. "If somebody has been listening to us all this time, we are sunk. Did you lock the front door when I came in?"

"I—I think so. But from what you are telling me, a lousy lock isn't going to stop these people," she whispered back.

"Put on some music."

Together they slipped silently into the mudroom, where Belinda grabbed her coat, boots, and purse. Luckily she'd made a habit of putting everything there when she came in. Closing the door quietly behind them, they snuck over to her car and tried to get in with as little noise as possible. Belinda flipped a small box hanging on her key chain into her hand and pointed it at the door they'd just came through. She pushed a button. A quiet snick filtered through the car.

"What's that?"

"Mom got me this for Christmas. It's a remote control that locks and unlocks the car, the front door, and the garage door. She said even though it was a new-fangled thing for convenience, a woman alone never knows when she may need it. She was right!"

Belinda aimed the control at the garage door. As it was rising, she slammed the key in the ignition and gunned the engine. "Hang on!" she shouted as she threw the car in reverse and put the pedal to the floor. They could barely hear a banging at the house door over the roar of the engine. The door burst open as they careened out of the garage and slid into the street. Without looking back, Belinda threw it into drive and sped down the road.

chapter twenty-eight

OU DIDN'T LEAVE THE POLICE BARRACKS until past nine that night. The call came in about Timothy Reed while he was delivering the photos and the place turned into a madhouse. With their photographer out with the flu, Lou found himself snapping the required pictures at the scene. After all, it wasn't every day the President of the Town Council dropped dead, so he didn't bitch about it too much, just enough to guarantee some extra cash and maybe a favor or two when the time came. It was rumored Timothy's son could not be found and the mother was in hysterics. Back at the station, Lou hung around until the message came through loud and clear there was no evidence of foul play in Reed's death.

He called Sam Renard to give him the news and made a pass at the receptionist, which was thwarted, as usual.

At home in his apartment, Lou made a few quick phone calls while munching on a microwaved pizza. He polished it off with a cup of coffee, rooting around in his desk for a piece of plain white paper and a pencil. Sucking down a second cup of coffee, he got out one of the close-ups of Binky's body and traced the tattoo, then purposefully spilled some coffee on the edges of the paper for effect. He folded and unfolded the paper several times so that it would look like it had been passed to him by someone else. He even took some dirt from his dying spider plant and rubbed it on the creases.

He snagged his tattered brown leather jacket from the hall closet. You didn't dress like you had money when you drove into the city. At the last minute he put Binky's picture with the others and shoved them in his camera bag. He didn't feel comfortable leaving the photos unguarded in his apartment. He was sure no one knew he had them, but one couldn't be too careful when there were multiple murders involved.

Dead. The road, the sidewalk, the entire area around his apartment— nothing moved.

He threw his camera bag in the trunk of his beat-up Dodge and waded through the snow to the driver's side. His toes were already too cold for comfort. He should have worn his boots. He didn't relish the thought of going back inside. Now that he had begun, he didn't want to waste time.

Whiskey Springs is an upstanding town. No bars (except for the VFW, of course), no bowling alleys, not even a movie theater. Lou threaded his way through its limited collection of streets without encountering another vehicle, save the borough salt truck. He swung off Main Street and on to Route 15, heading for Harrisburg. The snow decided to take a breather. When he crossed the bridge over the Susquehanna River, he could see it had finally iced up, topped with jeweled drifts of newfallen snow. The roads weren't as bad as he expected and the traffic was light. The front wheel drive didn't slip a bit. Count on his Dodge to get him anywhere, anytime.

He cruised the inner city, checking out the list from the information he'd gathered through the phone calls. One rather seedy establishment was closed and no one at the other two recognized the tattoo. The fourth was lit with whirling red and blue and he circumvented the three cop cars without wanting to get involved. He hoped the last two on the list would be more promising and not on the agenda of any twenty-four-hour district justice. If he felt an inkling of trouble at either place, he figured the cities of York or Chambersburg would be a better bet to investigate for now.

Rosie's Tattoo, as the gold lettering on the sign announced, was a little further uptown, right at the brink of the ever-creeping ghetto. Once a stately Victorian home, it now suffered the first stages of city blight. Even in the dark he could see that some of the storm windows on the first floor were broken and the top step leading to the wooden porch buckled precariously under his weight. The narrow porch, filled with small drifts of snow, was partially enclosed by rotting trellises—the onslaught of last summer's heat peeling

away large scabs of white paint. In some places only the dead vines held the
slats together.

Lou looked over his shoulder and checked out the street.

Dead quiet.

Not sure if this was a walk-in business, Lou rang the bell. It rang shrilly.
Although lights were burning all across the downstairs, the shades were
pulled and the place felt empty and void of human activity.

After a minute or two, the porch light clicked on, casting a dull yellow
tinge on everything. A dark-haired woman in a colorful house dress opened
the door. "Do ya want tattoo or reading?"

The light was bad and he struggled to make out her features. Heavy-
set, forties maybe, but in this part of town, she could be a lot younger. "I was
considering a tattoo. A friend had one done recently and he gave me a sketch;
he said you might be able to help me."

She didn't budge from the door nor did she make any motion to invite
him in. He shivered, but her black gaze held no sympathy. Shrugging, he
pulled out the tracing, trying to hold it steady so she could see it. He wasn't
sure if his hands were shaking from the cold or fear of being caught in a lie.
"Can you do something like that?"

She took it from him but didn't look at it. "I don't do tattoos. I do readings. I read your palm, your cards, your auras. I make candles, too. I find you
love and tell you your lucky numbers," she recited in a bored tone. When he
didn't answer her, she stated, "Mario does tattoos." She glanced at the drawing and shoved it back. "Mario's not here."

"Do you know when he will be back?"

"No." She stepped back, her gaze riveted a little above his right shoulder. It made him want to turn around to check if there was company, but he
saw her hand firmly gripping the door knob and was afraid that if he gave her
the chance, she'd slam the door in his face.

"Well," he shuffled for a moment then stepped closer to the opening
of the door, breaking her gaze and bringing back normal eye contact. The
warmth from inside filtered out and caressed his face. "Could I leave a message?" He stuffed the paper in his pocket and tried to look nonchalant.

She didn't answer immediately. She seemed to be weighing something
with great care. Maybe if he asked her for a card reading he could work on
her with less suspicion; besides, at least he could warm up. He opened his
mouth to ask, but she put a finger to her lips and looked—no, peered—just
beyond his shoulder. Whatever she saw, her face drained of color. "Be gone!"
she hissed, and shut the door swiftly in his face. He hardly had time to get his
nose out of the way.

He raised his fist to pound on the door but thought better of it. He
slid back into his car. The sound of the running engine was comforting as he
headed back toward the hub of the city. Everything seemed so unnaturally
still. Guess it was the snow.

His thoughts drifted over the short conversation with the woman he supposed was Rosie. She'd recognized that design, there was no doubt about it. Evidently this tattoo had a history, just as he thought. But what the hell had she kept looking at behind him?

He cruised by a row of neon-lighted bars on Cameron Street, searching for the next address, finally pulling in front of the last bar on the block. The opposite side of the street was dark, the buildings broken and deserted. Usually parking was a problem anywhere in Harrisburg, but the weather seemed to have damped all but the staunchest of drinkers on this block.

The empty street crouched before him.

Dead quiet.

Lou opened the trunk and took out his camera bag. He rummaged for a few minutes, connecting and disconnecting lenses until he was satisfied and stuck his light meter and a couple of rolls of film in his jacket pocket. He threw the bag back in the trunk and slung the camera over his shoulder, double-checking that he had closed the lid securely before he moved away from the car. He wasn't worried about anyone stripping it—he left it looking like a junk mobile on purpose.

The basement entrance to Tattoo World could be reached by a set of steps leading down from the sidewalk. It appeared walk-in trade was popular here because the door was ajar and puddles of muddy snow glazed the white linoleum inside the door. The thunder and whine of heavy metal music filtered past him, rumbling on its way up to street level.

Lou pushed open the door. Stale cigarette smoke clung to the air. The front room was decorated from floor to ceiling with colorful framed designs for tattoos and close-up photos of various body parts that already carried them. A bulletin board littered with newspaper clippings and magazine articles on subjects ranging from Harleys to tattoos leaned against the right wall. The white linoleum floor was surprisingly well kept (except for that spot by the door), and the owner of the place obviously took great pains to make it appear as antiseptic as possible under the circumstances. The ceiling was slung with white acoustical tiles, and the walls, what could be seen of them, were done in simulated birch paneling. Cheap but clean.

An invisible hand cut the music and a short, wiry fellow sidled out from the back room. Lou could see a young brunette, whose hair never seemed to stop, in the client chair, her shoulder exposed, a tattoo half completed. Her long legs clad in black leather wound around one chair leg. There was a large floor-to-ceiling mirror behind her. Lou figured it was as much for the customer's benefit as for the owner's, who could watch the front of the shop from the back room without any problem. Beside her was an old cafeteria-style table filled with paints and tools of the trade.

"Can I help you, fella?" Lou quickly sized up the artist, choosing his tactic. The artist sported a head of flaming red hair, temporarily squashed by a black leather cap that looked like it would spring off the curls at any given moment. He wore a black tee-shirt, sleeves rolled up to expose matching dragons spitting fire and snakes. A Marlboro pack clung tightly to his breast pocket. His eyes were sneaky-grey. They reminded Lou of bits of dirty ice.

"Just admiring your work," remarked Lou, motioning to some of the pictures on the wall. Lou took his time, carefully gazing at the full-color body art pictures on the wall. He watched the artist size him up out of the corner of his eye. Bushy-head's eyes stuck on the camera, moved on, then snapped back to it, like a moth to a flame. *Good,* thought Lou. *He's going for the bait.*

"You've got quite a collection here," chatted Lou.

"Been at it a long time. You want a tattoo?"

Lou grinned sheepishly. "To tell you the truth, I've always hated needles. I'm a freelance photographer, work for some of the newspapers around here." He handed Bushy-head his business card. "I'm looking for something different for a photo shoot. Do you mind if I watch you while you work?"

Bushy-head glanced back at the girl perched on the stool. "Don't mind if she don't."

The girl shrugged her bare shoulder. Bushy-head returned to the back room. Lou followed, removing his camera from his shoulder.

"Mind if I take a few pictures?" he asked the girl. She shook her head, her eyes never straying from the hand mirror she was using to bounce the reflection of the work in progress.

"Suit yourself," she said.

Lou busied himself with his light meter, and took several shots trying to work around that blasted mirror. He would be lucky if they didn't all flash out. He asked the appropriate photojournalist questions. Bushy-hair had been in the biz for over fifteen years. He rode with a local biker group in his younger days, his tattoo art scattered on human flesh from Maine to California. He'd even done a few rock stars and an assortment of Beverly Hills "bitches." A few years ago he hurt his back in an accident when some dumb fuck drunk hit him coming off an exit ramp on 15. The buddy he was riding with had to be peeled off the pavement—he wasn't that much luckier. His insurance gave him the usual hassle and if it wouldn't have been for the help he got from ABATE, the victims' rights group, he didn't know where he'd have wound up. As it was, he won a half-decent insurance claim, paid off his medical bills, and had a little left over to rent out this studio from the guy who owned the bar upstairs. He was one of the lucky ones, he said.

His story was practiced, as if he'd told it a thousand times. Before he'd finished, Lou was holding an application to join ABATE, and had forked over a ten-dollar donation for a tee-shirt and promised to canvass his friends for the Christmas toy drive next year. He also learned the guy's name—Paints.

The girl in the chair smiled. Her teeth were rotten around the edges, but other than that, she wasn't half bad. "He gets everybody," she said.

Paints finished up, gave the girl instructions for taking care of her portable art work, and told her to come back in sixty days for a touch-up, free of charge. Lou scrutinized her shoulder as Paints bandaged it. The guy did beautiful work. She had chosen a phoenix and the colors were so vivid it looked as if it were about to take flight from her creamy flesh.

By now it was quarter to one in the morning. The girl paid him and sauntered out, promising to send a friend of hers who wanted a pink unicorn with wings around to the studio next week. Lou capped up the lens of his camera and stuck the used rolls of film in his jacket pocket.

"How about a beer upstairs?" he asked.

"That's cool," said Paints. "Guess I can't interest you in a tattoo?"

"Maybe some other time," Lou grimaced at the tools scattered on the table. "Let me lock up my camera and I'll join you in a minute."

The bar was non-descript as bars go. A neon sign hanging in the greasy front window proclaimed the joint was "Moe's." Clientele must have been light because the heavy layers of smoke so prominent in a busy fleahole like this were virtually non-existent. The room was fairly large with dull light and grill smells drifting from the kitchen in the back. Two pool tables, vacant, took up the right side of the place; a long bar ran along the left. There was a jukebox, playing dumb, past the pool tables. Paints, perched on a wobbly stool, sloshed down his first beer. Lou ordered one for himself.

At round six Paints still hung tough, as if he hadn't consumed a drop. Lou's tolerance was good, but not that good. He hoped he could get enough down to keep Paints from noticing he was only nursing his fifth. He glanced at his watch and was surprised to see it was about two. For the last hour they had joked about women, bikes, and sports, and talked seriously about art and politics, which impressed Lou and almost made him forget why he was spending time in this obscure rathole.

He watched Moe mop up the bar and wash out a few glasses. There were only three other people in the bar, all men, all looking sloshed and bored.

Lou waited until two of the drunks shambled out and Moe angled for the back room—*probably to scrape the grill and shoo out the rats*, he thought wryly. When Moe was safely out of earshot he took a gamble and pulled out the drawing of the tattoo found on Binky and the Conner boy. It was now or never.

"Friend of mine says he might like to have this one done for him, but he's not sure if it belongs to any particular group. He says he doesn't want to mess with anybody's colors. You ever seen it before?"

Paints' eyes were glassy but his hand was steady. He unfolded the paper and stared at it for a long time, shifting his gaze momentarily around the room. "I already talked to the cops about this," he said in a low tone. "I don't know nothin'," he barked loud enough for the last remaining patron to hear. Paints slipped off the bar stool. It swirled on one leg and crashed to the cracked linoleum below. A piece of it spun across the floor. "Moe," he shouted, ignoring the wounded stool, "give this asshole his money back; I'll pay for my own brew." Moe popped his head around the corner, throwing a hard gaze at Lou. He nodded, looked at the broken stool, and shrugged. Paints slapped some money on the bar and started to walk out.

"Wait!" called Lou. "I'm not a cop!"

Paints stopped at the door. "I don't care who the hell you are, but one thing's for sure, you've got trouble in your hands and I don't want to be any part of it. And friend, if you've got any sense in your head, you'll let it be. If you don't, you won't be long for this planet!" He banged the door with his fist and walked out.

Lou caught up with him outside, slipping in a light layer of snow. He grabbed Paints' arm and whirled him around. Paints raised his fist and popped Lou squarely in the jaw. He may have been small but he wasn't soft. Lou lost his balance and fell backward in the snow, his rear end grazing a fire hydrant. He was having difficulty separating Paints from the traditional stars dancing in the air.

"Aw, shit, you didn't have to do that!" yelled Lou, his breath filling the cold air with a quick succession of moisture plumes.

Paints stood over him. "Shouldn't have touched me, man. I don't like nobody touching me." He stuck out his hand and helped Lou up. "Look, I value my life. I knew as soon as you walked in my place you were a snoop. Let's face it, no jerk would come out in this weather, at this time of night, to get a story on tattoos that he could get in the light of day. I also know that there are certain things in this world you don't mess with—and this is one of them."

He stood back, legs spread apart, arms across his chest, and regarded Lou with a penetrating eye. "You're really not that bad of a chump, so fer your own good, I'm tellin' ya to back the fuck off. I don't know why you're wavin' this paper around, but it's sure to bring you trouble. These people are nothing to mess with!"

"So it is an organization!" exclaimed Lou, brushing himself off and stamping his feet. "I knew it!"

"Shit, it doesn't take an advanced IQ to figure that one out. Even the cops know it's a group of mean fuckers. Look, man, I've told you enough already." Paints side-stepped and moved toward his shop.

"Wait! You didn't tell me anything I haven't thought of," pleaded Lou. "Can't you at least tell me if you ever done that tattoo for anyone?"

"Why would I tell you something like that? I told you, man, these fellows are not playing kiddie games. Leave it and go find some hot little numbers to photograph instead. Save the heroics for someone else. I can tell you right now you are not equipped to deal with these guys. When they get wind of you—and they will—you'll never know what hit you. For your sake, I hope your karma is clean. Besides, I couldn't do that tattoo anyway, if you are really that interested, which means I've never done one, doesn't it?"

"Can't or won't?" asked Lou, pressing as much as he dared because Paints kept moving away from him.

"Can't."

"What do you mean, you can't? It looks like a simple design."

"I mean I won't because the dyes they use are mixed with human blood. There. Are you happy? Now leave me alone!" Paints continued to back away. Lou kept inching to make up the distance between them.

"Blood?" Lou knew he was hammering but he couldn't help himself.

"Look, Lou, or whatever your name is, I'm not into kink. I've done some pretty wild shit in my time but murder is out of my line. These people are crazy and their group is as old as the hills. Over seven hundred years, my man. Now, you don't look dangerous to me but you are mighty stupid. How many other people have you shown this tattoo to?"

Lou tried not to look nervous. "Three tattoo joints, including Rosie's, why?"

"Shit, have you opened up a can of worms. Rosie's people hate the Dark Men."

"Dark Men? Is that the name of the group?"

Paints grabbed Lou's arm and moved him over to the shadows of the bar. "It's not their real name, stupid, it's what people who know them call them. In fact the only people who know it are either friends of the deceased who double-crossed them or other family trads."

"Family trads? Like the Mafia?" sputtered Lou.

"Worse, stupid. Family traditionals gone bad."

"Do the cops know about this?" Lou felt a little doubtful—what could be worse than the mob? Maybe Paints was just pulling his leg to get him off the real gang, maybe like a street thing.

"They know, but they're not going to do anything about it." Paints flicked his eyes nervously up and down the deserted street.

Dead quiet.

"Since you're so big on mysteries, bud," he sneered, "you figure out why the cops haven't moved in on anybody." Paints spun on his heel and moved toward the studio stairs.

"But how do I find them, these Dark Men?" Lou called.

Paints looked over his shoulder. "Find them? You better hope to hell they don't find you! And don't come back now, hear?" he hollered as he disappeared into the building, muttering to himself about human stupidity loud enough for Lou to catch.

Lou shook his head, staring at the empty sidewalk, listening to the resounding bang of Paints' door and the smack of a deadbolt being thrown into place.

And now, dead quiet.

Those last few beers were kicking in and he felt a little woozy. The closer he got to his car, the worse his head pounded. He was glad he'd already packed the camera away. He didn't think he could negotiate the trunk lock at this particular moment, given the fact he could hardly get the key into the damned driver's door. The lock finally gave and he checked the street one last time for any sign of life.

As cities go, Harrisburg wasn't too bad. Most murders were crimes of passion, results of domestic disputes or a slip of the tongue in a bar. Now and then the bad asses from Baltimore or Jersey plopped a body on the turnpike outside the city, but on the whole, it wasn't as bad as York. However, it was still risky business to be drunk and on the street at two in the morning.

Instead of waiting for the car to warm up, he pulled out and headed across the bridge to Route 15. The Dodge shook in complaint but didn't die on him. He checked his rearview mirror, coaxing the vehicle away from the curb. For a moment he thought he saw a black shadow slipping down the cement steps, but it melted before he could register anything other than snow and exhaust vapor.

chapter twenty-nine

SITTING QUIETLY IN HIS OPULENT OFFICE, Mason Trout, director and owner of Whiskey Springs' Serenity Funeral Home, busied himself with the last-minute touches for the day's funerals. It was only 8:30 AM, but he had a packed house (so to speak) and he wanted everything to run smoothly.

Five blocks away, Lou Strader slept off the booze, oblivious to the fact that his apartment had been searched and his list of leads on the tattoo taken. Nor was he aware of the morning headlines—namely the murder of a tattooist named Paints and a fire at a place called Rosie's in Harrisburg.

Mason examined his appointment book one last time. There would be five funerals during the daylight hours and two evening viewings at the sprawling limestone estate of Serenity. It was going to be a very tight squeeze. Mason was glad he bought that fourth hearse last summer. After Christmas, old people die like flies.

185

His finger ran down the schedule. All seemed to be in order, though there was that body the cops found in Harrisburg at a tattoo parlor this morning to be dealt with. The Dauphin County coroner had phoned him on the QT. Seemed like it belonged to one of those farm clans up top of South Mountain and he'd be getting that one too after the forensic team got done with it. That would be a closed casket. From the description, it was a bad one. No paints needed for this fellow. The last one on his list, scheduled for cremation, was that Binky Carlisle kid. Not a problem, though—no service, no nothing. Just trash and burn.

But it was the afternoon funerals, starting at one, that disturbed the usually calm Mason to the point where the smallest unfinished detail sent him into a mental tizzy. Outwardly, he remained the ever solid, ever constant Mason.

The first (and the one for which he felt the saddest, which was rare for him) was for Terry Anderson, with services officiated by Lee Becker. Thinking of Lee brought Elizabeyta uncomfortably to mind. He'd found the details on her feud for her and if he had time, he'd stop by her house this evening and give her the information. Of course, he could give it to Lee … He decided not to carry the thought any further. No point in it.

The funeral parlor had been in Mason's family for three generations and he took a great deal of grief (so to speak) for it. Most people didn't like to be friends with him because he was always knee deep in death. Elizabeyta was probably the same. He often wondered how he ended up doing this, considering how much he hated the thought of it as a kid. But his was the only funeral home within a twenty-mile radius. The money was good. He sure couldn't complain.

At two was Jeffrey Conner. His skin crawled on that puppy. A closed-casket affair, this one. There would be newspaper reporters, television people—he wiped his brow at the thought of it. And then, of course, there would be Brother Hank officiating the service. Mason's stomach flopped at the thought of it. Brother Hank was the biggest slimeball he'd ever known.

Actually, they were a bit alike, Brother Hank and himself. Mason didn't believe in all the religious clap trap he said every day to unfortunate mourners and he knew from past experience that Brother Hank was no better. Mason casually wondered if that woman Hank was playing with would be in attendance. Nothing was sacred in this town. He also knew Louise would politely walk all over the woman, should she get the chance.

Hank was five years younger than Mason, but acted every inch his superior when he was around. Mason abhorred Brother Hank and he was well aware that Lee Becker despised him, too. The last time Lee and Hank had back-to-back funerals, Mason could have sworn there would be a third one by the time the day was through. He wasn't sure who would have won, but he personally hoped the God he didn't believe in would choose Lee to be the victor.

He snapped the appointment book shut and drifted out into the main hall to find his wife at the front desk answering phone calls, fielding eager mourners, and directing the flower traffic. She was a peach but Christ was her true husband. Mason often felt the equivalent of a mistress, as sordid as it may sound. If Louise hadn't been brought up Lutheran, she would have made a great nun. She refused to have children, which Mason often held against her. Yep, they should have stuck her in a convent at birth. But she was so darn generous in every other aspect of her life he had trouble staying angry at her for long.

Today she was dressed in a navy blue suit. A white blouse spilled volumes of lace from the small starched collar right down to the black patent leather belt at her tiny waist. Her white-blonde hair, a gift from Lady Clairol, was pulled back too severely but it didn't detract from the overall femininity of the woman. She also had great legs and he smiled at the tippy-tap sound echoing from her stiletto heels as she marched across the blue and white linoleum, stringing a florist's driver by an invisible tether behind her.

He turned from his reverie when the driver of the morning's first hearse entered for last-minute instructions. Yes, things should go smoothly, at least until one.

The house started to rock at 12:30 when the driver of the second hearse called to report that the motor mounts in his vehicle had broken when he tried to beat out a diaper service truck at a green light. The massive jolt of the motor pounding at the hood sent a backlash through the car, leaving Mrs. Curry and her coffin smack in the center of Fifth and Main, where a cement truck promptly pulverized both the occupant and green metal housing together.

Mrs. Curry's coherent daughter was threatening to sue. The other one had been carted away to York Hospital after suffering a massive coronary at the sight of the marriage between her deceased mother and the cement truck.

It was at this moment of revelation, Mason was to discover later, that Brother Hank pulled up in a rented white limo, with at least fifteen or more cars trailing up the driveway behind. Mason turned to look out his office window to see Brother Hank postulating on the macadam, his parishioners joining him and leaving their cars smack in the middle of the driveway, blocking the hearse exit for the Anderson funeral, not yet in progress. Mason dropped the phone.

Louise appeared at his door, waving a message that Timothy Reed's body had disappeared from St. Joseph's morgue and they wanted to know, if by chance, a Serenity employee had picked it up early. That was a good one.

Louise flashed a look of prim dismay at Mason's open mouth, took in the dangling phone cord leading to the floor, and swung her gaze to the scene unfolding in the parking lot. Without a word, she turned neatly on one slender heel, her mouth set firmly in a much dreaded crease of holy determination, and clicked a hasty exit. The quick tappity-tap rhythm of her heels was a signal of battle to any employee and several moved out of her way as she marched out the front door.

Mason gulped, drew in much-needed air, and found his vocal chords. He made arrangements with the driver to have the hearse towed after relief arrived and buzzed the downstairs intercom, giving directions to one of his apprentices to take out the fourth hearse and sweep up what was left of Mrs. Curry, if anything. Shit and double shit, but thank God for that fourth hearse. And yes, thank God for Louise.

By the time he got off the phone, she was standing in the parking lot without a coat or a shiver. By the set of her shoulders and the rapid fire of her mouth, Mason knew she was insisting that Brother Hank would have to move his entourage. Brother Hank's expression was one of machismo in God and he wasn't budging.

Not in the least daunted, Louise stepped forward, stood on her patent leather tippy-toes, and whispered something in his ear. Brother Hank threw her a nasty look, but stepped back and called his people together. Louise officiously directed the cars, her nose stuck in the air, the lace dripping gracefully from her slender arm. Brother Hank hustled his winter-tinged flock into the tiled reception area with a red-nosed Louise bringing up the rear. Mason knew she was infuriated by the rude comments and noise in "her" holy sanctum—he hadn't been married to her for fifteen years without learning something.

Mr. and Mrs. Anderson had arrived a few minutes prior to the fiasco, and as Mason headed toward his wife to still the anger he saw simmering in her blue eyes, he saw Mr. Anderson frantically looking for somewhere to take poor Mrs. Anderson, who was being pivoted and wheeled about on his arm like a broken puppet. She looked pale and out of it—drugs, most likely. He doubted if she could even speak coherently.

Mason caught Louise's glare and nodded toward the floundering couple. The fire melted from her eyes and an unspoken message passed between them—Mason was to proceed to the Andersons; Louise was quite capable of herding the animal types to where they belonged, once she figured out where to put the growing crowd.

The interior of Mason's funeral home was unique, as motels for the dead go. In the seventies he had the old structure completely torn down. In its place he built a unique circular structure of grey stone with two above-ground levels and two underground levels. Level 2 basement was for the preparation of bodies, a kitchen, and sleeping quarters for a few of his assistants. Level 1 basement was a parking garage for his vehicles, which included the four hearses, three "company" black sedans, and room for the ministerial vehicles, early-bird customers, and whatever else the cat might drag in, including an occasional police officer or reporter. In general, anyone who would make family members of the deceased nervous.

Ground level consisted of seven receiving rooms, the large circular reception area, and his office. The second level housed a showroom of caskets (one grieving wife remarked that it looked like a showroom for Dracula's castle), but it was done tastefully. Louise also had an office up here but she rarely used it. She preferred the counter in the reception area. Mason didn't blame her. It was light and airy down there, with lots of windows across the front that looked out to a wide porch with six great white pillars and a pleasant view of South Mountain beyond. In light of this, the second floor was rather depressing.

Louise was now shoving the last of the wailing mourners into the spacious reception area. Across the circular expanse, Lee Becker emerged from the Daffodil Room, where Terry had been placed. Mason could see the anger creep from Lee's white collar up his throat and into his cheeks as he took in the chaos with Brother Hank blubbering in the lead. This was not good.

Mason again made eye contact with Louise and jerked his head toward the Gold Room. She raised a delicate eyebrow, but nodded. God, how he hated to do that—the place would probably be in shambles before the day was through, but he had no other place to put the growing number of people now entering the reception area. He idly thought of that battery commercial, "it keeps going and going …" On the heels of the mourners (Mason thought that Hank probably paid most of them to attend) were the news people.

Louise pasted on her most motherly "I am here to console your suffering" smile as soon as she saw the reporters, and led them through the double doors to the Gold Room. Mason crossed over to the Andersons, glad to see that Lee had kept his temper under control and busied himself with the unfortunate Mrs. Anderson. Mason uttered his apologies about Hank's entrance. Mrs. Anderson didn't appear to care one way or the other, as she was temporarily residing in another dimension. Mr. Anderson only shook his head. Lee swallowed hard and rolled his eyes. Mason saw the fury there and decided not to placate any further.

Lee took Mrs. Anderson's limp free arm and together, he and Mr. Anderson ushered her into the Daffodil Room. It was now five minutes to one. Once Mr. and Mrs. Anderson were seated near the front of the casket, several friends and relatives passed before them in the obligatory consoling line. Lee left the room and snagged Mason outside the doors.

"What the hell does he think he's doing?" Lee asked Mason incredulously as he pulled the double doors shut behind him.

"Honestly, Lee, I haven't the vaguest idea. He's doing the Conner boy's service, but that's not scheduled until two. The family didn't request a viewing so I guess he's getting his dibs in before the service. I'll bet you that scoundrel is passing the collection plate right now."

Louise emerged from the Gold Room, shutting the doors behind her with the snap of authority. She crossed the now empty reception area, filled with muddy footprints and pieces of slush, slipping a time or two before she reached her husband and Lee.

"Well, I never!" she exclaimed. Her usually perfect demeanor was ruffled. "I may be an upstanding Christian woman, but this is ridiculous! My

God would never stand for that!" she cried and thrust her arm in the direction of the closed Gold Room doors.

"Precisely my point," edged Mason, who loved it when his wife got a glimpse of the mottled mess of religious philosophy.

She threw him a wary glance, but he gave her a genuine smile and squeezed her arm. "You did wonderfully, Louise. Whatever did you say to Brother Hank out in the parking lot? I didn't think a tank would move him."

Louise looked momentarily guilty, but smiled in triumph. "I simply told him that first, I would call the police to physically remove him, and second, I would call my brother at the garage and tell him to bring over his tow truck. When neither of those threats worked I also told him that before I did any calling, as part owner of Serenity, I would not permit him to pass his collection plate, and if he did, I would confiscate all the money and give it to charity! Guess he didn't want to miss out on glories to come, so he moved."

"Praise the Lord!" said Mason flippantly, then regretted it as her expression soured. It was an old argument, after all, and this was neither the time nor the place to enjoy it.

Her disapproval fleeting, she turned to Lee and extended her hand. "Lee, I'm sorry I didn't see you come in. How are you doing? You don't look like you've been sleeping well."

Lee smiled and returned the handshake. Mason noted with amusement that Louise was using her "firm grip" handshake. It was so odd for such a small woman that it always managed to put her in control, as it did now. She was giving Lee a chance to recover from his anger and assuring him with her grip that everything was under control—at least for the moment. Again, Mason was grateful for Louise.

"Actually, it's been a pretty rough week," Lee answered. "Thanks for fielding the Mad Hatter's party out there. I don't think I could have kept my cool as well as you did."

Louise smiled her most heavenly smile. "That's the idea, Pastor Becker, to come to each other's aid when needed, to provide strength to those who deserve it ..."

"And to kick ass when the situation calls for it," interjected Mason with a grin.

Louise sniffed, rolling her eyes at Mason. "We can't all be perfect all the time. I'm sure you'll be there for me someday when I need it."

"What are they doing in there?" asked Mason.

Louise frowned. "Well, first they milled around a bit. Then they did a prayer where everybody held up their hands and moved their hips. When they finished that, Brother Hank passed the plate. Or, rather, she passed the plate." Louise rolled her eyes in obvious distaste.

"Maybe we should roll the casket in there to keep them occupied," suggested Mason.

Louise's snort was delicate. "I'll buzz Jim downstairs to bring it up. I'm also going to have Steve and Martin get dressed and get up here to keep the lid on the pressure cooker. Look at these floors, why don't you? What a disgrace. That will have to be cleaned up immediately!" She shook her head at the mess, then turned to Lee. "You've not been to dinner with us in ages and you can expect a call from me next week with an invitation."

Lee grinned. "I'd be delighted."

"Good!" She said her farewells to Lee and delicately picked her way across the wet tile until she reached firm ground, her tippy-taps becoming more rapid and pronounced.

Lee looked at his watch. "I'd better be getting in there. You think you can keep the dogs at bay until I take care of Terry?"

"No problem. I'm going to send Jim in with you after he delivers the Conner boy, and I'm keeping Martin and Steve with me in the Gold Room. We'll bar the doors if we have to," said Mason.

Lee slapped him on the shoulder in thanks. He hesitated at the door to the Daffodil Room, smiled at Mason, then stepped inside.

Mason loitered at the door, deciding to wait for Jim. He might need help negotiating the casket off the elevator and over to the Gold Room.

Something brushed his elbow, startling him. He was shocked to be standing face to face with a woman so colorless that he thought she would collapse at any moment. He quelled the thought and smiled his best funeral director smile.

"Mrs. Conner," he said kindly. "What are you doing out here? I thought you were already in the Gold Room."

"You're Mason Trout, aren't you?" she whispered, glancing furtively about.

"You know I am, Mrs. Conner," he said, keeping his tone gentle. He noticed an old bruise turning brown that ran across her jaw line. "How can I help you?"

She grabbed his shoulder with such force he thought she might dislocate it. Her dark eyes pierced him to his soul. "It's him who killed my boy!"

Mason looked about but saw no one. "I'm sorry, Mrs. Conner. I think you need to sit down and relax. Is the rest of your family in the Gold Room?" Mason looked around frantically for Louise. She was good at this sort of thing.

"I tell you it is the Dark Man who killed my boy and that foolish Brother Hank won't listen to me. Alls he cares about is the money he'll make off the publicity. My baby's dead and I want the man who killed him to pay, I do!" Her voice rose and he laid his hand lightly on hers, hoping to quell the rising electric whine he heard in her voice.

"What man, Mrs. Conner?"

"The Dark Man. I tell you, he killed my boy. I heard them talking on the phone. Jeffrey thought they were going to set up the Reed boy but it was

Jeffrey who was arranging his own death, and my baby didn't know it!" Her eyes were wild, the whites red. She was to the point of screeching now and Mason hoped Jim would get up here and help him. The woman was obviously insane with grief. Mrs. Conner grabbed him by the front of his black suit and hung on for dear life. "It's my cousin, you see; he's the Dark Man! I hate him. I've always hated him. The Witch. Only the Belladonna Witch can destroy him! I knows she's in town! I seen her for myself. And the Dark Man wants to get her. Get her and kill her. Get her and drain her blood. Get her and skin her alive, I tell you! He's going to drink her blood!"

Uh-oh, thought Mason. The best thing to do was humor her until help arrived, but the obvious reference to Elizabeyta stopped him cold. His brain slowed down.

"Why are you telling me all this, Mrs. Conner? Do you want me to get your husband?" He thought he'd seen him earlier, talking to Brother Hank.

"No!" she screamed. "He's part of them, too, but he don't know they killed his son yet. He's away. I cain't find him neither! I tell you because the Belladonna Witch is your woman!"

Mason stepped backward, tearing his suit from her grasp. "That's not true!" he sputtered, adjusting his suitcoat. "I'm a married man!"

Mrs. Conner all but danced around him. "It's true. It's true. I've got the gift. Had it since I was a babe. Jason don't know. I never told. You must tell the Witch!"

Mason looked out across her bobbing head to see Brother Hank standing quietly by the Gold Room door. Oh, shit. His expression showed avid interest with a glint of evil about the edges. Mason's stomach lurched toward his toes but before he could process a worthy thought, chaos swarmed about him. Later, Mason would have trouble putting the events at hand in their correct order.

Someone came off the elevator, presumably Jim, and rushed toward Mason and Mrs. Conner. Mrs. Conner got down on her knees and grasped Mason's legs with a bear grip from hell. Brother Hank ran forward. The Gold Room doors burst open and Louise and Steve strode out with several of the standing-room-only types on their heels, including a number of the reporters. Everyone converged on Mrs. Conner. Flash bulbs were popping, a woman screamed, and twittering voices raised to a sea of pandemonium.

A big man with wiggling jowls strode toward the chaos. He was encased in a rumpled suit that threatened to pop at every known seam. Mason thought for sure the man would be naked if he moved any faster. As he drew closer, the smell of alcohol surged before him. He pushed through the crowd, demanding to know what was the matter with his daughter, pointing a finger at Mrs. Conner. He seized her (Mason actually heard one of the seams of his suit tearing unceremoniously). Mrs. Conner promptly fainted. Mason instinctively snatched her limp form out of the fat man's grasp and into Louise's confused arms. Louise, without compunction, passed her back along to the fat man who she actually thought was one of her employees, until too late. The inebriated fellow slung Mrs. Conner over his shoulder like a rag doll and marched back to the Gold Room, Brother Hank striding quickly beside him, patting her limp hand.

Louise clapped her hands in the din of reporters and mourners. "That's enough now. That will be quite enough. This is a place to respect the dead, not participate in a three ring circus!"

Slowly the crowd broke apart. With the air of a queen, Louise led many of the scattered souls back to the Gold Room, leaving Mason to deal with the rest.

chapter thirty

EE THOUGHT THE AFTERNOON WOULD NEVER come to a close. A nasty wind swirled tentacles of ice and snow around the mourners as they huddled together in the cemetery. The sky overhead was as gloomy as the subject of the eulogy and Lee had to repeatedly remind himself not to lick his lips—they were already cracked and bleeding.

He felt disconnected from the scene before him. Both Mr. and Mrs. Anderson appeared to be barely breathing, their skin tones blending with the colorless landscape. He wondered if Terry was here, floating around somewhere in this cold and miserable air, overseeing the grief and pain of the occasion. Although there were times in the past when he wished the dead could watch, today he sincerely hoped they couldn't.

The snow began again. Would it never pass them by—this cold and humorless weather that claimed so many dead this season? The weather service said the front had stalled and the worst was yet to come. How many more would die in this world of endless white? The longer he gazed at the scene before him, the further his mind buried itself under the weight of white grief.

A young lady to his left, bundled from head to foot in winter gear so only her red and puffy eyes denoted a living being beneath, let out a muffled moan, snapping his mind to the duties at hand. He was not sure if it was the cold, the coming of yet another snowflake, or her grief that forced the mewing sound from her lips. His gaze swept the twenty or so who had bravely ignored the elements to gather here and he decided to cut this short. Enough was enough.

The last red rose was set atop the white and silver coffin, signaling the mourners to depart with speed. Only Lee stayed to watch it as it descended into the vault originally reserved for Mr. and Mrs. Anderson alone. He usually prided himself on the control he held over his emotions at these affairs, but this was different. He'd slept with her, for God's sake—enjoyed picnics, movies, books ... or maybe he was considering his own mortality ... he just didn't know any more. He cried, and as he did so, the tears froze to his cheeks. Small icicles attempted to form on his chin and melted as he buried it to his chest in wracking sobs. Through blurred vision he looked down at the casket, hearing the grinding of the winch, like a soul being torn from the body, while it descended to its final resting place. He saw the roses through a river of tears—resembling a puddle of rich and clotted blood.

A driving force hit him on the back of his neck. He crumpled to his knees in a snowdrift, his gloved hands clasped together tightly, his body doubling into a fetal position. The world rushed in shadows about him. He groggily wondered who, or what, had leveled him before he was lost in a tumult of muted greys and blacks.

When he regained his senses, he found himself lying in a clearing beside a roaring fire in what looked to be a forest. It was a far cry from the flat expanse of the cemetery he thought he was supposed to be in. Towering firs swung in muted breezes above him. Well, it certainly wasn't a graveyard, of that he was absolutely sure. An old woman with snow-white hair sat across from him, quietly watching through the flames of the inferno that separated them. No, that was wrong—it was a campfire between them, nothing more. Perhaps it was the heat that made her figure appear surreal and wavering.

He sat up, shaking his head to clear it. He rubbed the back of his neck, thinking to find a tender bruise or lump. There was nothing there.

"Won't work," she said.

"I beg your pardon?" he replied as he eyed her closely. Was her skin blue?

"Can't shake your head to get back, son." She grinned and a lonely fang protruded from her wrinkled lips. If it was possible, she really looked blue now.

Lee blinked in confusion. Something was different in this place. He wasn't cold, but that could be because of the proximity of the fire. No, there was something else. He didn't feel the heat from it, either. In fact, he felt nothing. And there was the sunshine! He looked overhead at the vaulted ceiling of tree branches and icicles to see the sun peeking through the limbs and bouncing off the ice. The entire view appeared to be a prism of rainbow color.

"Breathtaking, isn't it?" asked the old woman, following his gaze.

"Where am I?"

"In between, son … in between."

He studied her face and realized that she was not as old as she had first appeared, or was it a trick of the fantastic light and color that deceived him now? It didn't matter; she was still blue. There was no such thing as a blue person—unless, of course, the person was dead. This lady appeared far from it.

She was dressed in some sort of white and black animal skin with a massive wolf pelt for a cloak. He wondered if she was an Indian of some sort, but didn't have the energy or inclination to ask. Besides, he had never heard of a blue Indian with fangs.

"You'll not be here for long," she was saying. "I need to talk to you. Very soon the people of your time will take care of you and you must leave this place. We may only have a matter of minutes so I would appreciate it if you kept silent."

Lee nodded in agreement. What else could he do? Her voice carried both command and compassion.

"You are in a place that is not a place—a void in time."

He looked at her blankly.

She continued, "You are between birth and death, joy and sorrow, traveling on the wheel of existence." She shifted her weight and he realized she was sitting on a log. At her feet was a large, panting wolf. He started, his heart picking up pace, but the animal neither looked in his direction nor paid attention to the smell of fear Lee knew he was producing. Why hadn't he seen the wolf before now?

"My name," she said, "is Calliech Bleu." At the sound of her name, the wolf whined. She stroked its massive head. It yawned and relaxed back against her legs. "You can call me Cally."

Lee swallowed hard. She appeared to be growing younger with each syllable she spoke. "Pleased to meet you," he whispered.

She ignored him. "I'll get right to the purpose of this conversation. I'm concerned about Elizabeyta. You know Elizabeyta Belladonna, don't you?"

"Ah, yes."

"There's a monkey in the works and she has begun to block not only the training she brought with her to this lifetime, but many of the lessons my tradition taught her as well. This has put her in a great deal more danger than was initially planned. To put it bluntly, the plans of the universe have gone slightly awry."

Cally continued to stroke the animal at her feet. She was silent for a moment. "If Elizabeyta cannot move the blocks herself, she will die a most unfortunate death. She will not complete the tasks that have been set out for her, and hundreds of souls will have to reincarnate again because of her error. Lives on the earth plane are like school. Humans and others go there to learn lessons, acquire knowledge, and return here to hopefully travel forward."

"Where is here?" asked Lee. He knew he shouldn't interrupt, but he really was trying to understand.

The woman lowered silken white lashes over her black eyes only to open them again over brilliant violet eyes. Lee drew in his breath and decided to keep quiet from this point on.

"Here," she said shortly, "is where you left from before and where you will come back to again. It doesn't surprise me that you don't remember; few of your kind do. Actually, you should be damned glad you made it here at all—there are some unpleasant stops along the way. The fact that you are here now says a lot for you. However, I'm not in the least thrilled at your presence."

Well, thought Lee, *that was blunt enough.* Personally, he didn't want to be here either and he sure as hell wished her eyes would change back to black. That violet blaze was getting to him.

For the first time she smiled, as if she'd heard him. The tree tops overhead rattled slightly. Her smile vaporized as she glanced upward in irritation. The breeze didn't make it down to the clearing. She licked her lips and leaned forward. "Look, son, it's soon time for you to go, so I'll be quick about this. You are the monkey in the works. I'll be more than blunt—stay away from Elizabeyta. You can't help her, you haven't got any gifts, no power to speak of, and your God archetype is losing ground in your mind as well as in your world. Without connection to Divinity, no matter what the positive religion, you are worthless to her. You bought into technology and sold off your power of the Old Ways. If she gets any more involved with you than she already is, she will surely die at the hands of the Blackthorn. He takes many of us each lifetime. Without you, she can beat him and be done with him forever. Then I can get my hands on him." She stretched out hands that were now young, vibrant, and strong. With shock, Lee's gaze traveled back to the woman's face. His heart skipped a beat. Her white hair had been instantly colored. It glowed with a sanguine sheen.

She didn't miss a beat in her conversation. "With you in the picture—well, there are many who will have to travel that road again, and I, for one, do not wish to be burdened with another religious war. You can thank me for bailing you out back there at the graveyard. If I hadn't brought you here, they would have finished you off. It was because of her I did it. She's asked for my help. I thought it was the least I could do, under the circumstances."

She picked at the wolf's fur. After a time she said, "It was one of the Blackthorn's boys, you know, who struck you from behind with a tire iron. I snatched you fast. Right now they are checking your body. They're pretty sure you're dead and are nervous about getting caught. Blackthorn's shields can't last forever, and he knows it. Knocking you off is a very stupid mistake on his part, but he is getting desperate. Believe me, you're not worth it, but it wasn't your time. I'm very devoted to duty, you know."

She sucked on a long, curled fingernail absently, muttering to herself. Finally, she spoke. "Elizabeyta is our hope, our shining star, our redeemer. If you really love her, let her go."

"But I can't let her go!" exclaimed Lee, rising quickly. The world about him seemed to tilt. When he managed to make focused sense out of it, Cally was again a very blue, very wizened creature.

"So says your tongue, young man," she spat, "but what about your heart? I hate to remind you, but you had to make this determination before, and failed miserably. Do us all a favor and just bail out, a coward like the last time. Oh, does the word 'coward' bother you a bit? It shouldn't. She once burned while you hid behind your holy order." She spit forcefully into the fire, then swung her head around with a menacing stare. Saliva dripped off the wild tooth. She didn't bother to wipe it away. "You stood placidly by while she was sacrificed by those stupid Aztec priests! You let her get eaten by lions, though you knew she was steadfast in her beliefs. You are the fool who takes up any religion that promises order—lifetime after lifetime!" Cally slapped the wolf's side in anger. Instead of growling at her, it growled at him.

Lee could feel his jaw hardening. She hit a nerve, bad memories that he couldn't quite grasp. He did not consider himself a coward. Calculating, perhaps, but not a coward. "I'd do anything for her. I'd never, ever let anything happen to her!"

Her face remained stony blue.

"So be it, fool!" The impact of her voice literally threw him back on the snowy ground. "You are a coward even to your own truth!" The energy of rage swirled around them both. The campfire roared in anger, as if it, too, in this strange place, was a living being. He vaguely noticed the snow he was lying in didn't feel wet and cold as snow should. In fact, it didn't feel like anything.

"But should you change your mind," she said, her hair now turning black as raven's feathers, her face that of a woman in her twenties, "remember my name. It will be the last word you utter on the other side!" The breeze picked up, rattling the branches above, building to a roar. The fire between them rose and licked the sky. The wolf howled and Lee squinted painfully as the sudden impact of flying ice and snow exploded in his face.

Someone grabbed his shoulder and shook it hard, forcing him to open his eyes. The clearing was gone, the fire was gone, and the blue woman, nowhere to be seen. Mason slapped his face with a gloved hand, pulling him to his knees, grunting with the effort to get him to stand.

Snow tickled his eyelashes. Large flakes fell into the abyss of the open grave, the coffin out of view.

"I came back because I had this really bad feeling," said Mason in a rushed voice. "I don't know what hit me. I dropped off the Andersons at their home and remembered their car was still at Serenity. Then for some reason I remembered that I hadn't seen you leave the cemetery. I mean, I often leave before you do, but I don't know. I just felt I had to come back."

"I'm glad you did," whispered Lee as he hung on to Mason's wool top coat, trying to pull himself up like a monkey. Monkey?

Lee's foot struck something hard in the snow—a tire iron.

"What's this?" asked Mason as he picked it up. "Trying to fix an invisible car? Why would you bring a tire iron to a funeral?"

Lee raised his arm to check the back of his head where he had been struck. There was nothing there.

Mason put his arm around Lee and led him over to his gently purring black sedan. "Look, Lee, we'll leave your car here and get it later. Right now I'm going to take you home and get one of the ladies from the church to come over and warm up some food and coffee. You sure look terrible. What happened to you out there? Maybe we should call a doctor."

Lee settled himself on the passenger side of the front seat, extending his hands to the heater. Mason stowed the tire iron in the back seat. "I don't know what happened, Mason. One minute I was in control, and the next, I was down on the ground. I must have blacked out for a few minutes but I don't think a doctor is necessary. I haven't eaten all day and it just got to me."

Mason threw him a critical eye. "A few minutes—hell, it takes a good twenty minutes to get to the Anderson place and back. You could have frozen to death! The wind chill factor is at least thirty below in that cemetery. Don't you remember anything?" asked Mason.

"No, not a thing," lied Lee. *Monkey* ... whispered his brain.

"Well where the devil was the guy who was taking care of the casket? Didn't he see you?"

"Guess not," answered Lee. *Monkey* ... came the whisper again. This time he wasn't sure it came from his own mind.

"How the hell could he have missed you? You were only two feet from the damn grave. He had to see you there!"

"Maybe he thought I was praying and didn't want to bother me," suggested Lee. "Pastor types are known to do that, you know." He cracked a smile and blood trickled from his chapped lips. *Monkey* ...

Mason shook his head. "What? I don't think so, mate; you looked pretty blue and out of it to me."

Lee slid a suspicious gaze at Mason, but his friend held only an expression of concern. Lee closed his eyes and slouched back into the plush, black seats of the sedan.

The shakes had started to set in as Mason helped Lee into his house. For some reason, he wasn't surprised to see old Emma waiting patiently on the doorstep with a large soup kettle clutched protectively to her coated breast. She shifted heavily booted feet as he stumbled up the walk. Mason, on the other hand, muttered a "Well, I'll be …" as Emma informed him "a little birdie told me my services would be needed here today," and promptly hustled them both into the kitchen.

In five minutes, Lee was settled at the table with blanketed shoulders, nursing hot tea and brandy while Emma fluttered around in a clatter of domesticity. He was soaked to the skin; he could feel the fever rise and his chest fill with every breath. He should trundle upstairs and change into something dry, but his body simply would not obey. He knew before this week was done, he'd be spending several hours in bed struggling through a nasty bout of the flu or whatever this was that seemed to be squeezing his insides out from the pores. Too much stress, too little sleep, and a bed in the snow did not make for smart preventative health care.

Mason suggested calling a doctor, but Emma wouldn't hear of it. Her argument was valid. Doctors didn't make house calls anymore and it would be ludicrous to drag Lee back out in that awful weather just to see one of those pompous interns. She further informed Mason that she had stood by many a sickbed in her day. If antibiotics were necessary, they could be arranged for in the morning. Right now, the best thing for Lee was to "Git him abed! How did this happen?" Lee made an attempt to grin at Mason, who smiled at him and shrugged.

Mason rocked on his heels, briefly recounting his perceptions of Lee's predicament. He suppressed a snide remark as Emma manhandled his friend over to the sink to wash him up a bit. Head held high, Emma marched Lee back to his chair. "Hurry and get the bed turned down, Mason," she said. Obediently, Mason edged around the haphazard pair, taking the stairs two at a time.

This done, Mason used the phone in Lee's bedroom to make arrangements to get both the Andersons' vehicle and Lee's back to their owners, then hurried downstairs with a grin. He briefly called the funeral parlor. One of his employees told him that Louise had gone on home and would be waiting for him there. He didn't mention the slight difficulty Becker had gotten himself into. As he rounded the corner and into the kitchen, he hoped Emma had brought some of her famous chicken corn soup in the black kettle she was guarding there on the stove.

Lee smiled, reading the expression on his friend's face. "It's okay, Mason. I'll be fine. Just a touch of the flu or something. Emma here will take care of me." Although he'd really rather have Elizabeyta.

Monkey ... came the whisper. Emma's head snapped up from steaming kettle on the stove, the wooden spoon she had raised for a taste clattered on the porcelain top, spattering her with hot liquid. "Heavens!" she growled as she made haste to clean the mess, then pocketed the clean spoon in the smock she was wearing. "What on earth does 'monkey' have to do with how you feel?"

Lee sat up abruptly, wisely not denying he had said anything, though he knew he hadn't. The memories of Cally—and her warning—flashed before him. His head was pounding and he felt dizzy. Mason crossed the kitchen, looked at Lee, nodded to Emma, and together they hustled him up to his room without further protest.

Emma scratched the tickle at the back of her neck. Lee never heard her come in, nor did he acknowledge her presence as she sailed about the room, putting his wet clothes in a pile and folding a dry sweater. She fixed the bed clothes with a firm pat, and took a seat lightly on the edge of the bed, shaking her old head sadly. She figured that of anyone in this God-forsaken town, she knew best what mess Pastor Lee had gotten himself into. She knew from the moment the Belladonna Witch pulled into town with her U-Haul trailing behind her that they were all in for a bad spell. And, from the day she had spied him a-knockin' at the Belladonna woman's side door in the winter dusk while she was visiting her cousin down the street, she knew there was evil afoot.

It was just like a Witch to bring a pack of trouble with her. From what Mason told her downstairs, she'd bet her false teeth Pastor Lee had been bewitched, either by the Belladonna woman or somebody else. She hoped the old nonsense had slipped away as technology around her bolted forward. Putting her head in her hand, she sighed with disgust. Didn't seem hardly likely that a young, healthy soul like Pastor Lee simply laid down in the snow for twenty minutes for the sake of amusement. If it was the Witch, she could soon settle that one, but if it wasn't, that meant poor Pastor Lee here was in a ride for his life. It would be better for everybody if it was the Belladonna woman. Somehow, though, that line of thought, as pleasing as she wanted it to be, did not feel right to these old bones of hers. The tingling feelings in her gut simply weren't there. She always knew who the bad ones were; her innards never failed her.

Emma prided herself in being a strong and courageous woman, despite her frail physique that never managed to total much more than 100 pounds, except when she was pregnant, of course. That was, however, a very long time ago, a memory as feathery as the crumpled love letters hidden in Grandma's hope chest in her attic. Emma had been respected and honored as a healer all over South Mountain for over half a century, but the line had been drawn a while back, and she rarely used her talents in town. They had grown past her type, become educated and snotty. There wasn't much room for her kind in the world anymore, especially in Whiskey Springs. From that time onward, she stuck to the farm folk, but after a spell, they didn't seem to want her help, either. Oh, they were nice enough, but more than once she'd been turned away at the door because "why, the doctor was on the way. So kind of you, though, Emma, to take a trip here to help out." The screen door would promptly bang in her face.

She looked at Pastor Becker, his labored breathing, his sallow skin. Yep, there was black energy afoot here, sure enough, but he had to be tested first. It didn't do to make foolish mistakes in healing. Not one for an audience, she asked Mason if he would mind making a pot of tea and bringing it up. He nodded silently and walked to the bedroom door, turned slightly, as if hesitating to leave his friend. He must have thought better of it. Without a word, he left the room.

To the sound of his retreating footsteps on the padded carpet, Emma went about her business. She was assured that Mason would be a while because she had hid both the tea and the pot when she'd sent him to get the bed ready. With palms extended a few inches above Lee's body, like her granddaddy had taught her, she slowly moved her hands up and down his still form, feeling the energy currents of the man—where they were blocked, weak, or throbbing.

His heart center was blocked, his forehead weak, but she almost got jolted from the pelvic center. Whatever else his problems were, she smiled to herself, Pastor Becker was in love. The combination of the weak heart and powerful sex drive told her that. She vaguely wondered who it was, but there was more important business to consider. On second thought, she heaved a mighty prayer to the Almighty that the lady in question was not that Belladonna person. The overall feeling of his body, however, was sticky. It felt grey and gooey to her healing sense. This would have to be dealt with first.

She withdrew a small ball of red yarn from one of her many smock pockets and measured Pastor Lee from head to foot. He was out cold and didn't move a wink—all the better for it. She snipped the measured length with a small pair of silver scissors retrieved from a different pocket, then returned both the ball of yarn and the scissors back to their respective places. Didn't do to lose your healing tools.

With the cut yarn, she measured the length along the pastor's foot seven times. If the yarn came up short, he was surely bewitched. If long—well, he'd just outdone himself is all, and probably with the mysterious little tart. She'd have to ask him about that when he woke up. The yarn came up short, at least by a foot and a half. It'd been years since she'd seen something like this. She hoped it wasn't the same bunch responsible this time. But her guts were just a jumpin' like those little Mexican beans she'd seen once at the Christian missionary's booth at the harvest festival. Damn it all to hell! It still didn't rule out that Belladonna woman. Emma was sure she was tied to this mess somehow.

She sat down on the bed to think. She really didn't believe the Witch had that much power in her, but then that would mean, as her guts indicated, there were local dealings afoot. She snickered in spite of herself. No, this was serious business and now she had to do something about the pastor before he all but up and died on everybody, and wouldn't that be a fine mess? Death was definitely where he was heading. She checked his pulse. Too weak.

From the seemingly unending pockets, she withdrew a lighter and a rather large thimble. She stuffed the yarn in the thimble, placed it on the night table, and promptly set the yarn afire. She chanted under her breath until the flame burned out, leaving a small, sticky black mass in its wake. Lighter tucked neatly away, she next fished for the spool of red thread, unwound about a yard of it, and cut it with her lower teeth. (They were still the good ones.)

She wrapped the thread around both her gnarled hands and drew it taut, eyeing the tightness between her suspended hands—yep, that was about right. She leaned over the pastor and started on his right side, chanting and moving the thread in a counterclockwise motion to the left, in front of him, then over to the right.

"The weed and the dragon crossed the River Jordan," she intoned. "The weed sank and the dragon drank. In the name of the Maiden, the Mother, and the Crone." She then blew her breath softly on the pastor's face in three short bursts. She repeated this process twice more, then began all over again saying, "And these signs shall follow those that believe in my name. They shall cast out devils and they shall speak in new tongues and if they drink anything deadly, it shall not harm them. They shall lay hands on the sick, and they shall recover. In the name of the Father, the Son, and the Holy Ghost."

Pastor Becker stirred, but did not open his eyes. This was not a good sign. His fever continued to rage and his pulse was weaker than before. Emma got up from the bed, produced a lighter again, and lit the thread. She watched it fizzle and burn. Not good at all. The faster it burned, the heavier the enchantment. Her heart sunk; now she really didn't believe the Belladonna woman was involved in this one.

From yet another pocket she withdrew a smooth stone the size and shape of her little finger. On the largest face was painted the intricate figure of a wise old Crone. It had been her granddaddy's, and his grandmother's before him. This was her healing stone and had worked as a faithful tool for many years. Ever since she could remember, she had made a ritual of repainting the little blue Crone face, careful to be sure she hadn't changed a thing, including the tiny tooth that protruded from the wizened lips. Just like Granddaddy, God rest his soul, had taught her. She hoped it would do its job well now.

She laid her hand on Pastor Becker's chest, cupping the stone over his beating heart. "Hair and hide, flesh and blood, nerve and bone," she chanted, "No more pain than this stone. In the name of the Maiden, the Mother, and the Crone." Thrice done, he seemed to be breathing easier, but there was still more work to be done. Yes indeed!

She stood up by the side of the bed and set the stone on his forehead with her right hand, and pointed her left hand directly to the floorboards below her, feet spread slightly apart.

"Out of the marrow and into the bone," she began, shutting her eyes and imagining her own throat energy center opening like a camera lens and accepting the energy from God.

"Out of the bone and into the blood," she whispered as her hand on his head began to tremble.

"Out of the blood and into the skin." She increased the strength of the chant, her voice slowly rising. She could feel the energy pumping through her now, pulling from him and pushing out of her free hand onto the floor.

"Off the skin and into the hair." Her whole body began to tingle.

"Out of the hair and into the green forest. Out of the green forest and into dry sand as surely as the God made heaven and man! Blue Lady, servant of God, I beseech thee now to break the enchantment and bring this body in tune with the healing energy of the Holy Ghost!"

Granddaddy once told her the Holy Ghost was really a woman, but no one wanted to admit such a thing. He said he knew for sure, because he'd seen her with his own eyes, he did, when ministering to a little girl nigh on sixty years ago. Like an angel," he said, "but without the wings." And such love he felt from her. "Well, wasn't anything like it on man's corrupted earth." Emma concentrated on that Lady Holy Ghost now, and for lack of a good visualization, pictured the blue lady on her stone. Minus the protruding tooth, of course. Who ever heard of a heavenly one having an ugly old tooth hanging out of her mouth, for pity's sake? It was bad enough she didn't have respectable wings. But, if Granddaddy said she didn't have any, then she didn't.

Emma heard the howl of a big dog coming from underneath the bedroom window. She shivered, but didn't break her concentration. The morbid sound seemed to go on forever, but Emma refused to let fear tug at her consciousness. Then, when she thought she couldn't hold it another second, a surge of power like she had never felt before lasered through her body. A loud crack resounded about the room as the floorboard directly below her left hand split in two, a puff of tiny splinters and dust rising about her ankles.

She didn't move, but continued. "In the name of the Father, the Son, and the Holy Ghost. In the essence of the Maiden, the Mother, and the Crone. It is done!" She brought her hands, still clutching the stone, to her breast and hung her head. Her ears registered running footsteps, but her mind did not absorb the signal.

Elizabeyta burst into the room with Mason fretfully trailing behind her. Lee opened his eyes, and Emma jumped so high she lost her balance, tipping like an eighty-year-old teeter totter, her fall cushioned by the edge of the bed.

Lee gasped and coughed, trying to get air. Elizabeyta strode to the bed and yanked Emma up by the smock collar, towering over her like a Valkyrie ready to strike. "Just what the hell do you think you are doing?" she shrieked, the silver pentacle around her neck blazing like a newly born sun, blinding Emma's already flustered sight.

Emma, not one to be cowed by any Witch, quickly recovered, struggling valiantly in her grasp. "Put me down, you whore of hell!" she squealed. "God made thee, dog and hound, set your nose, oh Satan's minion, to the ground!" If she thought Elizabeyta would lose her grip on that one, she was sadly mistaken. She looked at Elizabeyta in disbelief. The younger woman didn't budge, nor did she relax her grip. Emma's feet were now dangling in the air.

Mason peered into the room, wishing he had the foresight to go home an hour earlier. This was just too bizarre to handle and as terrible as it was, he wanted to laugh until his guts came out. He felt something he had never felt before—whatever the essence about Elizabeyta, Mason wanted to drift toward her like a piece of fuzz to a vacuum cleaner. "Just suck me up," he though crazily, "and I'll be forever grateful." What was he thinking?

For a moment their eyes locked. All time suspended. The world around Mason did not exist—only Elizabeyta.

"Elizabeyta, put her down," croaked Lee.

Elizabeyta didn't move, and attempted to scan the woman she held like a puppet. Nothing. She couldn't get anything. This was definitely a magickal person she had by the throat—the woman was well shielded. On closer scrutiny, she deduced it was a natural shield, something the woman was born with and probably didn't have the slightest idea she possessed. Elizabeyta slit her eyes—the other woman's aura was sparkling blue and white, the definite sign of a healer, but she wasn't about to take any chances. "Not until I find out what she thought she was doing," she said.

Emma's head swiveled from Lee to Elizabeyta, then back to Lee. *Her old brain is doing cartwheels on this one*, thought Elizabeyta. Then it hit her: the old lady thought Elizabeyta had enchanted Lee! How truly preposterous.

"I was taking care of him," replied Emma primly. "Your love spell almost killed him, you evil spawn of hell!" she hissed.

Elizabeyta scowled, not knowing whether she should blast this woman with a psychic bolt or just drop her on the floor and guess which bones would break first. The other alternative was to laugh.

Mason piped up. "Yes, Emma is a good woman, here to take care of Lee. She's the friend I told you about … remember … that special friend?"

"It is Satan we are entreating here!" exclaimed Emma, again trying to twist away from Elizabeyta's iron hold on her. "Lee, you've been bewitched by this temple harlot!"

"The only devil in this room is the one in your old fool head!" spat Elizabeyta.

Lee sat up slowly. "Elizabeyta, I've known Emma for a long time. Let her go. Now."

"Listen, you bag of bones," said Elizabeyta. "I've never in my life cast a love spell on anyone, and I'm certainly not about to start now. I've got much more important things to occupy my time. Romance is for the idle!"

Mason frowned. *Now why is his aura spiking?* thought Elizabeyta, but she dismissed it in favor of the battle at hand.

"I'll bet," sneered Emma, "it's you who has been causing all the deaths, isn't it? Poor Terry, the council president, and who knows how many more until you're done! Admit it, daughter of Satan!"

Elizabeyta regarded her coolly. "Lee, I'm going to punch this woman. I've had enough of this lousy town, you, and the blind ignorance that seems to have a hold on the lot of you!"

Mason finally made his feet move and delicately walked over to the struggling Emma. "Emma, you shouldn't call people names like that. You don't even know Miss Belladonna. I don't exactly understand what is going on here, but it appears that Elizabeyta thought she was coming to the aid of the pastor. She bounded up the stairs so fast I thought she was going to lose her shoes. I believe, Emma, she's on our side since it appears someone is drawing the line. Are you so old that you have forgotten how many paths there are to God?"

Everyone looked at Mason in silence. Elizabeyta let go of Emma. Emma's shoulders sank. Lee collapsed back in the bed.

Emma edged toward the door, her intention to bolt clearly on her face. Elizabeyta glanced at Lee and said, "Emma, I think you and I need to talk. Would you mind joining me in the kitchen for a cup of tea? It is obvious that you did not harm Lee, and he is better for your work. I could not have healed him as quickly as you did. Would you take hold of your fear long enough for us to chat?"

Emma's eyes hardened. "I give my word I'll wait for you downstairs."

Mason eyed Elizabeyta and Lee. "I'll just be on my way," he said, and followed Emma down to the kitchen.

Elizabeyta, her face flushed with embarrassment, turned to Lee. He regarded her for a few moments in silence. "That was quite a show. Tell me, what do you do for an encore?"

She smiled, the tension visibly draining from her body. "Oh, I don't know, I might try whipping up a love spell after all."

"And to whom would you direct this spell?"

"Why to Emma, of course!" she smirked and flounced on the edge of the bed. "So, what trouble have you managed to get yourself into since I've seen you last? I'm sure Emma wouldn't have uncloaked herself in this town if the need wasn't serious."

"Your guess is as good as mine," answered Lee. "I did Terry Anderson's funeral today—it was a total disaster from start to finish. Then I guess I got sick at the end of the funeral and Mason had to haul me out of the cemetery and bring me home," he said.

Elizabeyta sensed that Lee's story bordered on untruth, but decided to let the conversation ride. "Ah, indeed. Poor Mason; I didn't even give him a chance to open his mouth when he answered the front door. I just bowled him right over and headed for the stairs at a dead run," she laughed.

"How did you know where my room was?"

"Windows work two ways, or haven't you noticed?" Elizabeyta saw the color leap on his face.

"Actually, it was the beacon that set me spinning your way," she said.

"Beacon?"

"Yes. When a person practices magick, he or she becomes like a beacon in the cosmos. Humans don't often acknowledge it, but it can be seen slicing through several, if not all the dimensions—and felt. Sometimes this magick draws darker entities looking to eat up energy, whether or not the intent in the first place was positive in nature. If the rules of protection have been followed, the positive magician or Witch will not be harmed. In any case, this beacon also lets other magickal people know there is work going on or a need is near. Sometimes this can be good, but not always. There are times when you don't want anyone aware of the magick you are performing for safety's sake. Then you cloak, which she didn't. Actually, I don't think she knows how."

Lee stretched and yawned. "You're really into this stuff, aren't you?"

Elizabeyta tossed her head. "Into it? It is my life! It is the essence of my self!"

"Not according to the old woman, it isn't," he said. His words hit her like a slap in the face and she visibly recoiled.

"What old woman?"

"I had a conversation with an old woman while I was in the cemetery, who wasn't really there. She says I'm supposed to stay away from you."

Elizabeyta looked at him suspiciously. Ah, the untruth border. Interesting territory. "What exactly did this old woman say?"

"In a nutshell, I'm a monkey screwing up the works."

"A what?"

"I'm not supposed to get involved with you."

"I see."

"News to me, too," he said. His smile twisted like a baby garter snake squashed in the middle.

Elizabeyta went on. "What else did she say?"

"Well, my memory isn't the best at this moment, but she also said that you are blocking yourself and you've forgotten about nearly everything you were taught at some 'stead place."

Elizabeyta didn't accept the chastisement well. "I'm not the one who got me into this absurd mess!"

Lee reached for her hand. His fingers were ice, hers fire. "I can't believe I'm talking to you about my hallucination like it is real. For what it's worth, she claims that you are in great danger and she says that many people are depending on you to make the right choice. What do you believe the right path is, Elizabeyta? Stay here. Give up this family mess and marry me." The words hummed quietly through corridors of time. They had been said before, but she could not consciously admit it.

For a long moment she refused to look at him, knowing if she did so, she wouldn't be able to think clearly. It was a familiar sensation, but not from any memory in childhood or since. A beforeness feeling. She briefly savored the passion in his body. It was as if she'd stuck her finger in a light socket and accepted every ounce of current it could give, even if it killed her. She fortified her shields and let the moment pass. It would never work, the two of them together. One of them was bound to be obliterated because of it. Again she slit her eyes, as if in thought, and watched the aura about his head. It glowed with honesty and passion—the man was a veritable powerhouse despite his physical condition. She scanned him and felt only desire. Thank the Goddess he didn't know how to shield, even if it did put her at an unfair advantage at the moment.

Well, all was fair in love and war, wasn't it?

She delicately removed her hand from his grasp. "I think that right now you are taking on the characteristics of a real monkey with those animal desires of yours, and therefore need plenty of rest to become human again. I'm going to go downstairs and put the fear of the Goddess into Emma. She did a good job on you, and you should be fine by morning, but now you should rest. Maybe we can talk later."

She stood up and lifted her necklace over her head. "Here," she said, "you wear this for now, but I'll want it back. It should protect you until Emma and I can get our heads together and find out what's going on. Later I'll ward your house. I should have done it before, but I was hoping you wouldn't get involved."

"Look," he said, "I'm just sick. I don't understand the big deal here, and I really don't think I need your necklace or any of that silly warding stuff."

"That's just the problem," she snapped. "It is not that you are incapable of understanding what happened, it is just that you refuse to acknowledge it. You are not simply sick. Some person or persons worked very hard to ensure you drew your last breath today. I have an idea that if Emma hadn't showed up when she did, you would be the next guest at the Serenity Funeral Parlor. And, believe me, if I saw the beacon, they may have, too. Or do you have a better explanation on why I blundered in here?" She angrily put her hands on her hips. "Why can't you just admit that you may not be aware of all things in heaven and earth? Or are you too pious for that? Believe me, you are not safe by a long shot!"

Lee faintly held up his hands and gave her a sheepish grin of temporary defeat. They both knew he wasn't in any shape to hold his end of an argument. Still flushed from her outburst, she leaned forward and lowered the necklace over his waiting head. Her black-sweatered breasts grazed his cheek as she did so. They both teetered on the edge of in between—she could feel it pulsating between them—but she moved gracefully away and tucked the quilt around him. She sensed that his heartbeat returned to normal.

"Get some sleep," she said and moved to the foot of his bed, thereby being in no danger of touching him again. She stood silently, her own breathing returning to normal. His eyes slid slowly shut. "I'm here now," she whispered. "No one can get to you tonight. Not even the Calliech Bleu, should she take it upon herself to be interested in you. I don't know who you saw in your so-called hallucination, but I certainly hope the old one is on our side. I dread to think what may have been awakened with all the energy swirling around on this side of the fence."

But Lee didn't hear her. He was already asleep, snoring softly.

chapter thirty-one

ELIZABEYTA EYED THE KITCHEN BRIEFLY. HER home and the parsonage appeared to have been built in the same style. Only minor additions made to suit various owners separated the overall theme of the structures now. The kitchen of the parsonage, like Elizabeyta's, was large and airy, though lacking a woman's eye in matters of matching tea towels and wall decorations. The wall facing her own house had been extended, allowing a larger trafficking area in the kitchen for church functions, should the minister in attendance be married and his wife take to the normal weekly entertaining. The sink was more of the industrial size and the refrigerator/freezer looked to be the biggest on the market, equipped with automatic water and ice contraptions melded into the front in a modern design. A large old stove, looking like it had just stepped out of a 1956 issue of *Better Homes and Gardens*, squatted in the far corner, sandwiched by floor-to-ceiling cupboards. Somehow the place looked almost clinical. Heavy-duty black and white linoleum covered the spacious floor, save for in front of the fireplace, where the flagstone hearth and red brick interior still survived.

Elizabeyta sat facing a very prim, white-faced Emma—the high wax gloss of the table mirroring their faces. Mums, their bright bowed heads casting a gaudy reflection on the polished surface, were positioned between the pair. Elizabeyta assumed the flowers were left over from last Sunday's church service and brought to the parsonage by one of the well-meaning women who took care of Lee. In her mind she wove a minor magick around them, touching the little energy left in them to promote peace in the room.

Emma's jaw was set in a determined square. She barely touched the tea before her. Elizabeyta, however, was relaxed. Her occult knowledge, though not complete, was vast where her opponent dealt only with superstition. Fact, reason, and a steady head were Elizabeyta's weapons. Emma had only her fear to protect her.

"I want to thank you again for taking care of Lee," began Elizabeyta. "He—he is a nice individual. Have you been a healer long?"

Emma's stern expression yelled loud and clear that she had no tolerance for platitudes. "Let's get down to business, shall we?" she said icily. She waited a moment, stirring her tea with vigor. "In my opinion, you should pack up, lock, stock, and whatever, and take your little self right back to where you came from. The devil's own are not welcome here!" She slammed her spoon down so hard one of the mums fell from the arrangement, scattering silent petals. She was frightened but it was obvious she was determined to hold her own.

Elizabeyta was prepared for Emma's temper and fear. She knew it was born of years of training by her church, and evidently reinforced by her own family. "Let me make myself perfectly clear, Emma. I will not leave this town until I am ready. Not you nor anyone else can make me leave."

"Then you will surely die by God's hand," said Emma, the hollows of her old cheeks flushing.

Elizabeyta only smiled at her aggressor. Shields up, she concentrated on sending loving thoughts to Emma. She kept her voice even and low. She knew if she sent positive energy to Emma long enough, it would get through. Her only worry was that Emma would bolt before they could get over her stubborn fallacies. To prevent this, Elizabeyta warded both exits of the kitchen with blazing pentacles that she hoped only she could see. It would be bad business if Emma had auric sight.

Emma looked directly at the back door, then concentrated on her tea. Her expression did not show alarm. Elizabeyta hid her relief. The woman was not trained and must be naturally blocked.

"I will not die at God's hand," said Elizabeyta carefully, "but I may die at the hand of evil. We are not so different, you and I. Actually, I believe in the same God you do, but I also believe in the Goddess as well. It takes two halves to make a whole—we see as it The Source, The All. Doesn't your religion teach good over evil? Well, I believe that good should triumph over evil, too; that's why I came here."

Emma looked at her worriedly. It was obvious she didn't like the direction the conversation was going. She didn't answer.

Elizabeyta shrugged and continued. "In my religion, we do not believe in Satan or the minions you speak of. But we are very well aware that where there is good, there is evil to balance. We do not practice evil, but we understand that it exists. To give it a name would be to give it power, Emma; surely you understand that."

Emma fiddled silently with her tea cup.

"We refuse to give that energy to the evil ones. Instead, we desire to make the world a better place for all people."

Emma picked up her spoon again and relentlessly stirred her tea. "Bad things have happened since you came here," she muttered.

"Bad things were happening here long before I came, and you know it!" said Elizabeyta firmly. "I believe, Emma, that you have some answers to puzzles I have been trying to unravel. Whether you wish to believe it or not, what you did upstairs is called magick where I come from. And magickal people know about other magickal people in their area, both the good ones and the bad ones. It is the only way they can survive—information. Anyone who has practiced as long as you have in the same area has got to know the good, the bad, and the ones who walk the line. I promise you that once I get those answers and solve my problems, I will be more than happy to leave this place."

"For good?" queried Emma. Elizabeyta could read her expression. She still didn't quite believe.

Elizabeyta smiled. "For good, Emma. One does not like to live where one is not welcome. You must know that in your own experience."

Emma nodded her head. "That I do. But I will tell you straight out that if I find you are enchanting me in any way and hiding the truth or hiding your evil from me, I will find out, and I will deal with you! I may be a healer, but I can kill you quick. My God is a mighty and avenging one and he doesn't take to magicians like yourself, young woman!"

"Fair enough," announced Elizabeyta. "First, I want to know how you knew I was in town. I have used a great deal of magick to hide myself, plus I have been very careful in the mundane realm. So tell me, when did you know I was here?"

"The day you pulled in with that trailer," stated Emma flatly.

"You're kidding!" Elizabeyta's eyelids fluttered and her thoughts scurried to who else might have known she was here all along. Mason wasn't kidding when he said this woman was "special." Was she being played for a fool?

"Nope. I don't lie, young lady! Mrs. Conner called me. She's a relative of mine. Most people think she's touched in the head, but it's because Rufus beats her all the time when he bothers to come into town. She lost so many babies from his abuse it's a wonder she managed to keep her wits about her to make a simple meal and take care of that boy of hers that did survive. Which doesn't matter now because he's dead. 'Course you know about that, don't you?" Emma gazed directly into Elizabeyta's eyes.

Elizabeyta did not flinch. "Yes, I know about the murder, but I had nothing to do with it," she said honestly.

Emma pursed her thin lips but continued. "Well, she's had the second sight since birth. I was there when she was born with the caul over her face, but we were all sworn to secrecy. Her side of the family tree delves into things a body shouldn't and her mother was afraid that the men folk would find out and use her up. She's a Blackthorn, you know. The last female with the sight in the Blackthorn clan was kept pregnant till it killed her—they thought they would make lots of boy babies with the gift. Unfortunately only three of that woman's babies lived past six months. So we never told, not one of us. The women at the birthing, they're all dead now, except her and me, and to this day, I never broke my oath. I don't think she's long for this world so it won't hurt my tellin' you. She's been abed since this afternoon and the doctors can'na do nothing for her. Her pa won't let me in to see her. I think they want her to die."

"Who's 'they,' Emma?"

"The Blackthorn boys. There's three of them who runs the family now. The eldest, he doesn't count 'cause he moved out to California when he was no more than eighteen. Just packed up and skedaddled with a Jewish girl a long time ago. A few people around here have heard from him now and then but he either calls without giving a number or sends letters without return addresses. They're both doing well with a passel of kids."

"You said there were three. What about the other two?"

"Well, there's the youngest, Lance. A real character, that one. I guess he's about twenty-four. I can't stand him myself, has those crazy eyes, you know. The boy has tattoos all over his body, rides a motorcycle, and has kept emergency room business alive at the clinic. A bad penny if I ever saw one, but he's not the worst of the lot—that's Jason. Oh, and then there's the adopted one, ah …" She looked at the ceiling trying to capture his name on her tongue. "Richard, that's it! Now Richard's an odd duck. I always thought he was such a good boy … Jason though, he's the piss-pot."

Elizabeyta's skin felt clammy, her heart skipped a beat, and shivers ran along her arms.

"Yeah, I know," said Emma. "Every time I mention his name I get the creeps. He's been mean and ornery since he was a kid, that one. He's thirty-five now. I wouldn't allow him on my farm after he killed both my dogs and a few cats back in '63. Said he was collecting their blood to wash away the sins of a woman. Born bad is Jason. Has evil straight through him. I told his parents that if they ever brought him to my place again I'd write them out of my will, I would. They were greedy people and didn't bring him by no more.

Not long after that his momma, my blood kin, dropped over dead while hang-ing out the wash. Hemorrhaged to death from havin' too many babies. She'd just lost one the week before. His papa remarried two weeks later and that's where Lance come from." Emma dabbed her lips with a hanky from one of her pockets and sat back resolutely in her chair.

"Then, when Jason reached manhood, he came by himself to my farm. Said only a woman of the family could give him the power of healing and that's what he wanted from me. Said he didn't need no other powers 'cause he already had 'em. Claimed he wasn't the child I'd seen growin' up, but a man who could move through time or some such nonsense. I personally think he was high on those new-fangled drugs they got out now. Alcohol ain't good enough for those no-accounts." She took a deep breath. "Anyhow, the new woman his papa had married didn't have any gifts. I told him flat out no, but he put up a nasty argument. He got pretty violent and thought he would grab hold of me and shake it out. But I've been training Chows for years. You know, them fancy dogs? I had two males then and they did a right nice job on his behind. Still carries the teeth marks, I hear." She giggled mischievously. "Don't have those Chows no more, though. Getting too old to take care of them right."

"After he left I did the only ritual I've ever done in my life. I sort of regretted it, but it had to be done. I built an altar to the Lord out of a hay bale, like my pa had taught me, and I sacrificed a black chicken on it. I hated doing it, but I was desperate. When I was finished, I dug a big hole at my doorstep and buried all the ashes, every last one I could pick up. If he's ever come back, I didn't know about it and when I see him now and again he looks straight through me, as if I'm not even there."

Emma rubbed her face with a wrinkled hand. "I guess sacrificing ani-mals is nothing to you. I felt guilty as hell, though."

"Actually, if it makes you feel any better, Emma, we don't believe in taking the life of any animal or human."

"You don't? I thought—"

"No." Elizabeyta reached across the table and took Emma's hand in hers. It was small and cold. "You would be surprised how much we really do share. I believe in healing, too, but I'm not as good as you. Maybe if I make it through this thing alive we can spend some time together before I leave. I can show you some things and you can help me be a better healer."

Emma shook her head. "I can't pass my power to another woman. It won't work."

"Have you ever tried it?"

"Well, no, that was the rule I was taught and I followed it."

"In magick, anything is possible. Years ago the people of the Craft set down that rule, even before they came to this country. It was to protect the integrity of the line and to keep the power in balance. The time has come, though, that positive knowledge should be shared. I'm sure that if we put our heads together, it will help both of us. I'm not saying you must pass your power to me; that would be unfair. It is your decision to make. However, perhaps there is a young woman you are fond of who you think may benefit from your teachings when this is all over."

Emma looked at her skeptically, but did not reply.

"Right now, I'm here to do a job," said Elizabeyta. The key to Emma's support lay in honesty, she knew. "And I think you are the only person in this town capable of understanding and of helping."

Emma shook her head. "You are on your own. There is nothing I can do."

"You're wrong. You have knowledge that may help me. Already you've told me in a few minutes information I've been searching for over three years!"

"I have?"

"Yes, isn't the proverb 'know your enemy' an important one?"

Emma eyed Elizabeyta suspiciously. "But I have told you little." It was Emma's turn to rise from the table and refill the tea cups. "By the way, where is Mason?"

"I'm right here." Both women raised their eyebrows and looked toward the kitchen doorway. Mason grinned and sauntered into the room, taking a chair beside Emma.

"You two have had quite a discussion. Are we friends?"

Elizabeyta smiled thinly. Why hadn't she known he was there?

Emma looked at Mason skeptically then glanced out the kitchen window. Elizabeyta followed her gaze; there appeared to be nothing there but a black window pane. They both shivered in unison. A nervous giggle escaped from Emma's wizened lips.

He turned to Emma. "I told you she was a nice woman."

"Hrumph!"

Elizabeyta sat back in her chair, picking at a mum petal on the table. "You mean you told Emma about me?" She turned her dark eyes on the old woman. "If Mason had already talked to you about me, why were you accusing me of such nonsense?"

"Testing."

"Did I pass or fail?"

"The jury's still out," replied Emma, her eyes narrowing. "I see a lot and I'm not inclined to share when I don't want to."

"You two remind me of two cats spitting at each other over a piece of fish," remarked Mason, a small smile dancing at the corners of his mouth.

"You!" Emma hit his arm lightly. "This here's my apt pupil," she said winking her eye.

"Pupil? You mean as in ..."

"As in country magick, girl. He's a fast learner. I swear he's done it all before and is just remembering."

Elizabeyta looked at Mason with new eyes. "Why didn't you tell me?"

"For the same reason you haven't told us much."

"Oh."

"So why are you so interested in Jason Blackthorn?" asked Emma.

Elizabeyta hesitated, then blurted, "I think he's the fellow who killed my grandmother, and I think I'm next."

Emma's expression was incredulous. "You mean he's come after you?"

"No, not yet," admitted Elizabeyta. "But he will."

"Well, how do you know that? What's he got to do with you? What do you mean, he killed your grandmother?"

Elizabeyta explained, trying not to leave out any details. She finished with, "I'm not sure, really, if it is Jason Blackthorn. He's seems like a likely candidate, but I just don't know. That's why I need you to help me put the pieces together. All I know at this point is that he is wants me dead, and if I understand my source right, it will be soon."

Emma rubbed her eyes with both hands, pulling the wrinkled skin taut with her palms. "I wonder if that Jason is responsible for the recent murders 'round here."

"I have no idea. I'm not sure how many people he really has killed. Some of the incidents could have been legitimate accidents, or there could be several that we don't know about. How many accidental deaths have there been around Whiskey Springs in the past ten years?"

"Oh my, I ain't the person to ask that. I don't rightly know. I never really thought about it. There have been some odd ones, to be sure, like that barn fire two years ago that killed the whole Tailor family, but nobody ever said anythin'. Jason bought that farm about six months later. What do you think, Mason?"

"There have been quite a few odd deaths lately. I don't know ... the Connor boy to be sure. Terry Anderson, she was a hit and run ... you know, she looked an awfully lot like you."

All three looked at each other in silence. "You don't think they tried to get Elizabeyta and hit Terry by mistake, do you?" asked Emma, an incredulous expression on her face.

"Oh Goddess, I hope not! Have there been any others, Mason?"

"Let's see. Timothy Reed ... definite heart attack. Though oddly enough, his teenaged son is missing."

"The Reed boy? Oh, what a shame!" said Emma.

Elizabeyta gasped. Mark Reed. The future she couldn't see. He must be somehow involved.

"And there is one more ... an old South Mountainer, Paints. Definite murder."

"Paints? Oh dear!" said Emma. "Why, I used to babysit him when he was just a tyke. Always into things with wheels, he was." She shook her head. "That's a darn shame."

Mason hesitated a moment. "Timothy Reed's body is missing from the morgue."

"Now who would want to take a dead body?" snapped Emma.

Mason shrugged his shoulders and turned to Elizabeyta. "I found some interesting information for you while going through my collection of letters."

"Letters?"

Emma grinned. "He collects letters. I've been helping him," she said proudly. "He has them from the Civil War, from the Big Ones, and from Korea ... even a few from the Viet Nam conflict. All written by residents of the town. Interesting stuff. Sometimes sad, sometimes funny."

Mason waited patiently until Emma finished. "Anyway, I found what you were looking for. According to my records there was and has always been a feud between the Blackthorns and the two Irish families you were talking about the other day—the Framptons and the Belladonnas."

"I knew that," said Emma, as if disappointed with Mason's information. Both Mason and Elizabeyta looked at her in disbelief.

"Well, sure! Started back when this town was only a settlement. Two doctors fighting over one patient. The patient died. Each blamed the other. The patient was a Blackthorn fellow, the head honcho of the family. Blackthorns swore they'd get even and stamp out every last Frampton and Belladonna. Heck, that feud lasted until those two Irish families up and left about thirty or forty years ago ... can't rightly remember when exactly ... they sort of just slipped out of town ..." A distraught expression crossed her face. Elizabeyta sensed she was hiding something.

"I believe that Jason, or his men, killed my grandmother and her sister. Emma, I bet you've lived around this town most of your life. Did you know my great aunt, Beth Ann Baxter?"

Emma's eyes snapped open. There was a mysterious gleam in them. "Beth Ann was your great aunt?"

"Yes. As I told you earlier, my grandmother, her sister, came out to see her about two years ago. I thought you understood we were talking about the Frampton and Belladonna families. I guess I didn't make myself clear. My grandmother never came home. When members of my family began making inquiries, they found out my great aunt was dead. There was no mention of my grandmother. She simply disappeared. We didn't file a report with the authorities for, shall I say, personal reasons."

"Beth Ann died of a heart attack. I know; I was at the funeral. And, little girlie, she was a fine upstanding woman in Christ!" said Emma.

"That may be so, but I think she was killed with magick! And, you know that is possible, don't you, Emma?"

Emma squirmed, a dark look crossing her old face.

"I also think that you knew my grandmother as well, didn't you?"

Emma retained a stoic expression. Mason looked at her quizzically.

"You can't tell me, in the town the size of Whiskey Springs, when you and my grandmother were young people, that you didn't know her."

Emma popped her dentures up and down in her mouth, swishing them around until they stayed firm. Still, she said nothing.

Elizabeyta could feel Emma warring with herself. Her aura shimmered with fear. She almost felt sorry for putting the old woman through all this, but she really needed the information. It was a matter of life and death. She bit down on her own lower lip, determined to push this as far as it would go. She glanced at Mason, who sat with his arms parked across his chest, rumpling his expensive suit, a curious look on his face.

Silence. Fear. Emma looked like she was going to pass out. Her shoulders were bowed, her face ashen as powdered bones. Waves of guilt engulfed Elizabeyta. Mason looked like he felt it too and reached out, putting his arm around Emma.

"It's okay. If you don't want to talk about it, I'll understand."

"Well I won't!" said Elizabeyta hotly. "The lives of children are at stake here! Please Emma, for Goddess' sake, tell me what you know."

Emma sighed deeply, the breath rattling her entire body. "Yes, I knew them all. Your grandmother, your grandfather, pretty near the whole Belladonna clan."

Elizabeyta realized the guilt she was feeling emanated from Emma.

"The Blackthorns ran 'em out of town, with the help of some of the rest … of us." She looked forlornly at the pitch-black window. "We were all young then, and foolish. I don't know how or when the fightin' got so bad. It seemed the Belladonnas were always trouble for the Blackthorns, or vice versa, ever since I was a babe. The Framptons, now they tried to be more neutral, but it didn't help. Just made matters worse. Most folks stayed out of it. In those days there was a lot of land, the farms were big, and it took most everybody's energy to run them. The town was fair near split atwixt the Blackthorns and the Belladonnas. Each owned about a third. The Blackthorns owned a third, together the Belladonnas and Framptons owned another third, and other folks owned the rest."

Elizabeyta leaned forward intently, concentrating on free energy flow and strength to Emma. Mason sat in total silence.

Emma, even if she did notice, kept going, as if once the story was begun, it had to be finished. "Part of the problem was that the Belladonnas and the Framptons were Catholic and the Blackthorns were River Baptist. There was always friction. Of course the other part was magick. The Blackthorns diddled in high-born German magick and the Belladonnas and Framptons, well, they used somethin' else. I was always taught they got their magick from the devil and to stay away from them, which wasn't difficult because they kept to themselves, schooling their little ones at home, 'stead of sending 'em to the schoolhouse. As soon as they were grown up some, they all went to college, girls and boys alike. The most we got to see the kids was at the county fair or some such other function."

"What forced my family out?" Elizabeyta held her breath for the answer. She knew part of it but didn't offer any information. Perhaps Emma had more information to give and if she interrupted her now with the facts as she knew them, Emma would clam up.

Emma fiddled with her smock, playing with the edges of this pocket and that. "At first, nobody thought much of it." She took a deep breath. "Little Tommy Belladonna was first, drowned in the creek. Everybody thought it was such a terrible accident. Then ten-year-old Martha Frampton fell off the overhang, about a mile past my place. Still, most of us figured it was just a bad accident, even though the deaths were only a month apart."

She shifted uncomfortably in her chair. "My dentures are getting loose from all this jawing. Could I have another cup of tea?"

Elizabeyta nodded and refilled her tea cup. Mason handed her the sugar.

Emma stirred the tea thoughtfully, as if trying to find her story in the swirling depths of the steaming liquid. "As I was saying ... that was late spring, moving into early summer. The twins was next, no—maybe it was Martin Frampton. Don't rightly recollect. Eight-year-old Martin just up and disappeared. Some thought a bear'd got him, but we never did find nothing. The twins, they was run over by a wagon. There were witnesses to that one, but the Blackthorn boy who drove it swore it was an accident."

She looked off into space. "There used to be a big revival every summer, up on South Mountain, not far from where my place is now. I know it would seem strange to a person of today, this bein' such a small town an' all, but remember we have the rail station and life was pretty dull for most folks around. The revival brought in near forty thousand people, I kid you not. Check the town records if you don't believe me. It lasted ten days and people would drive in their buggies, some brought their cars, and tons of 'em would come for a day on the train."

She took a deep breath and plunged on. "Well, there was no supervision in those days. Lots of the men would slip off into town and do a spell of drinkin' afore they joined their wives up on the mountain. We had three bars in town. Now, in case you've not noticed, we don't have any, save for the VFW. Anyhow, some of the bad ones, like Jason's granddaddy (who wasn't hitched then, of course, and a wild, big thing), would get pretty rowdy. Somehow they got hold of one of the Belladonna girls. If I recollect right, it would have been your grandmother's and great aunt's sister ..."

"My grandmother only had one sister, not two," interjected Elizabeyta.

"That's what you think. She had another one, the baby of the family. She was only thirteen. They called her Cally. Anyway, after ever'body had gone home and the revival was over, little Cally was missin'. They found her the next mornin' in one of the fields. What they'd done to her was not good. She lived long enough to tell her pa who did it, but nobody else heard what the girl said. They tried to press charges, but it fell through. After all, there were thousands of people there, and supposedly, no witnesses. There weren't no revival ever again and most folks blamed it on some outsider; they were too scared to blame it on a Blackthorn."

"Oh my Goddess ..." breathed Elizabeyta.

Mason nodded. "That's pretty much what I found. One letter in particular, though, claims there was a witness to the little girl's murder."

Emma took a sip of tea, the cup wobbling in her hand. "I ain't done."

"There's more?" asked Elizabeyta.

"Well, people started dyin' mysterious-like on both sides. It got to the point where nobody talked to anybody. Then one day, the post office got notice that both the Frampton and Belladonna clans were gone, and there was no need to forward any mail. Over twelve families had sold fifteen farms to three land developers. All the stores changed hands quiet-like. Heard they took the money and run. Of course, 'cause they lit out ever'body believed they were the devil's people all along, 'specially since they got out so slick. Some even said they kilt their own children, just to make the mess go away in their minds. The Blackthorns were furious, 'cause many of the properties ran along their own and new housing started to go up all over the place. To add insult to injury, we all eventually found out the big lake was donated to the state ..." she turned to Mason, "you know, Rinshot Lake—Gifford Rinchot was married to one of the Belladonna women—which meant the Blackthorns couldn't buy it from anyone. Which was what they was itching to do in the first place."

Mason nodded. "All that area around the lake is state game lands now."

"I wish I'd met you a while ago, Emma. You have no idea how much time I've spent researching this town, trying to find out what happened."

"Well, the upshot of this whole thing is that the Blackthorns followed suit, at least as the idea of sellin' went. They sold off half their farms, mostly the ones next to the proposed developments, and reeled in a pretty large sum of money, which they invested badly. The only thing left now is the family estate up on South Mountain. Jason and his brother Lance, and God knows who else, lives there. I heard tell Richard left for college. I thought he'd just skeedattle, but somebody told me the t'other day he'd come back."

The overpowering sense of guilt had not retreated from the room, rather it seemed to have grown in size. Elizabeyta surveyed her own thoughts, but they were angry, not guilty. Mason looked interested, but complacent. Her eyes turned to Emma.

"What's bothering you, Emma? I feel very much that you have a part in all this that you're not saying."

Very calmly, Emma folded her hands in her lap. "Well, if you are indeed the angel of the devil come to render justice, you'll find out eventually, so I might as well tell you and get it over with. I was with Cally that day. I know for sure who kilt her."

Mason's breath quickened. "You were the witness?"

She nodded slowly, her eyes filling with fat tears.

"I thought you said that no one got to know the Belladonna children?"

"Well, most didn't. But my pa's farm was next to theirs. We met when we were both workin' in the fields. We made a pact not to tell and would sneak out to meet each other. We spent several summers down by the creek, or over at the lake. Sometimes we'd go up to the mountain and see my granddaddy. He never tol' anybody and didn't seem to mind. He even hinted our families were somehow related a long time back ..." Emma's voice broke into small, hard sobs. She took a tissue out of one of her smock pockets, dabbed her eyes, then blew her nose. It took her several minutes to get under control.

"I saw what they did to her that night. She was screamin' my name, but I ran and ran and ran. I went to my granddaddy's and hid in the shed until mornin'. He found me 'round three and I told him everythin', but by the time I fessed up, it was too late. She was long dead. My family arranged for me to stay up on the mountain with him, and when the Belladonna family started askin' questions about me, my granddaddy swore that I'd been on the mountain with him the whole time, and naturally didn't know nothin' about nothin'. He may have been old, but he was still a powerful man. After a time, when I didn't say nothin' to the authorities, they left me be. I was still up on the mountain when the Belladonnas and Framptons lit out, and your great aunt married that missionary fellow and took off for India. There's a cliff up there, where if you sit on the edge, you can see for miles. Come dawn one mornin', I saw them, your great aunt and her husband, leave on the train. Then I looked out across the farms and watched the rest of the two families go, quiet-like. No one saw them go but me and God."

"Oh, Emma!"

"Yes, I know'd I should have said somethin' about Cally in the first place, but the years went by, most ever'one involved finally died. I thought I'd deal with it in heaven when the time came, should I be lucky enough to get there. In the meantime, I've set to helpin' people as best I could and hoped that nobody would remember or care anymore. Then you showed up and I knew it would have to come out and that you'd only bring the devil with you to take care of all them wrongs done."

Elizabeyta ran her fingers through her hair, pulling it back from her temples. "I'm not here to render any sort of justice, Emma. That's between you and your God. I came here to find out who killed my family, and keep them from hurting any more of us. I've pretty much figured out the who, but I'm not exactly sure of the why, other than some type of family feud that seems to have been going on forever. I think Cally's murder was just part of it. There's got to be another reason that I'm not seeing, one that makes this all fit together ..."

"You mean you ain't gonna kill me?"

Mason chuckled, a look of relief on his face. "For goodness sake, Emma, she's a woman, not the angel of death."

Elizabeyta shook her head sadly. "No, Emma, what's done is done. You were a little girl who witnessed a terrible thing. You couldn't have helped her, and you did keep quiet so the rest of my family could leave safely."

"Well now it appears I've done all the talkin' and you the listenin'. Tell me 'bout yourself and how you figure to take care of your family. You're just one little woman up against a passel of no-good menfolk. I hear tell they're runnin' drugs now up from Baltimore and down from New York. How is a little thing like you going to go up against a mess like that? Good Witch or bad Witch, you're still all alone."

"No she's not, she's got me and Lee!" said Mason.

"How do you know about the drugs, Emma?" asked Elizabeyta, ignoring Mason for the moment.

"Just the same as I knew you were here. The women know what's goin' on, but they're too scared to do anythin' about it—what few women there are left, that is. Why don't you just go home, while the goin's good, and let this mess die, like it rightly should?"

"I can't, Emma. If I don't deal with him here, he'll find our home. It will only take a matter of time. There are lots of little children there, Emma, just like Cally. Do you want the same thing to happen to them that happened to her? Do you want them to die like those other children long ago?"

Emma breathed deeply and collapsed back into her chair. "No, I don't want that to happen. I suppose it is right you are here and I'm tellin' you all this. I always wondered why I've lived so long. Maybe I had to wait until you got yourself here. What do you want me to do?"

"Nothing right now. You've told me a wealth of information, but I still have work to do tonight and honestly, you should go home and get some rest. I need to think about my next move."

"We all need to think about that," interjected Mason.

Elizabeyta smiled at him. "It would be nice to have three knights in shining armor, Mason, but you all could get hurt. We can talk some more tomorrow if you don't mind. Maybe you two could come over to my house in the afternoon. I doubt Lee will be up and around for awhile, but if he feels like it, Emma can ask him, too."

Elizabeyta smiled and sighed. Thinking about how tired the old woman must be made her realize her own fatigue. "Let's think on it until we all feel fresher."

Emma rose and went into the parlor to collect her coat and boots. Mason stayed in the kitchen a moment and put the tea cups in the sink, taking a deep breath over the soup kettle, still simmering on the stove.

"You can turn that off," said Elizabeyta to him as she followed Emma to the door.

Emma smiled and whispered. "No wonder Louise never had any babies; Mason is always out and about helping people. There ain't no time, I guess, to make any."

"Louise?"

"Mason and Louise have been married since the dawn of time with no little ones to boast about. Never could figure that one out. They both seem so healthy, even if he is on the pale side," she chuckled. "Now, if'n they'd come to me, I could have fixed her up. But," she sighed, "they're part of the new generation, you know—science and all that." She cupped her hand close to her mouth. "Real nice people, though she's a bit uppity, if you know what I mean, but the two of them are good. The trustable kind. Not many of them around these days. Louise is probably pitching a fit that he ain't home yet. She tries to keep him on a tight leash."

Elizabeyta laughed as she ushered Emma out the door, grabbing one of Lee's jackets from a peg in the hallway to take some of the chill out of her walk down to the gate. The cold wind blew past them. Elizabeyta glanced back to be sure Mason had not heard their conversation. He was busy in the hall, adjusting his suit and putting on his overcoat. Satisfied, Elizabeyta hurried after Emma.

At the front gate, Elizabeyta said, "Oh, Emma—one last thing."

Emma, five steps from the gate, turned to face Elizabeyta.

"Do you believe in ghosts?"

Emma's dark eyes sparkled. "Talk to them all the time, dearie."

Elizabeyta couldn't tell if she was smiling below her muffler, but when she heard the tinkle of the old woman's laugh she was greatly relieved. The two women turned in time to see Mason pulling on an orange ski cap. He looked a sight in his sober overcoat and black pants topped with the flash of orange striding sedately toward them. *There is something about him ...* thought Elizabeyta.

"Got to keep warm," he grinned. "When Lee wakes up, tell him I wish him well. I take it you and Emma are pals now?" All three of them looked toward the street as a Toyota roared around the corner and out of sight, almost skidding into a large oak tree.

"I wonder who that was?" said Mason.

Elizabeyta and Emma looked at each other darkly, but Mason missed the exchange.

"Anyway," chattered Mason, "I'm glad you two ladies are friends now; we don't need any wars going on in good old Whiskey Springs." Elizabeyta sensed a falseness here—something held back, missing.

"I'm going to warm up my buggy," said Emma. With a brief good-bye she trudged down the sidewalk, presumably toward her car. Elizabeyta saw a red Jeep parked down the block. In a moment, Emma reached it, put the key in the door and got in. A few moments later its motor roared to life.

Elizabeyta grinned and turned her attention to Mason. She shivered again. Lee's jacket was little comfort in this weather. "Time will tell. Mason, I appreciate all you did for Lee today—and for me."

Mason bowed. "My pleasure as well, my lady. Although you may think this is malarkey, I really do believe I may have known you in some other lifetime. However, I'm an agnostic, so I certainly don't have those ideas, do I?" He winked and stepped from the path onto the sidewalk.

"Why Mason, if I didn't know better, I'd think you were flirting. What would Louise think?"

"I think that if she met you, she'd keep me chained to the desk at Serenity. As it is, I've got a lot of explaining to do and I'd better get home to do it! Oh, tell Lee I'll return his tire iron next time I see him. I don't think he'll be needing it right away."

"Tire iron?"

"Yeah. It was the darndest thing. He had it at the cemetery with him." He patted her on the back and headed for his car.

Elizabeyta hurried after him. She caught up with Mason at his car. "Can I have that iron?"

Mason shook his head and grinned, retrieving it from the back seat. When she grabbed hold of it, she almost dropped it. "Yech!"

"Something wrong?"

"Oh, nothing." How could she explain to Mason about psychometry out here in the freezing cold? She smiled farewell and scampered back to the front porch. Mason moved to get in his car. As Elizabeyta reached the porch, she turned to see that he was still standing by the open car door, watching her. He smiled again, cocked his head, waved, and disappeared into the plush interior of the sedan. She watched him drive slowly down the street, past the Jeep where Emma still revved the engine.

The thermometer beside the front door read below twenty. Quaking with cold, she slipped back inside.

Elizabeyta made her way to the kitchen, picking up her black canvas backpack from under her coat on the way. She plopped it on the kitchen table. With Emma's cup cleared away and her own mug refilled, she eased into one of the chairs at the table. An unseen floor clock clicked monotonously from somewhere in the depths of the house. She checked her watch without really considering the time. It was 10:30 PM.

Sipping from her mug, Elizabeyta considered what she should do next. First on the agenda was to protect the house and Lee with psychic shields. She had always been very good at this, and for her, it took more time than effort. She began to empty the contents of the bag on the table, picking and choosing among the array of tools and herbs.

Her hand passed over a foot-long wooden stick with a crystal wired firmly to one end and a leather grip on the other. Although many of her friends back at the covenstead used wands, Elizabeyta found them cumbersome. The dagger, or athame as she called it, was a different matter. She slowly withdrew it from its leather sheath, its intricately etched, six-inch blade catching the reflection of the kitchen light.

Elizabeyta balanced the carved wooden handle in her right palm. Runes, Goddesses, and animals raced around the handle. Bright, powerful sensations traveled up her arm, filling her body with tingling energy. Unlike normal daggers, the edges of this one were dull, as ritual required. The blade was not used for material cutting, but for magick.

She used to hate knives. As a child, before she was initiated into the mysteries, she believed terrible things were done with the ritual knives of the adults. Perhaps it was because they glittered so in the moonlight that shone serenely in the outdoor circle when the Goddess or God was invoked. Now she knew better.

She lovingly set it down on top of its sheath, beside a clear fluted bottle of holy water and a capped shaker of salt from the Dead Sea. A vial of clove oil was next. Now, for the herbs. Her fingers traveled over several glass vials—vervain to make it all go, as well as protect. Rue? Good protective herb, but it had a tendency to bring obsession into focus and thereby force you to deal with it.

No, rue was not a good idea. Angelica—good, that makes two, but it takes three to charm. Asafetida was excellent for protection and getting rid of demons, but it stunk like hell. A little whiff of it sent many a Witch running for the bathroom. No, not a good idea in the house of a minister. She sorted through the vials of herbs for several minutes, discarding many on sight, pondering then rejecting others. Her have-Witch-will-travel selection was good; she'd been doing this for many years. Magick usually took a great deal of planning to avoid mistakes. Patience was a must.

Without quite deciding what the third ingredient should be, she rose and puttered around the kitchen. A quick check of the refrigerator confirmed Lee's bachelor status; only a quart of milk, a few dented apples, and assorted half-empty condiment containers. She found what she was looking for rolling around in the back of the vegetable drawer, alone and rather wilted—garlic. With another refill of tea, a chipped soup bowl filched from the dish drainer, and an odd crystal goblet found crammed in the corner of the dish cupboard, she turned back to the task at hand.

The floor clock continued to tick. It was now quarter past eleven by her watch and she was well aware she'd better get a move on. In her heart she knew Emma's work would not last forever. They would try again. Either Lee had somehow gotten too close to the truth or else they figured he was her weak link—perhaps both.

She settled on that third ingredient—rosemary. Carefully, she mixed the three herbs in the soup bowl, blessing the dried leaves and empowering them for protection. Next she crushed the garlic in the crystal goblet, reaching out to divinity for protection of Lee.

Although she didn't normally use incense (she was allergic to most of it), she decided to blend powdered frankincense and sandalwood, pouring them on top of a small, hollow charcoal brick. This she set carefully in a metal incense burner shaped like a dragon, a piece given to her by her first lover.

Supplies and tools ready, she leaned back in her chair to consider where the power point of the house was. Warding the house included all the windows and outside doors from attic to basement. She would also put up a temporary shield in Lee's bedroom, but she needed to know the power point to raise the shields around the entire house.

There were two ways to do this: either walk around the house or go into a meditative state and look for it astrally. Either way, she would have to explore the house, which didn't please her. She wasn't a snoop. At least she could go to Lee's room, and take it from there. She clipped the athame to her boot and checked the cupboards under the sink for a large tray, which she promptly found. With clove oil, she blessed and consecrated the tray. She rummaged in the backpack again, and whipped out a rolled cloth of black silk. Opened, it just covered the tray. With precision, she laid her supplies on the cloth, careful not to spill any of the herbs.

Most home power points were found on the first floor, where the family members spent most of their time and expended a great deal of energy. Often it would be the kitchen, dining room, or perhaps, family room. But Elizabeyta knew that in some cases, when one was dealing with a charismatic or very religious person, the power point would be where the person spent most of his or her time meditating, writing, and studying. Perhaps that was upstairs in a personal den. She would check after she looked in on Lee.

Lee slept peacefully, the fever broken, a slight smile lingering on his lips. Elizabeyta put her lips to his forehead. His temperature appeared normal. She raised her hand, palm extended about an inch from his skin, and ran it down the length of his body, checking for blocked energy vortexes. She found none. Emma was definitely worth her weight in magick. Lee slept on, oblivious to her presence as she busied herself with his protection.

First, she placed the goblet of garlic under his bed. This was to drive away any astral nasties that hankered to take a bite out of the sleeping pastor. Then she scoured the room for the sweater Emma had taken off the patient. She found it folded neatly in the corner by the closet. She unfurled it, turned it inside out, opened the closet door, and held it in the door frame. She closed the door with deliberation, pinching the sweater between the frame and the door.

Before she left his room, she called upon the Keeper of Visions and recited a simple charm for pleasant dreams, then drew pentacles with her left index finger, both in clove oil and holy water above each window and the door leading to the hallway. True, her right hand was her projective hand, as she had been taught years ago. Lately, though, she found she generated more power with her left. So be it. She shut his bedroom door quietly and padded down the thickly carpeted hall, balancing the tray of magickal goodies on her right arm.

The upstairs was designed much like her own. There was a spacious guest bedroom, definitely male in decor, and the energy she sensed here was only of men. No women had stayed in this room for quite some time, though she could feel the lingering presence—just a small whiff, mind you—of a singular female who was much loved by the present resident of the house. It did not feel like the essence of a lover. Elizabeyta realized she didn't know much about Lee's family background and made a mental note to check with Emma in the morning—without seeming too obvious, of course. Elizabeyta repeated the warding procedures on all the window frames and the door to the hallway, then did the same in the bathroom.

The third room was used for storage. Odds and ends of furniture from ministerial families gone by were heaped along one wall, fortified by boxes and packing crates. In one corner sat a chipped and discolored rocking horse. It eyed her forlornly. Although it was a pain, she managed to crawl over most of the junk in the room to complete her task.

The flick of the overhead light revealed that the fourth room had been made over into a personal study. It was not like the one she had passed downstairs, that took the place of the parlor in her own home. As that office was regal and plain, showing the designs of the church Lee oversaw, this room was vibrant and passionate in nature. A bit in awe, she set the tray down in the hall before she entered the room.

There were bookshelves with hardbacks and paperbacks stacked in haphazard fashion from Shakespeare to Campbell. Dozens of books on historical Egypt were stuffed in among an equal number of psychology manuals, all lumped on the floor in and beside several plastic crates. There were also stacks of science fiction and fantasy novels and a complete collection of Stephen King hardcovers—two of which were signed by the author. These sat on a shelf by themselves.

Several Native American blankets were suspended from brass rods on the walls, giving the room a warm and inviting feeling, their colors splashing gaily to the eye. A tightly woven throw, in the design of a large wolf, graced the back of an old and battered peacock chair, jammed in the corner closest to the window. There was also a leather shield that looked rather Mediterranean hanging behind a large, soft leather chair positioned in the opposite corner of the room. A modern standing light arched gracefully from behind the back of the chair. These things she caught with a single sweep of the eye.

It was his desk that captured her attention. On the right was a computer, with all its appropriate paraphernalia. Normal enough. It was the jumble of books in the center of his desk that held her eye. She moved to the chair behind it and sat down, pawing hurriedly through them. They were all new, some with covers just bent, many with notes penciled or penned in the margins. They were all on the Craft and the art of magick.

Beneath the book lay a notepad, also filled with notations, quotes, and personal thoughts. Her own mind vapor-locked and she was suspended for a moment, soaking in the intensity of his study. The yearning to know. The touching of mysteries and daring to hope they might be true. Her mind snapped back. What a wonderful High Priest he would make! She grimaced at her own folly. Well, at least she had found the power point she was looking for.

Personal ethics kept her from continuing to read his papers, nor did she venture into any of the desk drawers. Witches respect the personal space of others, if it can be helped.

She left the room momentarily to fetch the tray left in the hallway. It was time to go to work. The clock downstairs struck midnight.

chapter thirty-two

BELINDA ROLLED OVER AND LOOKED OUT THE motel room window through a small break in the worn curtains. The sliver of visible sky loomed cotton black. It was nearly forty-eight hours since they had run from God knew what—or more appropriately, who. She shivered and snuggled deeper under the threadbare blanket. Mark was probably freezing. Peeping over her blanket, she saw the soft rise and fall of his chest, barely visible in the gloom of this dive. Neither one of them had slept very well since their ordeal began, jumping at every car, every sound. They had been calling for snow again all day on the radio. She wondered vacantly how soon it would start. An easy thought to consider as all others were either too painful or too frightening to review. Bleakly, she figured all the funerals were over yesterday afternoon.

They said this snow would be the worst in twenty years. That would be fine. Then all would slow down to a mere crawl in the outside world, or maybe even stop for a while. Perhaps the evil could not find them in the slow motion of the weather. Then again, evil, like shadows, crept everywhere.

Mark stirred in sleep, his long legs battling the arm of the chair. He moaned softly. Holding her breath, she waited to see if he was awake, but he settled and grew quiet once again. Better to let him sleep; at least he could make good dreams if God was willing.

Belinda had just turned seventeen, but she felt as if she'd lived a lifetime.

What to do? In the end, she was glad she'd been driving, for surely had Mark had the wheel, he would have wrecked the little Toyota into a pancake-sized piece of metal with only their blood left for identification, for the first place they had gone was Mark's house. As she slowly drifted by the flashing lights, the small, hushed crowd of people, they both saw a body being carried out of the house and placed into the coroner's van. Mark's mother, her only defense against the cold a sweatshirt and a pair of jeans, trailed, dazed, behind the body. She fell once and a neighbor picked her up and threw his own coat around her shoulders. She shrugged him off, dropping the coat to the ground.

"Keep driving," whispered Mark.

"But Mark, your mother—she needs you!"

"I said, keep driving! They got to him. They'll get to us. They won't bother with her now," he argued.

His mouth rattled like a freight train. He was afraid. He swore his father's death was no accident—that they had done it. At first she chose only familiar roads and did several loops on and off the highway. More than once she felt unseen eyes boring into her skin. Close to 3:00 AM, on Route 15, she could have sworn a pick-up with a broken headlight was following them. To her relief, a cop pulled the truck over before the turnpike entrance.

She decided to avoid the pike. If someone really were following her, a highway with few controlled exits could be a trap. She drove down to Chambersburg and back, then on into Harrisburg and beyond. Through the night her Toyota sped on ice-glassed highways, Mark sometimes talking softly, sometimes screaming, and when doing neither—crying. Finally, he curled uncomfortably beside her until he slept the dreamless unconsciousness of grief.

They tried to sleep during the day, parked behind a clump of pines in a snow-covered field. Mark cried out in his sleep; Belinda watched him, heavy-eyed, clutching the manila folder to her chest, waiting for something to happen.

They drove back in to Whiskey Springs that evening, and sat for a half hour in front of the pastor's house, arguing. When the door opened and three strangers, two women and a man, stepped out on the porch, Mark screamed for her to take off. She obeyed without thinking, gunning the engine and again heading out to the outskirts of town. After fifteen minutes she headed back to the pastor's house again but parked two blocks away. At Mark's urging she snuck up to the pastor's mailbox, passing a red Jeep with the hood up, but no one was around. Belinda jammed the manila envelope in the mail box and ran all the way back to the car. Then they whirled out of town and onto the highway. She just drove and drove and drove. Mark refused to get out of the car.

Mark drifted into an uneasy sleep. Belinda drove. And she thought. And she planned.

In the early-morning darkness, she found a broken-down motel outside Lancaster. Dirty neon lights sputtered "Country Inn—Truckers Welcome." She pulled in, paid some disgusting old geezer for a room, and dragged Mark into the motel room. It was cold, it was dirty, but at least she didn't have to drive it anywhere.

They hadn't actually run away. It was agreed that they wanted to go home—when and to whom was the question. Perhaps they had made an error by disappearing. Belinda wasn't worried about being missed. Her mother was on that lecture tour.

It was Mark everyone was looking for. The good and the bad were homing in on him. Belinda crawled out of bed, shivered in the coolness of the room, and covered Mark up, tucking her blanket securely around him. Shadows leapt and crawled in the half-light of dawn.

Belinda was not into religion. Her thought to see the pastor was more a practical one than spiritual. He had often visited her home for Sunday dinners and she'd come to enjoy his infectious smile and probing mind. Many girls her age would have tried to woo him in girlish infatuation, but somehow it didn't seem right to her. Belinda loved her mother too much to make fools out of all of them and behaved accordingly.

She wished now, as she carefully gazed out of the window, alone in her thoughts, that there was really some greater power out there that gave a damn.

She'd heard her mother often talk about "Goddess Energy," but she had hardly listened. Something about it being the female side of God—an energy that women could turn to and be understood by.

Belinda placed her palms on the cold glass, giving her spirit and praying silently that this Goddess would come, or at least would listen to a frightened maiden deep in the bowels of a man's world and caught in the web of a man's dark magick.

She lost track of time, caught in personal grief like a rat in a trap with no escape. Something in her mind was breaking, pushing, shoving to get out. She clung to the veil between reality and something else—familiar, yet not. A memory of something lost, forgotten. What was it? Another time, another place, a grove of trees, an altar. A dream?

A lilting, female voice reached out and encompassed her. "And once every month, when the moon is full, you shall gather together, and I shall

come to you. For I am the Mother of All Creation and you are my children."
A sense of warm safety crept over Belinda. This must be a dream, a lovely,
secure vision of home long ago.

"And I will teach you the ways of the wise," whispered the voice. "Do
not fear death, because it is merely a cycle of life. The wheel turns, the cycle
moves, the spiral continues as you shall continue. Death to life to death and
rebirth. There is always a tomorrow."

Belinda's eyes snapped open. She had been to the card reader in town
last summer when everything had gone so wrong in her life, seeking answers
to problems she herself had created. Friends had convinced her to go, thinking perhaps they could pick up a love potion or something equally silly.

The woman who ran the shop, Terry something-or-other, was a piece of
work, smothering her friends with psychic buzz-words until they were properly impressed. Belinda stood near the door, wrinkling her nose in distaste. It
had taken some time, but the gauchely dressed woman finally wrangled a
rune reading fee from Belinda, at the student rate, of course. There hadn't
been much to it, leaving Belinda believing the woman didn't know what the
hell she was talking about. In fact, the only thing she could remember at this
moment, several months later, was the Death rune concluding the reading.

The Terry person had assured her that she was not going to die, only go
through some type of internal change. Although Belinda was no longer so
sure that death wasn't in her cards, she had reached the point where she was
no longer afraid. Nor did she flinch when the curtain rustled of its own
accord, spewing forth a man in black, snatching her into oblivion.

chapter thirty-three

ASON BLACKTHORN BIT VICIOUSLY ON THE filter of an unlit cigar. Timothy Reed was dead, without his assistance, and his man reported the Belladonna woman's file was not to be found, meaning she was wandering around somewhere, doing her everyday business for all he knew, without a care in the world. If she touched any of her financial business, like selling off property, moving stocks, changing bank accounts, everything would be lost.

He sucked on his cigar, his eyes slit and calculating.

Binky was dead. Ah, well, a slight misfortune. The silly ignoramus had killed the wrong woman anyway. Punishment would have been in order and Jason simply didn't have the time for such small matters.

He pressed the intercom button on his desk. "Richard, call Michael in from the field and tell him to stand by for my orders. He's to have his team ready. Where is he right now?"

"I believe he's in Oklahoma, sir," came the polite voice from the box.

"And where is Lance?"

"On his way back from Lowell, Massachusetts. He phoned in about an hour ago to tell you he has secured the funds. You will have access to them shortly."

"Good! As soon as he arrives give him something to eat, then come straight to me. That should be in about five hours, considering the way he drives."

"Yes, sir. Is there anything else, sir?"

"Have my lunch delivered here, in the drawing room. I don't like to take care of unfinished business on an empty stomach. I prefer seafood today. Have Harold prepare it accordingly."

"Will anyone be joining you, sir?"

Jason considered a moment, then smiled broadly. "Yes, I believe we'll have that Belinda creature as our guest. See to it she's cleaned up and appropriately dressed."

"Yes, sir."

"Oh, and Richard, were the boys able to get the computer from Reed's house?"

The intercom remained silent.

"Richard?"

"Yes, sir?" His voice was so soft that Jason could barely hear it.

"Were we able to get Reed's computer?"

"Ah, yes, sir."

"And?"

"Our man thinks the information is gone … sir."

"What do you mean, our man thinks the information is gone? Either it is, or it isn't!" shouted Jason.

"It is destroyed, sir. The hard drive has been reformatted in a special way. In other words, the information is not retrievable."

Jason slammed his fist on the desk, roaring in frustration. "What about the disks? Did he get those from the house, too?"

"Yes, sir, but they are all blank, every last one of them. Our man says it is definitely sabotage. Everything, including disks marked 'Reed family files,' is gone. We will get nothing from that end anymore."

Jason punched the intercom button to exclude Richard from his muttering and rose from the chair behind the desk, stroking his thin beard thoughtfully.

Of course, he had known where the Belladonna woman was all along, and had, up until now, felt confident that he could get rid of her whenever he wanted. He rather enjoyed her childish play as private investigator.

However, he didn't want the others to know where she was just yet. Hence the show with the fat woman and countless others. Unveiling his power on those evenings had been both entertaining and exhilarating.

One of his dark men reported that the minister next door, that Lee Becker fellow, was showing a little more interest than usual in Jason's intended prey. They had tried without success to remove him. Again, his men in the field had made a grave error.

Since Aunt Emma was so fond of the fellow, it was a given she'd probably helped him. Well, he'd see to the pastor in time. For now, it was not a pressing issue. Perhaps, with the Belladonna Witch out of the way, the pastor would no longer be a problem. He rolled the cigar filter around in his mouth. Of course, if the pastor managed to stay out of Jason's way—well, it was better to let him percolate on his own … he was too popular with the town at the moment.

But if Aunt Emma started snooping, too … well, the old bitch had been asking for it for years. She'd always been a thorn in his side, but she was old, and couldn't last forever. If he touched her now, the Elders would have a fit, many of them sentimental in their graying years and not enthusiastic about offing an old woman.

With jaw thrust forward, teeth clamped on the filter of the cigar, he paced like a caged animal back and forth across the blue Persian rug of the drawing room. He figured Reed's boy had the file, but when they brought the little brat and his two-bit whore in, it wasn't with them. His people had torn the car apart, had ransacked the girl's house to no avail. No file folder. No envelope. No nothing. His men had tried to extract the information through other means, but most he had chosen for their blind fealty and not their brain power.

If the Belladonna woman discovered she was being investigated, she may somehow obscure her financial information, though he doubted she knew how much she was worth. That sort of information was normally reserved for only the Elders. It had taken ten years to work out this plan of elimination and profit. He'd be damned if two teenagers stood in his way. Better had tried … and died.

He took a long, steady drag on the unlit cigar, flicking nonexistent ashes into the cold hearth. He was trying to quit. Which reminded him—he'd better get Richard in here to light a fire and arrange the room before they brought in the strumpet.

He'd finally discovered the location of the covenstead last evening. All was in readiness. He only needed one more piece—the Belladonna woman. The solitaries he'd ordered killed in over seven states were just fun to pass the time until he could smoke out someone important. Many didn't even know why they faced the wrath of Blackthorn. The few that did, well … too bad he couldn't get them to talk. Two had taken their own lives before his men had had the chance to get down and dirty. He pulled hard on the unlit cigar, smashed it into a perfectly clean ash tray, then spent several minutes wiping it out with a tissue.

Of course, he had hit pay dirt with the old bat, Elizabeyta's grandmother, but one of his men had gotten too zealous and she'd died before he could get anything out of her. If they'd let her live, he wouldn't have to be going through this now. Of course, now would be so much more amusing. The Belladonna woman was quite beautiful. She would be fun to play with. Damn fools. He'd had to dispose of the old woman's sister immediately, even though she obviously hadn't known anything. The men who botched the job were either stringing harps in heaven, which he highly doubted, or dancing a fire jig in Hades. He didn't care either way.

Back in the eighties, he'd thought some idiot wanna-be Pagan would flush them out of hiding, with a "we've been here all along" spiel, but they'd kept tomb silent while the rest of the country woke up to realize they had over half a million Witches and Pagans running around the cities and backwater country towns. At least he had managed to cultivate some interesting magickal cast-offs to add to his "family." The few who dabbled enjoyed the, ahem, left-hand path.

Ah, well, telecommunication links of the nineties being as fine as they are, even if he could not find that damnable report of Reed's, he could find someone else to do the job with the information he would most pleasurably pry out of those two teenagers. Unfortunately, his funds were rather low at the moment. He brushed an imaginary stray ash off his sleeve.

A soft rap at the door brought his attention back to the business at hand.

chapter thirty-four

SAM RENARD PATIENTLY DRUMMED HIS
fingers on his desk. He'd thought he'd gotten
rid of Sarah, but here she was, town scandal-
mouth, plopped unceremoniously in the chair
opposite his desk. It was times like these he
wished he was back in New York. The quartz clock
on his desk blinked at him hypnotically. It was
11:00 AM … 11:01 … 11:02 … 11:03 …

His attention was drawn once again to her
overly made-up face. Who was she trying to kid,
anyway? Everyone knew it was that husband of
hers, who'd finally popped her one. 'Course, she
claimed she'd fallen down the stairs. *Right, and there
isn't any ice in Alaska,* he thought irritably.

"So, as I was sayin'—Sam! are you listenin' to
me?" Sarah shifted her weight with care as to not
tip the chair over.

"Ah, yeah, Sarah. You were telling me about
Brother Hank sleeping with what's-her-name and

237

that there is a big revival scheduled for tonight. And you think it is, ah, news-worthy, and I ought to be there."

"Well, not because Brother Hank is sleepin' with that tart, for heaven's sake!" Sarah snorted and rolled her eyes.

Sam sat back heavily in his chair. "Then what, Sarah, what is so news-worthy that you felt you needed to pay me a personal call? Up to this moment you have told me about your bad dreams, your, hmmm, bad fall, and your bad experience in the church lot. Although I am sure these are momentous occa-sions in your life, they do nothing for me nor are they particularly newsworthy to anyone but yourself." He accentuated his frown so she would get the point.

Sarah squirmed in her chair, eyes flicking from Sam's computer to the papers on his desk, then over to the window. "I thought a big revival meet-ing would be interesting reading in the newspaper," she offered lamely.

Sam rolled his eyes. "Sarah, we have a freelance reporter who covers that sort of stuff, and if it's on the church bulletin board, she'll see to it that it gets in the paper. Nancy checks those things faithfully. She never misses anything that has to do with God, salvation, or any of that other claptrap. In fact, I believe you know Nancy. Why didn't you call her instead of coming in here and bothering me, or have you done something to piss her off, too?"

"Brother Hank says he's goin' to fight the devil tonight, at the revival," she said solemnly.

Sam guffawed. "What's he going to do, invoke the devil with a tam-bourine then run him through with a cross … sprinkle a little holy water on him?" He wiggled his fingers in the air as if spritzing water at her. She flinched.

"Ah, well … no. I think he's going to do somethin' to that girl." Tiny beads of perspiration trickled down Sarah's neck. She dabbed at them with a flowered hankie, produced from her oversized purse.

Leaning forward, Sam said, "You mean he's going to screw what's-her-name in front of everyone?"

Sarah flushed, growling under her breath. "No, you fool. I think he's goin' to do somethin' to that Belladonna woman."

"What Belladonna woman?" shouted Sam.

Sarah reminded him of their earlier conversation, finishing with, "You know, the one I told you about!"

Sam rubbed his forehead. "Now let me get this straight—you think that Brother Hank is going to try to abduct a town resident, drag her to a revival, and then somehow extract the devil out of her. How, may I ask, dear Sarah, do you think he is going to get away with such nonsense? I can't believe he'd try anything so stupid. He'd be arrested even before he got started, then sued to boot. It would be a suicidal move both financially and reputation-wise. How did you get such a ludicrous idea in the first place?"

Sarah moaned. "Because I told him the devil was the Belladonna woman, or at least she's in cahoots with him."

"You what? Oh, Sarah, how could you put someone you don't even know in such a predicament? That damn mouth of yours has gone too far this time. Sarah, I think you have been drinking too much. Do me a favor, go home and dry out!"

Sarah rose swiftly, towering over his desk. With one lunge of her arm she had him by the tie and halfway off his chair. "Now you listen to me, you son-of-a-whore, I don't drink. Never touched a drop of the stuff in my life. I think I made a real bad mistake—the nightmares gettin' to me and all. I know I done some mighty bad things in my time, gossipin' and such, but nothin' like this!"

She took a deep breath, nearly spitting in his face, tightening his tie until he gulped. "There's something real bad in this town. I've been tellin' ever'body I know and no one's listenin'. I already went to the cops and they don't believe me. Now, I'm comin' to you. You got pull here in town. Maybe if you just put the word out that you're doin' your usual snoopin', Brother Hank will change his mind. An' if you don't, I'll tell my sister about Miss Priss out there in the office!"

Jerking his tie from her clutches, Sam staggered backward, nearly flipping over his chair. "All right!" he said angrily. "I'll put the word out. But let me tell you something, Sarah, this is the last time you'll hold that over my head or there will be another dead body lying around town—yours!"

Sarah smiled sweetly, turned on her boot with heavy grace, and lumbered out of the office without a word, banging his office door behind her.

"Bitch!" he muttered at the closed door, adjusting his tie so he could breath normally again. His eyelids jerked in alarm as the door flew open. Grace, face flushed and her usual crispness slightly awry, burst into his office. "What did she do to you?" he moaned.

"She? Who? Oh, you mean Sarah. Why, nothing, she left without so much as a word. No, it's the scanner! Tiffany Parkins was found dead over at the truck stop about ten minutes ago!"

"Any word on how she bought it?"

"Rumor has it she got herself strangled."

"Thought she stopped going over there once she took up with Brother Hank?" Sam's voice died in his throat. "Get Lou out there on the double," he barked. "I'm heading there now." He rummaged in the desk drawer for his tape recorder, grabbed a pack of unopened batteries, some new tapes, and threw them into a small valise he kept by his desk for on-the-run jobs like this.

"Don't know when I'll be back, Grace. Probably not until you're gone. Lock up as usual. The typist isn't coming in until after midnight tonight. Heavy date or something."

Even though the truck stop was only a quarter-mile up Route 15, it took Sam almost an hour to get there. Vehicles were backed up a mile on either side of the highway. It would have been nice if Grace had warned him there was an accident right in front of the damned diner. Maybe she'd missed that part. Dead chickens, live chickens, blood, feathers, ice, snow, dirty slush, and angry motorists were everywhere. It was enough to give him a severe headache. By the time he arrived on the scene and produced his press pass, he had totally forgotten about the Belladonna woman.

Lou was already there, head bent in low conversation with one of the police brass. Since Lou stood behind the police lines, Sam figured the regular photographer was probably still off with the flu. Lucky break. He'd have great pictures for Monday's paper.

Tiffany's body had been found by a trucker's dog in a ditch that ran along the back of the stop, but by the time Sam arrived, the body had already been transported. The cops were now scouring the area. They were surly, cold, and non-communicative. Head pounding, Sam decided to kill two birds with one stone, heading for the diner end of the truck stop. If he was lucky, one of the waitresses could find him some aspirin and he could canvass the usual patrons, looking for a lead of his own.

He was not disappointed. Aspirin knocked back and coffee before him, he soon wrangled the details out of the waitresses and the counter regulars. Everyone was delighted to talk. Murder was a fun and interesting topic, as long as your own kin wasn't involved. Amid the din and clatter of diner noises, Sam listened to various accounts of Tiffany's last hours.

About nine Thursday evening, Tiffany had parked herself at the diner counter. Why, no one was really quite sure. She hadn't been in for several months, her time otherwise occupied by both her official church duties and her unofficial ones with Brother Hank. The waitress was fairly surprised when Tiffany strutted in, flirted with a few of the counter boys, and proceeded to drink coffee and banter for about two hours. She didn't appear to be waiting for anybody, nor did she mention where she would go whenever she decided to leave. After eating a piece of hot apple pie with chocolate ice cream, she picked up her purse and walked out into the night.

Nobody remembered her pulling in, or where she had parked. No one saw her drive away, either. The roads had been so bad, only a few regulars wandered into the diner after that, save for a trucker or two for take-out coffee. Of course, no one could say if she'd been at the pumps on the other side of the lot. They were always busy, no matter what the weather. But it was a fair way from the diner side of the lot to the pump side, and no one recalled Tiffany looking like she had done that trek in the bitter weather. She had entered the diner, smiling and fresh, as if she'd just alighted from her car.

The waitress, known as Babe to all the locals, remembered that Tiffany appeared in a fairly good mood. "She wasn't goin' no place," remarked Babe, "because she offered me a ride home. I said no, since my old man drives snowplow, and he was comin' to pick me up after his shift was over. I only come in here today because Linda is sick as a dog, poor thing. She's gonna be spit-fire mad she missed all the ruckus, 'specially since she didn't like Tiffany in the first place. There'd be no sadness in that girl's heart when she finds out! Me, I feel a bit sorry for the broad. Didn'a make nothin' of her life, and now look … dead and gone. Thank the good Lord she didn'a leave any babes behind. Now that would have been terrible sad, it would. Sort of makes a body think of their own life, don't it, Sam?"

Sam nodded, lost in his own thoughts as she moved on to the next customer, their conversation already shelved in her mind.

In a nutshell, then, Tiffany had been in a good mood, wasn't waiting for anyone, and didn't appear to have any place to go. Either she was a target of a psychotic trucker or someone she knew had it in for her. That, thought Sam, could have been a lot of people about a year ago, but since she had taken up with Brother Hank, she'd relegated her pleasures in other directions.

Sam stirred his coffee thoughtfully. Sarah may have been right after all. There was an awful lot of trouble around for a town the size of Whiskey Springs. It was no longer dullsville, it was deadsville. He didn't for a moment think that there was some sort of evil non-entity floating about, but he couldn't deny the fact that Whiskey Springs was stacking up corpses like Haynes' lumber mill was stacking cordwood for all the wood stoves in town.

Babe moved further down the counter, filling coffee cups and chatting politely. "Yes," he heard her say, "police have already been in here and taken statements from a few, mine included. Said that if they think of anythin' else, they'll be back. Lookin' for anyone in particular? Nawt' other than those that were here last night, but I think most of 'em were here this mornin' at one time and their statements were written down already."

Which suited Sam just fine, considering the rotten mood he had seen outside.

The bell atop the front door jingled for what seemed the thousandth time. Cold air wafted through the diner, curling around customers and furniture alike. Sam looked up to see Lou heading straight for him, a stony expression on his face. He took the empty stool beside Sam.

"So," remarked Sam, "how's the photo-detective doing these days? Saw you out there working. The other guy still have the flu?" His grin wasn't returned. Lou motioned at Babe, who brought a cup of coffee over for him. He waited until she hustled over to a booth, out of earshot.

"You're not going to believe it!" whispered Lou.

Sam leaned closer to Lou, turning his body to shield their conversation. "I'm all ears," he said.

"They found Tiffany's body naked as a jay-bird."

Sam grimaced. "Any sign of—well, you know …"

"No; of course the coroner will have to have the final say, but there were no bruises on the body, other than around the throat. But that's not the really weird part."

Sam's shoulders tensed as he leaned closer.

"She had one of those tattoos on the inside of her right thigh."

"No! You're joking!"

Lou gave him a searing glance, then straightened up as Babe rounded the corner of the counter and headed his way again with the coffee pot. He waited until she replaced the pot and went into the kitchen to pick up an order.

"I kid you not, and that's not all."

"You mean there's more?"

Lou nodded conspiratorially. "Get this. I did some scouting around the other night trying to get a line on that tattoo. Well, I met a guy named Paints and he was real scared-like. What do you know about a mountain family around here that operates like a gang?"

Sam looked at him blankly. "A gang? You mean like a city gang?" Things were beginning to click in his head. That's what had been bothering him about this whole mess—back in New York, there had been a big gang slaying with definite occult overtones. Cops had been in on it, city officials, it had been a real mess. In Sam's mind it never had shaken out properly. A deep shiver ran up and down Sam's arms. He didn't like this, not one bit.

"There's more." Lou looked over his shoulder. "The end booth is open down there; let's take our coffee over and order some food. I'm famished."

Sam grumbled, but followed the plan. He didn't realize how hungry he was until he bit into the Reuben sandwich. Mouth working and ears opened, he listened to the rest of Lou's story. Seemed that this fellow Paints ended up dead the day after Lou had spoken to him.

"City police claim it was robbery related, but I'm not so sure about that," said Lou between mouthfuls of bacon burger. "The other place I checked, that Rosie's joint, well don't you know it burned to the ground that night, along with a few other row homes. Nobody was injured, just missing. Word had it later they were all visiting relatives in Ohio, which I know is shit, because I talked to the woman right at the door and unless Ohio is over her doorstep, there's a mystery there, too."

Sam sopped up the Reuben juices with a piece of crust. "Anything else?"

Lou settled back and patted his stomach. "Other than Timothy Reed's body disappearing from the hospital morgue then reappearing again twelve hours later—no, I can't think of anything else."

"What do you mean, his body was missing for twelve hours?"

"Just what I said. It was there, then it wasn't, then it was. I don't think he went wandering around the hospital for one last jaunt on the planet earth. Hospital staff feels that he got delivered to the wrong funeral home by mistake and instead of someone fessing up, they just brought him back without a how-de-do and no thank you."

Babe interrupted their conversation to fill their cups again. "I'm goin' home now. I'm dog-tired and Susie will take over from here," she said.

Sam smiled and handed her a ten dollar bill. "Here you go, Babe; thanks for the conversation."

She grinned and pocketed the ten. A few minutes later, through the veil of steam congealing on the diner window, he saw her climb into the snowplow compartment with her husband. They appeared to be arguing, but with the lousy weather conditions, Sam couldn't be sure.

"Well, for heaven's sake," muttered Sam as he saw her jump out of the plow and run over to the pay phones near the road. She made a hasty call, then ran back to the plow. Eventually, it trundled out of the parking lot.

Lou wasn't paying any attention. He munched happily on his second burger. "Oh, by the way—Sam … Sam!"

Sam swung his head around from the window.

"The Reed kid is still missing. The cops think he might have argued with Tim right before he died. They still can't get much out of the wife, between her son missing and her husband dead she's gone loopty-loop in the thinking department. When the kid found out his dad was dead, he may have taken off thinking it was his fault or something. They're checking with relatives and friends of his at the moment, but nobody suspects foul play."

"Maybe we should be," muttered Sam.

"Huh?"

"I don't know, Lou, just too many bad things happening around here lately." Sam sighed; now he was talking like Sarah. Which brought up the issue of Elizabeyta Belladonna. Sam sat on it for awhile, allowing their talk to flow into regular newspaper banter. He had to digest the information Lou gave him. Arrangements were made for Lou to drop off non-sensitive pictures of the murder site, as well as a few other shots, including one of the Jack Frost champion ski team.

"Oh, and while you are at it, I hear Brother Hank is going to hold one of his revivals tonight, providing of course he'll still be doing it now that Tiffany is dead. You may want to stop in and snap a few. Keep the religious readers happy," grinned Sam.

Lou groaned. "Oh please, don't make me go there. I know he'll still do it. Money speaks to that man, not the dead, and certainly not any God I ever heard of."

"Now you never know just where good copy is going to spring up," chided Sam. "In fact, I'm not doing anything, so why don't we ride together?"

Lou looked at him in disbelief. "You, go to a revival meeting? What, that freelance reporter sick with the flu or something?"

Dabbing at his mouth with his crumpled napkin, Sam merely smiled and rose. He stretched his legs and picked up the check. "This one's on me, Lou, my boy, this one's on me."

Chapter Thirty-Five

SLEEPILY, ELIZABEYTA LIFTED HER HEAD; there were dustballs at eye level. At first she couldn't fathom where she was, until she saw Lee's hand hanging over the side of the bed. He was snoring.

"My stars and garters," she mumbled, "I must have slept here on the floor all night." She kicked off the comforter, with the vague remembrance of pulling it off a guest bed before collapsing in a heap of exhaustion on the floor. "Oh, my aching back," she groaned. She leaned over the bed and checked Lee's forehead. His color was good and he was certainly sleeping peacefully enough. She smiled as he grumbled in his sleep.

A small creak at the door made her whirl around. With pounding heart, she watched as it drifted open, only to reveal Emma's grey head pop around the corner.

"Oh, it's you," sighed Elizabeyta. "For a minute there ..."

"Well! It's about time you got awake, you lazy bones. Do you know it's past noon?"

"I never dreamed I would sleep here."

Emma shrugged. "Didn't think nothing of it. He ain't the one for you."

"I beg your pardon?"

"Never mind. Done a lot of thinking last night, is all." Emma slipped into the room and walked over to Lee's bed. "Looks pretty good for bein' near death, don't you think?"

Elizabeyta smiled. "Yes, Emma, you did a fine job. Remind me to call you the next time I get in trouble." She noticed Emma was wearing the same clothes as the night before. Either she was very poor, or she had a rough night, too.

Emma eyed her, shrugged her shoulders, and tip-toed out to the hall-way. Elizabeyta followed and shut the bedroom door quietly behind her. "Stew's simmerin' downstairs, should you have a mind to eat," said Emma softly. "Since it's past breakfast and all, thought I'd whip somethin' up for lunch. He'll be hungry as a bear when he wakes up and any man, pastor or no, thinks of his stomach before just about anythin' else." She nodded toward the closed door.

Elizabeyta realized Emma's mannerisms this morning were not those of an enemy. Since she didn't seem the type to speak her mind, Elizabeyta wondered what had gotten into her. The odor of stew drifted through the hallway, and her stomach rumbled in response. She scanned Emma, but could find no trace of deception.

"Before we get to talkin'," said Emma, "I think there's a woman's stomach that needs feedin', too." She grinned and hustled Elizabeyta down the stairs.

After Elizabeyta finished two bowls of stew and a dumpling, Emma cleared the table and brought out coffee, settling herself opposite Elizabeyta. "Seems this is where we left off last night," said Emma good-naturedly.

Elizabeyta eyed her with suspicion. This was definitely not the Emma she'd faced at this table last night. Although she thought they had parted friends, there was no use counting on things before you were sure of them.

"Okay, what gives? Last night you were ready to put a stake through my heart, cut off my head, and stuff my mouth with garlic. Then you thought I was here to render you unholy justice. Today you are feeding me until I'm ready to burst. I don't understand it."

"Well, I didn't go home last night."

That explained why Emma was wearing the same clothes. "If you didn't go home, where did you go?" asked Elizabeyta carefully.

"Oh, I meant to go home all right, but the Jeep kept cutting out on me. I meandered over to my cousin's house, but she had already gone to bed. She don't take to staying up late. I live up the mountain yonder so's it was too far to walk. I was tired to beat all, and I will tell ya right to yer face, I didn't believe all you tol' me."

Elizabeyta sipped her coffee, but didn't interrupt. Emma's tone was sincere; her aura was strong and bright.

"Anyhow, I came back here first, but by then most of the lights were out and I figured disturbing you wouldn't be wise. On the way down the walk, I slipped a good shot and would have kissed the Lord's ground, save for the mailbox. I'm afraid I jerked the handle so hard to save myself, I broke it clean off and the door flew open. And don't you know, this here came a-tumblin' out." She pushed a large manila envelope toward Elizabeyta, its edges dirty and rumpled.

"What's this? Looks like you cried over it," kidded Elizabeyta uneasily. "It also, well, feels yucky." *Like the tire iron but not like the tire iron,* she thought. By the way, what had she done with that tire iron? She'd been so preoccupied the night before. She'd have to go looking for it later.

"Just snow, of course, made it rumpled."

Her attention snapping back to the matter at hand, Elizabeyta held it for a moment.

"Well, ain't you goin' to open it?" snapped Emma irritably. "I'll have you know, I already read it." She folded her bony arms across her chest.

"First things first," frowned Elizabeyta. With a delicate hold on the envelope, she shut her eyes and concentrated. Breathing deeply, she relaxed and centered herself.

"What you doin'? I can tell you what's in it!" Patience was not one of Emma's virtues. Elizabeyta could feel how badly Emma wanted her to know the contents of the envelope, but she resisted the temptation. There was other information she needed to gather first. If she looked inside, she may draw inaccurate conclusions.

"Shhh!" spit Elizabeyta, here eyes still shut. "I'll look at it in a minute, I've got to do something important first."

Emma's sigh whooshed across the table.

Again she relaxed and centered. This time Emma didn't interrupt. Elizabeyta moved further into the task, letting the remnant energies attached to the envelope touch her mind. Initially nothing other than the slimy feeling touched her senses. Her mind flirted momentarily with the idea that she may not be able to do this anymore, and what she eventually came up with may be wrong. "There is no time for this," she thought angrily. She released her personal feelings and kicked in her training.

Psychometry, the art of trying to decipher who has touched an object last, its history, and events that have happened around an object, had been one of her better studies at the covenstead. If she failed now, then perhaps she had lost her touch. It came, but it came slowly.

"The last person to handle this envelope was you, Emma; of course I already know that because you told me. Before that, it was in the hands of a younger person, a female … I think. I can feel her fear. It is like she is running from something or someone. There is also a boy … no, a young man with her; I can feel his energy, too."

Emma gaped at Elizabeyta. "How you know that stuff?"

"Training," muttered Elizabeyta, her eyes still closed. "Try not to chime in, please. Let me try again." She was silent for a few moments. "This is a report of some kind and whoever put it together didn't want to. That was a man, older. He's in a lot of trouble. He's very unhappy. No, wait—the energy level is very low … no, there's a veil of some kind, but not magick; something else … that's all I can get." She opened her eyes and looked at Emma. "So, I know you are bursting at the seams to tell me. What's in this envelope?"

"I'm amazed. Do you see pictures?"

"Not very often. Mostly I feel things, like emotions and levels of energy. You didn't answer my question. What's in the envelope?"

"Well, honey, it's ever'thin' about you. Where you come from, your people, and—ah … how much you're worth."

"Excuse me?"

"Honey, you don't need to josh me. You're set pretty nice for yourself."

"I hate to break it to you, Emma, but I haven't got a dime. Everything I own is tied up with my family."

"Not by that, it ain't. It all belongs to you."

Elizabeyta fumbled with the envelope and withdrew the report, headed with her own name. Flipping through it nervously, she wondered who could have compiled it and why. It was a complete financial statement, including holdings of various family members, but it was the bottom line figure that knocked the air right out of her. According to this report, Elizabeyta owned seventy-five percent of everything, which added up to so many zeros after the initial figure that they seemed to run across the page in an endless line.

Emma stared at her.

"Oh my stars and garters," murmured Elizabeyta. "I never knew. No one ever told me." She held the report close to her chest for a few moments, then looked at it again. Addresses, phone numbers, private accounts of individual family members—it was all there, including purchases made by all of them in the past six months. Even her computer modem information was listed.

"This is not good," said Elizabeyta firmly. There was also the mystery of what the report was doing in Lee's mailbox. Why, if he had something to do with this she'd scratch his eyes out! "I wonder why it was in Lee's mailbox? How dare he order a report on me! And if you really must know, it isn't all my money, it belongs to everyone at home, equally!"

Emma patted her hand. "Now honey, I see the temper rising in you, but hold on a minute. Even if it was Lee who asked for that report, who could blame him? He's sweet on you and he has a reputation to protect."

Elizabeyta would not have any of Emma's banalities. "How dare he have me investigated? If this report got into the wrong hands, a lot of people could suffer! He has put my entire family at risk and I'll not forgive him for it! Ever!" She slammed the report down on the table. "And how do you know he's 'sweet' on me?"

Emma shrugged. "Mason told me … and well, I got me some special talents too, you know." Emma looked at her thoughtfully. "Even if he did have that report done, it doesn't explain who did it, or anything about the kids you seen. Now think a moment, dear; we can ask Lee when he wakes up. I'm sure he'll put it all to rights."

Lips smashed in a thin line, Elizabeyta slouched in her chair. "Okay. Fine. I will ask him, and he'd better have a terrific answer! And, speaking of answers, you still haven't told me where you stayed last night, Emma."

"How about we trade information? You tell me what that mark is on your hand and I'll tell you where I stayed."

Elizabeyta looked at her squarely. "You drive a hard bargain for an old lady."

"And you are too full of mystery for a young one."

Elizabeyta grinned. "Okay, I'll give. You've got good timing when you want to, Emma. The mark is called a Triskele, the triple spiral. It is very old, I guess about three thousand years. All members of my family, after they have taken the oath of responsibility, receive this mark. It is a sign of respect and fealty."

"Sounds rather barbaric to me," muttered Emma. "Why do it?"

Elizabeyta toyed with her hand. "Oh, I guess each person's reasoning is different. Where I come from, families are different. They are like a union and often work together. This symbol, to me, is proof of my union and my dedication to my family. It is a very serious thing to receive the mark."

Emma shook her head. "I'm not sayin' I understand what you are tellin' me, but I understand how you feel about family, I guess. Maybe someday I'll understand better."

Smiling shyly, Elizabeyta's dark eyes grew round with gratitude. "Thank you for being my friend, Emma. It means a lot to me. Now, I fulfilled my part of the bargain. Where did you sleep last night?"

"Why, your place, o' course."

"Excuse me?"

Emma hesitated, "Well, I didn't think you'd mind."

"But how did you get in? The place was locked; besides, I have it protected!"

"Oh that," Emma waved her thin hand, "The door just swung open. Before we chat about that, though, I think there is somethin' else you should see." She reached in her smock pocket and pulled out a neon yellow piece of paper, folded neatly in fourths. "Take a look at this, honey; I found one on your porch stoop and one on Lee's. I took the liberty of sneakin' a peek up and down the street, and every house had one that I could see. Must have just delivered 'em before I walked out the door at 5:30 this mornin'."

Elizabeyta unfolded the paper and read for a moment. "Oh, how awful!"

"That's what I thought," remarked Emma. "I'm a good Christian and a Godfearing soul, mind you, but I really think he's taken it too far this time. We better not show this to Pastor Becker or he'll be flying out from under the covers and borrowin' your broom."

"Very funny," growled Elizabeyta. She put the unfolded paper down in the middle of the table. They both stared at it glumly. "Who is this nutcase, anyway?" asked Elizabeyta.

"Well, now, he's a no-account that came back to town sellin' religion. They call him Brother Hank. Look's like he's fixin' to fight the devil tonight."

The bold lettering, proclaiming that "Satan Is In Town" was bad enough, but the poor drawing, a naked picture of Satan, complete with male body parts, goat legs, and monster face, was enough to set Elizabeyta's teeth on edge. "Come To Heavenly Springs Church," begged the flier, "And See Brother Hank Battle the Demon From Hell Who Has Descended Upon Our Town." She noticed the printing was the rub-on stuff, running across the page in an uneven line. "Hear the Truth About the Evil of WitchCraft, Wicca, Satanism, and Ceremonial Magick," continued the tirade. Under the picture, the caption read, "See the Demon From Hell Brought To Its Knees In Front Of Your Very Eyes—8:00 PM Heavenly Springs Church, Fairfax Lane. Brother Hank Officiating Pastor."

"Sounds like a circus con," said Elizabeyta, as she mimicked the words on the flier.

"It does that," said Emma sadly.

"This is disgusting." Elizabeyta frowned. "I wonder if he really knows what's going on or if he is just using the predicament the town is in to make money."

Emma shook her head. "Knowin' Brother Hank, he's probably going to try to make a load of money. He always does. Folks say he owes some pretty ornery fellas a lot of money these days with his gamblin' and drinkin'. One of my relatives has seen him bettin' on the ponies regular. Lost most of his flock, he has, but this is the kind of garbage that will bring some of 'em back. But that ain't the worst of your problems, unless he knows about you."

"No, I don't think so." Elizabeyta wrinkled her brow in thought. "No, I never met the man. I don't usually stay long in town, and try to shop in York. In fact, this is the longest stretch I've been here. The only person from here I know even slightly is Lee—I mean, Pastor Lee."

Emma smiled sardonically. "Right."

"Well, I don't know him that well!"

"That ain't the one I was thinkin' about. In fact, it's Mason that comes to my mind."

Elizabeyta looked horrified. "Mason means nothing to me. Besides, he's married. I don't have time for such nonsense and I certainly won't sit here and chat about it! And for pity's sake, don't tell Lee any such gossip.

You'd ruin their friendship. I don't want to be responsible for that. I have enough on my shoulders right now."

Emma patted her hand. "That's okay, dear; I won't say nothing. But I know what I think."

Elizabeyta was infuriated, but could sense that no matter what she told this old woman, it wasn't going to be heard.

"Sky looks clear today," remarked Emma casually.

Elizabeyta grinned despite herself. "So tell me about my ghosts."

Emma laughed and got them some more coffee. "Well, I didn't hear no ghosts at your place."

"I thought you said you could talk to ghosts."

"I can, dearie, when they have a mind to speak. Thing was, nobody said a peep. I slept like a log. Sure you ain't been hearin' things, the stress you're under and all?"

"I know they are there," snarled Elizabeyta, then stopped herself. "I'm sorry, Emma, I don't mean to snap at you. But I am sure they are there, or at least, there is one there."

"Maybe after a bit you and I can go over and check again. We was going to talk to Mason over at your place anyway. See if we can come up with a plan of some sort to stop Jason."

Elizabeyta couldn't mask her disappointment that Emma hadn't seen her ghosts. "Sure, Emma." A heavy despair settled on her shoulders. She now had some answers to her questions, but not enough. Attack could come at any time … at any time. She'd better go home to prepare herself before Emma and Mason dropped by. "How about 4:30 this afternoon? Could you call Mason for me? I have some things to take care of," she said.

Bundled up and ready to go, she asked Emma to take care of Lee, explaining she needed a few hours to herself. Besides, she didn't want to see Lee right now on the chance he had ordered that report. The thought that he may not trust her cut her deeply. She walked by the tire iron stuck in the umbrella stand by the door, forgetting all about it and her backpack shoved in the corner of Lee's room.

chapter thirty-six

DEPRIVED OF SLEEP, MIND REELING FROM whatever drug had been used to render her unconscious, forced to sit in a cold chapel on a hard pew for who knows how long (she wasn't sure, nor no longer cared), Belinda could hardly walk when she was escorted from the chapel through a long, ill-lit hallway and into a large foyer. One of the men had to pick her up and carry her up the stairs to a bedroom on the second floor. He dumped her unceremoniously on the floor.

"Bathroom's in there," he nodded to a closed door on her right. "Clothes are in there," he motioned to a closet on the other side of the room. "You have an hour to shower and dress." Without another word he turned and left the room. She heard the snick of an outside lock. Trapped, again.

Belinda staggered to her feet, half-walking, half-stumbling over to the bed. She collapsed and lay there for some time. All she really wanted to do was get some sleep, to curl up in a ball and let the world slip away. And where was Mark? Had they taken him to a room, too? When she awoke, dazed, in the chapel, she didn't remember seeing him, though there were muffled sounds echoing from the other side. There had been whimpers and a cry of pain, then silence.

The men watching her were dressed in solid black, their faces plain and shaven, their hair short. Looking at them, she felt dead minds in living bodies. They neither spoke nor smiled. One of them roughly sat her up on a pew and there she remained.

She knew she was in deep trouble, there was no way around it. No one had the vaguest idea where she was, and no one was even aware she was someplace she didn't belong, wherever someplace was.

The man said he would be back in about an hour. How much time had she wasted lying here? Shaking her head in desperation to clear it only made her more dizzy. Finally, she sat up and tried to stand on her feet. It took a couple of tries, but she made it. She worked her way to one of the draped windows. In case someone was watching her room from the outside, she slowly pulled the heavy material aside, to be met with disappointment. The window was painted black and nailed shut. She moved to the next window, and found the same. There were four windows in this room, which meant she was probably at the end of a hall in a corner bedroom. A lot of good it did her.

She investigated the closet and found a number of designer-label black dresses as well as black dress pants and black sweaters in a variety of sizes. Everything was neatly arranged by style. There were many black housecoats or robes of some sort. Too bad black wasn't really her color. She grabbed a sweater and a pair of pants and headed for the bathroom. Maybe a hot shower would clear her head.

The guard, or whatever he was, found her fifteen minutes later, sitting on the edge of the bed, showered, dressed, and waiting for him and God knew what else.

"Mr. Blackthorn has asked that you join him for a late lunch in the drawing room," he said shortly. "You'll be needing these." He shoved a pair of black slippers toward her.

A nasty reply rose to her lips, but his cold demeanor stifled it. She swallowed hard and put the slippers on her feet. Grabbing her arm, he steered her down the hall at a brisk clip (she had been right, she was in a corner bedroom), and down the wide, red-carpeted staircase. The drawing room doors slid silently open to expose opulence she had only read about in fairy tales. She honestly didn't know what to look at first, but had no chance to choose as Jason Blackthorn swept into her line of vision.

Her skin crawled. It wasn't his face exactly, or his build, which appeared normal as well—not too fat, not too slim; not too young, not too old. He was well groomed, and like all the others she had seen so far, dressed totally in black from his turtleneck sweater right down to his socks and shiny leather shoes. The first thing she thought was that he dyed his hair and beard; they both had that fake black sheen to them. In fact, so did his eyebrows. The second thought that crossed her mind was—this man is absolute evil.

"Ah, Miss Belinda, such a pleasure to meet you. I trust you've not had too difficult a time with us, although you do look a bit pale. My men assure me you have been well treated." He moved slightly to the side and waved his arm toward the fireplace, the light of a fire within playing gently across the room. Before it sat a small round table, set for two, flanked by two leather wing-backed chairs.

"You see, a banquet set for a queen; or in your case, should I say princess," he smiled sardonically and clicked his heels lightly.

The table was indeed set with a small feast, including wine chilling on the side. Belinda's eyes slid carefully around the room. The same heavy drapes were on all the windows here, too. Were these windows nailed shut and painted black? Belinda made no move. "Where is Mark?" she asked quietly.

"All your questions will eventually be answered," he crooned.

Belinda still didn't budge. This man was a major menace.

"You must not be so shy! I would be most happy if you joined me."

His teeth were so perfect, Belinda felt sure they were false, like everything about this guy.

The guard shoved her lightly from behind, propelling her in the direction of the table. Jason held the chair for her. She hesitated, then sunk into it.

"You may leave, but stay outside the door please, Richard."

The other man gave a slight nod and retreated, closing the drawing room doors quietly.

"I am a man who loves secrets; they are the foundation of my work," declared Jason brightly, taking the seat opposite her, and unfurling his napkin. "How about you, Belinda? Do you like secrets?"

Belinda didn't answer.

"Come now, my child, mustn't be shy. We have lots of secrets to share, you and I, but first, I'm famished and I'm sure you are, too. Don't hesitate, my dear, dig in. Would you care for some wine?" He reached over to the bottle, then withdrew his hand quickly. "My mistake, you are probably under drinking age. You don't mind if I help myself, do you?"

Belinda shook her head and he proceeded to uncork the wine and pour himself a glass. The blood red liquid gurgled into the glass.

"You know one should drink white wine with seafood, but I have always preferred the sanguine. Perhaps the excellent cuisine will loosen your tongue." He plopped two large, steaming crab legs on her plate. "I'm sure you are hungry. You've had quite an eventful time."

Belinda breathed in the tantalizing odor of seafood, melted butter, and baked potato all rolled into one, delicious aroma. Shutting her eyes, she internally said a small prayer. Jason may think she was asking for a blessing on her food; actually she was screaming for God to get her out of this jam. No, switch that—make it Goddess. Other people believed in her, maybe she'd take pity on Belinda and bail her out. Up until this point, all the problems in her life, including this one, had stemmed from dealing with men. Perhaps now was the time to get some feminine action in the picture.

Opening her eyes she saw Jason staring at her intently, then nodding his approval at her silence. She shakily picked up her fork and began to eat. In minutes her plate was cleared, and Jason was heaping it full again, this time with delicately sautéed vegetables and shrimp.

As Jason refilled her water glass, he said, "Now that you have something in your stomach and a clear head, perhaps we could discuss my favorite topic."

Belinda visibly withdrew. "I don't know any secrets," she muttered, setting her fork down quietly.

"But indeed you do, my child, and I am so hoping you will share those secrets with me."

"What have you done with Mark?"

"Well now, that is one of my secrets. If you are a good girl, and tell me what I want to know, I shall tell you where Mark is. I take it he is of some importance to you?" Jason delicately dabbed his still snow-white napkin at each corner of his mouth. "I had such high hopes for him, you know, being that his father and I had a—shall we say, close relationship. Unfortunately, Jeffrey managed to botch up my plans. I believe you knew Jeffrey; it appears he was a mutual acquaintance of ours. Of course, you knew him better than I … in the biblical sense, I mean." For a brief moment, his eyes glinted his intense hatred of her.

The depth of her situation instantly hit home. Her guts twisted.

"Have I offended you, dear? You look a bit taken back. I'm so sorry. Of course, Jeffrey wasn't the most reliable sort. Maybe it was only wishful thinking on his part."

"Jeffrey was a piece of shit," flew out of her mouth with no emotion—just a statement of fact. Where did that come from?

"Indeed, I agree with you. Which is why he had to be disposed of. I throw away used and dirty things. They disgust me." His eyes bored into hers, but she held his gaze steadily. "Satisfy my curiosity. Are you a Jezebel?"

There was a soft knock at the drawing room door. Richard appeared, looking rather flustered. "There is a phone call for you, sir."

"Now?"

"Yes, sir."

Jason excused himself, giving instructions to Richard to "keep her company," which consisted of Richard stoking the fire and presenting a dessert selection and coffee. He never once looked her in the eye, though he did clear his throat several times as if to say something to her, but nothing ever came out of his mouth.

Jason returned over twenty minutes later. By that time Belinda had downed two cups of coffee and a large piece of warm apple pie. She didn't know when she would be able to eat again, if ever. Jason strode briskly over to the table and sat down, rearranging his napkin on his lap.

"I'll have the Black Forest cake, please Richard ... thank you." He forked the chocolate cake topped with cherries into his mouth, savoring it for a moment.

"Time is growing short, princess. I have a proposition for you. I need a young, strong feline, such as yourself." He waved his hand expansively at her. "Your duties would be very light and all your needs met. If you want cars ... then a new car it shall be, every week if you desire. If you prefer clothes ... a shopping trip to New York or Paris whenever you want. All you need do in return—" he leaned over the table, his breath evilly caressing her face, "—is be my little Jezebel."

She withdrew in disgust. "You make me sick!" she spat. "You'll never get me to agree to anything. You are evil. A monster! I'd rather be dead!" she hissed. "I'm not going to tell you anything!"

"Your wish is my command," he said softly, the earlier cajoling attitude vaporized; his tone was hard and cutting. He stood behind her chair so she couldn't see him, his voice now floating over her head. "I'm in need of some basic information. If you answer me truthfully, I may find it in my heart to spare you. If you lie—you die."

The room seemed to loom before her. She swallowed hard. That pie threatened to find its way home to the ground. Richard was busy clearing the table and placing the dishes on a push cart. He never looked at her. She wondered how old he was and how he came to be here. He didn't seem to be more than twenty, but she didn't remember him around town. *How could a young man be so cruel and heartless?* she thought. Even better, what made her think she was anywhere near Whiskey Springs? She could be in another state, for all she knew. The panic rose in her throat, threatening a healthy scream. At least she knew sounds were closer to coming out than pie. She clenched her teeth and took a deep breath. To lose it would be to die. She was sorry to see Richard push the cart silently out of the room, not that he would have tried to help her.

Jason was speaking and she hadn't been paying attention. He was leading up to something, but she was surprised when it came.

"What do you know about Tiffany?"

Stunned into silence, she only sat there. He thumped the back of her chair.

"I said, what do you know about Tiffany?"

"Tiffany who?"

"You must be joking," he said icily. "Remember, I told you to lie is to die!" He violently kicked the back of her chair, snapping her head against the leather.

"I'm not kidding," she spat. "I don't know who you are talking about!" She clutched the arms of the chair, waiting for another blow that did not come.

His voice wafted from several feet behind her this time. "What did you do with the envelope?"

This was the question she had been expecting, but the conversation had taken such a quick twist, she didn't answer immediately. "I don't understand."

"Let me clarify for you, princess." The voice hadn't moved. "An envelope that belongs to me is missing from the Reed home. I want it. I thought you may know where it is. Do you?"

"No, I don't know where your report is."

"Ah, then you do know the report exists?"

Ooops. Belinda considered her options in answering. She'd just cut them in half. Her heartbeat was picking up speed. To lose it is to die. "Yes, I know there was a report."

"Indeed I thought you did. You are very wise in being truthful, you know. Now, you say you don't know where it is?"

"No."

"When did you see it last?"

"Why, Mark had it when we got in my car."

"Then you did read it?"

Now her heart was really thumping. "I know there was a report," she answered lamely. Shit. She realized she was gripping the arms of the chair so hard her knuckles were turning white. To lose it is to die. "I scanned it."

The voice moved closer to the back of her chair. "Did you read it before or after you got in the car?"

"I didn't read it, I told you, I only glanced at it before I got into the car."

"Then tell me your impression."

"It was a report on a woman who I don't know, about her financial business and some family background, I think. She's not from around here." It was hard to keep her voice from quivering.

"Do you remember the lady's name?"

Belinda opened her mouth and clamped it shut. She really couldn't think of the woman's name. To lose it is to die. She was losing it.

"Do you remember the lady's name?" The voice was so close now it almost brushed her right ear.

"I honestly can't remember her name. I don't understand it." Her palms were sweating.

"It does not surprise me."

Relief flooded through Belinda. Perhaps this wasn't going to be so bad after all. It was understandable, then, that she didn't know what had happened to her until after he slapped her. One moment he was behind her, the next he had pounded her face, then grabbed her by the throat, jerking her head back and forth.

"I want to know where that report is!" He released his grip slightly and she gasped for air, choking. The side of her face burned and began to swell.

To lose it is to die.

"To lie is to die!" he hissed.

Her mind went totally blank. "I—I don't know!" she squealed.

"Tell me now!"

"He may have put it in—"

A large log in the fireplace exploded, sending sparks flying into the room. Several landed on Jason's sweater. He dropped her immediately and danced about, smacking at his chest and arms. When he was through, she noticed several small burn holes. She glanced over at the carpet, realizing the smoke in the room was not coming from the fireplace, but from the carpet. It was on fire. Half the log was over two feet from the hearth. Smoke billowed and rolled into the room.

Coughing, he grabbed her by the neck of the sweater and pulled her to her feet. She could see Richard out of the corner of her eye rushing to handle the flames. Had he been there all the time? His face was a mask of stone as he beat at the rug. He never coughed once. What was this guy made of?

Several men, like clones, rushed into the room. "You," shouted Jason, "help Richard with that mess. You and you, take her to the chapel with the other one. I'll finish with her when Lance gets here. That should be in about three hours. See she is miserable until then, will you? If anyone wants me, I'll be in my den!" Jason shoved her toward one of the men, who grasped her roughly by the shoulders and marched her out of the room.

Although she couldn't consider her predicament any better, at least her demise had been held off for a few hours. Thank God—no, definitely Goddess—Jason hadn't heard what she was about to say. The problem was, now she remembered both the woman's name, how much she was worth, and precisely where her family was. That could be very unfortunate information for her to possess. She wished fervently she'd never seen that damned report. She sensed that if they knew she'd given the report to Pastor Becker, she'd be dead within the hour.

Jason's voice floated behind her, except this time she was not the focus of the conversation. "The stupid little cow doesn't know anything. It's the boy we have to get it from. Tell them to start working on him. Oh, and Richard, I want to know precisely what happened to Tiffany in less than one half hour. Is that understood?"

Richard nodded curtly, then herded Belinda out of the room. Her knees shook so badly she could hardly put one foot in front of the other.

CHAPTER THIRTY-SEVEN

BROTHER HANK NERVOUSLY PICKED HIS teeth. It was six hours until the meeting and he still had a lot to do. He'd had the Sisters of Heavenly Springs Choir distribute the fliers early this morning, door to door, all over town. The old fellow who did the regular newspaper run to the outskirt farms and housing developments offered to take care of the rest, so Brother Hank speculated local attendance would be fairly good. The flier was an invention of his own. He'd seen one in another town, about two hours over, where fundamentalist support was strong, and that got him to thinking about faxing these babies all over central Pennsylvania. By nightfall they would be busing them in; they always did. His Ohio and New York contacts had been notified, and a few from West Virginia had promised to make the trip. Yes indeed, it was going to be a hot crowd in the town tonight!

He rubbed his hands with glee, eyeing the master copy with satisfaction. If it worked, he may use it for his logo—now there was a thought. He could frame this copy and hang it in his new office after it was all over and he was rich and famous.

People certainly loved blood, guts, sex, and justice. Their order of priority depended upon the flavor of the moment. Right now the town was in an uproar—it was obvious that evil was afoot. Murder talk about the Conner boy was everywhere. With a little nudging on his part, he could make a great deal of money over it, then he could skip this stepping stone to nowhere, pay off his debts, and start over somewhere else. Southern California wouldn't be a bad place. He was sick of snow, anyway.

In the sanctuary, the cleaning team was just finishing up. Everything was perfect. The flowers—who knows where the church secretary managed to come up with them in this weather—were gorgeous and everywhere. Red roses and white lilies tumbled down from the pulpit; white roses encircling candelabras at the end of every pew sent their heady aroma throughout the sanctuary. He rubbed his palms together again. Each candelabra held thirteen spanking new candles. The church would be lit up like a Christmas tree!

Now for the tricky part.

Lee frowned, read the report, then frowned again. "And she thinks I had someone investigate her?"

"Yep," came Emma's reply as she filled his bowl for the third time with stew, then plopped another dumpling on top.

"How is it that she didn't take it with her?" asked Lee suspiciously.

"I don't rightly know," mused Emma. "She had it in her hand when she was heading for the door. I followed her out halfway, said good-bye, then turned around and came back into the kitchen. And there it was, smack in the middle of the kitchen table, right where you found it. I figured I'd just take it over around 4:30 when I visit her."

"You're friends now? Last night I thought you'd tear each other apart."

"Had some time to think, is all."

Lee was looking a lot better to her, and she was glad to see the color good on him. He'd come down the stairs about a half hour after the little one left. Of course, his voice was still filled with a cold, but that could be remedied easy enough. The stew had been doctored good with special herbs. Emma couldn't help but think of Elizabeyta as the little one—face so pale, body so slight. For her height, she didn't have enough meat on her, as far as Emma was concerned. She had a world of trouble on her shoulders, that one.

He twirled the report in his hands. "How could she think I'd have her investigated? I would never do such a thing!" He slammed the report down on the table and pushed the bowl away.

"She was so upset when she left she forgot her backpack," remarked Emma. She looked at Lee closely. "Now you're mad at her," said Emma.

"No, just hurt that she doesn't really trust me," he said.

Lee worked a neon yellow piece of paper out from under the leg of the chair beside him. "What's this?"

Emma rushed over and tried to snatch the paper. "Gimme that!"

"Not so fast, Emma. Keeping secrets from me?"

Emma wore an expression of one doomed to a firing squad. "Don't open that, Pastor Lee—it'll only make you angrier than fallin' in a pig pen." Maybe she'd better tell him the rest.

"A little anger is good for the psyche," he said, then opened the paper.

Emma watched his color rise from normal to rose red. "Uh-oh," she muttered.

"This is ludicrous!" he shouted. "How dare he do this, that scum-sucking piece of—"

"Pastor!"

"I don't care. I've had enough of this jerk. Emma, if you want me, I'll be in my office upstairs. I've got some calls to make!"

"But—" Emma found herself talking to an empty kitchen. "Well, I'll be," she grunted, then cleared his place at the table. She didn't get a chance to tell him that she was meeting Mason over at Elizabeyta's place after while, nor did she have a chance to tell him they'd figured out part of the mystery, though she was bursting to do so. "I think the angel Michael has just descended on this house," she said to herself. "That's good; I've a mind we're really going to need him before this thing is all over with."

Elizabeyta let herself into the house softly. Emma had been right; there wasn't a peep or noise that didn't belong with the old place. No ghostly raps, movements, nothing. She sighed, dropped her coat in the parlor, and headed toward the bathroom, dropping her clothes on the floor by the door. A shower and change of clothes was definitely in order. She felt like a hog.

There was a great deal to think about. First off, who ordered that report? After a great deal of consideration, she decided it probably wasn't Lee. That didn't feel right. Besides, she doubted he really had that much interest in her financial standing—he just wasn't the type. It was probably Jason Blackthorn. Thank the Goddess he didn't get it, but why would he want it? She never realized she could be tracked so easily, but this was the age of information and she'd often heard other people brag that there wasn't anyone in the world they couldn't find, if they looked hard enough in the right places.

In the shower she beseeched the element of water for continued protection. Dressed in a white pullover sweater and black jeans, she brushed her long wet hair before the bedroom mirror.

In her private space, she sat and stared at the blank computer screen. This piece of machinery and its dependent phone line had probably done more damage than anything else. Damn. In her bullheadedness she hadn't listened to the Elders. They were right. Her error could cost all of them dearly.

With tears in her eyes, she sent a message to the covenstead. DESCEND IMMEDIATELY. ALL POINTS KNOWN. She knew there would be no reply. The family would evacuate promptly. Since all their holdings were now known, she had no idea where they would go, but she was sure they would be safe—for now. The legal eagles of the family would fix it, if there was time.

If she was still alive when this was done, they'd find her.

Her next task was to box up all the computer disks. They would have to be sent today, overnight delivery to a post office box in California. When the owner discovered they were there, then the news would be out that she might not be long for this world. The box belonged to one of her few outside lovers—a professor she'd known in college. Above all others, he could be trusted; for years he'd had the instructions for what to do if he found something in that mailbox.

She carried a box of personal papers and files into the kitchen and burned every last bit of them. By the time she was done, there was no information anywhere in the house about the covenstead or herself. It all had to go. It was then she realized her backpack was missing and remembered leaving it in Lee's room. Emma would probably bring it over later, though it left her with a sense of disquiet to know it was not in her possession.

By late afternoon, everything was in order, and still no sign of Beth Ann. Maybe she had finally passed over to the other side. What a time to do it! Better get a move on, though, so she could get to the post office before it closed. She suited up for the weather to walk down to the post office.

On the way she spotted Emma, getting ready to come over. "Be back in ten minutes," she shouted. "Going to the post." Emma nodded, and retreated back into the parsonage. Several cars swished by on the main road, their tires munching through slush.

The mailing went off without a hitch, but it was barely light as she turned in her gate at the side of the house. Emma and Mason were nowhere in sight. The entire walk back she could think of nothing but Mason—his easy gait, how he always seemed to be adjusting his suitcoat, he slow smile and sea-green eyes. Why did she think about him so much? The man had never even touched her, or kissed her.

Elizabeyta fumbled with her keys. Frustration and unexplained desire for Mason overcame her psychic feelers, which she had been keeping open the entire trip to and from the post office. She took off her gloves in exasperation and aimed the key at the lock for the third time. With her earmuffs on, she once again did not hear an intruder.

chapter thirty-eight

IT TOOK UNDER FIFTEEN MINUTES FOR RICHARD to check the family network. "Babe was right—Tiffany is dead. And I checked with all our people. No one touched her, or at least is admitting to it."

Jason chewed on another unlit cigar, his expression heavy and foreboding. Richard stepped back involuntarily.

"Where is our man who was supposed to be keeping tabs on her?"

"He's missing, sir. We began looking for him when he didn't report in this morning. We never thought Tiffany would be … dead." Tiny beads of sweat glistened at his temples.

"Who was assigned to her?" growled Jason.

"Luther."

"Luther?" Jason shook his head, disbelief plainly showing. He's been with us for years. How is it the newspapers knew about Tiffany before I did?" he snapped.

Richard babbled for a moment, then lamely said, "I don't know."

"You don't know because whoever was supposed to be monitoring our people in the field was either otherwise entertained or sleeping!"

"I'll check, sir, but it may have been one of the men you assigned to watch the teenagers."

"Whose fault is that?" Jason seemed to grow a foot taller as he stepped menacingly toward Richard.

Richard dipped his head slightly. "Mine, sir. I should have double-checked the schedule."

"Indeed! Now that we have that settled, you can redeem yourself by finding out who killed one of my best people. What do you have so far?"

Richard pulled out a small notebook from his back pocket, perusing a few pages before he answered. "According to the night man on the phones, she called in about 9:00 PM, before she went to the truck stop. She said she had some interesting news about the Belladonna woman and Brother Hank, but she couldn't discuss it right then."

"I knew Hank would sniff something out. What else did she say?" Jason circled Richard like a cat ready to pounce.

Richard shifted from foot to foot, unconsciously trying to put as much distance between himself and his uncle. "That was about it. She reported Brother Hank was busy with a special project that she felt we would be interested in and she thought she could slip out for a few hours. We assumed Luther would trail her and she would relay any immediate information to him, then come here later on, but of course we know that didn't happen." Richard cleared his throat uncomfortably.

"And did we trace the call?" Jason's eyebrows arched like miniature pitch forks. Richard stepped backward defensively.

"Yes," he said, his voice slightly shaking. "She was calling from the Heavenly Springs Church office phone. It was logged as our procedure requires. Do you think the Witch has finally made her move?"

Jason smashed the cigar in the ash tray, then meticulously chose another from a box on the mantle. "I doubt very highly our little Witch was wandering around Heavenly Springs Church. In case you haven't figured it out yet, Witches are not particularly fond of zealots, especially ones who have, shall we say, criminal intent? Send a man over to the church, but tell him to be careful. Choose one of the more experienced fellows. Make sure he has magickal training as well. The back of my neck is tingling and I don't like that. Always a warning sign to me. Everyone in town knew Tiffany was sleeping with that bozo. I'm sure the cops will be looking to question him, if they haven't already."

"Yes, sir." Richard jotted a few lines in his notepad, then turned to leave.

"Don't go yet, Richard. I want a list of names of everyone who Tiffany has been in contact with for the last three months, including our people, and I want it in an hour. I also want the same type of list for our missing Luther."

Richard hesitated, then hastened out the door. If Jason let him off with just orders, he was lucky. Of course, he may suffer later. He was determined not to screw this up. Better get a move on.

An hour later, both lists and other items requested in hand, he found Jason, dressed in a black robe covered by a white sheepskin, kneeling in front of the fireplace. The electric lights had been extinguished. A single red candle burned on the hearth, overpowering the light of the dying embers that shone a murky scarlet on the stones. The hairs on the back of Richard's slender arms stood ramrod straight. He was petrified of the occult—had been since he was a kid, but he had grown up in this house and knew nothing else. He did, however, understand punishment.

"Give me the list of names for Luther first," said Jason without turning.

Richard obediently tip-toed to Jason's side and handed over the list of forty-three names. Jason held the paper to his lips, muttered something, then set it down neatly in the center of the hearth, atop a circular piece of sky blue silk. Jason gazed at the embers for several minutes. Without breaking his gaze, he said, "No matter what happens, what you see, or what you hear, do not move or speak. Do you understand?"

"You know I don't care for this sort of thing, sir. I'll just step out," Richard squeaked, backing toward the door.

"Remain!" ordered Jason.

Richard glanced around fearfully, but did as he was told.

Jason stood and removed a sheathed dagger from the mantle. With one swift movement he cast the covering aside and raised the glittering blade toward the fire. Richard's eyes rolled back in his head. At that moment he was convinced his uncle would splay him open with one deadly thrust. Every instinct told him to bolt—only fear of additional punishment, should he be wrong, kept him still.

Jason raised the dagger above his head, performing a salute of some kind. The air whooshed about the room as he cut a circular motion thrice with his right hand. The entire house seemed unnaturally still. Again, with both hands firmly on the hilt of the dagger, he raised it above his head. Richard strained to hear the words coming from Jason's lips, but they were uttered with such quick, quiet confidence that "I command thee now!" was all he managed to decipher.

Richard waited for the furniture to shake.

Nothing happened.

He waited for swift winds to tear the drapes from the windows.

Nothing happened.

He waited for a demon to rise from the blue silk.

Nothing happened.

Perhaps a bolt of lightning from the dagger?

Nothing.

For the first time in his life, Richard doubted the rumors of Jason's power. He immediately felt calm. Perhaps there was nothing to fear after all.

Jason kneeled again on the hearth, sheathing the dagger and setting it aside. With his eyes closed, he slowly ran his right hand down over the names on the list, pausing at some, skipping others completely. Eyes still closed, he shook his head and repeated the procedure.

"Nothing," he finally said, his eyelids snapping open. "No one here has anything to do with his disappearance. Either he ran off, which I highly doubt, or someone we don't know disposed of him."

"You think he is dead, don't you?"

"I don't think … I know. Give me the other list."

Jason closed his eyes and repeated the procedure, his hand stopping halfway down the list for a long moment, then traveling slowly to the end of the list. On the second pass his hand again stopped at the same place, continuing until he finished off the list. On the third time, he opened his eyes where his hand had stopped twice before and hovered now. The embers in the hearth settled with a soft crack.

"Brother Hank," whispered Richard in awe. "Your hand stopped all three times on his name!"

"Is his name on the other list as well?"

"Yes, sir. But your hand never stopped at his name on that list."

"Then he is innocent of the predicament of our Luther, but he is guilty of murdering Tiffany," remarked Jason flatly. "The astral beings are kind to me this day. They have given me his name as proof. Do we know where Brother Hank is at this moment?"

Richard's eyes grew round. "Our man called into the desk fifteen minutes ago. Brother Hank is not at the church, nor is he at home. However, there were fliers pasted all over the outside bulletin board proclaiming that he is leading a revival tonight at the church."

Jason thought for a moment, then unsheathed the dagger, uttered a few words of dismissal to the energies invoked, and rose from the hearth. "Tell our man to return to the church and watch it carefully, but do nothing until I give the word," he said quietly. "We are going to have to discover what our dear Brother Hank is up to. Perhaps the police have already picked him up for questioning—check it out. If they haven't, put a word in with our contacts. They'll understand. Tiffany must have gotten wind of something she felt was important enough to risk contacting us before her scheduled time. If he overheard her phone call and killed her for it, then he is dancing deep into the realms of the illegal. Is Lance in yet?"

"He is a half an hour out. He phoned in a few minutes ago."

"Good. Is there a monitor on duty now?"

"Yes, sir—Wilson."

"See to it that he pays close attention to the scanner. I want anything unusual reported immediately. I'll be here until Lance gets in. In the meantime, try to find out what happened to Luther, and call in the Council. I want everyone assembled in one hour."

Richard strode to the door, then turned. "What about the teenagers?"

"I haven't the time to play with them. Drug up the boy, find out where that report is, and then get rid of him. I don't want a trace of him found. Is that clear? Things are getting too hot for comfort and I don't want to add any fuel to the proverbial fire."

Richard nodded. "And the young woman?"

"Is anyone looking for her yet?"

"Not to my knowledge."

"Then your knowledge had better be good. Hold on to her. I'll decide that issue later, after I take care of Brother Hank. Lance may want to have a little fun before I dispose of her ..." He cocked his jaw, finger tapping at his temple. "Or perhaps I'll find some other use for her, once she knows the boy is dead. I'll meet the council at the cottage. This will be a work night. Have six Dark Man teams ready to roll at my word."

The cottage was nothing more than a rectangular, one-level building with black-painted windows and one door set deep in the estate woods, about a half-mile from the main building. Perched atop South Mountain, its view in daylight hours allowed one to survey a large portion of the county below. Smoke snaked from the chimney of the cottage.

Inside, Jason sat on a simple wooden chair at the far end, his back toward a floor-to-ceiling hearth. Around the room, in a semi-circular formation, sat fifteen silent men, ranging in ages from twenty-one to over eighty. Two chairs were empty. The one to the right of Jason was heaped with black roses.

Only wavering light from several sconces placed strategically on the walls, and the bouncing flames of the hearth fire, filled the room. In the center, on the glistening, hardwood floor, lay a larger version of the circular, sky blue cloth that Richard had seen earlier in the den. A ram's head skull was precisely arranged in the center of the cloth. To the right of it was a large silver breastplate, ringed by several copper discs. Each disk represented a planetary seal of the magick of Solomon. A silver chalice gleamed dully to the left of the skull.

Richard was familiar with each piece, though he did not understand their uses. One of his duties required the care and transportation of the artifacts. All had been in the family for generations.

He wasn't exactly sure why he was here. It had been the first time he was ordered to attend and he hoped his nervousness didn't show too badly. From his vantage point in the shadows behind Jason, he could see that many of the men had their eyes closed, and were breathing deeply. For a moment, he foolishly thought everyone had been drugged, then realized they were meditating. All the men were dressed in black.

He scanned their faces. Many of the elders he had known as a child died three years ago, during the roughest winter he could remember. Most had passed simply from old age, a few from cancer or other diseases. This had left several elder slots open, allowing Jason to hand-pick most of the group here today. Only Brother Samuel could really be considered an elder in age. He turned eighty-three last month and had never been one of Richard's favorites as a boy. His memories of Brother Samuel were of a cruel and blasphemous man who drove two wives insane—no one ever spoke about what happened to the third. The council forbade him to marry after that one, and the hushed fiasco led to his stepping down from active family leadership.

On Jason's left sat Lance, another thorn in Richard's side. He had hated Lance since he could remember. Lance had always been too beautiful for the male species, with luxurious dark hair and long lashes that belonged more appropriately on a woman. His dark eyes flashed with wicked malice that was both enticing and frightening. Many was the time an elder had kept Lance from literally killing slim, fair Richard in boyhood arguments. His years at college were a pleasant respite from Lance's constant cruelties. Secretly he wished that someday Lance would screw up badly enough to either be disposed of or disowned.

Lance turned in his chair and smiled knowingly at Richard, who felt the color draining from his face. Even with the roaring fire nearby, Richard's entire body stiffened with cold. Someday …

Lance looked up expectantly as Jason rose from his chair, signaling the beginning of the gathering. He moved to the center of the circle, knelt, and picked up the breastplate. Holding it before him, he slowly stood, and moved to the edge of the blue silk.

"I stand in the North, under the breasts of the mountain." He began circling the outer edge of the blue cloth, uttering a litany of angelic names as he walked clockwise about the room. Pausing at each quarter, he invoked elemental energies as well, then returned to the center, where he replaced the breastplate in its former position. All eyes turned to him expectantly.

"The plans we have so carefully laid to procure the lands and properties of the Belladonna clan are in danger." A low murmur of distress swept through the room. "One of our own has been killed," announced Jason over their voices. "And not a simple Dark Man, but our priestess, as I am sure most of you have already heard, judging from the number of black roses on her chair. We have much to do now and little time to do it. Although not immediately pressing, the female energy must be replaced as quickly as possible to please the father energy of the mountain." This time the murmur rose a few decibels.

Jason raised his hands for silence. "We know the killer of Sister Tiffany, and he will be dealt with. Lance will see to it," he said firmly. Lance curtly nodded his head.

"We now have access to the Witch," continued Jason forcefully. "However, we need the financial papers for our plan to be solidified. Thanks to Brother Lance, we have the cash for the required legal fees that our plan will entail. They are exorbitant, but must be paid. We have had to pull in several favors, and it will cost us. When we are full owners of the Belladonna moneys, the amount spent will be mere spittle."

"You know the whereabouts of the Witch?" came the question from a middle-aged man on his right. "Why is it you have not told us sooner?" The warmth of the small room was telling in his heavy face.

Jason smiled slightly. "Why Brother Michael, I've just been told this afternoon that our original suspicions are correct. She is at the home of the, shall we say, late Beth Ann Baxter. Who, as you all know, was once a part of the Belladonna clan until she was disinherited. I am also told, through information easily extracted approximately one hour ago, that the report was delivered to none other than Pastor Lee Becker, her next-door neighbor, who could have thought it was delivered to the church by mistake, given the proximity of the properties, and returned it to her."

This time the utterances of the group were louder. Jason held up his hands to calm them.

"Our men are collecting her now, no need to worry."

"Can she provide the female energy we need, perhaps placing it into the vessel of the girl we now hold?" came a soft, wizened voice from the opposite end of the room.

Jason shook his head, but there was no sting in his answer. "No, Elder Samuel, she has taken the oath of the Craft and has gone through the initiation procedure, I am sure, or they would not have allowed her to come here. Her energies would not be a wanted addition to our family. After we get what we need, she will have to be destroyed. Rest assured we will find a new, younger priestess to perform the necessary duties. The girl we hold now may be of some use. We will wait and see."

The old man nodded his head, settling back into his chair. He did not look happy.

Jason drew his attention to the others in the group. "Unfortunately, we have had to dispose of Paints, a former member of our family. I'm afraid he told a newspaper photographer too much. For those of you interested in the financial end, Paints' estate is small, but will be shared equally among the family accounts. The photographer is snooping for personal gain. He is not supported by anyone and will be easy to dispose of. Dark team number one will be dispatched this evening to take care of him before any significant damage can be done."

Sounds of approval floated through the room.

"What about his newspaper contacts?" asked Lance.

"Just the local paper, not a problem," answered Jason with a wave of his hand.

Lance drummed his fingers on his knee.

"Dark teams two and three will go with Lance to pick up Brother Hank. I understand he is putting on a show this evening. We have an edge with the police, arranged by Richard, and they will look the other way. The dispatcher has been paid heavily for his services. Brother Hank will be picked up after his little performance and brought here. Dark teams four and five will be dispatched to pick up the Witch. Dark team six is to find the financial report. Is anyone opposed to the decisions I have made or the information I have given you this evening?"

Silence.

"Does anyone have any questions?" asked Jason with confidence.

"The full moon is tonight," said Brother Michael. "Should we be ready for the Witch?"

"Yes, you all know your responsibilities as previously discussed. We will meet in the chapel at midnight. We will have her by then," replied Jason. "Which brings me to Richard's presence at the cottage with us today."

All eyes turned to Richard.

"As you know," continued Jason, "Richard has been educated for particular tasks the family requires. Last winter he completed his training and passed the bar with flying colors." Jason beckoned for Richard to come into the circle. Only with great effort could Richard get his feet to move forward.

Jason put his arm around Richard's slender shoulders. "We are all aware, Richard, that you have no interest in magic." A twitter escaped from a few of the members. However, you have served us well since entering the family business and have been completely loyal. Tonight, you will perform particular services to ensure the financial stability of the family for generations to come. Under your knowledgeable hand, the money and property will be procured and monitored—with my continued guidance, of course."

There were a few claps and sounds of approval. Only Lance sat sullenly, drumming his fingers on his knee and staring at the floor. Richard was flabbergasted and therefore said nothing. He did not miss Lance's disapproval or the meaning of his next comment.

"Will he be sworn, like the rest of us?" hissed Lance.

Richard felt his heart slip to his stomach. He was terrified of needles.

"He will be sworn, but not like the rest. He must have no marks on his body. There are certain circles he must move in, and the tattoo is not wise," said Jason patiently.

Richard breathed an internal sigh of relief, but also knew that Lance would continue to torment him until one of them drew his last breath.

Jason ignored the silent exchange between the two young men. He picked up the chalice and withdrew his dagger from the sheath on his belt. "Hold out your left hand, Richard."

Trembling, Richard did as he was told. After it was over and his hand was bandaged, the slice across his palm had been far better than the needles and the ritual tattoo.

Jason moved to again pick up the breastplate. Richard guessed he was calling the meeting to a close, but all eyes turned to Brother Samuel as he lurched from his chair, smacking an ornately carved cane on the floor several times. Brother Samuel was the oldest of the family, and therefore, though not the head, could speak his mind without retribution. It appeared he was going to take advantage of it now.

"It cannot be done!" he wheezed.

Jason whirled, his face quickly recovering from shock, filling with rage, yet his voice silky sweet. "Why not, Brother Samuel? Why do you object to the joining of Richard?"

"You know very well why not, and you've kept your mouth shut all these years. Tell the rest of them about this boy. Tell them now!" He waved the cane in the air, barely missing the man sitting beside him.

"It's too late, Brother Samuel, the joining is done. Let it be!" Jason's voice rose to a crescendo, but Samuel did not back down.

"The three things prophesied have come to pass, you blind fool, and you went ahead and helped it along!"

"The boy is now one of us," snapped Jason. "And those were your prophecies, Brother Samuel. Considering many of your so-called doomsday events have not come to pass, I'll not worry with them, or you, any further!"

Brother Samuel, stooped from age, pointed a bony finger at Richard. Richard held his breath, not knowing what either man was concerned about. "The boy is half Belladonna! You know it and I know it! He carries the energy of the Calliech in his lineage and her energy spells death for us all!"

Silence filled the room.

"That's right," screamed Brother Samuel. "Jason's sister fled one night, thinkin' she would be with her Belladonna lover. He came all the way cross-country to find her—said the Witches had sent him! We caught them in a barn in Lancaster, took her, killed him, and burned the barn. Nine months later she birthed this brat," he shook his cane at Richard. "We got rid of her, too! In those days a man was a man and a woman knowed her place, or her place would be taken permanently!" he screeched. "We should have gotten rid of this kid long ago!"

He turned to the shocked faces of the group. "That's right. The first prophecy came to pass when the old Belladonna woman brought her magick back here to meld it with her sister's. The second came to pass when the young Witch came to find her. Now, the third, the death of our beloved priestess! This Belladonna brat is in our midst and will spell the downfall of our clan. Richard's loyalties will lie with them, not us!"

Lance's eyes glittered.

Jason's face purpled.

Brother Samuel advanced on Richard, until he was nose to nose. "I killed your ma myself and I'm damned proud of it!"

Richard felt an immense wave of hatred for Brother Samuel, who promptly swooned on the spot. Richard sincerely hoped he was dead.

"The old man is a senile fool!" growled Jason as he kicked the still form viciously. "He's remembering what they did to his own sister, over sixty years ago. He's confused and mixing the two events. Your mother, Richard—my sister, was a fine woman and more dedicated to the clan than many. She died bravely in childbirth … of this you've often been told. Samuel's story has nothing to do with you, as well the others know. Enough of this nonsense. We all have work to do."

Jason's matter-of-fact explanation may have fooled most in the room, but not Richard. Upon finally hearing the truth, he knew it instinctively to be true.

Lance smirked.

chapter thirty-nine

ERRY ANDERSON SAT BY SARAH'S BED, watching the checkered quilt rise and fall with Sarah's heavy breathing. Beth Ann had said to look for someone with a bright, white aura. Terry floated gracefully in the air, then crossed her legs and slowly settled at the end of the bed.

She was getting pretty good at this ghost thing.

Actually, she enjoyed it.

And that was the problem.

Sarah was not having a good afternoon. She'd stumbled in here an hour ago for a nap. So far, she'd tossed and turned, tangling her legs in the comforter, moaning every five minutes or so. Sweat rolled. Sarah rolled. Time rolled forward.

Terry floated in the air, avoiding the flying quilt and Sarah's kicking legs. She knew Sarah couldn't hurt her, but she preferred the living not flail their appendages through her. It wasn't seemly.

After she left Beth Ann, she'd gone exploring. She almost forgot her promise. She'd seen her parents and spent a great deal of time with her mother, trying to get through to her, but to no avail. She'd visited her shop. Stopped by to see old friends. No one ever saw her. She'd also attended her own funeral but didn't go to the graveside service. She didn't think she could handle that.

Sometimes the living were a blur and she felt as if invisible walls closed in, blinding her to the events around her. The more living people in a contained area, the worse it was. At times, the world revolved only in a kaleidoscope of colors, energies, feelings …

She sighed.

Sarah moaned.

Time did not present itself in this new world. It wasn't until she wandered by the Heavenly Springs Church and happened to see Sarah that she'd remembered her promise to find someone to help. There was Sarah, getting into her battered Volvo. Her aura pulsated with brilliant white light. The promise she'd made grabbed her memory and held on.

And so she'd followed.

Unfortunately, like the others, Sarah couldn't see her.

But … Terry found out quickly, Sarah could be influenced easily. All it took was whispering in her ear. Over and over, until she finally got the point.

That's why she'd gone to that Renard fellow and told him about Brother Hank's plans to hurt Elizabeyta. Terry spent an entire evening getting her to make that move.

And that's why she was having such a bad dream now.

Terry floated beside the woman's ear again.

"Get up. Get up," she whispered kindly. (Thoughts got through better that way—being nice.) She'd tried screaming at her and that didn't work at all.

"Wake up, Sarah. Elizabeyta needs you. You have to go to the revival tonight."

"No," whispered Sarah, thrusting her arm out, as if to push Terry away. Terry persisted.

"It's time to help someone, Sarah. Time to do a good deed. You've got to stop Brother Hank."

Sarah mumbled in her sleep.

"Come. Sarah, come with me."

Sarah slowly opened her eyes.

Sarah awoke in a tangled mess of covers, tears streaming down her face. The clock on her night table read 4:30 PM.

"Got to get to that revival meeting," she muttered, throwing the covers off and struggling to her feet. "Got to stop Brother Hank."

It took better than an hour to clean herself up and get dressed for the harsh winter weather. She decided to go to the church early, just to sniff around a bit.

She found Morgan downstairs, watching television. "Where are you going?" he asked as she took her coat out of the hall closet.

"I'm going to a revival meeting at Heavenly Springs."

"I thought you gave that all up when you changed churches," he said, picking up the remote and changing channels.

Sarah pulled on her coat and adjusted the strap of her purse so she could wear it like a shoulder bag. "I just feel I need to go," she said lamely.

He aimed the remote at the television, flipping through a succession of channels. "Awful early for you to be leaving. Don't those things usually start at seven or eight?"

"I offered to help arrange the flowers," she lied.

The clock in her battered Volvo read 5:50 by the time she pulled into the Heavenly Springs parking lot, past the freshly painted banner announcing tonight's revival.

Sarah wasn't sure why she was here. It just seemed this was the best place to go. The lot was fairly deserted. She spied a few buses neatly lined up on the far side. They were empty. Those folks probably walked across the street to Denny's for supper. Sarah's stomach growled and it took some gumption not to start up the car again and go over to the restaurant herself.

She turned her attention to the church. Although the parking lot lights were blazing, the building itself squatted dark and foreboding. Even the sanctuary lights were out. One lone beam of yellow light snaked out onto the snow on the left. That must be Brother Hank's office. She sat for a few minutes, trying to decide what to do. Finally, she heaved herself out of the car and walked to the side of the church, where she could peek in the window of Brother Hank's office. She wasn't sure what she was looking for, but she thought she'd know once she found it.

chapter forty

MMA WAITED FOR ELIZABEYTA'S RETURN, NOW and then glancing out the back door. She'd called Mason over an hour ago and he said he'd meet her directly. Wonder where he'd gone?

Lee wandered into the kitchen. He still looked a little pale, but an afternoon of rallying the local ministers by phone didn't seem to hurt him.

"What smells so good, Emma?" he asked, wandering toward the stove.

"Oh, I fried up some chickens I found in the freezer. There'll be enough left over for ice box raids," she said absently.

"What's wrong?" asked Lee, as he lifted the lid of the large fry pan and savored the gently sizzling chicken.

"Elizabeyta went to the post office near an hour ago. I thought she'd be back by now. I've already called twice, but she doesn't answer. I must admit, with all the hocus-pocus talk we've had in the past twenty-four hours, I'm a mite worried."

Lee tried to pull a piece of chicken off with his fingers. "Ow!" he growled, licking his reddened fingertips. "She probably forgot and left her ear-muffs on," laughed Lee. "What hocus-pocus talk? If it makes you feel any better, I'll get dressed and go over to check on her."

Emma frowned. "You shouldn't be goin' out, Pastor Becker. I've been steeping some yarrow and peppermint tea on the stove there. Add some honey and pour yourself a cup. Good for what ails you, especially when you've been dealing with winter weather! I'm goin' over myself. I've tried to phone her, but she doesn't answer," she muttered as she drew on her coat.

Lee grabbed her arm lightly. "You didn't answer my question. What hocus-pocus talk?"

Emma tried to weasel away, but he held firm. "What's going on?"

"Well, Mason and Elizabeyta and I, we think we know who killed her grandmother."

"What?"

Emma looked at her brown oxford shoes. "Last night, while you was sleeping, Elizabeyta explained why she's here, and about her family … and how they's in trouble. I, well we, Mason and I, we got to talking and sharing history notes and such … and … well, we think the man who killed Elizabeyta's grandmother was—I mean is—Jason Blackthorn."

Lee's eyebrows shot up.

"You've heard rumors about him, I'm sure," Emma said quickly. "Last I heard, he was locked up somewhere, but I heard tell he's back."

"Why would he want to kill Elizabeyta's grandmother?"

"We're not really sure, other than it might be connected to a family feud of sorts."

Lee let go of her arm. "And what did Mason say?"

Emma swallowed with difficulty. "He appeared to believe her, and he's to meet me over at her place in a few minutes."

"Why wasn't I invited?"

"Well, you were sick and we didn't think you should go out."

"You didn't think I should walk a few hundred yards from my house to hers?"

"Now don't get your dander up. We were only thinking of your health."

"If you and Mason are going to have a pow-wow, I'm coming along."

Emma sighed. "Suit yourself. But why don't you let me see if she's back yet. In the meantime you can go change into something warmer."

The evening sprayed her cloak across the sky, studded with pinpricks of light. Emma shivered, her breath escaping in tiny plumes. The light snow that had graced the valley about an hour earlier had stopped, and with the clear sky overhead, the street glittered in icy beauty. If only her heart felt so serene.

Emma stood shivering at the side door of Elizabeyta's house. Not a single light shone through any of the windows. This immediately set Emma's heart beating faster. She clutched her coat, muttering at what appeared to be marks of an altercation in the snow. Emma looked closer at the bushes lining the walk. Large chunks of snow had been knocked from them and a few branches were broken. Lying beneath were Elizabeyta's earmuffs, twisted and broken. Emma's mittened hand flew to her mouth.

She had to tell Pastor Lee! But who took Elizabeyta? Emma peered through the glass panels beside the door. Only her own reflection peered back at her. Elizabeyta claimed she had ghosts. Well, she'd find out, she would. She had to get in the house. If there was a ghost there, maybe she, or they, knew where Elizabeyta was. She turned the knob of the door, but it wouldn't budge. Locked. She ran around to the front door; it was locked, too.

Retreating once again to the side door (it wouldn't do to have the neighbors watch her break into someone's house), she quickly pulled off her mitten and grabbed under her coat in her smock pockets, looking for her stone with the old lady on it. Cold fingers closing around its warmth, she shut her eyes and concentrated with all her might. "Elizabeyta says you are real. That the Woman Goddess is true. I've always been able to heal, and maybe it's been you helpin' me. Please, whoever you are, help this old woman now. Help me get into this house!"

When she opened her eyes, the door before her stood ajar. Warm air wafted past her, brushing her face. Swallowing hard, she took a deep breath and marched into the house, silently thanking the Woman God. My, that felt so good after all these years. Not that she didn't like her own God, for goodness sake, but now there was someone like her out there. Someone that was part of woman. Perhaps she knew it all along …

The house was totally dark. Emma wasn't afraid of ghosts; she'd talked to a score of them over the years—mostly in her head, though. Besides, she'd spent the night here last evening, and neither saw nor heard any ghosts. Over the years she'd only seen a few floating around, and they were relatives, so it wasn't really scary. She moved carefully in the dark, searching for a light switch, found the one in the kitchen. She wandered down the hall and into the parlor. The house was deserted. She didn't need to call out. It had that feeling of empty.

She sat primly on a horsehair sofa and glanced about the room. It reminded her of her parent's house when she was a child. It felt comfortable, yet auspicious. Good place to talk to a ghost.

Somewhere in the house, a door banged. She jumped up, whirling toward the stairs. "Elizabeyta? Elizabeyta, is that you?"

Cold air drifted down the staircase, encompassing her small form.

She walked closer to the stairway. Holding onto the banister, she put one foot on the stairs. "Elizabeyta, you up there?"

Not a sound.

She jammed her mittens in her coat pocket. Instinctively she knew she was the only living soul in the house. She turned and walked back into the parlor. "I know you are here," she said in a low, clear voice. "I ain't afraid of ghosts. You can talk to me in my mind, or you can poof yourself up so I can see ya. It don't matter to me." Once again she seated herself on the sofa, arranging her coat primly around her and setting her mittens by her side.

Silence.

"You needn't be shy. I'm a friend of Elizabeyta's and I think she's in trouble. Nobody could have taken her from inside this house. She said so herself, and I believe her. But I think somebody grabbed her outside the door. I got to find her."

Nothing.

Emma sat quietly for a moment, trying to think what to do. In her experience ghosts were a skittish lot. Sometimes they had a mind to jabber like a little kid and other times they was as quiet as the tomb. Of course, maybe this ghost couldn't get through. If that was the case, she'd never find Elizabeyta this way. She held up her stone to the empty air.

"This here's my healing stone. It has a picture of a Woman God on it. From what Elizabeyta says, this God Lady can help us. Ask the God Lady to let you talk to me."

This time she caught a faint whisper, but didn't see anything. Funny, where was that flower smell coming from?

"You're gettin' through, but I can't hear you proper. Try again. Don't talk in sentences, just tell me who took Elizabeyta."

There were several seconds of silence, then like a voice from a well, she distinctly heard—*Brother Hank.*

"Brother Hank took her? Why in tarnation would he do that?" Oh, no. The flier, the revival—what was that idiot going to do?

No more words came to her ears, but Emma felt a sense of urgency. The beautiful lamp on the end table beside her levitated a few seconds, then crashed to the hardwood floor, exploding in shards of glass. A skittering piece caught Emma on the side of the face. Her hand flew to her cheek and came away with her blood. She stood quickly, surveying the room. Still, she couldn't see anything, but the front door flew open, letting a blast of cold air scamper about her skirt.

"Hurry!" came a shout right in her ear that sent her flying from the parlor and heading for the door. "They are coming!"

Emma was thoroughly confused. If Brother Hank already had Elizabeyta, who was coming? "Who, who is coming?" she shouted to the air.

"The Dark Men," breathed the bodiless voice. "Run, run while you can, old woman!"

Emma sped out the door, slipping crazily toward the pastor's house.

CHAPTER FORTY-ONE

ASON FELT THE ANGER GROW IN HIS chest. Louise was keeping him here at the funeral home, constantly bringing all sorts of ridiculous tidbits to his attention. He knew why she was doing it. He'd made the mistake of telling her he was going over to Lee's house for awhile, and since it was over the supper hour, he'd probably eat there. Insulted that she'd not been invited, she'd purposefully made his life miserable all day.

"Just one more thing," she said, smiling demurely. "I'll need the car back by nine."

Mason pushed the papers she'd just handed him to the edge of his desk. "Why?"

"Because I promised my sister I'd visit later this evening."

What a crock, thought Mason angrily. "Take one of the sedans from the parlor."

"How gauche! I never drive those vehicles!"

279

"Fine," he said, rising from his chair and moving over the office closet. "I'll take one of the sedans. You keep the damn car!" He threw the car keys on the desk. They slid across the smooth surface. He checked his watch, then grabbed his overcoat from the depths of the closet. "I'm already late, Louise; can you find anything else to keep me here or have you made your point?"

Lou pushed his plate away, patting his stomach. "Sam, this was great. I don't often get home-cooked meals. It was nice of you to invite me over."

Sam grinned and began clearing the table. "With the wife gone visiting friends in New York, I figured I couldn't eat all the goodies she left me by myself. It would be unfair of me to enjoy all this stuff alone. This way, we can ride together to the revival and get it over with."

Lou nodded and sipped his coffee thoughtfully. "Do you think Sarah is on to something?"

Sam wiped his hands on a tea towel and sat opposite Lou. "I don't know if it is what Sarah said that got me to thinking, or Tiffany's murder, or all the other things rolled into one. What have you found in your snooping around?"

"Actually, I've pretty much hit a brick wall. Everyone has been cold as ice to me, including the cops. It is as if someone called in a blanket and smothered everything. This afternoon I found that our deceased town councilman's wife was taken to a private hospital in New Jersey. The house is locked up and already posted in the real estate listings. No sign of the boy and no one seems to be looking for him. The cops have him listed as a runaway. The whole thing is pretty funky. None of my contacts on the force want to talk to me. Do you know they confiscated all the cameras I had at Tiffany's murder site? They told me they would return them as soon as they developed the film. They've never done that before. Good thing I gave you those pictures to lock up in your office safe or my ass would have been grass."

"Points right to some type of underground, doesn't it? Do you have some cameras left?" said Sam.

"Yeah. I've got the new one I bought last week, but I've not had a chance to try it out. By the way, I also checked the Belladonna woman's house like you asked me this afternoon. I got there around 4:30 and it was locked up tighter than a drum. Maybe she got wind from someone that old Sarah had it in for her and split town."

Sam rubbed the stubble on his chin thoughtfully. With the wife gone, he'd forgotten to shave. Funny how a woman around made you remember details like that. "I don't know. I've never met the woman and don't really understand, other than Sarah's misbehavior, how she figures into all this, but I'm sure it's more than we think. We should have followed up on that lead much earlier. With this being a small town, I didn't want to make waves where they didn't belong."

Lou nodded and drained his cup. "I've got my gear packed. We should leave early and do some snooping around. We may find something interesting." He reached down and picked up his camera bag nestled against the dining room table leg. "I also brought a little something extra," he said, patting one of the outside pockets. "If we're dealing with killers tonight, I'll be ready."

Sam looked at him quizzically. "You packing a gun, Lou old boy?"

"Damn right," he exclaimed. "There are so many dead people popping up around here, next thing you know you'll be interviewing ghosts for stories. I just don't want one of them to be mine!"

Sam laughed. "Look, we'll probably spend the evening watching little old ladies yelling hallelujah."

Lou grinned. "Yeah, probably. Let's get going."

Beth Ann watched the old woman run like hell out her front door. Old memories resurfaced; she just couldn't quite place who the lady was. All this time she'd been trying to talk to humans, and now, when her prayers had been answered, Elizabeyta was gone. She sighed and collapsed into the parlor room sofa. The house was so silent. When did the clocks stop ticking? Where was Terry? Were there no bright souls out there for her to find?

"What would you give to save my granddaughter?"

Beth Ann whirled around, gazing at the room behind her. "My sister!" she gasped, not sure if she should be glad or frightened.

The other woman walked out of the shadows. Her features were surreal and glowing. "I said, Beth Ann, what would you give to save my granddaughter?"

Beth Ann wrung her hands. "I have nothing to give!"

"Think, Beth Ann, I am sure there is something." The radiant figure took a step closer, then hovered in the air.

Beth Ann simply shook her head.

"Think!" commanded her sister. "Has it been that long since you have cast a spell or sent positive energy into the universe?"

"I never thought ..."

"You never thought," snapped her sister, "because you've been too busy first feeling sorry for yourself, then using up your energy to bang things around. A lot of good you've done her. Now look at the fix she is in!"

Beth Ann whimpered, clutching her shawl tightly across her shoulders.

She began to cry. "I saw him take her and I couldn't stop him. I tried to get out of the house. I—I forgot all about magick ..."

"And about divinity," whispered her sister sadly.

"Yes, and about divinity. What can I do? I never thought that magick would work, now that I'm in between the planes."

"You fool! You are on a plane of your own. Did you think to experiment with it, other than to create your own reality?"

Beth Ann shook her head sadly.

Her sister sighed. "Do you remember the spell of snow?"

Beth Ann thought a moment, staring at the old rug on the floor. "Yes," she said excitedly, "I do remember!" She looked up, but her sister was gone. No matter. She knew what she had to do.

Lee wore both an expression of surprise and distaste as Emma barreled through the door. He put the empty cup with the dregs of yarrow tea down on the table with a deliberate bang. "This stuff tastes awful. What's with you?"

Emma clutched the edge of the kitchen table, heaving for air.

"Here," said Lee, standing and offering her a chair, an expression of deep concern etched around his eyes.

"He up and took her, just like that!" She snapped her cold and reddened fingers weakly.

"Hold on there, Emma. Who took whom?"

Emma shook her head, gasping for air. "Brother Hank! He up and took Elizabeyta!"

"Don't be absurd! Get a grip, Emma. All this mumbo-jumbo business has rattled your old brains."

Emma looked at him indignantly. "Young man, if I tell you a thing, then that thing is true. I've never been a liar and I don't intend to start now with you!"

Lee held up his hands in submission. "Okay, okay, I apologize. Let's start again."

Emma glared at him but related how she had gone next door, seen signs of a scuffle, and checked the house. For the moment, she left out the part about the ghost.

"What makes you think Brother Hank took her? You told me earlier that Jason Blackthorn was the monster."

Emma squirmed. Finally she said, "Stop being so difficult for once in your life, Lee, and listen to me when I tell you that Brother Hank has got her, and that's the long and the short of it."

She could tell he was taken back by her use of his first name without the ministerial credentials. Good! Time the boy grew up and faced the real world. She went to the refrigerator and started digging in the vegetable bins.

"Well then, say you are right, dear Emma. Where would he take her?"

"To the revival," she answered simply, and plopped the last of the garlic in the center of the table. She could feel Lee watching her as she pawed through one of the junk drawers beside the sink.

"Now what are you doing?" he asked.

"I'm a-gettin' ready," she said flatly.

"What, with a handful of safety pins and some garlic? What do you think Brother Hank is, a vampire with a torn hem? We should call the police!"

"For your information, this is country superstition. We pray over the safety pins and put one over the heart and one on the left sleeve of our coats. We put the garlic in our pockets to ward off bad spirits."

Lee looked ready to laugh, but held it well. "Brother Hank is a human being, Emma. Not an astral nasty."

Emma shrugged. "Then you'd better git yourself a gun. Got one?"

"No."

"Then don't laugh at my weapons, seein' as how you don't have any yerself! I suggest you skedaddle upstairs and put on somethin' warm. It's gonna be a blaster of a night. Be quick about it; we ain't got much time, boy! Meet me in the church sanctuary after you warm up the car. I left my mittens at Elizabeyta's house. I'm going to filch a pair of gloves from the lost and found box at the church. Don't think the Lord will see it as a sin, considering the circumstances. And stop starin' at me like you've seen a ghost. The girl is gone and she's in trouble. Or don't you give a damn?"

"I think you've gone crazy and I'm going to call the police." He left the kitchen. She could hear him picking up the phone in the hallway, talking to the 911 dispatcher. He came back to the kitchen, a black expression on his face.

"What's the matter?" asked Emma.

"The dispatcher accused me of making a crank call and hung up on me."

"What? I bet Jason Blackthorn had something to do with that!"

"You told me Brother Hank snatched her."

"Maybe they're in it together! I'm going to call Mason," said Emma quickly.

Lee hurried upstairs to get dressed.

Belinda sat alone on the bed. Dry-eyed, tears long spent, she wondered if she should try suicide, but she was so tired, she didn't think she could muster the energy. Curling up on the edge, she rested her head on a pillow. She knew Mark was dead. They had escorted her again to the chapel, back to the same, horrid bench. This time her guards were not silent. Instead, they talked among themselves in low, heated whispers. Something was wrong. One of the guards gave her a cup of tea and ordered her to drink it.

Fifteen minutes later they took Mark away. She didn't even get a chance to say good-bye. The guards kept them separated and stood purposefully to block their vision of each other. And now she was again in this stupid bedroom, not quite sure how she got here. She yawned, her eyelids threatening to droop. Groggily, she realized they must have drugged her. At least there was safety in sleep.

chapter forty-two

SARAH TRIPPED OVER A FALLEN TREE LIMB, caked with snow and ice. "Dang it!" she muttered, and picked it up. "Now where did this come from?" She used it to support herself and rubbed her ankle. She should have worn her boots instead of these dang rubbers. Her ankle ached something terrible. Stick in hand, she crept as well as she could over to Brother Hank's office window. The sill was about nose height, and if she stood on tippy-toes, she could get a good view of the room.

It was empty, its door hanging open into the darkened corridor. Papers were strewn everywhere. The light on the answering machine blinked methodically.

Sarah eased herself firmly on her feet, using the stick to balance, then leaned against the wall. All that walkin' for nothin'. Damn. Now what? A quick, shrill scream from somewhere in the depths of the church sent her head flying back against the wall in surprise. Double damn! She rubbed the back of her head. There would be a lump there tomorrow for sure. What the hell was she doing here, anyway? She heard the steady roar of bus engines and peaked around the corner of the building. More buses coming in. If anybody saw her slinkin' around the church, they'd think she went bonkers for sure. But she did hear that scream, and if it was Elizabeyta, then it was all her fault. Sarah believed in God and she knew of all the tricks she'd played in her lifetime, she would surely burn in hell for this one.

Maybe the devil really was Brother Hank? Sarah shivered at that twist of thought. All along she'd believed he was a man of God, overlooking some of his more bizarre tendencies. Didn't the Bible say somewhere that the devil liked to fool people, liked to act like he was good, when really he was bad through and through?

With a pronounced limp, she scurried to the back of the building, toward the service entrance. Speaking of keys, Sarah had one to the kitchen door on her key ring; she got it when she officiated the monthly covered dish suppers and never bothered to give it back. Why didn't she think of it before? After fumbling with the various keys, she found the right one, slowly inserted it into the lock, and turned the knob as to make as little noise as possible.

Sam and Lou pulled into the parking lot of Heavenly Springs Church around 6:15. "Oh, no," muttered Sam under his breath. "See those buses over there?"

Lou nodded his head.

"Well, that means he's arranged to bus an awful lot of happy glory-stompers in. Usually when they try that tactic, there's a behind-the-scenes battle being fought. If these people ever figured out they were being used for private wars, I bet a lot of them would take their tambourines elsewhere."

Lou tapped his fingers on the passenger window. "Believe me, these people don't want to wake up, Sam. If they did, and found out how the world really is, most of them would opt to jump off skyscrapers or bridges or something. The wolves need sheep and these people are delighted to give themselves over to it. They don't have to think anymore, just be ordered around."

As they were discussing the cycle of sheep and wolves in life, two more buses rumbled in and parked by the rest, disgorging a large number of chattering passengers. The bus drivers talked for a moment in the headlights of one of the buses, then moved to the front doors of the church.

"Look at that, Lou, the doors are locked and there's a sign there that says no admittance until 7:30. Guess Brother Hank doesn't want company too soon."

"You know, this is really weird. Wouldn't they have someone at the doors of the church to direct these people?"

"Sam checked his watch. "Well, it is only a little after six and the revival doesn't start until eight. Maybe they don't want any damage in the church."

They watched as the bus drivers talked, then made their way over to the milling passengers. By their hand motions and the movement of the crowd, Sam and Lou guessed they were taking the group over to one of the restaurants across the street. From their vantage point, they could see Denny's was full, but there was also a Pancake Barn and a Big Boy. Led by the bus drivers, the people separated between the other two restaurants.

The parking lot was again empty.

The windows were starting to get steamed. "Well, you up to some snooping?" asked Sam.

Lou grabbed his camera case and withdrew a .357 revolver. Sam whistled. "I hope you know how to use that thing. I don't feel like being an accidental victim here."

Lou smirked. "The safety is on," he said, holding the revolver, "Relax."

"There's a light on over by the side; let's check that out first," said Sam.

Halfway across the parking lot, Lou stopped short. "Hey, Sam! Isn't that Sarah's car?" He motioned toward the beat-up pea green Volvo in the far corner of the lot, near a garbage bin.

"Nah, what would she be doing here so early?" said Sam, hurrying on without looking at the car.

They both looked in the only lighted window. "Just an empty office," whispered Sam. "Take some pictures with the zoom, anyway; we may be able to pick something up later off the film. Close-ups of the desk, that sort of thing. You know what I think?"

"It could be anything …"

"I think that Brother Hank offed Tiffany," remarked Lou.

"What for?"

Lou shrugged. "Don't know. Just a feeling, I guess. Something stinks around here."

"I'll stand look-out," whispered Sam, moving closer to the edge of the building to a good vantage point.

"Right," answered Lou, already lining up for the first shot.

A few minutes later, Lou joined Sam at the corner of the building. "Anything?"

"Nah, not even a stray rabbit. It's too cold out here for man or beast," answered Sam. "Let's go around back and see if we can get in. If anyone catches us, we'll just say we're press, wanting to shoot pictures as the people come in. They'll buy it."

They stole around to the back of the church and found the kitchen door slightly ajar.

"All right!" said Lou. "Maybe there's a God after all!"

Lee hurried down the stairs, buttoning his black coat. Mason once told him he looked more like a range rider than clergy when he wore it. "It sure would be nice to have him along to keep things in balance," thought Lee. He stopped in the entrance way, wondering if any of this was real. If so, he didn't have a weapon, should he need one. Glancing at the umbrella stand, he saw the tire iron, picked it up with a firm grip, and headed out the door.

A few minutes later, he swung the car around to pick up Emma. She was waiting outside on the church steps. She got in the car without a word.

"Did you get hold of Mason?"

"His wife said he'd left about forty-five minutes ago." She looked worriedly out the window toward Elizabeyta's house. "I've not see hide nor hair of him. I don't think I missed him and even if I did, he would have come over to your place because I told him earlier that I'd made chicken for dinner."

"Should we wait for him?" asked Lee.

Emma continued to stare out the window. "Maybe they got him, too."

"I don't think so. Mason has always been able to take care of himself."

Emma knew her lack of confidence showed on her face. "These are killers, Lee, not little boys playing games."

"I hope you're wrong, Emma. I really do." He gunned the engine and headed for Heavenly Springs Church.

At the last red light she turned to Lee, an odd gleam in her eye.

"I've got to ask you something, pastor."

"Go ahead."

"That holy water in the sanctuary. Is is real?"

Lee cocked his eyebrows. "Real?"

Emma sighed with exasperation. "I mean, Protestants don't usually make good holy water, they just pour it into the bowl. Now Catholics, they do good prayers and such. What about you?"

Lee smiled. "I don't exactly understand why you are asking, but if there is a right way to make holy water, yes … I think I know how to do it. My family was Catholic, but I don't tell too many people that."

Emma whistled softly, "Well, I'll be. I bet most of your flock don't know that one."

"No," Lee shook his head. "They don't." The light turned green and Lee hit the gas too hard. The wheels spun on the ice and snow, gripped, and then lurched them forward.

"I hope you know holy water better than driving," mumbled Emma.

Richard rushed into the den. "We've found the covenstead," he shouted.

Jason looked up with surprise. "Who found it?"

"Lance brought back a new software program that traces phone connections. Once we knew where the Witch was staying, he checked to see how many phone lines she had, on the chance she'd installed a dedicated one for a computer. She did. Our hacker has the location of the covenstead. She sent a message this afternoon and we happened to be on line when she was. We've got them now."

"Good!" said Jason. "Call our men in the field; have them converge on the convenstead. I want it burned to the ground!"

Richard hesitated a moment. "Is is true what Brother Samuel said about my mother, Jason?"

"Absolutely not. The old fool can't remember what he had for breakfast today, but can recall minute details of deeds when he was young. He simply got confused. Terrible thing he did to his sister, but of course, I was not head of the family then … regardless, it's none of your concern."

By 6:30 PM, all the Dark Man teams had moved out. Richard checked in the monitor room to be sure the guard was on duty and awake. All the service staff was busy with the after-dinner clean-up. The girl, Belinda, was drugged and sleeping peacefully in the corner bedroom in the east wing. Jason, not one for getting his hands dirty, was in the den, awaiting word from the various teams.

Richard picked up the phone, then carefully set it back in the cradle. If he did not call to have the covenstead destroyed, then it would be eventually found out, and he would be dubbed a traitor to the family. There was no excuse reasonable enough to save him from Jason's wrath. If he did place the call, how many women and children would die? At college, he realized there was a world out there that did not work under traditional rules. He almost did not come back, but fear of being tracked down and brought here against his will did not set well.

What if Brother Samuel was not off his rocker—what if they really did kill his mother? What if he was half Belladonna, belonging to a family of loving and honest people? What then?

Seeing that Belinda girl and the boy, Mark, brought back how cruel and alien this environment was. They were like mice caught in a trap—not knowing or understanding why the fates had dealt them such a cruel blow. Other people did not live like this. But other people starved, toiled without a sense of belonging, worried about the rent, the utilities, and how to clothe their children. The family had none of these problems. They were taken care of by the source, and right now, the source was Jason. When the source gave an order, it was obeyed, lest one suffer as a normal human, or be punished by the family.

Richard's hand reached toward the phone again. Truly, there was no way out. If he did not make the call, he would be only buying them time they didn't know they had, so what use was the debate?

At 6:35 PM, Lee and Emma cruised slowly through the parking lot of the Heavenly Springs Church. A few empty cars were scattered in the parking lot, as well as several deserted buses.

"What do you think?" Lee asked Emma.

"I think it's awful funny that all the lights in the church are out, 'cept that one over there," she said, pointing to the left side of the building. "And lookie there at that sign on the front door. Says the church will not be open until 7:30. Ain't that odd."

"Maybe we should have checked his house first," mused Lee.

"Maybe," said Emma, "but somethin' tells me this is where he's gonna be. I have an idea he wants to use her somehow in the revival."

"How can he do that? It's illegal to snatch someone. No one in their right mind would expect Elizabeyta to stand up there and proclaim herself a Witch. Even if he got her this far, you know she'd run the first chance she could get."

"Not if he knocked her out or drugged her up," remarked Emma, a frown creasing her forehead.

"This is ridiculous, Emma! There's nothing going on here. Maybe Elizabeyta just went to the store or something. Maybe she simply slipped in front of her own house and there was no struggle at all! I am feeling more foolish by the minute."

"Hush!" hissed Emma. "Look over there!"

Lee glanced over to where her finger was pointing. Two shadows quickly ran across the front of the church, paused, then slipped around back. Emma gripped his arm. "I bet they're the Dark Men comin' here for somethin' no good."

"The Dark Men, Emma—you should be a screenplay writer."

Emma bit her lip to keep from telling the pastor off. He had a bad case of denial. Yes he did.

Strange, very strange. Sarah searched the main floor of the church. She didn't want to turn on any lights and cursed herself repeatedly for not bringing a flashlight. The entire place appeared deserted; her rubberized footsteps squeaked in the non-carpeted areas, no matter how lightly she tried to tread. The carpeted sanctuary, although prepared for tonight's revival, was empty. How could that be possible? Someone was always here before a revival. Getting ready, last-minute preparations ... but not tonight. No one was about.

Long shadows from the parking lot lights knifed silently across the pews in a kaleidoscope of colors from the stained glass windows across the west wall. All the Sunday school classrooms were vacant and dark, and many of the doors were locked.

This place didn't feel like the home of God any more. It felt cold … even cruel. She didn't like the feeling. She took a deep breath. The only place she left uninvestigated was the basement. She hated basements as much as she hated her nightmares. Maybe she should just go home and forget this nonsense. Maybe Brother Hank wasn't going to do somethin' terrible to Elizabeyta. On the other hand, maybe he was. Did she really want to take that chance, seein' as how it was mostly her fault in the first place?

With grim determination, stick still in hand, its crusted ice and snow melting with every step she took, she headed toward the janitorial rooms beside the kitchen, which she knew led to the basement of the church. Moving as silently as possible, she hurried across the expanse of the kitchen toward the janitorial room. The door was slightly ajar and opened noiselessly with a slight push of her stick. The room itself was dark, save for a band of light peeping out from underneath the basement door. She paused for a moment, thinking she heard an echo from the kitchen.

Silence.

Must be her imagination. She reached for the basement doorknob, slowly turning it, when the lights overhead flashed on, momentarily blinding her.

"Sarah! What in heaven's name are you doing here?"

Her stick clattered to the floor. It was her brother-in-law, Sam, and that photo man with him, standing in the doorway of the janitorial room, looking both shocked and disoriented at her presence.

"Shhh!" hissed Sarah, pointing to the basement door. "I think Brother Hank's got Elizabeyta down there!" She stooped and picked up her stick.

"Oh for Christ's sake, Sarah. Did you see either Brother Hank or this Elizabeyta?" whispered Sam harshly as Lou turned out the lights.

Sarah shook her head. "Nope, and I've been all over the church. Ain't hide nor hair of anybody as I can tell. Sure is strange, no one being here. But I haven't checked down here yet," she whispered back.

Lou looked at Sam, then grinned. "Sarah, what were you going to do all alone, if Brother Hank really is down there with the girl?"

Sarah shrugged.

"Step aside, Sarah; let us go down first. Your sister would have my backside if she knew you were traipsing around looking for a killer," complained Sam.

"A killer?" wheezed Sarah. "What do ya mean?"

"Lou says his instinct tells him your dear Brother Hank might have something to do with Tiffany's death. And take it from me, when Lou starts twitching, he's always right."

Sarah looked at Sam, wild-eyed. "Tiffany is dead?"

"Geez, Sarah, where have you been? It's all over the news!" said Sam with whispered irritation.

"I was sleepin' and I didn't listen to no radio or T.V."

"That's a first," muttered Sam. "Well, get out of the way, Sarah. We'll check the basement out. You wait up here." Sam turned the knob noiselessly, and slowly moved down the concrete stairs, Lou trailing behind him. Sarah, not one to be left alone in the dark, followed.

"We can't sit here all night," said Emma.

Lee was staring at her, trying to digest the information she'd just dumped on his head. "So, what you are saying is that some sort of family feud that has lasted over two hundred years is at the bottom of Elizabeyta's problems, and that this feud has resulted in countless deaths." His disbelief was more than evident.

"That's right."

"And you think Brother Hank is not part of this intrigue, and grabbed Elizabeyta for reasons of his own."

Emma couldn't decide if his tone of voice was simply incredulous or bordering on hysterical. "Yep."

Lee ran his fingers over the steering wheel. The long, soulful howl of a dog permeated the car, reminding him of yesterday's experience, which seemed so long ago and not so real at all. What had that woman said to him? He was to stay away from Elizabeyta, but what if she was really in trouble?

"I don't believe a word of it, but if you really think this bizarre story is true, let's go inside and check the place out. I should nose around, anyway. Maybe I can deter some of my own flock from participating in this charade."

Mason paced the chilly waiting area of the Sunoco station. He'd tried calling Lee to tell him he'd gotten hung up, but no one answered the phone.

The mechanic walked across the greasy cement of the garage and popped his head in the waiting room. "Sorry, Mason, but this is going to take awhile."

"What's the matter with it?"

The mechanic shrugged his shoulders. "Looks like your transmission up and went."

"You're joking! That car's almost brand new."

"Don't I know it," said the mechanic, rubbing his hands on a soiled rag. "I looked at that vehicle only last week and there wasn't a damn thing wrong with it. If I didn't know better, I'd think this isn't the same car."

"It is the same car," said Mason.

"Do you want one of my fellows to take you home?"

"Yeah. I suppose. Thanks."

chapter forty-three

THE SCENE THAT MET THREE PAIRS OF EYES halfway down the stairs left them all stock-still, mouths agape. There was an unconscious Elizabeyta, still dressed in coat and boots, about one hundred feet from the steps, gagged and bound to a water heater. A trickle of blood ran down her left temple. The right side of her face was bruised and scratched. Brother Hank was on his knees before her, praying in a sing-song litany, begging God above to fill this woman with the Holy Spirit so that she could testify at the revival tonight.

It wasn't his fault, he proclaimed to the basement ceiling. He thought that if he grabbed her and then offered her a fair sum of money she would jump at the chance to tell his congregation that she was a Witch who decided to switch. But she wouldn't listen to him, and fought like a wild woman. He couldn't get a word in edgewise and wasn't it the Lord who told him the demons of hell were running rampant in her vocal chords? In frustration, he clubbed her, and when she went down, he couldn't stop.

"And I know, Lord, you will fill her with your goodness. That she will turn away the evil of her heart and walk in the light of the Almighty. I know I hit her too hard, Lord, but it was the only way. She struggled valiantly, the evil in her strong, but I overcame the devil and I've brought her here, to take the demon out of her."

"Why you mangy bastard!" screamed Sarah, knocking the two men aside in one sweep of her arm and plowing down the stairs. Brother Hank looked up, startled. His hair stuck out in various directions. Sweat flowed down his neck in rivulets.

Like a mighty bull, Sarah barreled toward Brother Hank as he tried to rise to his feet, a look of wild determination in his eyes. She swung her stick in a giant arc, bringing him down in one blow. His face hit the concrete floor with a wet smack.

"You dog of hell!" she bellowed, and hit him again between the shoulder blades as he tried to get up.

He rolled over and grabbed the stick. "Bitch!" he screamed and yanked it from her grasp. Scrambling to his feet, he swung the stick and caught her in the chest. She stumbled backward into Sam and Lou, the three of them falling in a horrendous clatter. Sarah screamed, rising like a she-devil from the pile. Her eyes narrowed. Her nostrils flared.

"No man ever hits a woman; didn't your mother ever teach you that?"

Brother Hank flailed the stick in the air, saliva oozing from the corner of his mouth. "I never had a mother!" he screamed, trying to drive the stick in her face.

She ducked, tried to twirl on her feet, but her rubbers stuck to the cement. She teetered, at first toward the stick, then away from it … then slowly her legs gave under her, collapsing her large body on top of Brother Hank. He yelped as the stick clattered to the floor. Her body forcing him down, he jerked his head backward as her bulk snapped his neck.

"Lordy, I think I killed him!" yelped Sarah as she struggled to get up.

Sam and Lou scrambled over to Sarah as she looked down at Brother Hank's unusually crooked neck. His blank eyes were wide; the stare, dead.

"My God, Sarah!" whispered Sam.

"Served him right! Look at that poor girl. God knows what else he did to her," defended Sarah.

Lou was already untying Elizabeyta. Still unconscious, she slipped to the floor.

"Look at the bruises on her neck. Is she still breathin'?" asked Sarah as Sam helped her up.

Lou got the girl to a sitting position, holding his ear to Elizabeyta's chest, "She's breathing, but she needs to go to a hospital."

Sarah's ankle throbbed. "Where's my stick?" she whined. Sam picked it up and handed it to her.

"Brother Hank is as dead as a doornail. How are we going to explain this one?" moaned Sam.

"There will be no need," whispered a smooth, evil voice.

Again, three pairs of eyes moved in tandem to the stairs. Elizabeyta moaned, coming to consciousness. In moments, they were surrounded by several men dressed in black jeans and turtleneck sweaters.

"Get the girl," ordered the speaker. He was a tall, dark-haired man with silver eyes. Two men jumped to his command and gathered up Elizabeyta. "Take her to the van and get her to the estate; we'll take care of the others." They clambered up the stairs with Elizabeyta, half-conscious, between them.

"Well, what have we here?" cooed Lance, glancing at Brother Hank. "Check him," he barked to one of the men.

"He's dead."

Lance smirked. "Good, that'll cut down on our time." He turned his attention to his three captives. "What do you think you're doing here? Obviously you're not cops."

No one said a word.

A Dark Man spoke up. "That tall one's the photographer."

"Really?" said Lance, drawing out his breath. "Well. How lucky for us. You were next on my disposal list, anyway. How convenient." His silver eyes glittered in the basement light. "That would mean, if I took an educated guess, that you," he turned to Sam, "own the newspaper. I'd heard about you. Who's the woman, Annie Oakley past her prime?"

They didn't answer.

"I could waste my time and question you, but in all honesty it's not worth it. My cargo has been easily procured." Lance jerked his head at his men. "Get rid of them quickly."

Sam took a step toward Lance, and a Dark Man swiftly grabbed him. Sam did not resist, but relaxed, his eyes moving from one man to the next. The man holding him let him go. "You are one of the Blackthorns, aren't you?" he said, directing his comment to Lance.

"Won't make any difference to you, where you're heading."

"You're going to an awful lot of trouble just to snatch one woman. I bet there's more to it than that."

"How astute you are," he said, a wry smile playing across his lips. "Kill them!"

Lou and Sam exchanged glances, then Sam dove for the nearest man. Lou pulled out his gun, but the man closest to him jumped forward and knocked it out of his hand. It spun crazily across the concrete floor.

Sarah whirled her stick and clubbed the man closest to her over the head. He went down without a struggle. She hit him again for good measure, not at all surprised or shocked at the hole she put in his head. "Dead man number two," she said with triumph.

Sam knocked his assailant's head on the concrete stairs, rendering him senseless, then dove for the gun, rolled, and fired off one shot, bringing down the furthermost man on the left. Like a monstrous panther, Lance withdrew an ice pick from his belt with lightning speed, catapulted himself into the air toward Sam, and stabbed him squarely in the chest.

Sarah moved over to the man Lou had knocked silly and bashed him over the head with her stick. His skull collapsed with a sickening pop.

"Dead man number three," she said under her breath.

She glanced at the Dark Man with a bullet hole in his head.

Dead man number four.

Sarah lurched forward and grabbed Lance by the back of his black turtleneck, trying to pull him off Sam. When that didn't work, she cracked her stick over Lance's back. It split in two, with Lance only driving the pick deeper in Sam's chest. She lost her grip on Lance and stumbled backward.

Lou grabbed for the other man, missed, and slipped in someone's blood, giving his opponent the advantage. Knife in hand, he cut Lou's throat even as Sarah was trying to strangle the life out of him.

Lance leapt to his feet and punched Sarah squarely in the face. She loosened her grip on Lou's killer and went down without a struggle.

"Damn!" hissed Lance. "What a mess. At least we got the girl and got rid of the photographer." He looked at the remaining Dark Man slyly. "Torch the place, then go to the photographer's house and torch that, too. Don't come back to the estate until the job is finished."

"Yes, sir. What about the fat woman? I think she's still alive."

"Let her go; she won't wake up in time if you work it right." He kicked Sarah squarely in the head. She didn't move. "She should fry nicely. Move it!"

Mason alighted from the tow truck, thanked the driver, and unlocked the employee's entrance to the funeral home. Of all the times to have a car break down! He checked Louise's office and found it dark. She must have gone home. At this point, he didn't really care.

In his own office he tried to call Lee Becker again, but no one answered the phone. *He must be over at Elizabeyta's house,* mused Mason as he took the keys off the rack to sedan #4. This car was brand new. He should have taken it in the first place. He hurried down to the parking garage that took up the entire lower level of the funeral home to find that #4 slot was empty. He stared angrily at the empty space. Louise must have taken it. Well, he told her to, what did he expect? With irritation he marched back upstairs and replaced the key. Stupid, he should have noticed the other set of #4's keys were missing from the rack.

With the key to sedan #3 in his pocket he retraced his steps to the garage. In five minutes he was on the road, headed for Elizabeyta's house.

chapter forty-four

EE AND EMMA WALKED QUICKLY ACROSS THE
parking lot of Heavenly Springs Church. The
building was fairly dark. They tried the front
entrance, but it was locked. A van screeched around
the corner of the church, illuminated them with its
headlights for a few seconds, turned, and squealed
out of the lot. Emma and Lee exchanged glances.

"Let's try the back," said Lee after a
moment.

Halfway around the building, another vehicle sped past them, this one a low-slung sedan,
almost running them over. Lee and Emma
jumped out of the way, landing in a snow drift. It
zoomed out of the parking lot before either one of
them had a chance to recover.

"I swear, that car was aiming to hit us!"
exclaimed Emma, brushing the snow off her face.

"Sarah! Sarah, wake up!" screeched Terry, trying her best to move Sarah's inert form. Terry's ghostly hands only went through the woman's body.

"Get up, for God's sake, please get up!"

Sarah moaned, but did not open her eyes.

Terry sobbed, looking around the basement at the human carnage. She saw them all die. A white light surrounded the bodies of Sam and Lou; the other bodies were surrounded by a pea green goop.

"Sarah, please, there's a bomb. I heard the bad men talking. They've got a bomb in here and it will go off any moment. Please, Sarah, you've got to hear me. You've got to get out of here!"

Sarah opened her eyes groggily. "Can't move," she whispered.

"You've got to move. Please God, somebody help me."

"I'm gonna die," said Sarah simply.

"No, you're not. There's a window over there. Crawl to the window, Sarah; please crawl to the window."

Sarah shook her head back and forth, rising to her knees slowly.

"Hurry, hurry!"

With shaky movements she crawled a little at a time.

"Faster, Sarah, crawl faster!"

Sarah collapsed on the ground, weeping. "Can't."

"Yes you can, you can make it. Please, won't somebody help her?"

It was then the blue-faced hag appeared, her form advancing menacingly toward the shaking ghost and the crying woman.

Lee stood and reached over to help Emma up. A low rumble stopped them both.

"What—"

The sanctuary exploded first, showering flames and colored glass across the parking lot. Huge flames licked at the night sky; smoke rolled in waves toward the heavens. In moments, the entire church was engulfed.

"Oh my God!" shouted Emma, struggling in the snow to move away, keeping her face down as bits of flaming debris hit and sizzled in the snow around her. Lee picked her up, and together they stumbled further away from the building, smacking at sparks on each other's coats. They turned and looked at the spectacle before them.

"Elizabeyta!" screamed Lee, lurching toward the burning building.

Emma grabbed him hard. "No! She's not in there!"

Lee looked at her with confusion. People began streaming across the highway, the sounds of approaching sirens hidden in the roar of the fire.

"That van and the car—it must be Jason's people. They wouldn't leave Elizabeyta there. They need her. I'm sure she was in one of those vehicles," yelled Emma over the roar of the fire.

Lee looked at her blankly.

Emma grabbed the black tweed lapel of his coat, jerking him forward and backward with a mighty grip. "We've got to get to Elizabeyta, Lee!"

Lee nodded. Together they mixed with the growing crowd, maneuvering to the car. They slipped unnoticed out of the parking lot.

"Where to?" said Lee quietly, gripping the steering wheel as he guided the car onto Route 15.

"Up the mountain," said Emma. "Every magickal person has a home base, so to speak, and I think I know exactly where Jason's is. Take the next exit, there's a turn off 'bout half a mile. I know the way."

Mason wheeled the sedan into Lee's empty driveway. Where was Lee's vehicle? He got out of the car, looking to see if maybe it was parked along the street and he'd missed it. The car wasn't anywhere. He looked over at Elizabeyta's house. It stood dark and foreboding. Where was everyone?

First he knocked on Lee's door. No one answered. He tried the knob. Locked. He hurried over to Elizabeyta's and did the same thing. Tomb silent.

As he took the step down from Elizabeyta's front porch, two men quickly emerged from Lee's house. Both wore long, dark overcoats and wide brimmed hats. One had a manila folder in his hand, which he quickly shoved beneath his coat.

"You there!" shouted Mason, clambering down the steps of the porch. "Hey you! What do you think you're doing?"

Neither man looked in his direction as they hurried down the front walk. Mason rushed toward him. One minute he was just about to grab the bigger guy by the arm and the next the world around him crashed into darkness.

Richard knocked on the den door. "Enter!" came the muffled response.

Richard walked in. Jason had a chair pulled in front of the hearth, his feet propped on the flagstone, his elbows resting on the leather arms of the chair. Steepled fingers touched his lips. Richard maneuvered around to the far side of the chair. Still, he could only see Jason's profile.

"They just brought in the Witch," he said quietly.

"Why isn't she here with you?" Jason's profile barely moved.

Richard paused. "She's not conscious. They thought she was coming around, but she went out again. They have not been able to revive her."

"And why not?" came the controlled but seething response, fingers remaining in their position.

"Unfortunately, Brother Hank got to her first. He wanted to use her for his revival but it backfired. She has a serious head wound. Our men got on the scene too late. However, Lance reports that the photographer is dead, along with another man, identified by one of our men as the owner of the local newspaper."

Jason raised his lips from his fingers. "That isn't all, is it?"

"No," said Richard quietly. "Four of our men died in the altercation."

Jason's head snapped back into the broad back of the chair. "Brother Hank killed four of our men?"

"Well, no. Our teams found the newspaper man, the photographer, and a fat lady with the Witch. They think the fat lady killed Brother Hank."

Jason raised his left eyebrow. "And this resulted in an altercation where we lost four men?"

"Yes. The fat lady killed two of them."

"And the third?"

"Gun shot wound from the photographer."

Jason set a piercing gaze on Richard. "The fourth?"

Richard shrugged his shoulders.

Jason eyed him critically. "Perhaps we should be recruiting fat ladies as Dark Men."

Richard smiled uneasily.

"And what of this woman?" hissed Jason.

"Lance reports she died when the building was torched."

"Any witnesses?"

"An old woman and a younger man saw both the van and Lance's car. But no one thinks they can identify us. Lance tried to run them into a snow drift, and succeeded."

Jason ground his teeth. The sound was disconcerting.

"We also have the report," offered Richard quickly.

"Ah ..." Jason did not smile, but his mouth softened.

"Our team found it at the pastor's house."

"Anyone about?"

"Not in the house, sir. But ..."

"But what? Get on with it, man!"

"Someone, a man, saw two members of the team leave the house. The third member, posted as look-out, had to knock him out."

"And?"

"They didn't kill him," said Richard quickly. "They just dragged him into the bushes and got out of there quickly."

"Were they spotted by anyone else?"

"Not to our knowledge."

"Good. Have you had a chance to look at the report?" asked Jason, rising smoothly from his chair.

"No, it just came in. I'll be spending the next few hours tying up loose ends and preparing the information for transfer of the Belladonna holdings. It cannot be done, however, until the wedding ceremony is performed, and all the documents signed. Then I will fax them to the appropriate locations."

"And the covenstead. Has it been destroyed?"

Richard hesitated.

"Richard, has it been destroyed?"

"There has been no word yet, sir." Richard backed up slightly, unconsciously seeking the shadows of the room for protection.

Jason moved to his desk, picked up a letter opener, and flipped it in the air several times. "You do realize that the covenstead and the people in it must be removed for our plan to work. If it isn't, we will be tied up in court for years. I want everything done nice and neat—no strings, no one contesting the legalities of the marriage or the bequeathment of funds—is that clear? Don't make an idiot out of me, Richard." Jason advanced to a breath from Richard's face and held the letter opener to his throat. "Is that clear?"

Richard, eyes wide, swallowed hard. Acknowledging the order with a wordless nod, Richard fiddled unconsciously with his suitcoat pocket.

"Don't make me question your loyalty again, Richard. Make the call!"

"Yes, sir."

Jason removed the letter opener from its precarious position at Richard's throat. "Now, I believe one of our men is a paramedic. Have him see to the Witch. Where did you put her?"

"She's in the room beside that Belinda girl."

"Fine. Two pigeons in the same roost. Now get moving. I've got to get dressed for my wedding!"

Terry thought there must be a hundred fire trucks parked around the Heavenly Springs Church. People were running everywhere. The massive towers of flame had died back and the firemen were working desperately to finish the job. Sarah lay at Terry's feet, heaving, covered with cuts, bruises, and soot.

"You can leave now."

Terry's head shot up. Before her stood the blue-faced hag, her tattered clothing undulating about her.

"Who are you?"

"Who I am is not important." Quickly the ugly woman's form changed into that of a young, beautiful female with violet eyes. "You have done well. It's time for you to go. Your guides will come for you shortly."

"What about her?" asked Terry, looking down at Sarah.

"The medical people will find her and take care of her in a few minutes."

Terry sucked on her lower lip. "This place where I am going, is it nice?"

The other woman moved gracefully toward her. "Indeed it is. You will be most happy there. You have friends and family waiting to greet you."

Terry sighed.

"You don't look happy. Aren't you ready to go?"

"Well, I sort of like Sarah."

"Oh?" the woman arched a delicate eyebrow.

"I don't think I'm ready to go to that special place just yet. I'd like to stick around and help Sarah. She's really a nice person if you get to know her."

"Nice because you've helped her."

"I guess. I don't know …"

"Do you want to stay with her?"

Terry looked around her for a moment. "Yes. I'd like to remain on the earth plane until it's time for Sarah to go."

"That could be at least thirty years, maybe more."

"S'okay," shrugged Terry. "I like helping her. It makes me feel good … better than I've felt about myself in a long time."

Two paramedics rushed over to Sarah while the women watched. "She's going to need me," said Terry. "She's pretty messed up. I know I can help her through it. You know, I almost think she heard me in that church. Lucky thing you came along and pulled her out."

"I made a promise," said the other woman. "I keep my promises."

The paramedics were preparing to load Sarah onto a stretcher and put her in a waiting ambulance.

"Sure you won't change your mind?"

"No," said Terry with purpose. "I'll stay."

chapter forty-five

EE MANEUVERED THE CAR UP THE STEEP LANE with aggravating slowness, watching the slush-filled potholes as he slid around them. None of this made sense. Here he was, driving to someone's estate he didn't know, on the urgings of an eighty-year-old woman with tales of murder, mayhem, and kidnapping. Maybe the explosion at the church was the result of simple boiler failure and Elizabeyta wasn't involved at all. As the car hit a major bump, banging both their heads on the ceiling of the vehicle, he was more than tempted to turn back.

"Stop here!" shouted Emma.

Lee looked at her incredulously. "Here?" Now he was really baffled. There was nothing here but ice, snow, potholes, slush, and lots of trees.

"What," retorted Emma. "You expected to drive right up to their front door and announce you're here to collect a kidnapped Elizabeyta? I'm sure that would go over big," she said sarcastically.

"There's a pocket of macadam right over there," she said, motioning with a gloved finger to a treeless patch on the left. "It's a small lane that leads to a large turn-around a bit beyond those trees. Hunters use it to stash their cars before going out for deer. Looks like there might have been a poacher or two. See the tracks?"

Lee nodded and edged the car off the side of the road, trying to follow the partially covered indentations in the road. Sure enough, within two hundred feet there was a slight bend that opened into a fairly large clearing.

Emma let out a sigh of relief. "Thank God it's empty," she breathed.

Lee swung the vehicle around and killed the lights, keeping the engine running. Emma reached over the front seat and pulled out a backpack.

"That looks familiar," said Lee.

"It belongs to Elizabeyta," responded Emma. "She left it at the parsonage. She was pretty rattled when she left this afternoon, thinking that you had that report done on her." Emma glanced at Lee's stricken face. "You did lock up the report."

Lee did not answer.

"You mean you left it lyin' out where anybody could get a peek at it?"

Lee groaned.

"Boy, I think you have feathers in your head instead of brains. Just like a young one to think with his passion parts!"

Lee was glad Emma couldn't see him blush in the darkness of the vehicle. He cleared his throat. "So what's our plan of attack?" He was decidedly nervous. What chance did an old woman and one man have against a gang of cutthroats?

"Gettin' edgy, are we?" said Emma sagely. "Thinkin' we ain't got a snowball's chance in hell, huh?"

Lee nodded sheepishly.

"Well, we ain't, which is why it's a damn good thing we both left our common sense back at the parsonage!" With that she flung open her door, slipped out of the car, and slung the backpack over her old green ski coat. "We've got less than a quarter-mile hike as the crow flies. I hope you remembered to wear your boots, boy! Your choice of coat was less than intelligent."

Clutching the tire iron in gloved hands close to his coat, Lee followed Emma through a maze of ice-coated trees and snow-covered brambles. The full moon overhead lent a milky serenity to the bitter landscape, giving them both enough light to navigate by.

"Keep your eyes peeled for guards," said Emma in a tight undertone. "I don't usually come up this way, even when gathering herbs, so I don't rightly know what to expect." Just then her foot slipped, and she slid into a sturdy tree trunk. Lee grabbed her arm and righted her, nodding in assent.

When they reached a snow-covered, waist-high wall of field stone, Emma halted, a bit out of breath. "Here's where it's going to get tricky," she murmured. She crouched next to the wall and swung Elizabeyta's backpack between her knees. "The estate is just over yonder hill. Let's see what missy has in here." She rummaged through the bag, her hand feeling over bottles, a stick thing, and something else. "Ah," she said, a smile cracking her wizened face. "What's this?" She lifted the sheathed knife out of the bag.

Lee peered cautiously over her shoulder. "Don't tell me, eye of newt and tongue of adder, right?"

"Don't be a fool," snapped Emma. "It's some sort of fancy knife." She pulled the blade from the sheath; blue fire ran along the edge as she held it up for his inspection. "Lordy!" she breathed.

Lee looked at her quizzically. "It's a knife. So what?"

"Didn't you see the light?" asked Emma.

"I see moonlight bouncing off the blade. Big deal; it isn't even that big a blade."

Emma shook her head. "You ain't got no imagination, boy," she muttered, her breath hitting the air in small plumes. She sheathed the knife and stuck it in an oversized pocket of her ski coat. "Let's see what other goodies she's got in here with pointy ends—we might get lucky." Unable to make out anything else in the depths of the backpack, she finally turned it over and dumped the contents in the snow. Emma pawed through the pile of bottles and jars, pulling out some sort of metal tube wrapped in leather with a crystal on top.

"Wonder what this is for?" she muttered, raising it up toward the moonlight to get a better look. Instantly her arm tingled as the crystal caught the moonlight, holding her arm rigid. An odd feeling, a sort of tingling, moved from the wand into her hand and up her arm. Eyes wide, Emma felt the power of something old and ancient surge into her old body. For a brief moment, she felt like she was twenty again. She closed her eyes slowly. The vision of an old woman with a blue face and fangs peered at her from behind her eyelids. Emma jumped, eyes flying open.

"What?" whispered Lee hurriedly.

"You wouldn't believe me if I told you!" she said in awe, then pocketed the stick, too. "I don't see anything else that would be useful," fretted Emma, as she began putting various items back in the backpack. "Except maybe this." She held up a gold and copper medallion that was about two inches in diameter. "Big thing, ain't it?"

Lee eyed the necklace closely. It was hard to tell in this bad light, but it looked like one of the biblical seals he'd seen while in the seminary. The Hebrew letters embossed around the edges shown brightly. In the center was the familiar six-pointed star.

"I think it is one of the Seals of Solomon—some call it the Key."

"You put this on," Emma said, shoving it toward Lee.

Lee appeared dubious. Emma sighed. "Okay, I got me a nice knife and a pointy stick. All you got is that old tire iron. If it's in her bag, it means something. You put it on."

Lee's right hand went to his throat.

"What is it?" whispered Emma.

"I—I already have a necklace. Elizabeyta gave it to me when I was so sick." He fumbled with his coat and pulled out the silver pentacle suspended on its chain.

"Oh!" said Emma, taken aback. She swung the medallion into her hand, feeling a slight vibration from it through her glove. She unzipped her coat a bit. "Guess I'll wear this one, then," she remarked, and put the chain over her head, the medallion resting comfortably on her chest.

Backpack reslung, Emma scrambled over the wall, followed by Lee, swinging easily over it in one jump.

The estate was not exactly what Lee had expected. In the watery moonlight it appeared to be a rambling, two-story affair, much like three farmhouses smashed together in one structural lump. Each corner held an odd-looking stone turret, quite out of place with the rest of the building. As they drew nearer, Lee noticed every shutter, every step, and every wall was in excellent repair. The curved walkway, leading to a double set of large, oaken doors, was crisply shoveled. The second-story windows were black as pitch, many shuttered. Heavy curtains were drawn across the three bay windows in the front, but lemon light spilled onto the snow from a few windows on either end.

"She's here," whispered Emma, pointing to the right at a massive garage that could easily house five vehicles or more. A low-slung sedan and a van were parked in the round driveway. There were no guards visible, but Emma stopped dead at the line of ancient oaks.

"What's wrong?" asked Lee.

Emma's face held an odd look. She cocked her head, as if listening to a sound he couldn't hear. "If you must know," snapped Emma, "there's a blue-faced lady standin' right over there by the holly bush. She says that the place has special magickal lines all over it and if we walk through them, that no-good Jason will know we're here!"

A shiver ran across Lee's shoulder blades, but he could see nothing.

"She also says, and I quote: "You're still an ape!"

"Shit!" Lee sat down in the snow with a soft thump. "So, what do we do about it?"

"Shut up!" hissed Emma, clamping a gloved hand over his mouth. "I'm a-listenin' to what she has to say!"

After a few minutes she relaxed. "The lady says we have to wait."

Lee shivered again, this time from the sheer cold. It must be zero up here on the mountain. He gritted his teeth. "How long?"

"She said that Beth Ann is goin' to make some magick snow."

"Who's Beth Ann?"

"The other ghost!" said Emma with exasperation.

"What other ghost?" squawked Lee.

"The one other than the one I was just talkin' to!" Emma rolled her eyes.

"That's no ghost, Emma. That's a Goddess—oh, never mind!" growled Lee, slapping a gloved hand to his forehead. What was he saying?

"What do you mean she's not a ghost? Poor thing must have died out in the cold, her face all blue like that."

Lee shook his head. "Never mind. Did she say anything else?"

"We're to wait 'til it snows, but we have to hurry because Beth Ann is pretty rusty and the blue lady doesn't know how long Beth Ann can hold out. She says once we're inside, we only have to worry if we go either into Jason's study or the chapel."

Lee eyed the unusual structure. Where was the chapel?

As if hearing his question, Emma gave the details. "It's straight back from the front door, through the hall, into the kitchen, then through a door to the right. The chapel itself is in back of the main building with a connecting hallway."

"She told you all that?" asked Lee incredulously.

"Not exactly, she sort of showed me in my mind. Don't worry none, I've been talkin' to ghosts for years. A blue one don't make no difference to me."

They waited for several minutes.

No snow.

Lee looked over at Emma. She didn't seem to be minding the cold. "Did the blue ghost tell you if she is coming inside with us?" he asked through bloodless lips.

Emma looked at him oddly. "She said something kinda strange on that score. Something about not being able to go in until she was called, and that you knew how to do that, but you probably wouldn't because you're gutless. She said you don't understand the words 'Perfect Love and Perfect Trust.'"

Lee rolled that statement over in his mind for several minutes. Emma simply looked away, steadying her gaze on the house.

CHAPTER FORTY-SIX

RYING TO KEEP WARM, EMMA SLAPPED HER arms with her mittens, patiently waiting, while Lee checked his watch every five minutes with growing frustration. By close to 10:30, he figured they had been out here for more hours than his numbed mind could count. He looked at his watch again. This time it read 11:00. He couldn't feel his toes anymore and had long given up on his nose. Hopefully he wouldn't require plastic surgery if he lived through this.

One flake of white drifted into his left eye. He blinked and smashed it with his hand. Miniature drops of water rolled down his cheek. At first he thought it was an ash and he was back at the scene of the fire, but huge, successive flakes began to drift past his cheeks. Besides, ashes weren't normally flattened into water.

Emma, eyes half-closed for over an hour, snapped to attention and looked at the sky. A cloudless expanse full of sparkling stars and a silvery full moon met her gaze. Still, the massive flakes fell around them.

"We'd better move!" she said over her shoulder, relinquishing the protection of the trees.

Lee was about to shout after her about leaving footprints in the snow, but there were none. The magickal flakes obliterated every trace. Surging forward as not to be left behind, he found his knees tight and uncooperative. He floundered, setting his jaw. She was now several lengths ahead of him. He worried she would get too far and he would lose her.

He needn't have fretted. Emma waited for him, hunkered next to the east corner of the building. After a low debate, they decided to move around to the back, searching for the chapel, rather than heading through the house. Lee was afraid they would be outnumbered immediately and therefore of no use to anyone, including themselves. The word "gutless" crossed both their minds, with a different meaning for each of them.

There were fewer flakes now. If they didn't get inside the building soon, Jason would be alerted. Emma was beginning to slow down, now lagging behind Lee as they moved past what appeared to be the kitchen. Ahead, a stone annex that must be the chapel jutted haphazardly from the main structure. Tendrils of light slithered from small windows set high in the wall, close to the roof. From their angle, there didn't appear to be an entrance.

Hearts pounding, they quickened their pace, circling three sides of the chapel, looking feverishly for a way in. Only a flake or two fell intermittently. There were no windows or doors on the far side. Emma's heart sank. Lee's face was set with a grim cast.

Emma withdrew the medallion from under her coat. "Lee says you are a key to somethin'. If you are, find me an open door, or we are done for." The medallion trembled in her hand to the point where she feared for her safety. She thrust it out before her in case it had a mind to blow up. Instead, a golden thread of light slowly spiraled from its center, snaking across the chapel wall. In a moment the thread of light steadied into an outline of a small door on the side of the building.

Lee, eyes wide with disbelief, pushed where a door handle should be. The stones separated ever so slightly, showing it was a hidden door indeed. He pushed harder. It swung open without a sound, exposing the first few steps of a set of curved stone stairs. The gloom from the opening was so tangible, both of them stepped back involuntarily.

"Does she have a flashlight in that backpack?" muttered Lee.

Emma shook her head, straining her eyes to pierce the darkness.

"I guess it's now or never," offered Lee weakly.

Emma looked back over his broad shoulders. Only one large snow flake drifted to the ground behind him. "It's either go in, or run like hell," muttered Emma. "The snow's given out. Let's go."

Lee led the way, feeling out a path with his hands and feet as they moved down the depths of the staircase. Emma held the tail of his coat to judge her distance and keep from stumbling into him. A soft, dank breeze emanated from the darkness beyond.

Richard flew down the main staircase of the estate, eyes roving hysterically. He should have made that call right away. He should have done what he was told. Now what was he going to do? He paused at the bottom of the steps, gasping for breath. The entrance way of the estate remained empty.

His first response had been to run and tell Jason at once, but if he did that, Jason might lash out and kill him instantly. "Oh, my God," he moaned, grabbing at the polished banister at the bottom of the stairs for support. "What am I going to do? What have I done?"

It was true. The covenstead was gone, smashed to bits by a few well-placed bombs designed to create fires rather than level the place immediately. In fact, the inferno still raged—but there had been no one there. The spectacle was making the national news even as he stood here, wracked in the throes of fear, quaking at the bottom of the open staircase.

That Witch must have somehow let them know ... maybe in that last electronic mail she'd fired off from her damned computer. They were gone— every man, woman, and child. No trace of them anywhere.

And what was worse, Elizabeyta was no longer the controller of the family funds. She was penniless as of early this afternoon. How had they known? Perhaps it was simply a wise course of action, begun over a month ago when they knew Elizabeyta would not be under their protection. Sleuthing out the how and why was not going to help him now. When Jason learned he had missed seizing an incredible fortune by a few hours, he would be livid. He would be more than that, he would be murderous.

Richard trembled with despair. How could he have allowed himself to stay tied to this monstrous family? What was he thinking? Money? Power? Or was it simply old fears wound too tight around his being? He was just as bad as Jason, if not worse. He had carried out Jason's orders. He had arranged countless deaths. Jason was insane—what was his excuse? Self-analysis aside, what was he going to do now?

Muffled footsteps in the hallway above alerted him to the presence of one of the Men in Black. In moments, the young man was clattering down the stairs, black satchel in hand. Richard reigned in his emotions, turning to face the paramedic.

"The woman is recovering, though not fully aware of her surroundings," the man said curtly as he rounded the landing and stood in front of Richard. "I didn't want to give her any medication, as I don't know the extent of the internal damage. I've checked her thoroughly and don't think she will have major complications, but with that head wound, I didn't want to push it."

Richard nodded. "I'll relay your information to Jason. Will we be able to move her?"

"Personally, I'd advise against it, but I understand the need for her presence at the ritual. It would be best not to disturb her until then. I'm not sure if she can even walk right now. The guards may have to carry her. Call me if there is a change in her condition. I'll be in the monitor room." Without further comment, he stepped brusquely past Richard.

Richard turned to mount the stairs and came face to face with Jason, dressed immaculately in a black silk shirt, suitcoat, and black dress pants. "And where are you headed, Richard?"

"As a matter of fact, I was just coming to see you," lied Richard, stepping aside to allow Jason to pass. Jason moved slightly to the right and smoothed his hair in front of a large gilded mirror. Richard stood behind him, watching the mirrored image uneasily.

"Any updates I should be aware of?" asked Jason, turning to one side to check his profile.

"The covenstead has been obliterated."

"Very good!" said Jason crisply as he removed a speck of dirt from his cheekbone, then brushed off his suit coat. "Anything else?"

Richard related the status of Elizabeyta's condition, carefully calling her "the Witch," so as not to become personal with Jason's next intended victim, while Jason adjusted his tie. He then nodded his satisfaction, straightening his shoulders and bending backward to remove a supposed kink.

"Is the paperwork ready to go?" he asked, turning once again to face Richard. "By midnight I wish to remove both her power and her fortune in tandem. Is there a problem, Richard? You look a bit pale."

Richard shifted slightly, then said, "Only a delay in bank transmissions. I should be accomplishing the task by midnight as planned."

Jason raised his eyebrows. "A delay?"

Richard turned and tilted his head slightly, knowing that the shadows in the large entrance way would momentarily obscure his eyes. Jason had a knack of reading the truth through the dilations of one's pupils, and he didn't want to raise his suspicions. Richard had learned much in his years at the estate. "No problem; a small computer glitch at one of the banks. Nothing we can't get around," he said, putting a foot on the first riser of the stairs. "If this task is to be completed according to schedule, I'd better go about my duties. I thought, however, that you should be updated."

"Indeed," remarked Jason. "Get back to it, then. We will begin the ritual at midnight. One of the men in the chapel will radio you at the precise moment to complete transfer."

Richard nodded, eager to be away, but something inside held him back. "Jason, we never needed the Witch here for the business end of this. We could have destroyed her like the others, completed the transaction, and taken care of the legalities. Why bring her here?"

Jason slapped him lightly on the back. "You stick to business, and I will deal with the remainder. There is much power in lineage, as you will some-day understand and perhaps enjoy yourself. In fact, several of our elders are in the chapel as we speak, preparing the way."

Richard recoiled internally, but his face remained passive, almost sub-servient. "As you say," he said, and turned his back on Jason, carefully mea-suring the ascent of his own feet on the stairs. Whatever Jason proposed for the Witch, Richard knew it wasn't going to be humane.

CHAPTER FORTY-SEVEN

"CAN YOU SEE ANYTHING?" WHISPERED EMMA as Lee halted at the bottom of the stone steps, not daring to move further in the inky blackness.

"No. Don't you have some matches in all those smock pockets of yours?"

"I've got something better. There are candles and a lighter in Elizabeyta's backpack. Do you think we should risk it?"

"Why didn't you say something when I asked you for a flashlight?" grumbled Lee.

"I didn't think of it," retorted Emma, already fumbling to produce two candles and the lighter. The wavering illumination revealed a small underground storage area, filled with several large boxes and a few unmarked crates and barrels. The packed dirt beneath their feet eagerly consumed the caked snow on their boots. Although Emma thought herself silly, the dark chill of the place hampered her breathing.

"You feel it, too?" asked Lee, taking an extra-deep breath trying to satisfy his lungs. His candle wavered as he forgot and exhaled too close to it.

Emma nodded. "This must have been an old cold cellar," she noted. "The kind we used to store taters in when I was a kid. Looks like they used it later on to store coal." She pointed her finger at a small mass of black rubble underneath a metal shoot to their left. "Could be that's why it's so hard to breathe—coal dust in the air. What is all this stuff?" She prodded at a box or two, but they were all sealed with new fiber packing tape.

"Could be anything." Lee held his candle up and played the light around the room. A set of rickety wooden stairs caught his eye. He moved forward to get a better view. There was a wooden door, firmly closed, at the top. The candlelight picked up intricately laced cobwebs woven from the door to several of the top steps.

"That must lead to the chapel," whispered Emma.

"If they don't use those stairs, where did these boxes come from?" remarked Lee. "Do you think they used the door we came through?"

"Maybe," said Emma, moving further to the right. "In my recollection, most cold cellars in these parts have a door leading to the main basement over here somewhere. In fact, both those sets of stairs are unusual in a cold cellar. The place could have been used as an underground railroad during the Civil War. There were a few of those around here then. Good folks takin' care of all kinds of runaways, which means that chapel door has a trick to it. Like the one outside, it's probably hidden by a walled panel or a closet on the other side."

Emma picked her way around the boxes and crates, looking for the basement door. "Ah, here it is," she whispered, motioning Lee to take a closer look. "Don't hold your candle too close to the door; it's old wood and the light may shine out into the main basement."

The door, supported by rusty hinges, was only half a man's height but unusually wide. There were no cobwebs obstructing the opening here.

The floorboards creaked overhead, forcing them both to flinch. Emma put out her candle without thinking.

Lee played the light over the exposed rafters. The planking was thick, the boards tight together.

"Shhh!" spat Emma. "Did you hear that?"

Lee shook his head. "What? Footsteps?"

"No, quiet—listen!"

They both cocked their heads in silence.

"There! Again! I thought I heard chanting."

"I didn't hear anything!" Lee complained.

Mason pulled himself groggily to his feet. Where was he? His eyes roamed the bushes beside Lee's house. Then he remembered everything. The men dressed in black hurrying down the walk. How he tried to stop them … and ouch—he rubbed the back of his head—how someone must have hit him and knocked him out. Damn.

He wobbled to his sedan, got in and turned the ignition, then turned the heater up full blast. God, it was cold.

He drummed his fingers on the steering wheel. Where could they all have gone?

Warm air began to filter through the car. Still, he felt cold inside, gripped by some unknown fear. Instinctively he knew his friends were in trouble. His head turned to the passenger seat beside him, eyes growing round with shock.

A blue hag with ratty hair and soiled clothing sat beside him. She grinned, exposing thick fangs. "You'll find them up on the mountain at Jason Blackthorn's. But you're going to be too late."

She disappeared, her cackle filling the interior of the car.

Richard paused at the top of the stairs, glancing below. The first floor entrance was now empty. Instead of turning left and retreating into the haven of his office in the west wing, he pivoted right, moving slowly toward the rooms in the east wing. A Dark Man rested nonchalantly against the door to the Witch's room, smoking a cigarette and blowing intricate rings at the ceiling.

Richard nodded curtly and passed on. What did he think he was doing? A torrent of feminine anger drifted into the hallway from behind the Witch's door. The guard slowly moved from his post, knocked on the door, and disappeared into the Witch's room, giving Richard the chance to duck into the room next to it. In the darkness, he could hear Belinda's steady breathing.

He couldn't do anything about the Witch, there was too much action revolving around her, but maybe he could do something about this girl. It took several minutes to rouse her and he hoped the sedative she'd been given had mostly worked its way out of her system. The racket next door helped to rouse the girl. The Witch, now fully awake, was stirring up a fair ruckus.

Belinda attempted to scream, but Richard clamped his hand tightly over her mouth.

"Keep quiet; your life depends on it," he hissed, helping her sit up.

Belinda, slightly groggy, tried to slump back on the bed.

"You've got to move! Come on, try to walk it off a bit," murmured Richard, heaving her to her feet, guiding her a few steps forward and backward.

The racket next door was getting louder. Belinda looked at him questioningly and he simply shook his head. "I'm only one person and we have a long way to go to get you out of here. Don't make any noise! There's nothing we can do for her."

Confused, Belinda simply stared at the wall. There were banging sounds now, a woman's high-pitched stream of angry words, and muffled male voices. It sounded like they were heading for the hallway.

Richard stood at the bedroom door, cracking it open slightly. Two Dark Men emerged from the other room, hauling a slim, mouthy, auburn-haired woman between them. Their burly shoulders concealed her face. No one noticed Richard. He waited until the three of them made slow headway down the hall, and began the treacherous descent of the steps.

Gripped by the scene unfolding, Richard forgot about Belinda, and jumped when she moved softly behind him. Still, he couldn't tear his eyes away. As the trio moved from the top step, the guard closest to Richard moved first, allowing him to see the profile of the woman's face. At that moment she turned and stared directly at Richard. His breath caught in his throat. Her facial features, though a bit distorted by some nasty bruises, were much like his own—far more feminine, of course. Added to her body structure and hair color, Richard immediately recognized the family similarity.

Then surely, the bizarre story told by Brother Samuel was true.

Elizabeyta's distraught gaze flicked to Belinda still cowing behind Richard, then back to Richard himself. The most intelligent thing to do would be to silently shut the door, but he found himself frozen. The guard closest to Richard raised his head to see what held the Witch captive.

Elizabeyta grinned mischievously, stuck out her foot, and leaned into him. He tumbled head over heels, down the long flight of stairs, dragging Elizabeyta and the other guard along with him. They landed in a squalling jumble at the foot of the stairs. Richard quickly closed the door.

"Idiot!" squealed Elizabeyta as she shrugged off the guards and teetered to her feet. The room spun for a moment, then righted itself, though a bit blurry around the edges. A quick scan of those kids upstairs told her that while the entire household was otherwise occupied (presumably with her), those kids were going to make a break for it. Well, whoever they were, Goddess bless them; she'd see to it that at least someone escaped this hell hole.

The guard she'd tripped was still down, possibly out, but the other, larger one was already on his feet and attempting to hustle her out of the hall and into the kitchen. From the commotion behind her, she could tell the injured guard was being escorted from the hallway in another direction. Good. That left it clear for those kids ... but she'd make enough noise with this guard to ensure their escape, just in case.

Richard waited until there were no sounds drifting up from the hallway below. He motioned for Belinda to wait at the door, then walked quickly down the hallway to the edge of the open staircase. No one was about, either on this floor or the one below. He raised his arm, beckoning to her. She hesitated, then hurriedly met him at the top of the stairs. Quietly, they descended, Richard's eyes roving the area with every step they took. At the bottom of the stairs they paused. Footsteps echoed from the kitchen area. At first, Richard thought they were heading for the entrance way, but a large commotion in the kitchen struck up, and the footsteps receded.

Richard heaved a sigh of relief, grabbed Belinda's hand, and together they made a mad dash for the front door, then slipped out, unnoticed.

Elizabeyta was smiling wildly, backing slowly toward the outside kitchen door. The big guard, now groaning on his knees, looked up to see his prey escaping. Instead of looking worried, a slow look of satisfaction moved across his face.

"Why, good evening, Miss Belladonna," hissed a silken voice behind her. She whirled as a young man, perhaps in his mid-twenties, with silver eyes and a raven pony-tail, stepped in through her door of intended escape. A cold breeze blew past her as he carefully shut the door and turned the lock. Her gaze traveled up his husky six-foot frame. Shit.

"My name is Lance Blackthorn, and I am so pleased to see that you have recovered from your recent misfortune."

Elizabeyta stepped back involuntarily, right into the arms of another guard. Where did these people vaporize from?

"What's the problem here?" asked Lance, shooting a distasteful stare at the downed guard, clutching his bleeding hand.

"She hit me with something and then—then she bit me!" howled the guard angrily.

Lance raised his eyebrows, looking at Elizabeyta and the guard. "She hit you? She doesn't weigh more than 120 pounds. You must be mistaken."

Elizabeyta straightened her shoulders but said nothing.

The guard remained silent as well.

"I believe your name is Elizabeyta, is it not?" said Lance, moving toward her. "You've indeed had an unfortunate evening; why not sit down here in the kitchen and enjoy a hot cup of tea with me until my brother is ready to make his appearance. Most likely he is preening in front of a mirror somewhere or removing some lint from his clothing. He can be such a bore at times, you know."

Deftly he guided her over to a chair and held it out for her. Without really wanting to, Elizabeyta collapsed into it, every muscle stiff and sore.

Lance looked over at the injured guard. "Find Jason," he barked. "Then for heaven's sake, fix yourself up. It's time we get this show moving."

He glanced at the other guard. "You, remain here, but stay out of the way. I'd like to get to know our little Witch better. It may be my last chance."

The injured guard left without a response.

A kitchen staffer appeared from seemingly out of the air and served them both a cup of steaming tea. "Chamomile relaxes one so," remarked Lance, his gaze boring into hers. "You know, magick is such an interesting tool. It was highly unfair of you to use it on our guard. He doesn't understand that sort of thing, you know, and we certainly don't want him to realize that a little thing like you can outfox him with magick. Then they would all want to learn it and we would have too many chiefs around here. We have quite enough as it is." He shrugged off his sheepskin-lined jean jacket and tossed it on the chair beside him. He wore a black turtleneck, like all the others. A heavy silver cross glittered as he inclined his head slightly.

Elizabeyta remained mute.

"Go ahead and drink the tea," urged Lance. "I assure you it is natural. Just chamomile and honey—nothing more. It wouldn't do to have you unconscious at this point."

Elizabeyta tried to scan him, but his shields were very good. She got nothing. Sitting back, pretending to fiddle with her cup, she checked his aura: pea green and murky, not a good sign. Definitely not retrievable in only a few minutes.

"You'll be happy to know that your original abductor is dead," remarked Lance, sipping his tea.

Elizabeyta threw him a sharp glance.

"Yes, Brother Hank met his demise. Oh, not at our hands, I assure you," he chuckled perversely. "A fat lady sat on him in an attempt to rescue you." He burst out laughing at her expression of shock. "I swear, it's true. Unfortunately, we had to dispense with the woman and her ... friends. Tell me," he leaned close to her, "do you know who she was?"

Elizabeyta shook her head.

"Surely you knew one of the two gentlemen with her. Ah, I see you are worried. Perhaps I will leave their names as a surprise. You can find out when you meet the big Witchmaker in the sky, then." He rose perfunctorily, as Jason entered the room.

"Jason, I'm just getting to know your little pot of gold here."

Jason was not smiling. "Get to the chapel and make sure all is ready, then check the area around the house. Something is not right. I can feel it."

Elizabeyta kept her mind perfectly focused, not daring to consider why Jason should be nervous. He leveled his gaze in her direction. Where his brother's aura was merely murky, this man's contained an oddity she had never seen before—red and black spikes, pulsing in an irregular rhythm. It was definitely shields-up time. Mentally she enclosed herself in a mirrored shield, where everything sent to her would be immediately sent back.

Although Jason didn't flinch, he dropped his gaze and irritably crossed the room in wide strides.

"Shields are child's play, Witch!" he hissed, flexing his long fingers into fists. "I will have you, and all that is yours, very soon!" He banged both fists on the table in front of her.

She didn't flinch, either; instead she threw the hot tea in his face, cup and all.

"Bitch!" he screamed, hands flying to his face. The guard stepped forward, but Jason called him off. "No, her last great act of defiance. And believe me," he wheezed, wiping his face with a snowy handkerchief, "it will be her very last."

From the second Elizabeyta saw Jason's face, she perceived an old memory of pain and suffering. Throughout the ages this man had been the nemesis of many. She grimly understood her life was in jeopardy, as well as the lives of her family. He may have her financial history investigated, but he wouldn't get his rotten paws on her family. She had seen to that. By now, they were long gone and not even she knew where.

Lance returned to tell Jason all was ready. "So long, sweetie," he said to Elizabeyta with a wink. "I doubt I'll be seeing you again, but I sure will enjoy your money—honey. Thanks for stopping by." He reached over and patted the bruise on her face. He laughed when she winced in pain.

"Lance, check the grounds now!" ordered Jason.

"Yeah, sure; just thought I'd thank the little Witch for putting us on easy street," muttered Lance, slamming the back door behind him.

"We're no strangers, Jason," mumbled Elizabeyta. "But I will tell you now, you will not succeed."

"No?" he leered. "Your family is dead, your home is burned, I have control of your money, and soon, very soon, I'll have control of your lineage."

Elizabeyta scoffed. "Yes, perhaps the covenstead is gone, but my family is not dead, nor do you have control of their money."

"Indeed," he circled the table, now towering over her. "You seem so certain, but my sources tell me differently."

"Your sources are wrong!" seethed Elizabeyta.

"Impossible!"

"Not at all," it was her turn to leer. "I'm a Witch, you know that. I would immediately know if my family was dead, and I tell you—they are not!"

Jason stepped back a moment, caressing his thin beard in mock contemplation.

"And I'll tell you something else, you incompetent from hell, you've not got my money, either. The whole lot of it was transferred this afternoon. I haven't got a damn dime and control nothing!" she spat as she teetered to her feet, her own hands balled into fists. "You may get satisfaction out of killing me, but I swear to you in the end, you will have earned nothing for it.

With the transfer of the money went the transfer of my lineage. Your evil machinations have given you nothing but worse karma than you had before!" she screeched. "The blood of a solitary Witch is all you've got!"

Jason grew pale. He reached inside his suit coat and retrieved a hand-held radio. "Richard—Richard, answer me at once." When there was no reply, he radioed the monitor room, demanding to know where Richard was. They informed him Richard was last seen in the east wing, over twenty minutes ago.

"The east wing?" he roared. "What the devil was he doing there?"

"Those young people," breathed Elizabeyta.

"What about them?" snapped Jason.

Elizabeyta only smiled. "Why not find out for yourself? This is your stronghold. You look for them!"

He shoved her back into her chair, then turned to the guard. "Escort her to the chapel," he barked, "and wait for me there. I will be along as soon as I find Richard. What time is it?"

"Why, near midnight, sir."

"Blast!" muttered Jason as he strode toward the entrance way, then turned momentarily. "If what you say is true, Witch, I will take great pains in disposing of you very slowly."

chapter forty-eight

LIZABEYTA, ESCORTED INTO THE CHAPEL BY two guards, was taken by surprise. She was expecting a horrid, dank room, filled with foul smells and guttering candles. Instead, she found a most pleasant chamber loaded with highly polished pews. The floor, patterned in the old way, was of stone. Oil lamps every few feet on the walls cast warm pools of steady light. The only darkness in the place was here, at the back of the chapel, and immediately at the front. That area was empty save for two dark candelabrum, flanking the pews on either side. There was no pulpit. A deep piled black carpet led down through the center of the chapel. Every row of pews ended in a cascading arrangement of white and red roses, their aroma filling the room.

The pews were not empty. Approximately fifteen men, different sizes and shapes but all dressed in black turtlenecks or suitcoats, sat remarkably still, their backs to her, heads bowed.

320

Their chanting circulated the room in a low monotone of words that escaped her. It was from them the dark energy emanated—woven with their words and their minds. Much like a giant black web, it wove its way toward her, circling with predatory intent. Mentally, she redoubled her shields, but she knew she couldn't hold out forever. She had no tools, none of her magickal paraphernalia, not even her necklace.

Her grandmother had often told her tools were only props, and someday she may need to perform an entire magickal operation in her head. She had practiced this and often succeeded, but the pressure was on and she was not up to her normal self. A growing pain in her temple told her there was more damage than she'd earlier thought. She was sure at least one of her ribs was cracked, possibly two. By the grace of the Goddess would she get out of this one. The adrenaline rush she'd been riding on was flagging.

It was then she thought of Ankou, and his odd gift—the problem, of course, was that she didn't know how to activate it. Perhaps if she aspected the appropriate energies … She slumped against one of the guards, who obligingly led her to the last pew. She sat there, eyes closed, and began the simple countdown that would take her into trance. With her poor medical state, it was risky, but what did she have to lose?

In level one, she scanned her own body. It was bad, but not irreparable with the proper care. Mentally she shifted the energy patterns in her body, feeding vital, healing energy from the various chakra levels to the injured areas. She took as long as she dared, patching the worst and leaving the more minor problems for later—if there was a later.

At level two, she performed a short stress-relieving procedure, then fed more energies into her personal shields. The outside assault would eventually break them down, but they would hold out a little longer now. She fervently wished she'd kept her pentacle, as it had been empowered with an infinity shield. This thought led her to Lee. It was a sad thought indeed. She would probably never see him again.

She began the mental countdown into level three. Ordinarily, she could reach this level of mind with ease, but tonight, it was not an easy task. Unusual and bizarre thoughts crossed her internal vision. At one point she thought that Emma and Lee were beneath her feet. What a silly thought!

More stridently now she shaped her mental powers, guiding herself deeper and deeper into a trance state. The familiar feeling of the ability to project slowly came into grasp, flitted away, then eased back into her control. The moment was right to program her mind, but first, she decided to see how much time she really had.

It was a bit difficult to leave her body, but her spirit finally struggled free, drifting toward the vaulted ceiling of the chapel. Now she could actually see the black, pulsating energy of the chanting. It undulated in tendrils, wrapping itself around its vehicles and even the guards, who stood slightly dazed, one beside her body on the pew, the other behind. Both men were firmly grounded and had no magickal expertise at all.

The tendrils attempted to surround her physical body, but she noted with satisfaction that her shields were strong, and mirroring brightly. The blackness slithered around it, tiny sparks sizzling when one would get too close, quivering as if they had suffered severe burns. The shields would hold while she investigated elsewhere. If they didn't, then it wouldn't matter, anyway—the energy would splice the silver cord that tethered her spirit to her body. As long as the shields were intact, the cord would hold.

She drifted through the empty kitchen, drawn to the entrance by a loud commotion. Angry energy swarmed and filled the entire area. In its midst were Jason and several men dressed in black, all yelling and marching around. She kept to the shadows in case Jason had "the sight," but if he did, he appeared not to notice, such was his emotional state. His aura bulged with violent reds, interspersed by black bolts and something else … something living with grotesque tentacles. Elizabeyta shivered, though she could feel no cold. It was obvious that Jason was not as human as he appeared to all the others. She'd heard of negative energies and thought forms coalescing into monsters in old tales, but she had never witnessed such a thing first-hand. Always the elders warned their young students not to be enticed by the darkness, foretelling the consuming hunger of negative magick. This was an interesting twist indeed. She briefly wondered how much of the human Jason was really left, and how much was the living aspect of evil.

The young people had escaped, hence the turbulence in the entrance way. Everyone was blaming everyone else. They were interrupted by a short, fat fellow, who bustled into their midst. Elizabeyta floated further into the shadows of the vaulted ceiling. The man tried to draw Jason aside, but he would have nothing of it. In frustration and embarrassment, the heavy fellow related that the Witch's family had indeed disappeared before the fire and that the estate in her keeping had been transferred, not once, but several times, since this afternoon. Elizabeyta was most definitely penniless—her family thoroughly underground and presumed safe. It could be assumed also that her family had ritually separated her—therefore, no lineage to the power Jason sought. She was nothing but a woman on her own, with only her karmic gifts, which could not be taken under the laws of this plane.

In rage, Jason ran out the front door, screaming his fury at the starlit sky. It was the roar of a demon. How does one fight a denizen of hell? If she had some holy water right now, she'd throw it in his face—cut and be damned—though she doubted such a simple remedy would cure the illness.

Jason turned, heading for the front door. Elizabeyta zapped back into her body, which jumped with her sudden return. The guards didn't appear to notice. Breathing deeply, she began the countdown again. It was now or never to try and access the gift of shadows.

Lee and Emma stood at the top of the wooden stairs, both of them praying silently that they wouldn't suddenly wind up in a pile of rotten timbers and broken bones. Emma put her finger to her lips and Lee nodded. The chanting was louder up here, but still muffled. Although the storage room was directly under the chapel, the stairway must somehow lead past it, perhaps into the hallway the old ghost mentioned. She withdrew the stick with the crystal on the end and pointed it at the door. If the medallion worked, why not the wand?

"Ready, aim, fire!" she muttered softly.

Nothing happened.

Emma shrugged and Lee looked disgusted.

"Maybe you're supposed to say something," he whispered.

She nodded, but shrugged her shoulders again.

"You're the minister," she breathed. "Elizabeyta says Witchcraft is a religion. If that's so, you ought to be able to talk to some higher power to get it to work. Why not say a prayer or something?"

Lee looked sheepish. "Should I pray to her God or mine?"

Emma cocked an eyebrow. "Actually, the way Elizabeyta was talkin', I think they are pretty much the same."

Lee thought a moment, remembering what his sister had told him about Witchcraft only a few days ago. *They believe in a higher, positive power, Lee, just like we do*, echoed in his mind.

"I'll help you," offered Emma, closing her eyes and tilting her head.

He gently wrapped his hands around Emma's firm grip on the stick, and prayed his guts out.

Nothing happened.

At first.

There wasn't a pop or a bang. There wasn't any noise at all. They both watched as the cobwebs surrounding the door disintegrated.

"Now what?" asked Lee. "Maybe it's only a Witches' cleaning product or something."

"Turn the knob," urged Emma.

Lee reached out and captured the knob with his palm, turning it easily. The lock gave with a slight sound only a mouse could hear.

Emma stood on her toes, trying to make out what lay beyond the door—an empty hall.

Elizabeyta relaxed, taking a deep breath. She floated within the confines of her body, neither restricted nor free. She began programming her mind with statements of affirmation on the powers she sought—to blend with the shadows, to meld with the universe. Halfway into the procedure, her mind broke free of the litany, throwing her into a pathworking experience she didn't want. She traveled a forested stone path, seeking the One who held the energy she needed. Perhaps this was what Ankou had intended … she may meet him along the way where the gift would be bestowed.

Emerging from the trees, she gasped. Before her was a vast field, filled with many dead soldiers. Her hand flew to shield her eyes from the gory sight. Though there were no smells or sounds of death, a picket line of spears had been erected, each carrying a head that once belonged to one of the bodies scattered before her.

Swallowing hard, she ran her sweaty palms over her long dress. Looking down, she found herself in medieval garb. Perhaps the clothing was dated even before that, she was not sure. No living thing moved on the battlefield.

With every thread of courage she possessed, she picked her way through the carnage, stopping finally at the line of spears. A raven circled overhead, then another, and another. Silently they winged smooth patterns in the air, swooping between the spears, wing feathers just touching a spear or a head, then soaring to the heavens once more, disappearing as silently as they had come.

Elizabeyta sensed she should not breach the line of death, but how long would she have to wait? There was little time left for her on the earth plane.

"Time, time, time," muttered a seductive female voice.

Elizabeyta's head snapped up, but she saw no one. "Who is there?" she called.

"Why are you humans always so concerned with time? You know it doesn't exist, never did … it is a convenience, an illusion, nothing more. As a Witch, you should have learned that long ago, Elizabeyta."

Still, there was no one to be seen. She feared it was one of the heads talking, but noted with relief that none appeared to be female, or moving.

"Who are you?" cried Elizabeyta.

"I don't know what you are in such a blather about, I don't. After all, you came looking for me. Let's play a game. Yes, let's do! I'll give you clues, and you guess. If you guess wrong, you die. But, should the lassie guess right, I'll see to it she gets what she wants. Is it a deal?"

Elizabeyta was confused. Never in pathworking had she met an obstacle quite like this—and of all the bloody times! Normally she would have dismissed such a character, but it was too late to go back and begin again.

"All right," said Elizabeyta firmly.

There was no answer.

"This is ridiculous," muttered Elizabeyta, as she turned from the spears to gaze out across the field. The dead were gone and only the gentle grasses wavered in a slight breeze. The silent ravens returned, remaining a good distance above her. She quickly looked behind her. The spears, and those grisly heads, had also disappeared.

She walked further into the field, totally mystified. She stopped at an elevated spot, hands on her hips. "I suppose a clue is out of the question?" she called.

Gentle breezes kissed her hair. Growing in strength, they began to whip at her skirt. The sky darkened; the ravens departed. The clouds above undulated and billowed, darkening in a mad array of deep purples and crimson fog. For a moment she thought the heavens held three female faces, then the lightning flared and cracked into the ground inches from her feet. She jumped in surprise, struggling to hold her balance.

"You don't have to get pissed off!" she snapped. "It was a simple question! No. Wait. Battle, spears, heads, ravens, weather magick … the three faces of the Morrigan!" she shouted. "You are the descendent of the Calliech!"

The sky did not clear; the wind intensified. Perhaps her guess had been wrong. Crazy laughter rising to an inhuman scream buffeted her, sending Elizabeyta to her knees, clutching her ears in pain. Dizzying hysteria rose from her throat as the pounding of hooves shook the ground beneath her. Still holding her ears, she tilted her head to look skyward, the pain unbearable.

Astride a black stallion, green eyes blazing and red hair streaming, the apparition swooped from the heavens. Her right hand wielded a bloody battle axe above her head, while her left hand leveled a lightning bolt at Elizabeyta's skull.

Elizabeyta's eyes popped open. Jason's face was inches from hers as he grabbed the front of her sweater and jerked her to her feet. "We'll have none of that, little Witch!" he snarled, slapping her once with his free hand. Her head ricocheted back. She brought it forward with great effort.

His aura was totally black, seething with inhuman energies. Both the guards involuntarily moved aside, as if they could sense the monster within.

"You've ruined everything!" screamed Jason. The chanting stopped. Heads jerked around to view this unusual display of wrath.

"Jason!" whispered one of the men. "What is the meaning of this?"

"Shut up, you fool!" he shrieked. "This piece of flesh has destroyed us all!" He grabbed her by the throat, hauling her out into the carpeted aisle. A few of the men in black rose, varied looks of disgust among them.

Elizabeyta wasn't sure if their reaction was to her or to Jason. She was certain, however, that she had failed in her otherworldly contact, losing any chance of the gift promised by Ankou, her last shred of hope gone. Only seething anger remained, and she would use it for whatever it was worth.

"You filthy demon pig!" she hissed at him. "It is you who have destroyed the light of your people time and again! It is you who surround them with darkness, who has allowed the evil to penetrate your soul and attach itself to the Blackthorn offspring. And this is not the first time!" She gripped his wrist with her right hand, willing all her energy to displace it. His grip loosened. The entire chapel seemed to hold its breath as she slowly pulled his arm away from her throat. A few of the men began to back off. Jason did not notice, the fire of consuming hatred blinding his sight of anyone but her.

"You are a dead woman!"

A distant rumble answered his promise of death.

"You see," he smirked, "my power is far greater than yours, it has always been so."

He grabbed her by the hair on the back of her head, but instead of a raised fist, the dance of light on steel caught her eyes. Sidestepping, he bent her backward against his chest, exposing her throat.

There was a gasp and several shouts as two people barreled their way through the chapel door. Out of the corner of her watering eyes, Elizabeyta couldn't believe what she was seeing. Old Emma was shouting the Lord's Prayer, brandishing what looked like Elizabeyta's athame at the nearest guard, while Lee struck out with a tire iron at another.

Another rumble shook the heavens. Jason smiled maniacally. "Watch your precious Witch die!"

A Dark Man surged forward and punched Lee squarely in the face. Another reached out and tore the pentacle necklace from his neck, then threw it on the black carpet, its silver sheen dead against the dark pile. Elizabeyta gasped. Lee went down on one knee, shook his head once, then came up in full force with the tire iron, splitting the man's skull asunder. Three more surged in his direction. Emma stuck out her foot, tripping one, who fell into the pews, striking his head on the fluted wooden edge. He didn't move.

Emma continued screaming the Lords' Prayer. "Our kingdom come. Your will be done!" she yelled at the top of her lungs.

Jason drew the blade closer to Elizabeyta's throat. "Watch her bleed. The blood of royals on my body. I shall drink her blood, and I shall rejoice."

"On Earth!" shrilled Emma.

"And I shall mutilate every piece of her," spat Jason, jiggling the knife beside Elizabeyta's throat.

Lee pushed through the other two men, knocking one to the side. The other stumbled against the first, leaving the path clear.

Jason nicked Elizabeyta's throat with the knife, laughing maniacally.

"As it is in heaven!" screamed Emma.

Fearing he would not reach her side in time, Lee screamed the only name he thought could save her—"Calliech!"—while he plowed forward, coming within a breath of Jason's blade as it moved to cut Elizabeyta's throat. Emma screamed in horror as a man in black clubbed Lee on the back of the head. He crumpled into Elizabeyta and the blade, knocking all three of them to the ground.

A third booming sound echoed throughout the chapel.

Head bent forward, Elizabeyta rose precariously to her feet, the front of her white sweater covered in Lee's blood, her hands outstretched to either side, bloody palms extended. Lee grabbed onto the front of her clothing, coughing and spitting blood, a gaping wound in his chest from the blade that had been at Elizabeyta's neck.

Elizabeyta rolled her head, gnashing her teeth, cutting her own lips. Eyes crazed, she screamed a chilling howl. "Dark Goddess, descend upon your servant in her hour of need!"

Emma's hand flew to her mouth, her eyes wide with disbelief. The athame she held clattered on the stone floor. Jason hurriedly extricated himself from the motionless, dying Lee.

No one else in the chamber moved.

A low, guttural echo circled the room, moving in speed, rising in tempo.

"I commit myself to thee, oh Lord," whispered Lee, his grip on Elizabeyta slowly relaxing. He slumped lifeless to the floor, the black carpet sucking greedily at his free-flowing blood.

Elizabeyta lifted her head, mouth open, teeth red with her own blood, continuing to emit the sound, now rising into a holy battle cry. Some of the men ran from the room, others went down on their knees, cowering at the crimson woman with blazing black eyes.

Jason only grinned and continued to rise.

Emma, her escape now unhampered, stepped into the shadows, ignoring the few men still able to rush past her and out the chapel door. She held her woman stone and prayed for all she was worth to the Woman God, eyes fixed on the Lady who was no longer Elizabeyta, but something divinely terrible. She was determined not to leave, no matter what Elizabeyta had become. Emma may be old, but when she found a friend, she was loyal as hell.

"No one chooses the Morrigan," howled the female creature. "The Morrigan chooses them!" She raised her right arm to the heavens, catching a lightning bolt as it crashed through the ceiling. Cold air and snow rushed through the opening, guttering the lamps. The spear of energy glowed in her hand as she pivoted, glaring at Jason, who sidestepped toward the door.

For the first time in her life, Emma saw what must be the energy of a person, for as the Morrigan glowed a brilliant white, Jason was surrounded by a mist of black.

"Who dares to touch one of my chosen?" screeched the Dark Goddess as she leveled the energy bolt directly at Jason.

Jason remained undaunted. Even in the face of possible death, his facial muscles hardened in his hatred. The hysteria was gone, replaced by the lust of power.

"Choose me," whispered Jason to the Dark Goddess in Elizabeyta's body. "Why bother with a mere—such a shoddy vehicle? You cannot possibly be a guardian of the light, for you hold a dark and terrible countenance. Choose me ..." he whispered.

"Fool," spat the Dark Goddess. "The light does not consist of bubbles and childish wishes! It is the strength and union of uncountable souls of various beliefs, and of all levels of life, forged together to combat the powers you serve. You are a selfish little speck in the universe and you have tried my patience to its limit!" she stormed, then opened her mouth wide, screaming till Emma's bones shook and her eardrums rang in pain.

Jason took another step backward, an odd expression on his face.

"Where is your power now?" queried the Dark Goddess.

In answer, Jason scooped up the athame Emma had dropped and lunged toward the body the Dark Goddess now commanded. The knife was smitten from his hand in seconds, exploding in mid-air, as the energy bolt bounced off his shields, knocking him to the floor as well. His shields crackled, small bolts of light bouncing from it about the room, but they held. Grinning, he scrambled backward, regaining his feet and raising his own hand toward the heavens. Speaking his words of power, he formed a large, gyrating mass of black energy and threw it at the Goddess. It exploded on her shoulder but did no damage, bits of black mist vaporizing in the air.

She opened her mouth and howled without sound. White light spewed forth into the air, taking the shape of a giant, undulating snake. It hissed and slithered above their heads, slowly coiling itself around Jason's shields. With a shower of sparks and a great cracking sound, the black mist enveloping him hardened and crumpled to the ground in a small pile of dust. The Dark Goddess took a deep breath and blew the last traces of the shield away, her laughter echoing in the chapel.

Jason, realizing his position, turned chalk white.

The Morrigan addressed Emma, eyes blazing. "Remember me, old woman, for I am the Lady on the stone you now carry. You think your life is over, but I say to you, there are more than a few years of life in your future. Go now, and do not reveal to a living soul what you have seen here today, but endeavor to protect those in need. I choose you!"

Emma's eyes darted from Jason to the Dark Goddess, then to the still form of Lee on the floor. The Morrigan shook her head, and pointed in the direction of the door. "Go now!"

"Elizabeyta," she murmured, "and Lee ..."

"They are beyond your help. Leave. It is not yet your time."

Emma's heart pumped madly in her chest. "I ain't goin' until I do this!" She thrust her hand in the backpack, withdrew a bottle of holy water, and flung it at Jason. It struck his left shoulder, shattering. He screamed as the blessed droplets ate into his body. Steam and goo dripped from the wound.

Falling to his knees, he screamed, "You think a little holy water is going to hurt me? Think again, you old bat!"

"Stay away from her," snarled the Dark Goddess as Emma scrambled toward the door. "I'm not finished with you yet."

Arms outstretched, the Goddess threw back her head, feet apart in a battle stance. "Spirits of land, sea, and sky," she screamed, "be now obedient unto the Morrigan. I call upon the Light of the Universe and the energies of this plane to meld in strength and purpose!"

The rumbling began again, this time from under the chapel floor. Another cold wind blasted through the chapel, bringing snow and hundreds of beating wings. Jason raised his arms above his head in horror as the birds pounded at the air around him, the room full of the sound of a massive heartbeat. The flock of ravens swooped about the chapel ceiling, shrieking as one.

"Cauldron of Death!" shouted the Dark Goddess. "Open now to admit this traitorous evil that stands before me!" The stone floor jerked, undulated, then split in one long fissure running toward Jason's feet. He screamed as the floor beneath him gave two inches, paused, then opened swiftly, rising up to swallow him whole. His hands scrabbled like the paws of a small animal as he fought to regain his footing, snatching at anything. Pews slid and overturned, inching toward the opening that spread wider to capture anything in the room.

Jason, legs swinging precariously in the chasm, made one final effort to grab safety, his hands curling around Lee's body. Not enough weight to stop his descent, Jason continued to slip into the depths of the earth, Lee's body trailing behind him. The last thing he saw were the three faces of the Morrigan leering above him, astride a giant black stallion floating on clouds of snow.

"I'll get you!" he croaked, teetering at the edge.

"No, little man, thou shalt be imprisoned, alive, in the bowels of our mother!" she snarled.

"You have still lost; I have the priest!"

"The priest is long dead, fool, gone to the Summerland and out of your grasp. He has fulfilled his destiny, and you shall now fulfill yours."

The Morrigan looked up at the heavens, commanding the ravens to search out the Dark Men still on the premises. "Destroy them!" the Dark Goddess screamed. With a sharp snap, she pulled in the reigns and wheeled the horse, its back feet sending a mighty blow to Lee's body, kicking both the living and the dead into the chasm.

Jason's scream drifted up through the opening for several seconds. She laughed wildly, spurred the horse, then disappeared in a wavering whirlwind of snow.

Emma backed slowly though the kitchen; she had not left as instructed, but peered around the door in time to see Jason and Lee's body slip into the depths of the earth. Quickly she backed away into the kitchen. Nothing moved around her. She thought about returning, perhaps to find an injured Elizabeyta, but as she hesitated, a mighty crack shook the entire estate, rattling walls, sending loose items flying. Emma gripped the edge of the kitchen table until the disturbance subsided. A large opening in the floor now separated her from the chapel hallway. There was no way she could jump it. Another tremor hit the house. She moved quickly, stumbling over furniture and broken glass, slipping to her knees in the entrance way.

"Just where do you think you're going, old woman?" whispered a calm voice.

Still on her knees, Emma looked up to see Lance blocking her way to freedom.

"Get out of my way and let me pass, young man!" she spat. "You don't know what happened. You better run if you know what's good for you!"

"I've never run from anything, Auntie Emma, and I don't intend to start now." He reached forward and hauled her to her feet, dragging her back toward the kitchen, with Emma beating on his arm.

"You don't want to go back there!" said Emma hoarsely. "Believe me, you don't want to go back!"

Lance ignored her, shoving her about like a rag doll.

Emma looked down. Her hand still held the stone. Squeezing it, she prayed to the Morrigan to help her. Immediately a flock of ravens burst into the kitchen from the chapel, surrounding Lance. In his fury at the attack, he let Emma go. Another tremor hit the house, knocking them both to the floor. Emma crawled in the direction of the entrance, her stone still clutched tightly in her extended hand. Lance squealed as one of the ravens snipped off his ear, swooping off to the chapel. He lunged for it, slipped, and fell into the chasm between the kitchen and the chapel hallway.

"Another one bites the dust," mumbled Emma as she crawled toward the entrance once again. The tremors came more rapidly now. Behind her, ceiling tiles crashed, splitting in pieces that skittered across the floor. Dishes and small appliances hopped from their places, joining the debris. Emma half-crawled, half-ran to the front door. A ceiling light crashed in her path, sending her veering into the wall. She grabbed for the door, yanked it open, and plummeted onto the sidewalk and into the snow. She lay there, breathing heavily, as the mortar began popping out of the joints and into the snow. Fearing for her safety, she floundered further away.

In seconds, the walls crumbled, echoes of the destruction booming out across South Mountain. The gas main exploded into a secondary roar, sending sheets of flame clawing at the night sky, yet no flame or spark touched the iced trees of the mountainside. Concerned about the fate of Lee and Elizabeyta, Emma trudged around the fallen, burning structure, in search of the chapel. There was no need for secrecy or silence, yet she cried without sound.

Rounding the corner, her breath caught in her ancient chest. There was nothing. Not a stone, a piece of wood—nothing. A large hole, the size of the chapel foundation, stood gaping in the darkness. The ground trembled again, sending pieces of snow tumbling into the chasm. Emma moved closer, crying out the names of her friends. Abruptly she was thrown backward into the snow, as the walls of the gaping hole rumbled together.

When she looked up again, the old blue lady was standing where the hole had been, clutching the hand of a little girl. The child's face was awfully familiar … Cally! The little girl smiled and waved at Emma. "I love you, Emma … and I forgive you," she whispered.

The blue ghost shook her head. Turning to the girl, she said, "Guess he wasn't a monkey after all."

They melted into the night.

Sirens screamed, playing multi-colored lights across the trees.

The cavalry had arrived.

Emma simply sat in the snow, waiting for them to find her.

epilogue

EMMA AND MASON STARED AT THE EVENING sunset, rocking quietly on Emma's caned rockers, sipping last year's elderberry wine.

"Not real fancy," said Emma as she refilled Mason's jelly jar. The last warm rays of the sun danced along the edge of her high collar, softening her elderly chin.

"I've never known the glass to affect good wine," Mason said. He savored the tangy liquid, playing with it, tossing it around on his tongue.

"Right nice of you to keep comin' up here. I know the parlor keeps you busy and all, but I enjoy the company." She passed a chipped dinner plate of assorted cheeses squatting on saltine crackers under his nose. He carefully chose three and nodded for her to take the plate away.

"You'll not get fat on three pieces of cheese." He shifted uncomfortably under Emma's boring eyes. It was true; he'd lost enough weight for runner-up in the Jack Sprat look-alike contest. To satisfy her, he grabbed two more. She smiled, shoved the plate on the rusted T.V. table beside her rocker, and handed him a paper napkin.

"Balance them on this. If you want any more, help yourself."

The red-gold light of the setting sun played mischievously across the property, licking the edges of the water pump displayed prominently in the center of the yard, then dipped behind the mountains. The valley below, shrouded in twilight, sent up a sparkling panorama of electric lights. Mason reveled in the kiss of the May evening. So peaceful. So … deep.

"Pump looks nice this year," said Mason.

"Yep. Don't work no more, but I like plantin' the flowers all around. Like a gift for the Lady God. I picked them moon flowers. They bloom only at night about this time, but it's too early for the blooms. They've only grown a good foot or two since I planted them. Repainted the pump myself last week, though. Thanks for noticing."

Mason grinned, running his fingernail along the smooth grain of the rocker arm.

"She's a-gonna be full tonight," said Emma.

Mason nodded in acknowledgment. Every full moon since the mess on the mountain two years ago, Mason journeyed to Emma's house. Together, they chatted of local news, sometimes enjoying a minor sparring match on world issues, but mostly … mostly they got around to talking about Elizabeyta, Lee, and magick. The full moon does things like that to you.

It always started like this: a little bit of wine, a little bit of cheese, a little bit of chat. Then dinner. More wine. More chat. When it was warm enough, they would sit out here on the porch for most of the evening. If too cold, they would huddle near the fireplace in the center room of the cabin. Emma taught him how to look for firedrakes last winter, and he'd spent several hours over successive full moons practicing.

"Better be careful," Emma said one night. "Or you'll conjure somethin' fearful, with all that emotion you're puttin' in that fire. It's for fun, not for lust, you know."

For a while, his wife thought he had a mistress on the side. To placate her, he'd brought her along one evening last winter. Louise was a kind but controlling woman. She couldn't stomach country living, the wood stove heating, chatter, or the dark. When the next month rolled around, she'd sent him on his way alone, administering a pat on the back and handing him a grocery bag of things she felt Emma needed. Mason knew most of those things would wind up in gift bags for the needy. The way of Emma …

"Oh, I almost forgot, Louise sent you another bag of goodies." He reached beside his rocker and handed over the folded grocery bag. Emma smiled and set the unopened bag under the T.V. table.

"The Sorensons are bad off," she said, and settled into the repetitive movement of her rocker.

Mason nodded.

In silence they watched the skies darken around the moon. The sky deepened to plum. Birds chittered, lacing the air with their wings, which touched the moon like a bas-relief painting.

In the beginning, their monthly chats, livened with animated news, sealed their friendship. Most of the locals feigned ignorance of the South Mountain Disaster, as all the papers referred to it. The police questioned Emma intensely the first three months, but she claimed old age and senility. They finally left her alone. Newspaper reporters soon gave up the chase, beelining to fresh news and more immediate tales of the horrifying—like the candidates for local elections.

"They're talking about running a tour up here on Halloween," said Emma, staring at the moon.

"I heard."

"T'was the Jaycees. Wantin' to scare folks for money with a hay ride and tales of magick and monsters and such."

"I heard that, too."

"They'll vote on it next Tuesday at the town meeting," said Emma.

"I'm not going."

"Me neither."

There wasn't a single Blackthorn in the county. They all disappeared, quietly, slowly—drifting out of town. No one was sad to see them go. The Blackthorn estate went up for auction last year, bought out by some rich guy in New York State who planned to use it for a hunting getaway. The buildings themselves were long gone. The fellow wanted to rebuild; however, no local contractor would take the job.

"If the mountain has Her way, no man'll step foot for permanent squatting for awhile." Mason didn't disagree with her.

Mason and Emma made one last visit to the parsonage, about a week before the new minister moved in. The church board all claimed they were too busy to help. Together, Mason and Emma packed up Lee's things and shipped them off to his sister, who in turn, wrote a pleasant note telling them she and her policeman boyfriend were getting married and moving out of state. She thanked them profusely, saying she couldn't bring herself to come down and do it herself. The note didn't mention when she planned on moving or where. A check for a thousand dollars flittered like a bat out of the envelope. Would Mason mind taking care of Lee's memorial in the local graveyard?

The Belladonna house remained deserted. Town gossip said it was up for sale, though there wasn't a sign on the lot. Emma said she visited it once, but nothing out of the ordinary floated about—only memories. A moving van came the following spring and emptied out the place. An odd-looking bunch, remarked the new pastor next door, yet polite and respectful. Someone said the church was considering buying the property for a self-contained youth center, whatever that was.

At first, these visits on the mountain were to tie up loose ends, to heal wounds, to speculate and understand the inexplicable. Despite their age difference, Mason and Emma were sturdy friends. *The world won't be the same,* thought Mason, *when Emma passes.*

"About ready for supper?" asked Emma, pulling her green shawl closer around her thin frame.

"I'd like to sit here a moment or two longer, if you don't mind. You can go ahead and set it out. I'll be in shortly," said Mason.

Emma nodded and rose stiffly from the rocker. "Zip up your jacket. It's a mite chilly yet after the sun goes down here on the mountain." She paused at the screen door. "It may not be tonight, Mason," she said softly, and drifted into the cabin. The screen door banged comfortably, echoing over the mountain.

In the end, the police and the papers lay the blame for all the known murders at the dead feet of poor Brother Hank. Embarrassed, his family moved far south, leaving no forwarding address. Some said Georgia, others said West Virginia. Nobody really cared. His parishioners, those who had the guts to go to another church, did so meekly, heads bowed, eyes ferreting to the church doors, planning a speedy escape if anyone declared their ungodliness. No one ever did. Others, who couldn't get over the shock, stayed home.

Sarah Goodling did cause quit a stir. Who would have thought? She'd survived the explosion and spent almost nine months in the hospital. No one ever figured out how she crawled out that window, her escape compounded by her size, but she'd made it, and became a heroine overnight. For some reason neither Mason nor Emma could fathom, Sarah did not tell police or the papers about the Men in Black, and who really killed the photographer and her brother-in-law. She visited Emma once, no longer a hefty woman with a big mouth, but a much thinner, contrite lady. "Hospital food is a perfect diet," she said quietly. Sarah confided in Emma, telling her the details of her attempted rescue of Elizabeyta, but Emma did not budge, offering nothing but condolences and best wishes. Sarah claimed she had a guardian angel who stayed by her side in the hospital all the time, talking to her in her dreams. And once, once she was sure she saw her sitting Indian-style at the foot of the bed—a beautiful young girl, she was. Emma didn't dispute it. Though Sarah left disappointed, she claimed she held no hard feelings.

A month later, Sarah's sister sold the newspaper, packed up both their homes, and the two sisters took themselves to Florida, Sarah's husband and cat in tow.

"You're still in love with her, aren't you, Mason?" asked Emma the night of their first full moon visit. They almost got into a real fight. Mason knew Emma prided herself in going after the naked truth. It was her style. "I saw the way you looked at her that night you brought him back so sick, when we was sitting around the kitchen table. I was sure she'd bewitched you, too." A light smile played across her wizened lips.

Mason felt his heart beat faster. He took a deep breath through his nose, letting it out slowly, deliberately shutting his eyes. He wanted to bolt. To run. To hide. Manners held him in check—or maybe, just maybe, he was relieved the truth was finally out. At least Emma would not share her suspicions with anyone.

Emma tossed her old head, a few strands of grey hair escaping across her wrinkled cheek. "You're hopin' she'll come back. Walk out of that mountain mist, like some Goddess back from the dead. In my experience, the dead only come back to make things right."

"You think that she is dead?" He swallowed hard; he couldn't look at Emma's knowing eyes. He dealt with death every day, who knew more of its finality than he? But he had also lived through the bizarre.

"I saw you there that night, on the grounds. What were you doing there, Mason?" Her old eyes seduced him. His breathing became agitated. "I need an answer."

Mason's hands shook. He stuffed them in his lap. How ridiculous! He felt like a schoolboy, facing the ridicule of his peers. "You won't believe me." His eyes downcast, he sucked on his lower lip.

"At this point," said Emma, "I'd believe just about anything. Try me." She leaned her skinny rump against the porch rail opposite Mason, arms crossed over her chest. "I'm waitin'."

"I'd been dreaming about Elizabeyta off and on since the day I met her. At first, I thought it was because of Lee's attraction to her. We were good friends, apt to confide in one another when the mood was upon us. I thought I was simply internalizing his desires, since … well, my life isn't the greatest." Mason shifted uncomfortably. Emma's eyes didn't blink, boring into him, commanding him to talk.

"I was jealous—God, was I jealous. It ate at me, day and night. Look at me, a man who works with dead people, whose life is surrounded by despair. And, of course, I'm married, for God's sake. It simply wasn't realistic." He could feel the hysterics wanting to seize him, to make his body do something stupid, like cry.

"I wish I knew if she felt the same way about me." Mason sobbed, covering his face in his hands. "I—I can't believe now, but I did then. I thought she was here for me. That it was all a mistake. That she would turn to me and realize it was me she was waiting for. I would have gone with her. I would have gone anywhere with her." Garnering a level of control he didn't know he had, he took a deep breath and sat up straight. "I felt I'd always known her, that she was a part of me, which of course, is ridiculous." He looked over Emma's shoulder, at the rising moon, and for the first time in many weeks, felt calm and reassured.

"None of this answers my question," barked Emma. "What were you doing there that night? How did you know where we were? I saw you try to blend in with the emergency crew at first, then you walked out in the open, big as you please, said you'd heard about the emergency and could you be of any help? I may be old, but I'm not demented."

He told her how the car had broken down, how he'd gotten another and driven straight to Lee's house only to discover them all gone. "I saw the Dark Men and went after them. One of them hit me over the head. When I came to, I stumbled to the car, trying to figure out what was going on. I knew you all were in trouble and I was at a loss. And then, you wouldn't believe it, but a blue-faced hag was sitting in the passenger seat beside me. She told me where you were. She also said I wouldn't make it in time."

He took a deep breath and plunged on. "I tried to catch up with you two, but you were always one step ahead of me. It was as if something was holding me back. I thought for sure I would meet you on the mountain, but by the time I got on that back road I hit one hellacious pothole and got a flat. Can you believe it? There was no spare in the trunk! I pushed the car off the road and walked. By the time I got near your car, you must have already been up at the house. I lost you in that snowstorm. I caught one more glimpse of you as you disappeared around the house a few minutes later." Mason got up from the rocker, pacing back and forth.

"I wanted to shout," he continued, "but was afraid of raising the alarm. I turned around to find another way when, wham! Lance found my face with his fist." Mason rubbed his jaw. "Sleeping Beauty came alive to find you on your knees and a jillion cops and emergency personnel swarming the place."

"You're lucky he didn't kill you," said Emma.

Mason winced disgustedly. "Guess I've got a guardian angel."

Emma eventually accepted Mason's explanation. She fired more questions; got more answers. She didn't say too much about it after that.

There were loose ends, though, around town. The council president's son never turned up—dead or alive. The mother died from grief the following December, locked in the psychiatric ward of a state hospital. A teenage girl was also missing. Some said she'd run off with the boy; others, the old ones who populated the senior citizen center for a little action, decided they were both dead, victims of mountain magick. Emma shook her head on that one. "My psychic sense says she ain't dead. She's away somewhere, gettin' on with life. She'll be okie-dokie. The boy, though, ain't on this earth no more."

It was true. Mason noticed it immediately. Emma had changed. When she was around, there was a presence, an otherworldly strength, that hadn't been there before. She could predict things, and had done so correctly, on more than one occasion. He'd teased her, telling her she could take over his stock portfolio anytime. She'd just grinned and waved a bony hand. Emma set up what she called an altar on the mate to the old T.V. table inside.

"I light a candle for that Morrigan every night," she said softly. "Maybe some night, she'll let Elizabeyta come back."

Which is why Mason kept coming back. There was magick here. Where there was magick, he might find Elizabeyta. He leaned back in the rocker, drinking in the full moon, letting its energy caress him, relax him. With a sigh, he closed his eyes.

Emma busied herself in the kitchen, flitting from cabinet to stove to the table and back. She removed the ham from the oven. It oozed brown sugar and cherries. Her stomach growled as its rising steam hit her nostrils. More than once she stopped in mid-step, agonizing over her friend out there on the porch. Damn shame, it was. Unrequited love and all that. She'd known it to kill the best of men and women.

She'd done her best to perk him up these last two years, but he kept gettin' thinner and thinner, sadder and sadder. Heard tell last week Louise had filed for divorce. Funny, Mason didn't say nothing yet. He'd get around to it. A cryin' shame, that's what it was. Gossip said Mason had gone moody on her and finally cut that leash she'd kept him on.

A look at the mantle clock set her stepping. My, goin' on 9:30. No wonder her belly chattered like a magpie. Such a pleasant sound it was, the tickin' of that clock. Had it since—my, her eleventh birthday. She remembered her ma had been in such a tizzy when Aunt Agatha gave it to her. Seemed her mother believed Emma's life could get tied to that clock. Some Appalachian superstition that Emma never took stock in.

Today was May 1. Her books said it was Beltainne Eve. Okay, so they weren't her books, they were the books she found in Lee's study and kept. She'd returned the ones that belonged in that fancy university library, but she took all the ones that had his name in them. She didn't think anyone would care.

These books claimed that Beltainne was a time for lovers, mating, and children. A gay time. A time of ribbons, flowers, dancing, and, well—things she no longer thought of at her age.

Oh, never mind. She took the cornbread out of the oven and set it on the counter to cool, wiped her hands on a tea towel, and fished for her matches in one of her deep smock pockets. There, with the hankie and her woman stone.

Without hesitation, she walked over to her altar and lit the red candle. Fire, her grandfather'd said, was a living entity—a part of the magick. Every morning, just after her coffee, she would put out a fresh candle. Sometimes she would burn it then and replace it later in the evening with another. With it being full moon and all, and Mason coming, she'd not bothered to light the new candle in the morning.

Tsk, tsk. Her altar was awful dusty. She'd have to give it a good cleanin' later. Hmmm. Beltainne had a Maypole. Well, she didn't have one of those, but she had some ribbon, yes she did. She hurried into her bedroom and rooted in a dresser drawer. Among her sewing things she found some red, black, and white ribbon. Not the prettiest, but they would do.

At the altar she tied the ribbons around the base of the candleholder and stepped back. Holding the woman stone with both her hands, she slowly raised it to her old forehead.

"I stand here, an old woman," she said softly, lest Mason overhear her silliness.

"I've seen just about all an old body can handle." She looked over her shoulder. Mason was a-rockin' back and forth, not appearing to pay attention.

"I've done a lot of good in my time. Healed friend and foe." She took a deep breath.

"You said I got a good few years, that was two years ago, and I think I have some left. I don't rightly know what to do with them." Her antiquated eyes filled with tears. Could she really do this? She clutched the woman stone tighter now.

"I seen you do all kinds of magick. I seen you defeat a murderous fiend. I seen you in battle, so's you can appreciate the battle I'm havin' right now. I'm fightin' for that poor man out there, who's lost." She drew her body up straight and tall.

"And I'm a-callin' on you," she whispered, "Woman of the Mountain, to make your magick work for Mason. I'm a-callin' on you, Dark Goddess of Women, to bring balance, like they say you do. I'm a-callin' on you to take my last years as sacrifice and put Elizabeyta where she belongs, in the arms of her mate. The one she would have had, if you'd not taken her away. My feelings tell me. I know how it would have gone, had she refused to take care of her people. Well, to me, I say she's paid. She did the right thing. I can't believe you would take her happiness from her after all this."

Emma shut her eyes tight and concentrated with all her might on the memory of Elizabeyta. Higher and higher climbed her emotions, louder and louder she screamed in her mind, pushing her life essence into her desire. She flung her arms out wide and jumped for all she was worth, landing a little off-balance with a thud on the old oak flooring. "Make it so!" she screamed.

The rocking chair stopped rocking.

The clock stopped ticking.

The lights went out.

The candle fell over, spit, and died.

The mountain beneath her feet rumbled.

The echo of this rumble touched the entire chain.

The surrounding mountains gently shook in unison.

The echo felt everlasting.

In the dark, Emma turned slowly around to face the open front door. The full moon poured around her, spilling luminescent beams and shadows thick as chocolate pudding. Mason stood at the porch rail, leaning way over. Emma thought he was going to topple off the porch.

Mason straightened, his shoulders cupped in shock.

"Dear Lady," thought Emma, "I've killed him." She rushed forward, seizing his arm. His name formed on her lips, until she looked past him.

From the belly of the mountains rose a hiss of mist, rolling into the valley, obscuring vision. In seconds, Emma could hardly see her pump, five feet out in the yard. A dog howled somewhere. *Not again*, thought Emma. *How much can this old heart stand, anyway?*

"I was out and about," called a male voice from the right, "and thought I felt the tingle of magick. Magick, of course, always makes me curious."

Mason and Emma looked at each other, matching wide eyes.

"Who's there?" shouted Emma.

"Well, you needn't sound so hostile, my dear woman," came the quick answer, still disembodied. "After all, you are the reason I am here. I believe I'm supposed to collect something. Don't be afraid. Think of me as a travel agent."

"Show yourself!" shouted Mason.

"I don't think that will be necessary, Mason. Yes indeed, I've heard all about you. Seems someone's memory has returned. She's not extremely happy at the moment. Though I find her unique and challenging, I'm afraid her life force doesn't command easily, if you know what I mean. She's tough even for an angel to handle."

A stifled female giggle floated somewhere in the mist.

"So, I've made a bargain, as it were. You there, Emma, you know all about bargains, don't you?"

Emma's heart fluttered against her breastbone. Tendrils of mist shot around them both—heavy, gentle, lulling …

"Stop playing with her. It's not fair," whispered the feminine accomplice from somewhere near the pump. "You said true love, now get on with it—true love is at hand."

"You there, Mason. Come down off the porch. If you can face Death, then I will be satisfied," said the male voice, closer now. Too close for Emma's comfort. She squirmed and held onto Mason's arm.

"Don't go!"

She looked into Mason's hollow eyes, noted his pain. Slowly she released her grip. Mason moved along the porch, one step at a time. The floorboards creaked.

Maybe the Woman God was raisin' the dead, she thought.

Mason hesitated at the top stair, running his hand up and down the smooth column.

He looked back once, smiled weakly at Emma, then descended into the mist.

Nothing happened.

He simply disappeared.

Into the mist.

The mountain rumbled.

Emma grabbed onto the railing.

The mist lifted.

And she caught a glimpse, as the vapor curled into nothingness, of Mason and Elizabeyta, tearfully clasped together. There was the pump, the moon flowers planted around it grown four feet, their blooms opened the span of a man's hand, glittering with moonlight. Nothing in the yard moved.

"They are not dead," came a male whisper from atop the porch roof. "Only together again."

Emma shuddered in both delight and pain.

The lights in the house came on.

Her clock started ticking again.

The yard was empty.

She turned and walked into the house, picking up her candle and relighting it in thanksgiving. Her arm stopped halfway to the altar. In the dust was scrawled: "You've got a few good years left. Use them wisely. —M."

In a daze, Emma shuffled back out on the front porch, lifting her head to the canopy of stars above her. She held the woman stone to her breast, then out to the milk-white orb in the sky.

Joy rose in her throat; a single tear drifted lazily down her cheek. "I guess anything can happen ... beneath a mountain moon," she whispered.

AUThOR'S NOTE

HAVE ALWAYS BEEN AN AVID READER OF FICTION. Well, almost always. Okay, I'll confess. When I was a kid, I hated to read. I found it distasteful, boring, and an absolute waste of my time. Of course, now at age thirty-eight, I'm not precisely sure how I was spending my time, but that is neither here nor there.

My mother, Goddess rest her soul, was at her wit's end on what to do with me. Naturally, since I couldn't read well, my studies suffered. All her friends' children were excelling—she couldn't brag. Since I didn't have any sisters or brothers I couldn't fade away into anonymity, hence my mother's search for the golden fleece of reading.

She didn't go to expensive schools or training seminars to find the answer. These things were a little out of our league. Instead, she went to the furniture flea market and purchased a huge, overstuffed chair. I'll never forget the feel of it (deep and soft), or its horrid color (peach with pink blobs imitating roses). It was placed beside our picture window in the dining room where there was oodles of light (so I wouldn't go blind). Next, she took me to the library and told me to pick three books that might interest me. I chose a Nancy Drew mystery (remember those?), a book on Lipizan stallions, and something else I can't remember.

Now came the tricky part. She had to get me to read them. I was to sit in that chair every day for half an hour and read. If I did not, I was told I may find myself permanently glued there. My pool privileges would also be revoked for the entire summer. (I believe the threat about the pool was the clincher.)

So, there I sat, every day, miserable and grumpy. I started with the book on horses. It had a lot of pictures in it; unfortunately, it was a big book.

The first week my mother and I hardly spoke. In my mind she had sentenced me to living hell, small print-style. She did not relent. The second week was not much better. My father decided that there was no winning my side of the argument, and completely ignored my pleas for release.

There must have been magick in the air the third week. Perhaps it was a full moon, an astrological manifestation, lunar eclipse, or high-voltage sun spots. Who knows? My mother decided it was a miracle, because in the middle of the third week, when my time was up, I asked her if I could stay a little longer and finish the chapter. I not only finished it, I read until supper.

These days, I can plow through a novel in record time, which is really what I want to tell you about. I don't know about you, but I practice magick. I'm tired of books written by people who don't practice magick, but try to convince the reader that the characters do. I like to think there is some solid basis to the magickal theories practiced.

In this novel, Witchcraft is the prevalent magickal practice of the "good guys," and the "bad guys" dabble in a mixture of ceremonial Pow-Wow. No one likes to think any magickal person is bad, but we've got to have a story, right? I tried to employ as many standard practices as possible to make the story both interesting and believable. However, someone out there is going to get their dander up because I didn't spend as much time as I could on the religious aspects of the Craft. Yes, Witchcraft is a positive religion and its practitioners are very serious about the divinity aspect of the faith. More so, I think, than most. True, too, is the fact that Witchcraft is the fastest-growing religion in the United States today. We've come a long way.

To my friends and neighbors who visited me during the germination of this book: See, I told you there was nothing wrong with my "Mountain Moon Kill List." People would look at my bulletin board above my computer and casually ask me why there was a hit list prominently displayed. I received a number of odd glances when I told them it was only for my fiction manuscript.

I hope you enjoyed this tale of magick and mystery. I know I enjoyed writing it. I'll also tell you a secret. I think somewhere out there in the astral, these characters are sitting around having a great time, shooting the you-know-what and talking about their parts in the book. They are the ones who decided the ending, I simply did them a favor by writing it.

Murder at Witches' Bluff
A Novel of Suspense and Magick

SILVER RAVENWOLF

Welcome to the historic hamlet of Cold Springs, Penn., where interpersonal relationships are as chilly as the pond the town is named after, where a stalker chooses his victims carefully, and where the waters eat children and the fires consume homes.

Siren McKay, gutsy five-foot-two ex-mistress of a dead New York drug lord, is drawn to her backwater hometown determined to start a new life. Still stalked by her past, Siren soon learns that she is the ultimate prize of a hunter's revenge.

Teaming up with Tanner, a seasoned firefighter of mysterious family lineage; Billy, a no-nonsense cop; and Lexi, a flamboyant retired stage magician, Siren seeks to find and bring to justice the man she begins to refer to as "her killer."

At the foot of Hag's Head Mountain, the foursome discovers the terrifying secrets that boil in a cauldron of local legend, including a monster that lusts after human souls. With the help of Tanner's country magick and Lexi's psychic abilities, Siren battles her enemies in a waking nightmare of sibling rivalry, dark family secrets, and hidden personal desires.

1-56718-727-7
480 pp., 6 x 9 $14.95

Witches' Night Out

SILVER RAVENWOLF

Now, from the author of *Teen Witch*—the wildly popular guide to Witchcraft—comes the first in a new series of spellbinders written specifically for teens. Featuring the five characters on the cover of Teen Witch, these fictional books will focus on the strength, courage, and willpower of the teens to overcome seemingly insurmountable obstacles, with enough authentic magickal practice thrown in to keep you on the edge of your seat. Every book features a spell that readers can do themselves.

Main character Bethany Salem, 16, is on her own most of the time. Five years ago her mother died, leaving her in the care of her father, a New York City cop, who has deposited her in the suburbs with their Santerian housekeeper.

The adventure begins when enterprising Bethany starts a coven with her friends. In *Witches' Night Out*, the teens find themselves sleuthing to determine who caused the fatal automobile wreck of their friend Joe.

1-56718-728-5
240 pp., 4 ⅛ x 6 ¾ $4.99

Witches' Night of Fear

Silver RavenWolf

From the author of *Teen Witch*—the wildly popular guide to Witch-craft—comes another installment in the "Witches' Chillers" series of spellbinders. Featuring the five characters on the cover of *Teen Witch*, these fictional books focus on the strength, courage, and willpower of the teens to overcome seemingly insurmountable obstacles, with enough authentic magickal practice thrown in to keep you on the edge of your seat. Every book features a spell that readers can do themselves.

Main character Bethany Salem, 16, is on her own most of the time. Five years ago her mother died, leaving her in the care of her father, a New York City cop, who has deposited her in the suburbs with their Santerian housekeeper. The adventures begin when enterprising Bethany starts a coven with her friends.

In the first book, *Witches' Night Out*, the teens find themselves sleuthing to determine the cause of the fatal car crash of a friend. Now, in Witches' Night of Fear, they are pulled into a local homicide of a convenience store clerk and an active case in New York City.

> *A shadow darted out from underneath the direction of the willow tree, sending a thrill of fear up her spine. Had someone seen her? Magick done in front of non-believers lost some, if not all, of its power. Bethany backed up to slam the window shut, but the wind caught her hair and whipped the ends in her eyes, making her hesitate. In that split second a black, gloved hand reached out from the darkness beyond the window and grabbed her by the throat. She couldn't see the face…*

1-56718-718-8
368 pp., 4 ³⁄₁₆ x 6 ⅞, illus. $5.99

To order, call 1-800-THE MOON
Prices subject to change without notice

Witches' Key to Terror

Silver RavenWolf

More occult fiction just for teens!
From the author of Teen Witch—the wildly popular guide to Witchcraft—comes the third installment in the "Witches' Chillers" series of spellbinders. Feisty teens of different races and different backgrounds make up the WNO (Witches' Night Out coven). Can they withstand the pressures of growing up and working magick at the same time? Each book focuses on their strength, courage, and willpower to overcome seemingly insurmountable obstacles, with enough authentic magickal practice thrown in to keep you on the edge of your seat.

In this newest installment, 16-year-old Cricket Bindart finds a dead rabbit hanging from her mailbox, with a threatening note attached. Since she is home schooled at her family's orchard and not allowed to associate with public school kids, she calls on the Goddess of the Fields to bring her Witches who can help her find the stalker and save her farm from foreclosure. Enter the WNO coven. Do you dare to join them?

> In anger and fear she whirled, screaming at the harvest moon, "Great Mother of the Fields! Bring me the Witches!"
> A crash in the bushes. Her eyes widened. From the exact place that she had thrown the dead rabbit, a live one appeared, bursting from the thicket and tearing across the field. She watched the fleet-footed animal meld with frozen corn stubble and night-mist darkness, heading toward the county line, full force toward the face of the moon.

0-7387-0049-5

4³⁄₁₆ x 6⁷⁄₈, 272 pp. $5.99

To order, call 1-800-THE MOON
Prices subject to change without notice

To Stir A Magick Cauldron
A Witch's Guide to Casting and Conjuring

Silver RavenWolf

The sequel to the enormously popular *To Ride a Silver Broomstick: New Generation Witchcraft*. This upbeat and down-to-earth guide to intermediate-level witchery was written for all Witches—solitaries, eclectics, and traditionalists. In her warm, straight-from-the-hip, eminently knowledgeable manner, Silver provides explanations, techniques, exercises, anecdotes, and guidance on traditional and modern aspects of the Craft, both as a science and as a religion.

Find out why you should practice daily devotions and how to create a sacred space. Learn six ways to cast a magick circle. Explore the complete art of spell-casting. Examine the hows and whys of Craft laws, oaths, degrees, lineage, traditions, and more. Explore the ten paths of power, and harness this wisdom for your own spell-craft. This book offers you dozens of techniques—some never before published—to help you uncover the benefits of natural magick and ritual and make them work for you—without spending a dime!

Silver is a "working Witch" who has successfully used each and every technique and spell in this book. By the time you have done the exercises in each chapter, you will be well trained in the first level of initiate studies. Test your knowledge with the Wicca 101 test provided at the back of the book and become a certified Witch! Learn to live life to its fullest through this positive spiritual path.

1-56718-424-3
320 pp., 7 x 10, illus. $14.95

To order, call 1-800-THE MOON
Prices subject to change without notice

To Light a Sacred Flame

Practical WitchCraft for the Millennium

SILVER RAVENWOLF

Silver RavenWolf continues to unveil the mysteries of the Craft with *To Light a Sacred Flame*, which follows her best-selling *To Ride a Silver Broomstick* and *To Stir a Magick Cauldron* as the third in the "New Generation WitchCraft" series, guides to magickal practices based on the personal experiences and successes of a third-degree working Witch.

Written for today's seeker, this book contains techniques that unite divinity with magick, knowledge, and humor. Not structured for any particular tradition, the lessons present unique and insightful material for the solitary as well as the group. Explore the fascinating realms of your inner power, sacred shrines, magickal formularies, spiritual housecleaning, and the intricacies of ritual. This book reveals new information that includes a complete discussion on the laws of the Craft, glamouries, and shamanic Craft rituals, including a handfasting and wiccaning (saining).

1-56718-721-8
320 pp., 7 x 10 $14.95

Silver's Spells for Prosperity

SILVER RAVENWOLF

Take charge of your finances the Silver way! Now one of the most famous Witches in the world today shows you how to get the upper hand on your cash flow with techniques personally designed and tested by the author herself. She will show you how to banish those awful old debts without heartache, get money back from someone who owes you, and transform your money energy so it flows in the the right direction—toward you! An abundance of spells can aid you in everything from winning a court case to getting creditors off your back. You'll also find a wealth of historical and practical information on spell elements and ingredients.

Silver's Spells for Prosperity is the first in a new series of five books by best-selling Wiccan author Silver RavenWolf.

- Uncover the one secret to great prosperity magick
- Find out why magick doesn't always work
- Create abundance in your life with the help of specific goddess, ancestors, and angels
- Concoct incense powders and oils to help you manifest what you desire
- Cast spells from time-honored folkloric traditions as well as those tried and tested by Silver
- Increase your odds for success in any endeavor
- Banish poverty and negative financial energies

1-56718-726-9
240 pp., 5 ³⁄₁₆ x 6, illus. $7.95

To order, call 1-800-THE MOON

Prices subject to change without notice

Silver's Spells for Protection

SILVER RAVENWOLF

What do you do when you discover that your best friend at work sabotaged your promotion? Or if a neighbor suddenly decides that you don't belong in his town? What if a group of teens sets out to make your life a living hell? What if . . . *Silver's Spells for Protection* contains tips for dealing with all these situations, and more.

This book covers how to handle stalkers, abusers, and other nasties with practical information as well as magickal techniques. It also covers some of the smaller irritants in life—like protecting yourself from your mother-in-law's caustic tongue and how to avoid that guy who's out to take your job from you.

Silver's Spells for Protection is the second in a new series of five books by best-selling Wiccan author Silver RavenWolf.

1-56718-729-3
264 pp., 5 ³⁄₁₆ x 6, illus.   **$7.95**

To order, call 1-800-THE MOON
Prices subject to change without notice